ORTHOGONAL BOOK TWO

THE

ETERNAL FLAME

Other books by Greg Egan:

An Unusual Angle
Quarantine
Permutation City
Distress
Diaspora
Teranesia
Schild's Ladder
Incandescence
Zendegi

Orthogonal: Book One: The Clockwork Rocket

ORTHOGONAL BOOK TWO

THE

ETERNAL FLAME

GREG EGAN

NIGHT SHADE BOOKS
San Francisco

First Edition

ISBN: 978-1-59780-293-2

Night Shade Books
http://www.nightshadebooks.com

CONTENTS

BOOK TWO:
THE ETERNAL FLAME

1

"Carlo! I need your help!"

Carlo opened his rear eyes to see his friend Silvano halfway down the ladder that led into the workshop. From the tone of his words this was not a casual request.

"What is it?" Carlo turned away from the microscope. A bright after-image of the fragment of wheat petal he'd been examining hovered for a moment against the soft red light from the walls.

Silvano halted his descent. "I need you to kill two of my children," he said. "I can't do it myself. I'm not that strong."

Carlo struggled to make sense of these words. He had seen his friend's co just a few days before, and she'd been as emaciated as any woman on the *Peerless*.

"How could there be four?" he asked, not wanting to believe that there were any, that Silvana had given birth at all. As far as he knew she'd still been studying, and if the event had been planned they'd never mentioned it to him. Maybe this request was some kind of sick prank. He'd drag himself all the way to their apartment and there Silvana would be, whole as ever.

"I don't know," Silvano replied. He offered no why-would-you-doubt-me bluster, no theories about the reason for the calamity—none of the adornments it would be tempting to add to bolster a fabrication. Carlo scrutinized his face as well as he could in the moss-light, and lost hope of any kind of deception.

He extinguished the microscope's lamp, then pulled himself away from the bench and moved quickly around the workshop, two hands on the guide ropes as he gathered the drugs and equipment he'd need.

He knew exactly what doses would euthanize a vole or a shrew by body mass, and it didn't take much calculating to extrapolate from that. He wasn't committed to any course of action, but if he ended up doing what Silvano had asked of him any delay would only make it harder.

Carlo grabbed a small box to hold the paraphernalia and moved toward the ladder, packing as he went. Silvano ascended quickly ahead of him. It was only when they were traveling side by side down the corridor, their ropes emitting the same forlorn twang, that Carlo dared to start searching for a way out.

"Are you sure no one's offering an entitlement?" he asked. It was a desperately slim chance, but they could detour to the relay station and check.

"I spent the last three stints looking," Silvano replied. "No one's selling at any price."

A small group of people had entered the corridor behind them; their voices echoed off the gently curved walls. Carlo increased his pace, then asked quietly, "So you were planning to have children?"

"No! I just wanted to find a way for Silvana to stop starving herself."

"Oh." Everyone craved the same kind of ease, but to put too much hope in such a slender prospect was asking for disappointment.

"Her studies were becoming harder and harder," Silvano continued. "She couldn't concentrate at all. I thought it would be worth it, just to let her stop worrying and eat normally. An extra entitlement wouldn't have committed us to anything, and I could have re-sold it if we'd ended up not needing it."

"So why didn't you wait?" Carlo demanded angrily. "How many people did you expect to die in *three stints*?"

Silvano began humming and shivering. "She couldn't take the hunger any more. She kept saying, 'Let's do it now, and at least my daughter will have a few years before it's her turn to suffer.'"

Carlo didn't reply. It was hard enough watching someone you loved tormented by the need to convince her body that it was living in a time of famine, but to learn now that all of this self-deprivation had been to no avail was cruel beyond belief.

They reached the ladder leading inward to the apartments. Carlo forced himself to continue. A generation ago, anyone in his place would have offered to forego a twelfth of their own entitlement to help out their friend, and with enough contributors the extra mouths would have been fed. That was what his parents had done. But the crop yields hadn't risen since, and he wasn't prepared to diminish his family's share any further, forcing his own descendants into an even more precarious state. As for the chance of Silvano finding a dozen such benefactors, it was nonexistent.

At the top of the ladder it was Silvano who hung back. Carlo said, "You stay here. I'll come and get you." He started down the corridor.

Silvano said, "Wait."

Carlo halted, fearful without quite knowing what he dreaded. What could make this worse? Some complicated directive on how he should choose which pair should survive?

"You don't think you and Carla might…?" Silvano began haltingly.

"You left that too late," Carlo said. He spoke gently, but he made sure not to offer his friend the slightest hope.

"Yes," Silvano agreed wretchedly.

Carlo said, "I won't be long."

The corridor was empty as he approached the apartment, but the fixed gaze of the same three faces kept repeating as he dragged himself past a long row of election posters, all bearing the slogan MAKE THE ANCESTORS PROUD. The fact that he was still in Silvano's sight made hesitation unthinkable: he pushed the curtains aside and followed the guide ropes in. There were no lamps burning, but even by moss-light Carlo could see at a glance that the front room was deserted. Silvana's notebooks were stacked neatly in a cabinet. He felt a pang of grief and anger, but this wasn't the time to indulge it. He made his way into the bedroom.

Silvano had left the children encased in a tarpaulin that was tethered to two of the ropes that crossed the room. Carlo couldn't help imagining the couple themselves inside the same enclosure, steadying their bodies for the bittersweet end. He had never had the courage to ask any of his older friends—let alone his father—what they believed had passed through their co's mind in those final moments, what comfort the women took from the knowledge that they were creating new lives. But at least Silvana would have had no way of knowing that nature in its capriciousness was about to deliver twice the consolation she'd been expecting.

Carlo dragged himself closer to the bundle. He could see movement, but mercifully there was still no sound. The tarpaulin had been rolled into a rough cylinder, with the cord that threaded through the holes along two of the sides pulled tight to close the ends. He unknotted the cord at one end and began loosening it, his hands trembling as he felt the infants respond to the disturbance. Part of his mind skidded away from the task, conjuring fantasies of a different remedy. What if he could call on, not a dozen friends, but the entire crew? When a woman scourged her body with hunger to protect the *Peerless*, surely they all owed her children a simple act of decency—whether they were close to her family or not. A few crumbs less in so many meals wouldn't be missed.

But he was deluding himself. Sharing the load among strangers wouldn't diminish it: when the pleas started coming from every corner of the mountain—once every stint, not once in a lifetime—all those lesser demands would still add up the same way. In the long run nothing mattered but the size of the harvest and the number of mouths to be fed. If the rations were spread any thinner one bad harvest could see the entitlements torn up—and a war over the crops would leave no survivors.

One end of the tarpaulin was open now. Carlo peered into the gloom of the tunnel, then reached in and took the nearest infant in his hands. She was a tiny limbless thing, her eyes still closed, her mouth gaping for food. Her tympanum fluttered, but the membranes were not yet stiff enough to make a sound.

The child squirmed in his grip. Carlo emitted a series of soothing chirps, but they had no effect. This girl knew that he was not her father, not the one who had promised to protect her. He reached down and placed her on the bed below, where a second tarpaulin covered the sand.

The next one he extracted was her sister, not her co. Both were distressingly undersized, but both appeared equally healthy. Carlo had been clinging to the hope that with so little maternal flesh to go around one of the pairs would have died of natural causes already, or failing that a stark asymmetry in their prospects might have spared him any need to make the choice himself.

He placed the second girl on the bed; her sister was already drifting, her wriggling launching her up from the tarp. "Stay there," Carlo entreated them both, pointlessly.

Some instinct had driven their brothers to retreat into the dark depths of the birth tent; Carlo pulled the cord out completely at his end and opened up the whole thing to the moss-light. Against the spread of the gaily patterned cloth the boys looked impossibly diminutive and fragile, and they chose this moment to become audible, humming plaintively for their father. Carlo wished he'd sent Silvano further away. If these children had been his own, this was the point when he might have lost his mind and tried to kill the man he'd sent to halve their number.

This was wrong, it was insane, it was unforgivable. If he reneged now, what would happen? A few of Silvano's friends would take pity on him, and help keep the family of five from starving. But once those friends had children of their own, the cost of their charity would grow much steeper—and once *Silvano's children* had children, the situation would be impossible. Unless Carlo was willing to declare to his co: "These two belong to us now, to raise as our own. You'd better stuff yourself with holin, because in my weakness this is what I've done to you: your flesh that was made for the ages will perish now, just like mine."

Carlo dragged himself along the rope and snatched the nearest of the boys. The child writhed and hummed; Carlo spread his hand wide to deaden the boy's tympanum. "Which one is your co?" he muttered angrily. He grabbed the side of the bed and pulled himself down. Co recognized co from the earliest age, and their fathers could always see the link, but how was a stranger who hadn't witnessed the fission itself meant to be certain?

He held the boy beside each female sibling in turn. Carlo was humming now himself, though not as loudly as the unrestrained brother. He tried to picture all four bodies still in contact, before the partitions softened into skin and split apart: first the primary one dividing the pairs, then the secondary ones dividing co from co. He'd watched the whole process often enough in animals. With a free hand he prodded the underside of the boy's torso, the place where he would have been connected to his co more recently than he'd been joined side by side with his brother. Just beneath the skin there was a patch of unusual rigidity, flat but irregularly shaped. Carlo probed the same spot on one of the girls. Nothing. He checked her sister, and found the mirror image of the boy's fragment of the partition.

He hesitated, crouched above the bed, still trying to imagine how this could have ended differently. What if the four friends had made a pact, long ago, to feed each other's children and forego their own, if it ever came to that? Was that the stark, simple answer they'd all failed to see—or would the promise of security have poisoned them against each other, leaving them afraid that it would be exploited? Carla had never starved herself quite as diligently as Silvana, so what kind of life would she have had if she'd been endlessly harangued by a woman with every reason to urge her to show more restraint?

Carlo scooped up the chosen boy's co and pulled himself along the rope into the front room, a child clutched awkwardly in each free hand. From the box, he took two clearstone vials and a syringe. He extruded an extra pair of arms, uncapped the first vial and filled the syringe with its orange powder. When he held the sharp mirrorstone tip to the base of the boy's skull he felt his own body start shuddering in revulsion, but he stared down his urge to take the child in his arms and soothe him, to promise him as much love and protection as he would lavish on any child of his own. He pushed the needle into the skin and searched for the angle that would take it between two plates of bone—he knew the invariant anatomy here was not that different from a vole's—but then the tip suddenly plunged deeper without the drop in resistance he'd been expecting upon finding the narrow corridor of flesh. The child's skull wasn't fully ossified, and his probing had forced the needle right through it.

Carlo turned the boy to face him, then squeezed the plunger on the syringe. The child's eyes snapped open, but they were sightless, rolling erratically, with flashes of yellow light diffusing all the way through the orbs. The drug itself could only reach a small region of the brain, but those parts it touched were emitting a barrage of meaningless signals that elicited an equally frenzied response much farther afield. Soon the tissue's capacity to make light would be depleted throughout the whole organ. In this state, Carlo believed, there could be no capacity for thought or sensation.

When the boy's eyes were still Carlo withdrew the needle. His co's tympanum had been fluttering for a while, and now her humming grew audible. "I'm sorry," Carlo whispered. "I'm sorry." He stroked the side of her body with his thumb, but it only made her more agitated. He refilled the syringe with the orange powder, quickly drove the needle through the back of her skull, and watched the light of her nascent mind blaze like a wildfire, then die away.

Carlo released the limp children and let them drift toward the floor while he resorbed the arms he'd used to hold them. His whole body felt weak and battered. He spent a few pauses steadying himself, then he pushed out two fresh arms and filled the syringe from the second vial. When a speck of the blue powder spilled onto his palm the sensation was like passing his hand above a flame. He gathered the damaged patch of skin into a small clump, then hardened the tips of two of his fingers and sliced it off.

He picked up the boy. A world away, his brother was still calling out for help. Carlo reinserted the needle, and forced himself to take his time delivering the poison lest it burst from the wound and escape into the room. The boy's eyes had already been dull, but now the smooth white skin of the orbs began to turn purplish gray.

When the plunger could be driven no further, Carlo withdrew the needle carefully and set the dead boy down beside the cabinet. He refilled the syringe and turned to the boy's co. When he gripped her a spasm passed through her body; he waited to see if there was any more activity, but she remained still. He slid the needle into her brain and sent the blue powder trickling through.

Carlo returned to the inner room. He set the boy he'd spared down on the bed beside his co, then unknotted the end of the tarpaulin that had remained attached to the guide rope. In the front room he brought the bodies together, positioning them as they would have been before they'd separated, and rolled them into the tarpaulin. He folded the empty parts of the cloth together and secured the shroud with cord. Then he packed the syringe and vials back into the box he'd used to bring them.

As he approached Silvano in the corridor, his friend's whole body contorted with anguish. "Let me see them!" he begged Carlo.

"Go and tend to your children," Carlo replied. A woman was approaching them—one of Silvano's neighbors on her way home—but then she saw what Carlo was holding and she retreated without a word.

"What have I done?" Silvano wailed. "What have I done?" Carlo pushed past him and moved quickly down the corridor, but he waited by the ladder until Silvano finally entered the apartment. Comforting the surviving children—holding them, feeding them, letting them know that they were safe—was the only thing that could help him now.

Carlo descended past the level of his workshop, past the test fields where the seedlings he was studying grew, past the shuddering machinery of the cooling pumps, until he reached the base of the ladder. He dragged himself along the outer corridor, picturing the void beneath the rock.

A man was emerging from the airlock as Carlo approached. He removed his helmet and glanced at the tarpaulin, then averted his eyes. Carlo recognized him: he was a miller named Rino.

"There's no greater waste of time than the fire watch," Rino carped, climbing out of his cooling bag. "I've lost count of how many shifts I've done, and I still haven't seen so much as a flash."

Carlo placed the children's bodies on the floor and Rino helped him fit into a six-limbed cooling bag. Carlo hadn't been outside for years; agronomy was considered important enough to keep him off the roster entirely.

Rino snapped a fresh canister of air into place and checked that it was flowing smoothly over Carlo's skin.

"Helmet?"

Carlo said, "I won't be out that long."

"You want a safety harness?"

"Yes."

Rino took one from a peg on the wall and handed it to him. Carlo slipped it over his torso and cinched it tight.

"Be careful, brother," Rino said. There was no hint of irony in his form of address, but Carlo had always found it grimly inane that the friendliest appellation some people could offer was a death sentence.

He carried the bodies into the airlock with him, slid the door closed and started laboriously pumping down the pressure. A loose edge of the shroud flapped in the surge of air across the confined space as he delivered each stroke. He unreeled a suitable length of the safety rope, engaged the brake on the reel and hooked the rope into his harness. Then he crouched down, braced himself against the outrush of residual air and pulled open the hatch in the floor.

A short stone ladder rising up beside the hatch made the descent onto the external rope ladder easier. Carlo used four hands on the rungs and held the children in the other two. As his head passed below the hatch the trails of the old stars were suddenly right in front of him—long, garish streaks of color gouged out of the sky—while behind him the orthogonal stars were almost point-like. He glanced down and saw the fire-watch platform silhouetted against the transition circle, where the old stars blazed brightest before their light cut out.

Carlo descended until he felt the safety rope grow taut. He clung to the children, unsure what he should say before releasing them. This boy should have lived for three dozen years, and died with children of his own to mourn him. This girl should have survived in those children, her flesh outliving every man's. What was life, if that pattern was broken? What was life, when a father had to plead for an assassin to murder half his family, just to save the rest from starvation?

So who had failed them? Not their mother, that was sure. The idiot ancestors who squatted on the home world, waiting to be rescued from their own problems? The three generations of agronomists who had barely increased the yield from the crops? But then, what good would it do if the fourth generation triumphed? If he and his colleagues found a way to raise the yield, that would bring a brief respite. But it would also bring more four-child families, and in time the population would rise again until all the same problems returned.

What miracle could put an end to hunger and infanticide? However many solos and widows chose to go the way of men, most women would rather starve themselves in the hope of having only one daughter than contemplate a regime where for every two sisters, one would be compelled to die childless.

And if he was honest, it was not just down to the women. Even if Carla, given her say, had proved willing, he would not have been prepared to throw away his chance of fatherhood to raise these children as his own.

"Forgive us," Carlo pleaded. He stared down at the lifeless bundle. "Forgive us all. We've lost our way."

He let the children slip from his arms, and watched the shroud descend into the void.

2

Straining against the harness that held her to the observation bench, Tamara cranked the azimuth wheel of the telescope mount. Each laborious turn of the handle beside her nudged the huge contraption by just one arc-chime, and though she still had strength to spare there was nothing to be gained from it: a governor limited the speed of rotation to prevent excessive torques that might damage the gears. The soft, steady clicking of the wheel, usually a reassuring, meditative sound, drove home the machine's serene indifference to her impatience.

When the telescope was finally pointed in the direction of her last sighting of the Object, she lay flat on the bench and wriggled into place beneath the eyepiece. As she brought the image into focus she was granted as glorious a vision as she could have hoped for: there was nothing to be seen here but the usual mundane star trails.

The trails were exactly as Tamara remembered them, so she knew that she hadn't mis-set the coordinates. Twice now, the Object had escaped the field of view that had framed it just one day earlier. Such elusiveness proved that it was crossing the sky faster than anything she'd seen before.

Tamara turned the secondary azimuth wheel until she was rewarded with a small gray smudge of light at the top of the field, then she adjusted the altitude to center it. To the limits of the telescope's resolving power, the Object was simply a point. Nothing in the cosmos was close enough to the *Peerless* to reveal its width, but even those orthogonal stars that had remained fixed in the sky for three generations showed color trails at this magnification. To possess a point-like image the Object had to be moving slowly—but the only way a slow-moving body could cross the sky as rapidly as this was by virtue of its proximity.

She ran her fingertips over the embossed coordinate wheels, recorded the numbers on her chest, then computed the angle between the Object's last two bearings. Symbols blossomed on her forearm as she worked through the calculation. In both of the intervals between sightings the gray smudge had moved about two arc-pauses—but the second shift was slightly greater than the first. The true speed of the Object was unlikely to have changed, so its quickening progress against the background of stars could only mean that it had already moved measurably closer.

The change was far too small to yield accurate predictions, but Tamara couldn't resist working through some crude estimates. Within a period perhaps as short as four stints—or perhaps as long as five dozen—the Object would make its closest approach to the *Peerless*. Just how close that would be was impossible to say, without knowing how fast the thing was moving through the void, but the lack of a discernible color trail put a ceiling on its speed. The upshot was, the Object would pass by at a distance of, at most, nine gross severances. In astronomical terms that was positively propinquitous: about a twelfth the distance of the home world from its star. No living traveler among them had ever been so close to another solid body.

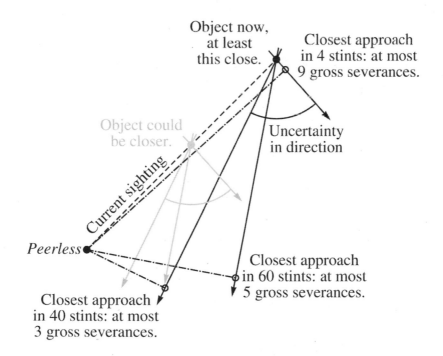

Object now, at least this close.

Closest approach in 4 stints: at most 9 gross severances.

Object could be closer.

Current sighting

Uncertainty in direction

Peerless

Closest approach in 60 stints: at most 5 gross severances.

Closest approach in 40 stints: at most 3 gross severances.

Tamara resisted the urge to bolt from the observatory and start spreading the news; the protocols dictated that she should complete her shift in the face of anything less than an imminent collision. But it would not be wasted time; the Object could easily be accompanied by fellow travelers, fragments from the same parent body with similar trajectories. So she duly worked her way across her allotted segment of the sky, hunting for another speck of light or a dark silhouette against a star's band of colors. Field after field was unblemished, as usual, but whenever the tedium of the search reached the point where her thoughts began to stray to the emptiness in her gut, she turned her mind back to the Object itself and savored again the thrill of discovery.

When she'd done her duty—with no further revelations—Tamara slipped out of the harness and pushed herself through the hatch at the base of the observatory. She drifted across the gap that separated the telescope's stabilized mount from the imperceptibly spinning rock below, and her momentum carried her into the entrance tunnel, returning her to the *Peerless* proper. She grabbed a guide rope and dragged herself along to the office. Roberto was there, ready to start his own shift, while Ada was studying for an assessment, poring over a tattered set of notes on the art of navigational astrometry.

"I do believe we should expect company!" Tamara announced. She gave her fellow observers the three data points and waited while they made their own calculations.

"It does look close," Roberto confirmed.

"How bright is it?" Ada asked.

"Five," Tamara said.

"And you've only just seen it?"

"You know what it's like, trying to spot things close to the horizon."

To Tamara, they both sounded a shade resentful. She knew there'd been no special skill in what she'd done, and her luck would attract no great esteem. But what lay ahead now was open to everyone: the chance to observe a body of orthogonal matter in unprecedented detail.

"I wish we had some way to pin down the distance," Roberto lamented.

"Do I detect a hint of parallax envy?" Tamara joked. On the home world, astronomers had had it easy: wait half a day and your viewpoint moved by the planet's width; wait half a year and that became the width of the orbit. Once those baselines had been measured, the shifting angles they created had been revelatory. But whether you imagined it was the *Peerless* itself that was moving day by day, or the Object, without knowing the relative velocity to fix the baseline between successive views the most you could glean from the angles alone was the timing of the encounter, not the distance.

Roberto hummed with frustration. "This thing might come close enough for us to resolve its shape—and maybe even structural features, impact craters... who knows? Think how much more valuable all that would be if we knew their scale!"

Ada said, "It sounds like the perfect job for an infrared color trail."

"What kind of gratitude is this?" Tamara demanded. "I bring my two friends the find of a lifetime, and all I get are fantasies about how things could be better!"

Ada was indignant. "What fantasy? I'm serious! The chemists have never made infrared a priority before, because they've never had a good enough reason."

Chemicals sensitive to ultraviolet light had been known since before the launch, but no one had managed to achieve the same feat at the infrared end of the spectrum. Imaging a slow-moving object's color trail in ultraviolet wasn't all that helpful; even infinitely fast UV would lie closer to violet in the trail than violet was to red. But an infrared trail could stretch out to many times the length of the visible portion.

"And this will count as a good reason?" Roberto was amused. "The last time I asked for a favor from the chemists, I was told to wait until they'd solved the fuel problem."

Ada said, "Maybe we can find a chemist who's itching for a break. If you've spent half your life bashing your head against the same old problem, why not try something easier?"

"No, they all want the glory too badly for that," Roberto declared. "Who's going to waste their time inventing *infrared-sensitive paper* when they might be on the verge of inventing a way home?"

Tamara tried to put herself inside a chemist's skin. The *Peerless*'s reserves of sunstone, burned in the usual manner, would barely be enough to bring the mountain to a halt, let alone carry their descendants back to the home world. She'd understood that unsettling fact since childhood, but to someone who'd made the fuel problem their vocation what interest could there be in the astronomers' petty concerns? The orthogonal cluster and the debris that surrounded it were just obstacles to be avoided, and while gathering statistics on the distribution of this hazard was a worthwhile activity, it wouldn't take an infrared color trail to recognize a head-on collision.

Then again, surely every chemist was at least a little curious as to how the sprinkling of orthogonal dust that had adhered to the surface of the *Peerless* had threatened to set the rock on fire, in the days before spin. Tamara wondered if she could sell them on the notion that establishing the size of any craters on the Object might shed light on that mysterious reaction. The trouble was, any ordinary rock that *had* struck the Object would have done so at such a great speed that the most likely result would have been, not a crater, but an all-obliterating fireball. The *Peerless* itself was almost certainly the only ordinary object in the region that had ended up more or less matching velocities with the orthogonal material—and if a leisurely encounter between the two kinds of matter was ever to be repeated, the *Peerless* would have to be involved again.

Tamara looked up at her friends and realized just how blind she'd been. Roberto had been right to refuse to accept the same old regime of half-useless observations; Ada had been right to insist that there could easily be better methods within their reach. But all three of them had been too timid by far.

Tamara said, "Why don't we go there?"

Roberto blinked. "What?"

Ada emitted an excited chirp. "You mean start the engines and...?"

"No, no!" Tamara cut her off. "The *Peerless* is too big and unwieldy, and it would be insane to waste that much fuel. We should build a smaller rocket, just for this journey—something we can take as close to the Object as we dare. Then we can measure what we like, observe what we like... carry out experiments, maybe even bring back samples."

Ada held up her navigator's manual, regarding it with an almost fearful new respect. When Tamara had studied the same notes, she'd assumed that the only use she'd ever make of them would be to teach the theory to the next generation, keeping the knowledge from withering away while they waited for the infinitely remote prospect of commencing the journey home.

Roberto's stunned expression gave way to one of pure delight. "If the tiniest speck of orthogonal rock is a liberator for calmstone," he said, "who knows what the same material in bulk could do to our fuel?"

Tamara said, "I think we might be able to interest the chemists in helping us find the answer to *that.*"

3

arla opened the valve at the top of the lamp, allowing a trickle of liberator to fall onto the sunstone. She started at the sudden hissing sound and the dazzling eruption of radiance, and her hand moved quickly to the dousing lever that would bury the flame in sand. But after a moment the noise settled to a steady splutter, and though the beam escaping through the aperture in the lamp's cover retained its formidable intensity, it appeared to be stable.

Carla had prepared the liberator herself, extracting the active ingredient from sawflower roots, then diluting it with crushed powderstone, checking the proportions three times and running the mixture through an agitator to be sure there were no clumps. But even these precautions couldn't assuage her fears entirely. Fire of every kind crossed the Cornelio line into positive temperatures, but the act of igniting sunstone felt like summoning a malevolent creature out of the sagas. It might sit on the bench and amuse you with its tricks, but you knew that what it really wanted was to bring its whole world of bright chaos through the crack you'd opened up between the realms.

A lens over the lamp's aperture partly countered the natural spreading of the light. Carla placed a small mirror in its path; mounted diagonally on a pegged holder, it sent the beam straight down through a hole in the bench-top. She knelt and fitted a triangular prism into place to intercept the vertical beam, then she ran an upturned hand through the space below it, to watch the brilliant spectrum glide over her skin. Sunstone disquieted her, but no other source produced such pure, intense colors.

A robust clearstone container sat on the floor beneath the bench. Apart from the corners, rounded for strength, it was almost box-like in shape, and the gravity here was strong enough to hold it in place by friction alone. At the bottom of the container was a flat rectangular mirror, freshly polished. The spectrum from the prism fell along the length of the mirror, with a thin strip of colors spilling off one edge onto a sheet of gridded paper, making it easy to see the position of every hue. Carla noted the locations of the red and violet ends; some space remained beyond them where the mirrorstone would be exposed to invisible wavelengths. Half of the spectrum reflecting off the mirror showed up on the underside of the bench-top, with the rest reaching an adjacent wall, but Carla felt no urge to contain the spilt light. It was no longer part of the experiment, and the streak on the wall made a cheerful decoration.

The prism she was using had been calibrated against a light comb by an earlier custodian of the workshop—the neatly written table was dated just a dozen and four years after the launch—allowing her to assign a precise wavelength to each line on the grid. She verified the overall calibration with half a dozen spot checks, then glanced at the clock. Going on what Marzio had told her, and accounting for the strength of the beam, she had planned for an initial exposure of one day.

Marzio was one of the most respected instrument builders on the *Peerless*. Four years ago, he'd been asked by the astronomers to construct a wide-field camera that could function in the void, in the hope of capturing sharper images than those taken behind the clearstone panels of the observatory domes. Like most such cameras his design had included a mirror to divert the light path, making it easier to keep the gas that activated the sensitized paper from leaving a residue on the lens. The device he'd built had been successful enough, but when Carla had run into him recently he'd told her something curious: the mirror had grown tarnished more rapidly than the corresponding part in any camera he'd built before. This was not what anyone would have expected; the gradual loss of reflectivity in polished mirrorstone had always been attributed to some kind of slow chemical reaction with the air.

Marzio had speculated that perhaps the activating gas, which seemed to cause no problems with the mirrors in air-filled cameras, was behaving differently in the vacuum—although it still did its job perfectly well. And the tarnish on the mirror, he admitted, bore no signs of being an entirely new phenomenon: it was indistinguishable from the patina that appeared under ordinary conditions. It merely arrived sooner in the absence of air.

Carla had had no good theories about any of this, but Marzio's observation had nagged at her. *If it wasn't air that tarnished mirrors, what was it?* Exposure to light, or simply the passage of time? It would have been absurd to ask Marzio to build a whole new camera for her to play with, so she'd set up this simple test. To measure the effect of time alone, a second mirror in its own evacuated container had been shut away in a light-proof box.

Carla stood by the bench, eyeing the lamp warily. She'd had to beg Assunto to approve the use of sunstone, though this handful was nothing to the quantity the *Peerless*'s cooling system burned up every day. "What's the purpose of this experiment?" he'd asked irritably. He'd have to justify his decision to the Council in person at the next meeting, so he needed as pithy a summary as possible.

"Understanding the stability of matter."

"And how exactly will a tarnished mirror help with that?"

"If the surface of a mirror can change in a vacuum," Carla had argued, "that's not a chemical reaction, it's something simpler. If the luxagens in the mirrorstone are rearranging themselves in response to light, that could provide us with a *mildly* unstable system that we'd have a chance to manipulate and study—"

"As opposed to the kind that explodes in your face." Assunto was of the school that believed luxagens would turn out to be pure fiction—he preferred to think of matter as a continuum rather than a collection of discrete particles—but in the end he'd signed the requisition for six scroods of sunstone.

Carla had re-read and signed the safety regulations. A sunstone lamp could not be left unattended. She went and stood at her desk, but kept her rear eyes on the lamp's fizzing crucible as she marked her optics students' assignments. After the first half-dozen it was tedious work, but she forced herself to wait as long as she could before taking a break.

Carla had been told that she'd have to share this cramped workshop with Onesto, the archivist, until one of the senior experimentalists in the main facility retired and freed up a bench there. But she and Onesto usually managed to choose shifts with as little overlap as possible, to avoid disturbing each other, and there were advantages to working on her own.

When the clock struck the fourth bell she stopped to wind it, then she went to the cupboard and took out a bag of groundnuts. She cupped one hand and tipped three of the aromatic delicacies onto her palm, then closed her fingers over them to trap the exhilarating scent. Her whole body tingled with anticipatory pleasure, casting off the lethargy that had begun to afflict her. But Carla had the timing down to an art: just before the muscles in her throat threatened to start gulping down an unsatisfying emptiness, she tossed the nuts back into the bag and quickly returned them to the cupboard.

I did swallow them, she told herself, wiping her hand over her lips, slipping three fingers into her mouth. *That's the aftertaste.*

She picked up the stack of assignments again, then glanced back over the ones she'd marked so far. The men were doing better than the women, she realized—not by a lot, and not in every case, but it was impossible to miss the pattern. Carla thumped the side of the desk angrily; the lamp three strides away hissed and flickered in response. After seeing so many women slip behind in her final year, she'd promised herself that the same thing wouldn't happen to her own students. She always pushed the women in her class to participate, to ask and answer questions so they couldn't glide through the lesson in a hunger daze, but she was going to have to pay more attention and pick out the ones who were losing focus.

The ones who might be headed where Silvana had gone.

"Yeah," she muttered. "Then I'll hand out bags of nuts. Problem solved."

"Are you sure you'll be all right with this?" Carla asked Onesto.

He looked over the apparatus, respectful but not intimidated. "If in doubt, I'll just kill the flame," he said, gesturing at the lamp's dousing lever. "You can always complete the experiment with a second exposure, can't you?"

"Of course," Carla replied. It was kind of him to agree to take responsibility for the lamp; she could have enlisted one of her students, but since Onesto was going to be at his desk a few strides away regardless, it did make sense.

"Are you seeing your co tonight?" he asked, doing his best to make it sound as if he viewed the question as nothing more than ordinary small talk.

"In a couple of days." Carla had been open about the arrangement; she was hoping more people would try the same strategy, but most of her colleagues had greeted the news with embarrassment or confusion.

"Ah." Having broached the subject Onesto backed away from it. "I put my name down for the *Gnat* yesterday. For the lottery."

"The *Gnat*?"

"That's what they're calling the little rocket now," Onesto explained.

"Isn't this all a bit premature? We still don't even know how far away the Object is." Carla caught the tone of irritation in her voice. Why should she be annoyed that the astronomers' plans were progressing, as they waited for the tools they'd need to bring the project to fruition? When she'd first heard of the discovery she'd been thrilled.

She could smell Onesto's last meal through his skin.

Onesto glanced down at the mirror in its container. "I don't suppose *that* will be sensitive to infrared?"

Carla said, "If it is, it would still take half a year's exposure to record any kind of color trail."

"Right." Onesto stretched his arms behind his back. "You seem tired, Carla. You should go. I'll look after everything, I promise."

Carla's new apartment was six levels closer to the axis than the workshop. She climbed ladder after ladder in the walls' red glow; all the shafts looked the same, and at some point in the journey she lost track of where she was, unsure how much of her growing sense of lightness was down to her location and how much to hunger.

At home she took her holin dose, chewing the green flakes slowly. Her body begged for something more, but she lay down in the sand of her bed and pulled the tarpaulin into place.

She woke a bell earlier than she'd intended, thinking about the loaf in the cupboard barely four strides away. *What difference would it make, to eat the same meal a little earlier on the very same day?*

But she knew the answer. She'd be hungry again, from habit alone, at the time she was accustomed to eating. Then she'd be twice as hungry in the middle of the day, and so ravenous by the evening that she'd be struggling not to eat again. Her body had never experienced the home world's cycle of plant light by night and sunshine by day, but it could still be pushed to follow a diurnal schedule more easily than any other routine. If she let the timing of her meals slip out of synch with that internal rhythm she would have lost her best and strongest ally.

She lay half awake beneath the tarpaulin, watching the clock in the moss-light, imagining Carlo beside her. Taking her in his arms, naming their children, promising to love and protect them as he drove her hunger away.

Onesto said, "No fireworks, no down-time, no problems at all."

Carla was relieved. "Thank you. I hope the lighting didn't distract you from your work." The spillage from the lamp's beam filled the room with patches of brightness and deep shadow, and though she'd become used to it the day before the contrast now made her eyes hurt.

"Not at all." Onesto was trying to reconstruct a notebook belonging to one of the first-generation physicists, Sabino. It had turned up recently in a woeful state, and Carla didn't envy him the days he was spending squinting at the torn sheets with their smudged dye.

Onesto put away his materials and left. Carla had no more marking to do, so she stood and reviewed her notes for the next optics lesson, trying to think of ways she could convey to the students the maddening intractability of the field's unsolved problems without scaring them off completely. Most of what she taught hadn't changed since Sabino's day—and while much of that legacy possessed an indisputable elegance and consistency, and might well deserve to be passed unaltered down the ages, the rest was a perplexing mess.

No one had been able to improve on Nereo's equation, which connected light to the "source strength" of the hypothetical particles he'd called luxagens, much as Vittorio's equation connected gravity to mass. Sabino had demonstrated that the force implied by Nereo's equation was real, by showing that it could hold two tiny mineral grains together, despite a visible gap between them. But taking all of Nereo's ideas at face value soon led to predictions that simply weren't true.

Whatever the fundamental constituents of a rock or a flower were, they either possessed the light-making property or they didn't; it wasn't something that could come and go. A few lines of mathematics proved that "source strength" was conserved, as surely as energy itself. So matter had to be made of *something* that possessed source strength, or no flower could glow, no fuel could burn. The trouble was, anything with source strength should give off *some* light, visible or invisible, all the time; only absolute stillness—or the equally unlikely contrivance of a pure high-frequency oscillation—could keep it from radiating. But a substance that emitted light could not be left unchanged by the process: the energy of the light had to be balanced by the creation of energy of the opposite kind. A flower could use its newfound energy to make food, but what was a rock to do? With a sprinkling of liberator a rock went up in flames, but why should it need that push? Why hadn't every lode of sunstone simply blown itself apart, eons ago?

Carla disciplined herself not to so much as peek at the experiment before the exposure was complete. When the full twelve bells had passed, she knelt beside the clearstone container and checked that the spectrum had remained aligned with the same marks on the paper as before, then she stood and extinguished the sunstone lamp. Onesto had lit an ordinary firestone lamp in the corner of the workshop; now she turned up its light to help her see clearly.

She slid the container out from under the bench and tipped it for a better view; the clearstone caught the light and confused her with its own reflections, but she was almost certain that the mirror's sheen had been diminished. She fetched a needle and made a tiny hole in the container's resin seal, then waited impatiently while the air squealed back in.

With the pressure safely equalised, she cut the seal away completely, removed the lid and took out the mirror, careful not to detach the gridded paper that she'd glued beneath it.

Carla held the mirror up to catch the light. There was an unmistakable dull white patina, uniform and complete across the width of the mirror—but not its length. It stretched from one end of the rectangle to a point about halfway along, where it disappeared abruptly. She summoned the calibration notes for the grid onto her thigh. The tarnished region corresponded to a portion of the spectrum running from infrared to green.

Why stop at green? The intense light from the sunstone beam would have shaken the luxagens, making them vibrate, making them radiate their own light in turn... giving them the energy they needed to break out of the mirrorstone's regular structure, damaging the surface, spoiling the sheen. But why should the color of the light have such a sharply delineated effect? The theory of solids held that a material's only hope of stability was for its luxagens to sit in energy valleys whose natural frequency of vibration was greater than the *maximum* frequency of light—so at least that favored, resonant frequency couldn't generate radiation and aid in the material's destruction. So why should light have the power to shake luxagens loose on the red side of green but not the blue side? Since *every* color was far below the resonant frequency, the response should have varied smoothly across the spectrum, without any sudden jumps.

Carla turned the mirror back and forth in front of her eyes, wondering if it could all be an error, an artifact. Maybe an obstacle outside the container had intruded into the blue end of the spectrum—something Onesto had stashed under the bench for part of the night? But that was ridiculous; why would he have done that? And even if he'd set out deliberately to sabotage the experiment, she'd been present for the greater part of the exposure. Blue light *had* reached the mirror. The color-dependence was real.

As the mirror flared in the firestone's light, a new feature marring the surface jumped out for an instant and then vanished. It was like glimpsing a white thread on a white floor, only to lose it again. Carla cursed and repeated the motion, over and over, until she found herself staring at a second, faint edge. In the half of the mirror that had seemed to her before to be uniformly shiny and new, there was in fact another, very subtle change in its reflectivity. The tarnish that she'd thought had ended completely at green actually continued—vastly diminished—along a section that stretched almost down to violet. *And beyond that?* She was no longer prepared to assume that the surface remained pristine; all she could be sure of was that she'd exhausted the discriminatory powers of her vision.

But there were *at least* two abrupt transitions in the density of the tarnish: two sudden changes in the damage the light had done, depending on its color.

Next to the calibration notes on her thigh, Carla wrote the wavelengths that marked these transitions. She committed them to memory, then started sketching luxagen arrays, doodling calculations, trying to make sense of the numbers. Maybe there was some kind of shift in the response of the mirrorstone when the light's wavelength crossed some natural length scales dictated by its structure. Luxagens were expected to be separated from their nearest neighbors by roughly the same distance as light's minimum wavelength, but other regularities showed up at greater distances.

There was no fit, though, between her two numbers and any of the known array geometries.

Carla paced the workshop. If not the wavelengths, what about the frequencies? She did the conversion: the green edge was at three dozen and three generoso-cycles per pause, the violet edge at two dozen and seven. But the frequencies at which luxagens were expected to vibrate, in mirrorstone or any other substance, could only be pinned down to within an order of magnitude—crudely constrained by the known properties of solids and the strength of Nereo's force. So to what should she compare these frequencies?

To each other. They were in a ratio of five to four. Not exactly, but it was very close.

Carla remeasured the locations of the edges in the tarnish with scrupulous care, then recalculated everything.

Within the range of uncertainty imposed by the measurements, the ratio was indistinguishable from five to four.

4

arlo said, "I'd like to come back to your team, if you'll have me. I'm giving up on wheat. I want to work with animals again."

Tosco reached out for a guide rope and pulled himself away from his workbench. "What's brought this on?" he asked. "I never thought of you as easily discouraged."

Carlo tried to block out the anxious humming of the voles; there must have been three or four dozen of the animals in the cages attached to the far wall. It hadn't taken him long to grow accustomed to the blissful silence of the plant kingdom.

He said, "Do you know what my biggest achievement in the last three years has been? Understanding why some farms end up with all of their wheat-flowers synchronized, while in others the plants split into two groups that take turns producing light."

"I wouldn't belittle that," Tosco said. "Surely the yield is higher when there are staggered shifts?"

"It is," Carlo replied. "Having half your neighbors sleeping means less ambient light to inhibit production. But the difference is tiny, it's marginal. What I was really looking for was a way to keep the flowers open for a greater portion of each day—and nothing I tried brought me any closer to that. If I'm getting nowhere, maybe I should admit that I made a mistake by switching fields in the first place."

Tosco stretched out his top pair of arms in a gesture encompassing the workshop. "So what exactly would you do, if you rejoined us?" One of Carlo's old colleagues, Amanda, was dissecting a lizard on a bench nearby, with a huddle of students looking on. In the corner behind them another researcher, Macaria, who'd been loading a centrifuge with tissue samples, swung down the safety shield and retreated. Sometimes the different density fractions in organic matter weren't stable on their own, and the endpoint could be explosive.

Carlo took a moment to summon up his courage; until now he hadn't put this into words for anyone. "I want to find a way to inhibit quadraparity."

"I see." Tosco's tone was not enthusiastic. "Do you know how many drugs they tested for that, before either of us were born? The only thing that kept the vole population stable in that program was the fact that the fatal treatments balanced the merely ineffectual ones."

"So it might require something other than a drug," Carlo ventured.

"We know how to inhibit quadraparity," Tosco said. "The solution might not be as pleasant as we'd wish—"

"Or as reliable," Carlo interjected.

"It's not perfect," Tosco conceded. "But no treatment is perfect. It's an innate property of women's bodies that they produce four offspring under ordinary conditions. Anything that interferes with such a fundamental process is doing damage to their health, by definition."

"Holin isn't perfect," Carlo protested, "but where's the damage or the pain from that?"

"Putting reproduction on hold isn't the same as modifying the outcome."

Carlo couldn't argue with that, but he couldn't accept the larger claim either. "Women's bodies have an innate ability to be biparous, too. It makes sense that it's normally only triggered by famine; the question is, *triggered how?* If we could understand that process in detail, why shouldn't we be able to push the same lever without the usual antecedents?"

Tosco said, "Our bodies don't come with levers attached. If you're not going to throw random drugs at the problem, where would you start?"

Carlo hesitated, but there was no point underselling his plans now. "What I want to do is investigate the whole process of fission as thoroughly as possible. Unravel the mechanism in both biparous and quadraparous species—right down to the signaling level—then look for the safest, most effective point to intervene."

Tosco buzzed wryly. "That's a lofty proposal. Do you think it's going to be easier than improving the crop yields?"

"Probably not," Carlo admitted. "But to succeed at this would count for much more."

"When you left here," Tosco reminded him, "you told me you were going to double the wheat entitlements, then retire to raise your children."

Carlo cringed. If he'd made some real progress toward that goal his youthful boast might have seemed less vain, but it would have done nothing to redeem his misdirected ambition. "And what would happen if someone actually achieved that?" he said. "We'd get a generation or two of plenty before the increased population overtook the increase in the harvest. What we *need* is stability. If I've read the history correctly, at the time of the launch so many women on the *Peerless* had escaped from coercive families and were committed to dying childless that it must have looked as if a balance could be maintained that way: for every woman who had four children, another would willingly have none at all. But that's not the culture any more."

"No." Tosco regarded him with bemusement, but didn't spell out what Carlo suspected he was thinking: *The culture now is to accept the women's famine. That works well enough, so why not let it be?*

"Let me try this," Carlo pleaded. If he had no other choice he could work on his own, but everything would be easier with the support of his former mentor and his team. "What's the worst that can happen? We learn something useless about the reproductive cycle in voles?"

Tosco said, "The worst thing would be if the harvest fails, and you start wishing you'd persisted with your last career. But if you really believe you have the patience to carry this through—"

"I'm certain of that," Carlo insisted.

Tosco looked skeptical, but he was done with arguing. He said, "How can I turn down an agronomist who's willing to step off his pedestal and rejoin his old friends?"

It was Carlo's turn to travel down the axis, to meet his co in the new home she'd made for herself. Most of his friends had told him that a partial separation sounded like the worst of both worlds, but he'd studied the numbers from the last census. Total separation was a bad idea: it left women at an elevated risk of spontaneous fission, and no amount of holin could eliminate that entirely. But living together and relying on willpower alone to delay reproduction was even worse; more than half the recorded births in those circumstances had come earlier than planned. The trick was to let your co's body know that you hadn't abandoned her—that if it waited, her children would be cared for—while doing all you could to minimize the risk of delivering on that promise prematurely.

Carla wasn't home when he arrived at the apartment. The moss-light was enough for him to see his way around, so he didn't light a lamp. He'd brought four loaves for them to share, for the evening meal and breakfast; he packed them away in the empty cupboard.

Passing the entrance to the bedroom, he saw a spare tarpaulin floating in the air, suspended against the weak gravity by a faint updraft from a cooling vent.

When he heard the guide rope twanging in the corridor he went to the doorway and parted the curtains. Carla saw him and chirped excitedly. "Get ready to hear some good news," she said.

"What—you've won a place on the *Gnat*?"

"That would be something." She followed him back into the apartment. "But this is better."

Carlo lit a lamp in the front room, then clung to the rope beside her as she described her tarnishing experiment. She'd had to refresh his hazy memories of Nereo's force and Yalda's puzzles countless times before, so he knew she'd forgive him if he didn't immediately grasp the significance of the results.

"Five to four," he said. "What's so special about that?"

"A ratio of small integers isn't likely to be a coincidence," Carla replied. "If it was dozens and something to dozens and something else, that would be meaningless, but this suggests very strongly that the numbers in the ratio really are lurking in the physics itself. Four of something, then five of something... the transitions mark a kind of succession."

Carlo could only understand physics by translating it into geometry; he started raising undulating lines on his chest. "So can I draw it like this, fitting different numbers of cycles into the same amount of time?"

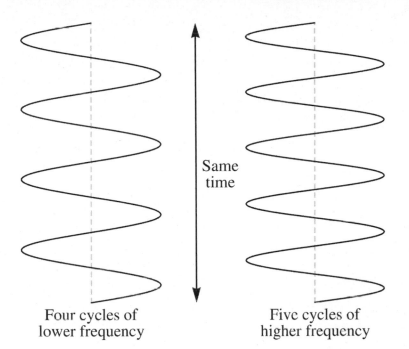

Four cycles of
lower frequency

Same
time

Five cycles of
higher frequency

"No, no, no!" Carla chided him. "You've got it backward!"

"What's wrong?" he asked. "Doesn't that give a five to four frequency ratio?"

"It does," she conceded. "But I'm working on the assumption that the frequency goes *down* as the associated integer goes up, and you've described the opposite trend. Going your way, there'd be another transition at a higher frequency—'frequency six', out in the infrared—beyond which mirrors would start tarnishing at an even greater rate. The trouble with that is, if the pattern in tarnishing rates held up then Marzio's mirrors would have needed re-polishing after a couple of stints, not a couple of years."

"All right," Carlo said. "So how should I picture it?"

"I don't know yet," Carla admitted. "All I can say is that light produces a strong tarnishing effect when four times the frequency exceeds a certain number. When the frequency falls so low that you need to multiply it by *five* to meet the same target, the effect suddenly becomes drastically weaker—and when you need to multiply it by six, it becomes weaker still. It might even vanish entirely at that point; I'd need to do a much longer exposure to be sure."

Carlo pondered this. "Wouldn't it be easier to follow the pattern in the other direction? If the effect grows *weaker* as the magic number goes from four to five to six… what about three? Shouldn't you get super-fast tarnishing from waves where you can reach the target merely by *tripling* the frequency?"

"There are no such waves," Carla replied. "The target is more than three times the maximum frequency of light, so you can never reach it by tripling."

"Aha." Carlo had a glimmer of comprehension. "Which is a good thing for mirrorstone, isn't it? If it was that easy to damage, it probably wouldn't be around at all."

"Exactly!" Carla's eyes widened with pleasure. "Whatever's going on here, it's showing us the border of stability. And maybe every mineral, every solid, has its own 'target number' like this—but in the case of something like hardstone, it could be so high that even six times the maximum frequency of light doesn't reach it."

Carlo said, "The empirical rule sounds simple enough. I suppose the hard part will be making it mesh with the theory—with Nereo's equation and the luxagen model?"

"Yes."

"And…?" he prompted her.

"And right now," she admitted, "I have no idea how to do that."

Carlo told her about his meeting with Tosco. He'd given her no warning of his plan to return to the animal physiology group—and he offered no justification now, but he watched her face as he spoke. Carla listened politely, in silence, but she almost flinched when he reached the point of describing his new research program. And this was from the subject in its most abstract, impersonal form: comparing biparous and quadraparous fission, hunting for the mechanism that allowed some species to switch between the two.

He understood why it was painful for her to hear. Behind these calm career announcements he was whispering a promise that he had no right to make: *I'll find a way out of the famine—if not for you, for our daughter.* He had no right, because people had tried and failed before: countless women driven by hunger, countless men driven by the suffering they'd seen. There was a terrible equilibrium now, and an unspoken consensus that the only real option was to cling to their hard-won resilience and endure what had to be endured.

Carlo couldn't live like that any more, but he understood that he had to follow this new path quietly, making it as easy as possible for everyone around him to avert their gaze. When he'd said all he needed to say for the sake of honesty, he steered the conversation back to the mysteries of light and matter. Failure there might leave them stranded, doom their whole mission and kill off all their ancestors—but at least they hadn't been cursed with some wretched half-solution that sapped their resolve and kept them from reaching the real thing.

5

"Lizard skin?" Tamara asked incredulously.

"Lizard skin," Ivo confirmed. "The jungle has its uses."

"Is that where you go looking, when nothing else works?"

Ivo said, "That depends on what I'm after. When people think of light they usually think of flowers, but most animal tissues have some kind of optical activity too."

Tamara managed a murmur of concurrence, as if the first course of action that anyone should consider when faced with the need to find a new chemical would be to pop a lizard in a centrifuge and see what oozed out.

"What kind of wavelengths are we talking about? What kind of sensitivity?"

"Come and see for yourself." Ivo led her deeper into the chemists' domain, four hands shuttling him swiftly along the guide rope.

As they moved down the center of the cylindrical chamber, Tamara watched his colleagues at work around them. Most were harnessed to benches fixed to the walls, or were attending to various spinning or vibrating contraptions, but one eight-armed chemist was blithely floating in mid-air as he snatched vials of reagents from a weightless cluster in front of him, mixing the contents in a dizzyingly rapid sequence that Tamara could only assume was essential to the success of the procedure. When his rear gaze fell on her she quickly averted her eyes, afraid she might distract him and end up turning the whole chamber into an inferno.

Ivo switched to a cross-rope that took them to his own bench, where he slipped into the harness. A large lightproof box was attached to the bench-top; he swung up the lid to allow Tamara, still hanging on the cross-rope, to inspect the contents.

"That's just an ordinary lamp in there," he explained, gesturing at a spherical hardstone enclosure. "Lens, prism... it's all standard equipment." Ivo pulled the prism out of its slot and passed it to her for approval, as if he feared she might suspect him of some sleight of hand. The prize she was offering wouldn't be much use to a cheat: any attempt to visit the Object would be an awful anticlimax if they failed to calculate its distance correctly. But Tamara obliged her host out of courtesy, and held the prism up to the light of the nearest lamp. The shimmering sequence of colors that appeared in front of her as she rotated it around its axis was no different from that produced by any piece of clearstone similarly cut.

She returned the prism to Ivo. He replaced it, then pointed out an unprepossessing piece of yellowish, resin-coated paper, positioned about a span from the light source. "This won't make a permanent record itself; it will need to be supplemented with an ordinary camera. It doesn't need any activating gas, but it only retains its potency for a few days after preparation."

"I see." Tamara made a mental note to start factoring that into her plans, hoping it wouldn't lead to the *Gnat* having to carry a lizard-press.

Ivo tapped the lamp's enclosure, shaking some liberator into contact with the firestone until the hot gas from the flames themselves started scattering the powder back onto the fuel. He closed the lid, then gestured to Tamara to peek through a slit in the box, opposite the lamp.

She moved back along the rope so she could bring her head down closer, self-conscious for a moment at her contortions. When she was in place, the first thing she noticed was an ordinary spectrum, muted by the paper through which she was seeing it but no different in scale and orientation than she would have expected from the prism's geometry.

She closed all her eyes but one, ridding herself of distractions. Ivo said, "If you want to block the visible spectrum, there's a lever on your right." She found it, and slid an opaque screen across the band of colors. Then she waited while her vision adapted to whatever remained.

Out of the grayness, a blurred vertical bar of shimmering yellow light appeared—far beyond the red end of the hidden spectrum.

Tamara gauged the strength of the fluorescence. Assuming the effect scaled linearly, infrared light from the Object would produce far too weak a response in this lizard paper to see with the naked eye, but they could probably capture it with a camera and a long enough exposure.

"What wavelength is this?" she asked Ivo, without moving away from the slit. She was prepared to take his word for it, and hoped he wouldn't insist on her verifying his answer immediately with protractors and calibration curves.

"About two scarso-scants."

She did some quick calculations on her forearm. Light of that wavelength traveled at about an eighth the speed of red light, and it would extend a visible color trail by a factor of a dozen. If that wasn't good enough to let them measure the Object's speed, it would have to be moving at little more than a jogging pace. Any slower—and nearer—and they'd be able to toss a rope out to it and make the whole journey by hand.

"Congratulations," Tamara said. "You've won yourself a trip into the void." She drew away from the box, and Ivo opened it and shut off the lamp, contemplating her announcement in silence. Everyone had been outside the *Peerless* for at least a few shifts of fire watch, but traveling across the void until the mountain vanished from sight had to be a daunting prospect for anyone.

"More immediately," she added, "we'll be needing you at all the planning meetings, to ensure that the *Gnat*'s capable of supporting whatever experiments you have in mind. There's only going to be one chance to get this right."

"Only one chance?" he replied. "I hope not."

"The Object's on a linear trajectory," Tamara said. "Once it passes us, it's never coming back."

Ivo said, "Exactly. And this might be the only substantial body of orthogonal matter to come within our reach for generations. However diligently we prepare for this trip, however large the samples we're able to bring back, it's not going to be enough for everything we need to do."

Tamara said, "What do you suggest then? If the *Peerless* matches velocities with the Object we'll slip out of orthogonality with the home world. Not by much—but do we really want to be under pressure to solve their problems any faster?" The whole point of the *Peerless* was to grant its inhabitants as long as they needed to find a way to deal with the Hurtlers. If time on the endangered planet began to creep forward for the travelers, however slowly, that advantage would be lost.

"I don't want the *Peerless* changing course," Ivo said. "But that doesn't mean we can't match velocities."

Tamara gazed at him uncomprehendingly for a moment, but then she grasped his meaning.

She said, "Why is it that whatever you ask a chemist, the answer invariably entails an explosion?"

Ivo buzzed delightedly. "A *small* explosion," he said, "could correct the Object's course, transforming it from a fleeting marvel whose passing we might recount to our grandchildren into a resource that they can study and exploit for as long as they wish. And if this thing is made of the same material that caused spot ignitions on the mountainside before spin… all we'll need to do is toss the right amount of calmstone at the Object and it will become a kind of rocket in its own right."

"No doubt," Tamara replied. "But how do we discover what *the right amount* is—without blowing the whole thing into fragments, or creating a brand new star?"

"Calorimetry," Ivo replied. "We'll need to take samples and carry them a safe distance away from the Object itself, then determine just how much energy is released in the reaction with calmstone."

Tamara had a vision of the two of them in the void, drifting along beside a jagged mountain of orthogonal matter. While she struggled to steer the *Gnat*, Ivo would be juggling vials of reagents—trying to calibrate a detonation that would either kill them both and obliterate their quarry, or grant their descendants a storehouse of energy that could pave the way for their return from exile.

6

atrizia took the guide rope to the front of the room, then turned and addressed the class. "Suppose there are some luxagens in the mirrorstone that are bound so loosely that they can easily be freed from their energy valleys by a light wave. Suppose they get swept along by that wave, until they're moving as fast as the light itself. If you compare the geometry of the light with the geometry of the luxagens' motion, you can see that each of these luxagens ends up with an energy that's proportional to the frequency of the light."

Carla watched as the usually shy student sketched a diagram on her chest illustrating the relationship.

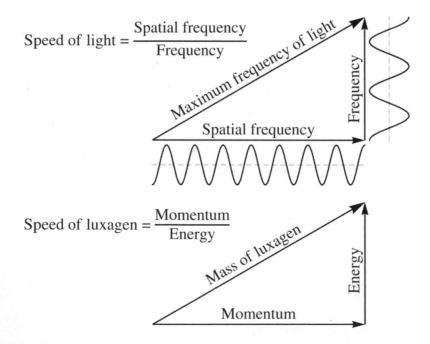

"To tarnish the mirrorstone at a given location," Patrizia continued, "will require a certain amount of energy. Suppose that for light of the highest frequency, four luxagens can deliver that amount—so if a site in the mirrorstone is struck four times by these luxagens it will suffer the damage that we see as tarnishing. But as the frequency of the light falls, the energy per luxagen will fall too, so there'll come a point where *five* luxagens would be needed to reach the same threshold. The tarnishing will still occur—but it will suddenly take much longer, and for a given exposure time it will be much fainter."

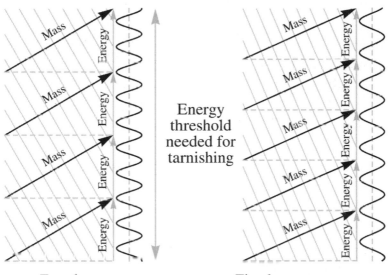

Four luxagens
moving with speed
of higher frequency light

Five luxagens
moving with speed
of lower frequency light

Patrizia drew four stacked energy vectors for luxagens at the transition point, then added a second stack that reached the same threshold with five particles. "Eventually the same thing will happen again: there'll be a frequency below which even five luxagens won't be sufficient. And the ratio of the two critical frequencies will be exactly *five to four*."

Carla could only marvel at the young woman's ingenuity. Yalda's great discovery—on Mount Peerless, no less—was that the frequencies of light in time and in space formed two sides of a right triangle—with the ratio between these sides determined by the speed at which the light traveled, while the length of the hypotenuse remained fixed, regardless of whatever else was changed.

But the energy, momentum and mass of a solid object formed a right triangle too. This triangle's hypotenuse was also fixed, by the object's mass, while the speed of the object set the ratio between the other two sides.

Arrange for the speed to be the same in both cases—make a luxagen, a particle of matter, match speeds with a pulse of light—and the two triangles adopted the same shape, with corresponding sides locked into a fixed relationship. The energy of the particle became proportional to the frequency of the wave. And instead of the shifts in tarnishing being tied, inexplicably, to integer multiples of the light's frequency, these particles in lock-step with the light would naturally carry *energy* in integer multiples.

Carla had set aside her planned lesson and invited her optics class to debate the tarnishing results. "This is your chance to argue for any wild idea you're willing to defend," she'd urged them, "even if you can't make it perfect, even if there are gaps and flaws you can't fix. There have been gaps and flaws in everything I've taught you, and mysteries people have struggled with since before the launch—but this time no one's been there before you; Yalda, Nereo and Sabino can't offer us their guesses. So this is your chance to go beyond everything you've learned: to see what's missing in the old ideas, or to tear them down and start building something new."

It had started slowly, with everyone tentative and wary—and the usual people needing prodding to get them to engage at all. But after half a bell of meandering, of questions and clarifications and increasingly passionate claims, three of her students had been brave enough to sketch their own novel explanations for the strange pattern in the tarnishing.

Romolo had suggested that the light striking the mirrorstone could be generating sound waves within the material, and some small nonlinearity in the equations for those waves was allowing energy to move between different harmonics, all the way up to the natural frequency of vibration of the luxagens. Palladio had proposed that light with the right frequency could give suitably timed kicks to the oscillating luxagens in such a manner that neighbors in the array were pushed together close enough to drag each other out of their energy valleys. But it was hard to see how either of these theories could predict a *tiered* pattern, rather than isolated bands of tarnish confined to a few special resonant frequencies.

Patrizia's account certainly explained the tiers—and the analogy she'd used between energy and frequency was so simple and elegant that Carla was ashamed not to have thought of it herself. But for all its virtues, the theory as a whole didn't quite hang together.

Carla broached the first problem as gently as she could. "You're relying on some of the luxagens to get swept up by the light?"

"Yes," Patrizia agreed. "Pushed along faster and faster, until they're moving at the speed of the wave itself."

"So how would that look, if we were moving alongside them? If we matched velocities with the luxagen, what would we see?"

"It would appear motionless to us," Patrizia replied, puzzled. Wasn't that obvious?

"And how would the light wave appear?"

"Motionless too. Everything's moving with the same speed."

"The light *pulse* is moving with the same speed," Carla said, "the way you've envisioned this. But the history of a pulse is perpendicular in four-space to the wavefronts. So what are the wavefronts doing?"

"Oh." Patrizia lowered her gaze and slumped away from the guide rope. "They're going backward. And so the luxagen wouldn't be moving with the pulse—it would be trapped in an energy valley between two wavefronts, moving backward at a completely different speed."

Carla said, "Right. The motion of the pulse is *not* the motion of the wavefronts! It's an easy mistake to make: I still get confused by the difference sometimes."

She sketched the situation Patrizia had described. "For the luxagen to end up moving with a constant velocity, it has to be sitting in an energy valley. In fact, I'd only expect that to happen with a very high intensity light source, otherwise the valley wouldn't be deep enough. But if it *did* happen, the luxagen would be motionless with respect to the wavefronts, not the pulse."

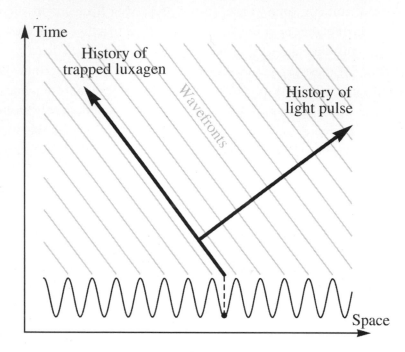

"I understand," Patrizia said sadly. She began to move away.

Carla said, "Wait. There's another problem here, and it's worth discussing that as well."

Patrizia was mortified now. "Isn't the first flaw bad enough?"

"Bear with me for a moment," Carla suggested. "Sometimes two errors actually cancel each other out."

"Only sign errors!" Romolo interjected. Carla raised a hand to hush him, then turned back to Patrizia. "You had four or five mobile luxagens able to cause tarnishing when they reached a threshold in their total energy," she said. "But if they're going to strike another luxagen trapped in an energy valley, knocking that luxagen free will require a transfer of kinetic energy equal to the depth of the valley. Kinetic energy goes *down* as true energy increases, so your original idea, with the mobile luxagens matching the speed of the light pulse, wouldn't have worked. But if the luxagens are moving with the wavefronts, not the light pulse, everything is reversed: the higher the frequency of the light, the slower the light pulse, but the faster the wavefronts. So luxagens trapped between wavefronts will be moving faster and carrying more kinetic energy when the frequency of the light is higher."

Patrizia thought it through. "The trend ends up pointing the right way," she said, "but the numbers don't work out any more, do they? The frequencies at which four or five luxagens cross a threshold for *kinetic* energy won't be in a five to four ratio."

"No," Carla conceded. "And of course there are other problems that would have to be solved to make this work: you'd have to analyze the collisions in detail to see just how much kinetic energy was transferred from the mobile luxagens to the trapped ones, and also account for any radiation being produced. It's hard to see how all those effects could conspire to leave a simple five to four ratio."

Patrizia said, "You're right, it was foolish." She started back to her position in the class.

"It wasn't foolish at all!" Carla called after her. Though she couldn't see how to salvage the whole elaborate scenario, its complications had been wrapped around an insight as beautiful as any from the glory days of rotational physics.

"All right," she said. "We still have no good theory of tarnishing. So what we do now is try to think up a new experiment: something that might help us make sense of the first one."

Romolo said, "Whatever knocks these luxagens out of their usual sites in the mirrorstone... where do they all go?"

"They must find a new kind of stable configuration," Carla said. "That's all that tarnish can be, after all: luxagens rearranged so that they no longer form the normal structure of mirrorstone."

"But then why don't we see two different kinds of tarnish?" Romolo protested. "Mirrorstone that's lost some of its luxagens, and mirrorstone that's gained what the other parts have lost?"

"The tarnish might well be heterogeneous," Carla replied, "but I'd expect that to be on a scale too small to see, even under a microscope."

Azelia—who'd spent most of the class staring blankly into mid-air— suddenly interjected, "Why does all of this happen faster in a vacuum? What difference does the air make?"

Carla said, "I think the air must react with the polished surface in a way that protects it against tarnishing. We used to think air *created* the tarnish, but now it seems more likely that what it creates is a thin layer that's immune to the effect."

Azelia wasn't satisfied. "If this layer doesn't stop the mirrorstone being a mirror, then surely light must still be interacting with the material in the same way. So why wouldn't it rearrange the luxagens in the same way?"

Carla had no reply. The truth was, she'd been so entranced by the astonishing simplicity of the frequency cut-off that she'd given very little thought to the messy details of the tarnished material itself.

She caught the look of elation crossing Romolo's face before he even spoke. "The luxagens go into the vacuum!" he declared. "Surely that's it? Air must modify the surface of the mirrorstone in a way that makes it harder for the luxagens to escape—but when there's no air, the light can send them drifting off into the void!"

Free luxagens? Carla felt her tympanum tightening in preparation for a skeptical retort, but then she realized that the idea wasn't so absurd. It had long been conjectured that flames contained a smattering of free luxagens, but they'd be impossible to detect among all the unstable debris of combustion, and there was no reason to expect them to remain free for long when they were constantly colliding with other things. But a thin breeze comprised of *nothing but luxagens* wafting off a slab of mirrorstone into the vacuum was a very different scenario.

"You could be right," she said. "So how do we test this idea? If there's a dilute gas of free luxagens in the container that holds the mirrorstone, how could we tell?"

There was silence for several pauses, then Azelia demanded irritably, "Can't we just look? Most gases are transparent, but luxagens would be nothing like an ordinary gas."

"Luxagens should scatter light," Carla agreed. "In fact, every one of you should be able to calculate what happens when light of moderate intensity meets a free luxagen. So come back in three days with the answer to that, and some suggestions for how we could try to observe it."

When the classroom was empty, Carla felt a sudden pang of anxiety. Now that she'd torn up the curriculum, where was she heading? She'd made one tantalizing discovery—and for a while that in itself had been exhilarating—but she couldn't begin to explain what she'd found, and in the aftermath the whole subject seemed murkier than ever. What pride could she take in leaving the next generation with one more problem than she'd inherited herself?

She fumbled in the cupboard for the groundnuts she'd hidden behind a stack of worn textbooks. *How many holes were there now, in Nereo's theory?* Too many, and not enough. One anomaly was an embarrassment, two were perplexing… but a dozen or so might come together to reveal a whole new vision of the world. What she should be fearing was not mess and confusion, but the possibility that she'd only see enough of it to take the process halfway.

7

Carlo spun the syringe between his thumb and forefinger, suddenly unsure whether or not he'd identified the right spot to insert it. The male vole adhering to the immobilized female glared up at him balefully, unable to do anything for his trapped co but promising her tormentor a suitable punishment once he was detached. Carlo could only sympathize. Over the years, biologists had managed to produce a strain that would breed, not merely in captivity, but in the face of stresses and indignities that would have seen their wild ancestors prudently deferring the act. With no hope of privacy, the caged voles could not afford to miss an opportunity.

"Do you want me to do this?" Amanda offered. "You might be a bit out of practice."

The protocol Carlo had prepared referred to landmarks on the skin patterns that were shared by every member of this strain of voles, but his notes had been based on a stylized reference version of the pattern. Now that he was facing a real animal again after a three-year hiatus, he was beginning to recall just how tricky it could be to identify the features on each individual.

The reference pattern showed a junction between three crisp dark stripes, just behind each shoulder. For this subject, the injection was meant to go in the top corner of that junction. But the stripes on the clamped female in front of him were diffuse, and the corner between them showed a gradient of diminishing pigment at least half a scant wide. This didn't mean the task was hopeless; if you took your bearings from the entire hide it was still possible to get an accurate fix. But he hadn't had to do that for a very long time.

"Actually, if you don't mind—" Carlo moved aside and handed the syringe to Amanda. She quickly thrust the needle into the female's skin, up to the depth calibration mark, then pushed the plunger, delivering a small dose of suppressant. The male emitted an angry chirp; Amanda withdrew the needle and closed the lid of the cage. Carlo reached over and shifted a lever that loosened the clamp on the female. He didn't want any confounding mechanical effects interfering with the fission process.

"Thank you," he said. "I'm still waiting for the old instincts to come back."

"I can believe that," Amanda replied. "I have the opposite problem: you could put a rock in front of me and I'd start to see hide markings on it."

Carlo had thought he'd be the one confidently demonstrating the protocol to *her*, as a first step in convincing himself that he could rely on her to perform some of the trials without his supervision. But he'd only been two years her senior the last time they'd worked together, and he felt foolish now for assuming that he'd somehow retained his old advantage in experience. His own world wasn't full of imaginary voles; it was strewn with hallucinatory wheat petals.

The male began squirming and thrashing about, eager to be unencumbered. Apparently the exchange of signals was over to his satisfaction, but the skin of his chest was still stuck in place. He grabbed the transitioning female with all four paws and forced himself apart from her, then he scampered around in a frenzy, clinging to the twigs that crisscrossed the cage like guide ropes, chirping loud warnings.

"No one's tried this before during fission?" Amanda asked.

"A long time ago, with a much coarser suppressant." If she hadn't heard of that work it was because nothing much had come of it. Carlo didn't want to waste time repeating other people's experiments, but the new preparation Tosco had discovered blocked signaling in a smaller volume of tissue, and also seemed to have fewer side effects. "I'm not expecting to find some magic spot where we can interrupt transmission and see the number of offspring halved," he said. "But to get anywhere, we're going to need the best map we can make of the pathways that influence fission. Even these tiny doses will probably interfere with a dozen individual pathways, but that will still be a big improvement on the last map."

Amanda said, "I've had some success with microsurgery, for identifying phalangeal control pathways in lizards."

Carlo was intrigued. "So you cut into the leg under a microscope… and managed to paralyze a particular *toe*?"

"Almost," she replied. "I have to infer things from incremental damage—I can't actually sever the pathway for any given toe without severing other things as well. And of course the lizards either re-route the signals within a chime or two, or resorb the whole limb and reconstruct it."

The female vole had already been limbless in her mating posture, but now her body was deforming further into an almost featureless ellipsoid. Carlo could just make out a shallow longitudinal trench that marked the beginning of the primary partition. Whatever change the injection had wrought, it hadn't suppressed the start of fission itself.

"So you know how to paralyze a lizard," Carlo said, "but have you ever thought of doing the reverse?"

Amanda buzzed softly. "The old yellow flash muscle twitch? I know it impresses students, but I'm not sure that there's much to be learned that way."

"I was thinking of something subtler than a twitch," he said. "Imagine severing the pathways from the brain… but then introducing motor signals of your own."

Amanda was skeptical. "Even if we could manage the mechanics of an intervention like that, we'd have no way of knowing the proper time sequences for the signals. Believe me, I've stared down a microscope at enough flickering lizard tissue to know that I'm never going to be able to transcribe what's happening."

"I have some ideas about that," Carlo confided. Faint lines could now be seen neatly dividing each half of the vole blastula, displaced to the usual degree above the midline to guarantee an extra quota of flesh to the daughters. The father-to-be screeched triumphantly, as if he knew that his captors had been thwarted. But any celebration was premature; in the old studies a similarly placed dose of suppressant had led to stillborn males.

"What ideas?" Amanda pressed him.

"Run a long strip of light-sensitive paper past a probe into the tissue," Carlo replied. "Turn the variation of light over time into a variation over space. You could have the whole history of a motor sequence spread out in front of you, to read at your leisure."

Amanda thought it over. "I suppose that might work." She shifted her grip on one of the ropes they shared, sending a brief shudder through Carlo's body.

"You could copy the pattern," he said. "Maybe modify it too. Then send it back into the body using a strip of paper of variable transparency, moving in front of a light source. But the beauty of it is, you could send it back to a completely different site, if you wanted to. Maybe even send it into a completely different animal."

Amanda buzzed softly, not quite mocking him but amused at his audacity. "So that's the plan? Record the way a biparous animal initiates fission, then feed those signals into a quadraparous species in place of their own version of the sequence?"

"I don't know," Carlo said. "Maybe that's naïve. The difference might not come down to anything we can localize that way."

"Still, it makes more sense than a drug," Amanda conceded. "I wouldn't say it's not worth trying."

They watched in silence as the primary partition began to fracture, cracking into plates of shiny brittle tissue that stuck to one side or the other. The male approached and started pawing at the structure, trying to hasten the separation.

Carlo glanced over at his colleague, wondering what her reaction would be if he dared to ask her: *On a scale of one to twelve, how much comfort does it give you to know that this is the fate of your flesh?*

When the blastula had split completely, the male took hold of one of the halves and carried it across the cage, backing away awkwardly with its two hind-paws gripping the scaffolding of twigs before extruding another pair to make the task easier. Carlo wasn't sure why the animals were so emphatic about the separation. So far as he knew co always recognized co, whatever the first sights and smells they encountered, and in any case when a crossed mating was contrived it appeared to cause no problems. Maybe it was simply advantageous for the male vole to have the strongest possible instinct to aid the process of fission—rather than standing by uselessly if the blastula became stuck—and it did no harm to take this sentiment further than was strictly necessary.

The secondary partitions were still intact, but one pair of young voles were already beginning to twitch and squirm, limbless balls of conjoined flesh struggling to wake into their own separate identities.

Amanda said, "They all look healthy so far."

"Yes." Now the other pair were wriggling too, and Carlo couldn't help feeling a visceral sense of relief. The experiment had told him nothing—except that the new suppressant hadn't been crude enough to do as much damage as the old one when delivered in the same spot. He should have been disappointed. But the sight of the four live infants was impossible to receive with anything but joy.

The father approached the tardier of the pairs, stroking his children's skin with his paws and tugging at the partition that still glued them together.

Carlo turned to Amanda. "We'd better move on. We can check the whole brood for deformities tomorrow, but we need to set a pace of six matings a day or this map's going to take forever to complete."

8

"The nozzle's fixed," Marzio told Tamara. "We're ready to launch, just name the time."

Tamara did the calculations on her forearm. The rotational period of the *Peerless* was close to seven lapses, but apparently no one had thought it was worth the fuel to tweak it to an exact multiple, just to simplify the arithmetic whenever the cycle needed to be converted into clock time. When she'd finished she pressed her arm against Marzio's, letting him feel the numbers so he could check them himself.

"That looks right," he said. "Can you get notice to your people in time?"

Tamara glanced across the workshop at the clock again. "Yes." She hurried over to the signal ropes and sent a message to each of the observatories; unless the relay clerks were dozing this would be warning enough. Roberto would just be starting his shift at the summit; she wasn't sure who'd be on duty at the antipodal dome, but every observer had been prepared for this for days. She'd wanted to help track the first beacon herself, but it would have been an absurd vanity to delay the launch any further for the sake of that privilege. Besides, this way she'd be able to watch the event itself, with all of the excitement and none of the hard work.

Marzio's children, Viviana and Viviano, maneuvered the beacon onto a trolley and began wheeling it toward the airlock. The device was built into a cubical frame of hardstone beams about two strides wide. Cylindrical tanks of powdered sunstone, liberator and compressed air were arranged around an open flare chamber, while all the pipes and clockwork were tucked away neatly behind clearstone panels.

Marzio followed his children, gesturing to Tamara to accompany him. Aside from the wheat fields this workshop had the largest floor in the *Peerless*—and spread out along its arc a dozen teams of instrument builders were assembling similar beacons. Groups of workers stopped to cheer as the trolley passed, celebrating their common cause.

Marzio said, "Don't be too dismayed if something goes wrong. We'll have plenty of opportunity to vary the design if we have to."

"Unlike the *Gnat*."

"Oh, the *Gnat* will be fine," he promised her. "It'll be carrying its own repair crew. The hardest thing to build is a machine that needs to function perfectly without any supervision—without the chance to make a single adjustment once it's out of your hands."

They reached the ramp leading down into the airlock. As Viviana and Viviano donned helmets and cooling bags, Tamara hung back, not wanting to interfere with their preparations. She was just a spectator here; the launch could go ahead with or without her.

Viviana raised the airlock door, standing aside to keep it open as her co wheeled the beacon into the chamber. Then she joined him inside, and the spring-loaded door slammed shut. Tamara watched them through the window as they worked the pumps.

"What could still go wrong?" she asked Marzio. "You've fixed the nozzle; the rest is just clockwork."

"Clockwork in the void," Marzio replied. "You might think it would simplify a machine's behavior when there's no air or gravity to contend with—but there's still heat, there's still friction, there's still grit that can hang around to jam moving parts. Odd things can happen to surfaces that turn them unexpectedly sticky, or opaque. In fact a friend of mine has grown very excited over the way mirrorstone tarnishes in the absence of air."

Tamara had heard about Carla's discovery, but she didn't think other physicists were taking it too seriously. "Some people can find patterns in anything," she replied.

Viviana and Viviano were through the airlock now. Tamara walked down to the rack of cooling bags and selected one for herself. In her rear gaze she saw that Marzio hadn't followed her.

"You're not coming out to watch?"

"I'm an old man," he said. "It makes me queasy."

"To see the stars below you?"

"No, being in a cooling bag."

"Oh." Tamara found the fabric against her skin a bit irritating, but other than that the devices didn't bother her. She climbed into the one she'd chosen, redistributed some flesh from her shoulders to her chest to accommodate its shape, then asked Marzio to check the fit before she attached the cylinder of air that would carry her body heat off into the void.

Once she was through the airlock, standing at the top of the exterior ramp, she pulled a safety harness from a slot beside her, checked that it was tied securely to the guide rail that ran along the side of the ramp, then stepped into the harness and cinched it tight.

Marzio's children were further down the ramp, their harnesses tied to opposite rails so they wouldn't get tangled in each other's ropes. They had already cranked back the spring-loaded launch plate, and as they slid the beacon off its trolley and moved it into place the scraping sound came faintly through Tamara's feet, almost overwhelmed by the reassuring susurration of air leaking from her cooling bag. When they'd finished she raised a hand in greeting, and they returned the gesture. The springs would help the beacon clear the ramp safely, but most of its velocity would come from the rotation of the *Peerless*. In less than a year it would be three gross separations away—by then, Tamara hoped, just one point in a huge, sparse grid of identical devices drifting out across the void, all flashing in a miserly but predictable fashion. Anyone could orient themselves by the stars, but knowing your position was something else entirely. The ancestors had had their sun and their sister worlds to help them navigate, but if the travelers wanted to leave the *Peerless* without losing their way they would have to create their own guiding lights, on a scale commensurate with their intended journey.

Viviana set the triggering time on the clock beside the launch plate. It was impossible to choose the beacon's trajectory as precisely as they'd need to know it, but the timing of its launch would be enough to ensure that it was traveling in more or less the right direction. Viviano reached into the beacon and disengaged the safety lever, allowing sunstone and liberator to enter the flare chamber the next time the air valve was opened. Then they both moved back behind the plate, out of harm's way.

Tamara watched by starlight as the launch clock's three fastest dials spun toward the chosen alignment. The figures on her skin tingled with recognition just before the faint shudder of the springs reached her through the rock. The beacon shot clear of the ramp and plummeted out of sight. Tamara rushed forward to the edge and peered down, but the machine was already invisible, a speck of darkness lost among the star trails. She glanced back at the clock and pictured Roberto's fingertips on the same dials spinning beside the observer's bench: one hand following the time, one on the scope's coordinate wheels. At the other end of the *Peerless* another colleague would be doing the same.

When the flash came Tamara raised an arm to cover her eyes, though the light was already fading before she'd moved a muscle. Powdered sunstone burned fast and bright; Roberto would have been using a filter, but the stab of light would have burned the measurements at his fingertips into his brain. Tamara was dazed and half-blinded, but now she could believe that the beacon's light would be visible across the void, even through the *Gnat*'s modest instruments—so long as nothing broke, nothing jammed, and no speck of orthogonal matter turned the machine into a fireball before the *Gnat* had even been launched.

There was no point waiting for the second flash; the rotation of the *Peerless* was tipping the ramp up, hiding the beacon behind her. But Roberto and his opposite number would have dozens of chances to repeat their measurements, triangulating a whole series of points along the beacon's trajectory before the machine switched to its dormant state. After that, the next flash wouldn't come until a stint before the *Gnat*'s launch.

Viviana and Viviano were already headed back to the airlock with the empty trolley. Tamara stayed at the edge of the ramp, one hand around her safety rope, gauging its reassuring tension. She would not be embarking on a fool's mission; they would not be going blindly into the void. Long before the journey began they would have wrapped the space around them in light, in geometry, in numbers.

The wheat-flowers were opening as Tamara strode along the path that ran down the middle of the farm, the limp gray sacs unfurling until the petals' red glow filled the whole chamber, overpowering the moss-light from the walls and ceiling. A faint scent of smoke hung over the field but no sign of the burn-off was visible.

Tamara reached out to brush the plants' yellow stalks with her fingertips. Though the crops rose and fell, the farm itself seemed ageless, unchangeable. But she remembered her grandfather telling her that in his own parents' life-time the sheer wall of rock on her left had been a soil-covered field. There had been no low ceilings then, no second, third and fourth farms stacked above them; no one had planned for centrifugal gravity when they'd first carved these chambers out of the mountain. Tamara sometimes found herself scandalously wishing that it would be as long as possible before the engines were fired again, sparing any of her immediate descendants the tedious job of reconfiguring the farm for a second and third time. Or perhaps by then some brilliant agronomist would have boosted the crop yield to the point where everyone could live off stored grain for the whole reversal stage, and the farmers could take a three-year holiday.

"Hello!" she called out, as she approached the clearing. There was no one in sight. She went to the store-hole and took out a small bag of flour, left over from grain she'd milled the day before.

Tamaro and Erminio arrived as she was finishing the loaves; they were both carrying scythes and lamps. The lamps were extinguished, but she could smell the smoke that still clung to their skin from a different kind of fire.

"How bad is it?" she asked.

"It's under control," her father assured her. "All within a few square strides, and all of that's ash now."

Tamara widened her eyes in relief. The wheat blight appeared on the back of the petals, close to the stem, making it almost impossible to spot when the flowers were open. The only way to catch it was to go around with lamps in the moss-light, inspecting the dormant flowers—and the only cure was to incinerate the afflicted plants immediately.

The two men sat and joined her in the meal she'd prepared. Tamara knew that they had their own store-hole nearby, and that they'd eat again as soon as she left in the morning, but a part of her was still able to ignore that abstract knowledge and stitch together a version of the family's daily life comprised of nothing but her direct experience. Every evening she made three loaves and shared them with her father and her co, and her stores of grain and flour were always the same when she returned as when she'd left them, so she could tell herself a perfectly believable story where the three of them were all living in an equally austere fashion. She never for a moment forgot that it was fiction, but it still did more to make the situation tolerable than any amount of time spent pondering the ultimate consequences of giving in to her hunger.

"What's happening with the beacon?" Tamaro asked her.

"It's out there, at last!" Tamara recounted the details of the launch. "I heard from Roberto afterward, and it looks as if we got a good fix on the trajectory. So we'll go ahead and follow with the others. The next one should be ready in less than a stint."

As she spoke, she could see Tamaro growing uneasy. "I'm sure you can get the navigation system working," he said. "But I'm still worried about that idiot Ivo."

Tamara wondered if she'd unwittingly libeled the man; it was hard to resist joking about his lizard paper, but he certainly knew his field. "He's a bit eccentric," she said, "but he's not an idiot."

"He's reckless." Tamaro brushed crumbs from his tympanum. "Once a man's seen his grandchildren, his own life means nothing to him."

"That's a stupid generalization," Tamara replied, irritated. "Anyway, he's not making all the decisions about the *Gnat*. The Council has appointed its own experts to vet everything we're planning to do: people who won't be on the expedition themselves, so they'll have a different perspective."

Erminio said, "How does someone get to be an expert in a substance they've never even seen?"

"And if they won't be on the *Gnat*," Tamaro added, "why should they care what happens to its passengers?"

"Make up your mind," Tamara retorted. "Is it Ivo who's reckless, or the advisers who'll be staying behind?"

"They'll both be more worried about capturing the Object than they will be about who lives or dies," Tamaro replied heatedly. "Once this precious lode of orthogonal matter is suspended in the void, the *Gnat* will have done its job, won't it?"

Tamara hummed with frustration. "Will you listen to yourself? Capturing the Object will require an exercise in precision rocketry. The

Gnat will only end up damaged if we lose control of the situation. The two outcomes are mutually exclusive! You don't achieve the first one by risking the second."

Tamaro tipped his head slightly, conceding that he might have gone too far. "The fact remains, though: Ivo's an old man, he's lived his life. I'm not saying that he's planning a suicide mission, but when he weighs up the risks against his chances of glory, he's not going to take the most cautious route."

"So what do you want me to do?" Tamara demanded. "Renege on my offer to bring him along? Tell him to delegate the job to a younger colleague with *more to lose*?"

Tamaro said, "No. But you could stay behind yourself. Find another old man to take your place."

Tamara looked to her father, hoping he might raise some objection to this sorting of the population into two distinct categories: expendable old men and people with lives worth living. But he gazed back at her with an expression of mild reproof, as if to say: *Listen to your co, he has your interests in mind.*

"I'm the chief navigator," Tamara said evenly. "Without me there is no mission."

"I thought every astronomer studied navigation," Tamaro countered.

"Yes, but not with these methods! They learn what was used to set the *Peerless* on its course, and what we'll need to bring it home one day. None of that applies here."

Tamaro was unswayed. "So you devised a new system, especially for the *Gnat*. Are you saying it's unteachable? That no other astronomer has the observational skills or the ability to perform the calculations?"

Tamara hesitated, unsure how she'd backed herself into this corner. "Of course not," she admitted. She'd already taught Ada everything she'd need to take over her role, if it came to that. "But I found the Object, I proposed the voyage. Unless there's someone better qualified than I am, I have a right to a place on that rocket. My colleagues accept that, the Council accepts that. And if you think Ivo will be such a danger to the mission, you should be glad I'll be there to keep him in check!"

Erminio said, "You're upset now. We can talk about this later, when everyone's calm."

"I'm perfectly calm!" Tamara replied. But her father rose to his feet; the conversation was over.

She fetched her dose of holin from the store-hole as the family prepared to retire to the flower bed. Erminio bid his children good night and lay down behind the wormbane. Tamaro brushed loose petals and straw out of their shared indentation, then placed his scythe along the middle of the bed.

Tamara settled into the soil beside him, the long hardstone blade between them. "You should trust me," she whispered. "I won't let Ivo do anything stupid."

She received no reply, so she closed her eyes. Would she have been just as angry herself, she wondered, if she'd believed Tamaro was putting his own life at risk? Risking grief and pain for his family, risking turning their children into orphans? She had to admit that the thought of giving birth alone would have terrified her.

If he'd gone rushing into some dangerous, vainglorious folly, of course she would have tried to argue him out of it. But if the goal had been a worthy one, and if he'd had his reasons for wanting to play a part, she hoped she would have listened to him.

9

As the dozen and three students from her optics class squeezed into the tiny workshop, Carla glanced anxiously down the corridor, wondering how much attention the gathering would attract. One rule Assunto had impressed upon her before assigning her to teach the class had been that she should never perform a demonstration whose outcome she could not predict in advance. "Practice each experiment first, as often as you need to," he'd urged her, "until you're sure you can make the whole thing run like clockwork. Researchers know that things go awry in their workshops all the time—and the greater part of their job is uncovering the reasons. But you don't want to be confusing these youngsters with the messiness of real science when they're still trying to learn the basics."

Carla wasn't entirely sure that his advice had been misguided. Whatever authority she had in her students' eyes came from her ability to explain the phenomena she chose to put in front of them. *This is where the lens focuses its image—just as our equations predicted! This is the angle at which the light comb diffracts red light—in perfect agreement with Giorgio's formula!* Talking to the class about her tarnishing experiments might have been a good way to assure them that the field was far from moribund—that new discoveries were still being made, and if they persisted with their studies they could be part of the vanguard themselves—but now here they were chasing free luxagens, and she had absolutely no idea what they'd find.

But it was too late to cancel the experiment. All she could do was try to get through the session without making a fool of herself.

Carla joined the students, called them to order, and began allocating tasks, starting with the polishing of the mirrorstone they'd use as a luxagen source. "We don't have a lot of space here, so *please* move slowly and carefully. If you break something, tell me straight away. And if anyone touches the sunstone, they're going straight out the airlock."

The experiment they'd designed required a simple variation on the tarnishing apparatus: since they were aiming to maximize luxagen production while minimizing stray visible light, the mirrorstone surface would be exposed to nothing but infrared. A second beam from the same lamp—this one undivided by color, in order that it remain as bright as possible—would be directed across the vacuum above the mirrorstone, and an eyepiece on a semicircular rail would be used to check for light scattered from the beam at various angles.

Carla stood back and watched as everything came together, only having to intervene physically when Azelia became confused by the vacuum supply. "The low-pressure chamber we use is shared by other workshops and factories," she explained. "It's vented after each use— that's why the access valve is locked now. If you'd managed to force it open, you would have made a direct path between the interior of the *Peerless* and the void, which is something we try to discourage."

When all the apparatus was finally in place, Carla approached and double-checked the alignment of the optics. "Good job, everyone!" She managed to ignite the sunstone without flinching, then she called on Patrizia to extinguish the firestone lamp in the corner. They had taken care to block most of the spillage, and the beam that crossed the evacuated container ended up striking an unreflective black screen, so the moss-free workshop was in almost total darkness now.

Romolo was already in place beside the swiveling eyepiece, ready to do the honors. When Carla heard no movement from his direction she urged him to go ahead. He was probably as anxious as she was, having put his pride at stake with such a bold prediction. *Light blasting luxagens out of a solid and into the void.*

"First observation, three arc-bells from the beam axis," Romolo began. There was a long silence. "I can't see anything," he said.

"Adjust the focus on the eyepiece, very slowly," Carla suggested. "When your eyes have nothing to look at, they can end up focused beyond the point where the eyepiece is presenting the light. You can stare right through a weak image without even knowing it's there."

She waited while Romolo tried this. If there *were* luxagens in the container they should be scattering light in all directions, and the view perpendicular to the beam would be unlikely to include any stray reflections from the container walls. The primary lens of the eyepiece was as wide as the beam itself, so it could gather light over a much greater area than the pupil of an unaided observer, but if there were simply too few luxagens for the scatter to be visible, that was that.

"Still nothing," Romolo admitted.

"All right," Carla said. "Change the angle." She couldn't see how that would make any difference, but having gone to so much trouble it would be absurd not to collect a full set of observations.

The class stood in the dark, listening patiently as Romolo announced negative result after negative result. According to calculations that stretched all the way back to Nereo, any luxagen jiggling back and forth at a suitable frequency should live up to its name and *create light*. Individually, each particle would emit a bit more light parallel to the axis of its vibrations than in other directions—but if those vibrations were being driven by randomly polarized light all the individual biases would average out, so whatever pale glow the thin gas of luxagens produced, it should have been visible from any angle.

"Ah, I can see something! There's a reddish light!" Romolo sounded even more surprised than Carla. He was down to an angle of six arc-chimes, almost staring into the beam itself, so he was probably just seeing light scattered by the container's walls, rather than by anything in its interior.

Carla said, "Reach out and pull the lever that brings the shutter down over the infrared." If the glow persisted, then it was nothing to do with any hypothetical luxagen wind rising off the mirrorstone.

Carla heard the click of the lever. "The red light's gone," Romolo said. "There's nothing."

"Lift the shutter again," Carla suggested.

"Yes. Now the light's back."

"You must be blocking the visible light, not the IR!" Carla declared. She slipped past the students in front of her, then felt her way around the edges of the bench. She could see a faint splotch of gray where the beam came to an end, and once she was oriented she knew where everything was.

She put one hand on the lever that would bring the shutter down over the visible beam, then reached for the IR lever; Romolo's hand was still on it. He buzzed in surprise and pulled his hand away. "Did I have the wrong one?" he asked, embarrassed.

"No," Carla replied. "You didn't."

She asked Romolo to move aside, then she peered through the eyepiece herself and tried blocking each beam in turn. Shutting off either one made the reddish glow disappear. There was no escaping the conclusion, then: *something* that the infrared light was driving off the mirrorstone into the vacuum was scattering the visible light through a small angle—and showing a preference for red in the process.

Luxagen scattering was predicted to be stronger at the red end of the spectrum, but the small angle made no sense. Perhaps the mirrorstone was giving off a very fine dust, reactive enough to be absorbed by the container walls as soon as the IR was shut off. If these dust particles were transparent they could be refracting some light away from the beam axis.

Carla explained her hunch to the students, then swung the eyepiece around by almost half a revolution, in the hope of seeing some back-scatter reflected off the dust. There was nothing. She went back to the light Romolo had found; as she moved the eyepiece even closer to the beam axis, the red tinge became less pronounced while the overall brightness grew a little.

But it was hard to quantify the changes in this complex mixture of hues. Carla asked Patrizia to relight the firestone lamp. "I don't know what we're seeing here," she admitted, "but I think it will be easier to study if we try scattering a single color at a time."

Following her instructions, Palladio and Dina fitted a prism and a color-selecting slot into the visible beam. "Let's start with green," Carla suggested.

With the workshop in darkness again, Carla bent down and looked through the eyepiece. She'd left it in the position where the scatter had first appeared, as far from the axis as you could go while still seeing anything at all. It took almost a lapse for her eyes to adapt sufficiently to pick up the weaker glow now that most of the beam was being blocked, but the glow was still there.

And it was red. Pure red. The green light crossing the container was being scattered—and in the process it was *turning red*.

Carla felt utterly lost. If nature had deliberately set out to mock her—to prove to her students once and for all that their optics teacher knew nothing about light—it could not have done a better job.

She steadied herself. This would make sense, somehow; she just needed to be patient. "Who's got good vision in low light?" she asked. After a moment Eulalia replied, "I've been doing fire-watch shifts lately, if that's any help."

"Perfect."

Carla had Eulalia take her place at the eyepiece.

"What do you see?" she asked.

"Red light," Eulalia confirmed.

Carla found the lever for the visible light shutter and closed it about halfway. "What now?"

Eulalia was silent for a pause or two. "A dimmer red light."

"Is the color any different?"

"Not as far as I can tell."

Carla addressed the students in the darkness. "Why did I reduce the intensity?" she asked.

Patrizia replied from the corner of the workshop. "If the luxagens were getting trapped in the light wave's energy valleys, they'd be rolling back and forth in those valleys—giving off light of their own at a different frequency to the frequency of the beam."

"So what does it mean that the scatter remained red when I made the beam dimmer?" Carla pressed her.

Patrizia said, "It means that explanation can't be right. The exact shape of those valleys would depend on the strength of the light. A weaker beam would have made the valleys shallower... making the luxagens roll back and forth more slowly, reducing the frequency of the light they emitted."

"Exactly," Carla replied. But she knew of no other way that one pure color could give rise to a completely different hue. *White light* could end up being filtered selectively, changing its appearance in all kinds of ways, but when you started out with a wave of a single frequency it was supposed to make everything it touched oscillate at the very same pace, generating more light of the very same hue.

Carla opened the shutter fully again. Then she groped her way around the bench and adjusted the slotted screen in front of the prism that determined the color of the visible beam, changing it from green to blue.

"What do you see now?" she asked Eulalia.

"The light's turned green."

She pushed the slot back in the other direction, until the beam was yellow.

"And now?"

"Nothing," Eulalia replied. "It's gone dark."

Carla buzzed, delighted in spite of herself. "Blue becomes green, green becomes red, yellow becomes infrared." At least the shift was in the same direction each time. She'd given up all hope of impressing the class with a simple explanation for these strange results. They'd found a completely new anomaly, a mystery to rank with the stability puzzle itself. There was nothing to be done now but to accept that.

And to gather more data.

She called for the workshop to be lit again, and asked Palladio and Dina to add a second prism to the light path, this time directly behind the eyepiece. Then for each color beamed across the container, she had the students take turns measuring the frequency of the light that was scattered at a variety of angles.

The experiment had one more surprise for her. At the smallest angles, violet light produced *two* distinct colors in the scatter: one only slightly altered in hue, the other shifted far toward the red. At larger angles the two colors moved closer together—just before the scatter disappeared completely. Blue light showed signs of doing something similar, though in that case the second color moved beyond the visible range, at a point not far below the maximum scattering angle.

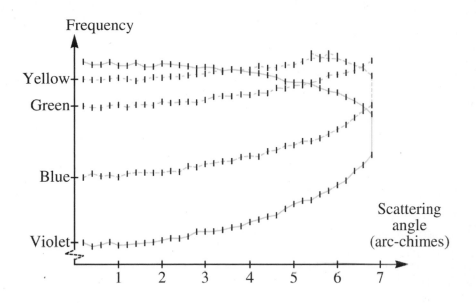

Carla plotted all the measurements on her chest, then dusted her skin with dye and made copies for the students to keep. "Think of this as a souvenir," she told Romolo. "Maybe by the time your grandchildren are studying optics, this experiment will be as famous as those Sabino did to measure Nereo's force."

"I'm confused," Romolo said. "Did we find free luxagens in the container, or didn't we?"

Carla said, "Ask me that again in six years' time."

10

Carlo stiffened his tympanum to keep himself silent, then plunged the probe deep into the flesh of his wrist. As he struggled to force the needle all the way down to the calibration mark the pain became excruciating, but once the thing was in place and motionless the sensation was tolerable.

"The voles of the *Peerless* thank you for your sacrifice," Amanda said wryly.

Carlo managed a dismissive buzz. Loath as he was to inflict needless suffering on the animals, he was stabbing himself more out of expediency than compassion. The current version of the probe was so large that he could not have expected the creatures to endure it without an elaborate routine of anesthesia and recovery—and by the time he'd also trained the voles to perform specific movements on cue he would have ended up with a protocol where every trivial experiment took half a dozen stints to complete.

He waited a lapse or so for his skewered flesh to recover from the shock, then wiggled his fingers cautiously. He hadn't paralyzed any of them. The question now was whether he'd erred in the other direction; if the probe was too far from the bundle of motor pathways he'd have no chance to spy on its traffic.

Amanda was harnessed to the bench beside the light recorder. Carlo gestured to her to look through the eyepiece, then he moved all his fingers at once.

She said, "Nothing."

"All right. Let me turn it a little."

The hardstone tube protruding from his wrist had a cross-hatched ring at the top, attached to the inner sleeve that held the primary mirror within the probe's clearstone tip. Above the ring, the same sleeve slotted into the side of a much longer tube that carried the light across into the recorder. Carefully, Carlo began to turn the ring, aiming the mirror below in a new direction. Since none of the moving parts were in contact with his flesh the adjustment ought to have been painless, but in fact there was enough friction between the sleeve and the outer tube to make the whole probe start twisting, so he had to stop and sprout a new hand to hold the thing steady.

He wiggled the fingers of his impaled hand again. Amanda said, "Yes! There's light now!"

He tried the six fingers one by one. Amanda could catch glimpses of his brain's messages to all of them, but the second finger from the right gave the best results. Carlo adjusted the mirror further, turning it back and forth by ever smaller angles until the light coming through was as bright as he could make it. He might have been able to do better still if he'd been willing to yank the probe out and reinsert it closer to the pathway, but that didn't seem worth the pain. So long as he had a visible signal, that would be enough to tell him whether or not the machine was going to be useful.

He began tracing out a circle with the tip of the chosen finger, repeating the motion as smoothly as he could. "Can you see that?" he asked Amanda.

"Yes. Don't ask me what the sequence is, but I'd swear it's periodic."

This was not an unbiased judgment: she was watching his hand with her rear gaze even as she peered through the eyepiece. But with luck they'd soon have a more objective way of assessing the signal's properties.

"Start the recorder," he said.

Amanda flipped the lever to retract the mirror that was diverting light into the eyepiece, then she disengaged the brake on the drive wheel. Carlo tried to keep his mind on his rotating finger and ignore the machine's whir, surprised by the strength of his urge to hold his whole body expectantly motionless. When he'd first been testing the recorder—with a slab of lamp-lit translucent resin taking the place of his flesh—he'd usually ended up waiting, tensed, for the sound of tearing paper.

"It's finished," Amanda announced. She opened the device and extracted the spool, then stretched out a portion of the strip so they could both see it.

It was blank.

Carlo was disappointed, but not greatly surprised. With every trained instrument builder busy on the *Gnat* or some ancillary project, he'd had to use salvaged components for most of the optics and clockwork, while the way the parts had been brought together was unmistakably a product of his own inexpert hands. The failure he'd been dreading most was that the temperamental system for dispensing the activation gas might stop working again, leaving the paper to run through the machine without being properly sensitized.

"Maybe the viewing mirror's stuck," he suggested hopefully.

Amanda bent toward the eyepiece. Carlo was still mechanically twiddling his finger. She said, "Not unless it stuck halfway, because I can't see anything." She pushed the lever to reinsert the mirror. "And I still can't."

"So I've been torturing myself for nothing?" Carlo joked. "The voles will be pleased. Maybe something else has slipped out of alignment."

"Wait, what was that? You stopped—"

He'd stilled his finger. "Yes."

Amanda said, "When you *stopped*, there was a burst of light."

Carlo started up the motion again, slowly and deliberately. "What do you see now?"

"That's... back to how it was at the start."

He said, "Show me the rest of the recording strip."

Amanda unspooled it completely. At the start of the recording the paper displayed a long sequence of dark streaks, the density of the pigment rising and falling in a complex pattern. Only the last quarter of the strip was blank.

Carlo said, "Check the eyepiece again."

Amanda complied. "The signal's still visible."

Carlo tried to distract himself, to think of anything but his rotating finger. "How's your co?" he asked.

"He's fine," Amanda replied, surprised by the question. "He's just switched to a new job, doing maintenance on the main cooling system—ah, the signal's gone again."

"Either there's an intermittent fault in the optics," Carlo said, "or my finger doesn't really need to be told what to do all the time. If the instructions follow a simple pattern, the flesh soon gets the message and the brain stops repeating itself. Until—"

He halted the twirling.

Amanda said, "There's that burst again. A 'stop what you were doing' signal?"

"That's what it looks like."

"We should get that on tape," she suggested.

Carlo agreed. They spent the next bell and a half capturing the signals that initiated and halted dozens of different movements, trying to exhaust all the possibilities while the probe was in place and the recorder was still working. They ran out of paper before Carlo was entirely satisfied, but by then he was glad of any excuse to extract the probe and resorb his abused limb.

Amanda left him; she had two pairs of voles ready to mate in the pathway suppression experiments. Carlo stayed harnessed to the bench, looking over the recordings.

The patterns for all the repetitive motions he'd tried were, gratifyingly, roughly periodic. In fact, if he coiled each strip into a broad helix of just the right width he could place each cycle right beside its successor, and see the same instructions arriving again and again. Then the pattern faded out until the "stop" signal came—and that was virtually identical in every case.

On a finer scale, though, the sequences remained mysterious. The brightness and duration of the individual pulses varied enormously, and there were no obvious recurring motifs. So how did his flesh interpret these instructions? Were there detailed commands for each muscle fiber, spelling out every contraction? Or was this more like a sequence of symbols or sounds, strung together to form words in some ancient somatic language?

Tosco had conducted an ingenious study where he'd dyed the flesh in a lizard's extremities, color-coded by its initial position, and shown that after being resorbed it could turn up in any other labile region. The flesh that had comprised a certain toe one day could easily find itself in the middle of a limb the day after. But that didn't settle the question as to whether the flesh "knew" which role it was playing at any given moment, or whether that responsibility fell entirely to the brain. Each time the body reshaped itself, did the brain tell the new toe-flesh "Now you are a toe", allowing them both in later conversations to take certain toe-ish understandings for granted? The signals Carlo had recorded for repeated motions—spelled out the first few times, then left to his finger's own initiative—suggested that the brain didn't micro-manage everything, but the initial instructions seemed far more detailed and complex than he would have expected if they were merely specifying a selection from a pre-existing repertoire of possible finger movements.

Carlo looked across the workshop toward Tosco's bench. Nine years after his first dye studies, he was still repeating the experiments—and that wasn't out of laziness or inertia. He kept refining the techniques and gathering more data, painstakingly building up maps that showed the way flesh moved within a lizard's body as it adopted various postures.

Nine years was nothing in the history of this field. A lifetime was nothing. Carlo gazed at the streaks of pigment on the paper in front of him, and realized that he still hadn't solved one simple, practical problem: the paper was darkest when the light had been most bright. If he ever hoped to send these recorded signals back into his body, he'd need a way to modulate the light source in precisely the opposite fashion: making it bright when the paper was dark.

Amanda returned with the preliminary results from her two vole matings. The whole brood in the second suppression test had been stillborn—but as ever it had been a brood of four.

She took one of the strips of paper from the bench and held it up to the light from a nearby lamp.

"So... you'll run this beside a second, sensitized strip?" she asked. "To duplicate the pattern with the density reversed?"

Carlo stared at her in silence, dumbstruck for a moment. Then he came to his senses and replied, "Of course."

11

"Air," said Ivo. "Air is what remains when the fiercest flame has consumed its fuel entirely. There's nothing safer, nothing more stable. In the worst case imaginable—if the orthogonal rock acts as a liberator for all of our solids—we should still be able to manipulate it with jets of air."

Tamara looked around the small chamber, wondering if anyone else shared the secret thrill she felt at the prospect Ivo was raising. What could be more terrifying than a universal liberator: a substance that could set anything on fire? And what could be more exhilarating than finding a way to cheat that danger, to grasp the ungraspable in invisible hands?

Massima, the lottery winner, appeared to be growing less at ease with each word she heard. When she'd first put her name down for a chance at this jaunt there'd been a lot less talk of explosions. Ulfa, the chemist appointed by the Council to oversee the project, was as calm and businesslike as ever, raising neat rows of notes on her chest as Ivo spoke. Only Ada, who'd beaten six other astronomers in their own mini-lottery for deputy navigator, showed any sign of excitement.

Ada said, "What if we can't break a sample free with air alone? If the Object is made of something like hardstone, and there are no loose fragments… you can't carve hardstone with a jet of air, however high the pressure."

"If that's the situation," Ivo replied, "we'll have to cut into the surface with airborne dust. If we add a small amount of crushed powderstone to the jet, the reaction between the powderstone and the orthogonal rock will render the jet far more potent."

"You're assuming that the rock itself will be consumed, and not just the powderstone," Ulfa pointed out.

"Do you know of any liberator that *isn't* consumed in the flame it creates?" Ivo asked her.

"No," Ulfa conceded. "But the liberators we know about are fragile plant extracts. We can't assume that a slab of solid rock will act the same way."

"If there's a flame produced at all, the heat should at least weaken the rock," Ivo said. "And if that's not sufficient, we could replace the powderstone with hardstone, making the jet more abrasive."

Ulfa said, "This is a material we've never encountered before. What if it can't be abraded, even by burning hardstone?"

Ivo emitted a soft hum of frustration. "There's no reason to believe that orthogonal matter will be endowed with magical powers of durability! Reversing the arrows of its luxagens might influence its chemical properties with respect to ordinary matter, but it can't make the rock itself harder, or more resistant to heat."

Tamara had to side with him on that: it was basic rotational physics. For a rock to be rendered tougher just because its "future"—according to Nereo's arrow—had ended up facing their past was as absurd as expecting a rope to become stronger if you turned around and traversed it in the opposite direction.

Ulfa remained calm, but unswayed. "I understand that, Ivo. But it's my job to ask what will happen if these assumptions are wrong."

"If the rock can't be cut by any method at all... then we won't cut it," Ivo replied. "What else can I say?"

"And if you can't take a sample," Ulfa pressed him, "how will you calibrate the process that you're hoping to use to capture the Object?"

Ivo was silent for a few pauses. Then he said, "We'll have no choice but to perform the reaction in the wild. We'll throw calmstone at the Object and observe the effects—scaling up the quantity gradually so we don't take undue risks."

"But you'll have no way to measure the force you're producing," Ulfa said.

"Not immediately," Ivo agreed. "Not until it starts to change the Object's trajectory. We'll simply have to work by trial and error, incrementally: dropping calmstone on the site where we want to deliver a push, until the cumulative effect is large enough to observe."

Ulfa paused to dust her chest with dye and press a sheet of paper to her skin. Then she addressed Tamara. "Do you think that's feasible?"

"It will be difficult," Tamara admitted. "Each beacon will only be visible once a bell, so if we're going to have to nudge the Object repeatedly and check its motion each time, it will be a slow process. We could be there for as long as a couple of stints."

"So you'll need more cooling air, more food," Ulfa said. "What's that going to do to your flight plan?"

"The mass of any extra food would be negligible," Tamara said, resisting a joke about the proportion of women on the crew. "But it might be worth making allowances to bring more cooling air. Hyperthermia is a horrible way to go."

Massima said, "Forgive me for interrupting."

At the sound of her voice everyone turned to face her. In all the planning meetings she'd attended, she'd barely spoken a word.

Tamara tried to counter the alarm she'd inadvertently created. "I only meant that we needed to be sure of our air supplies. I promise you, we won't be taking any foolish risks—"

Massima raised a hand to silence her. "I accept that. But the truth is, I have no expertise to contribute to this task, so why should I be there with you, using up precious air? It was generous of you to offer a place on the *Gnat* to an onlooker. This could have been the experience of a lifetime, the perfect story to leave to my children. But in all conscience, after what I've heard these last few stints I can't take that role any more. I wish you luck, but I'll have to hear about the journey upon your return."

Tamara didn't know how to respond. Imploring the woman to reconsider would only embarrass her.

Ada said, "I respect your decision, Massima. And I'll be happy to tell you everything as soon as we get back."

As Massima left the chamber, Tamara wondered if the Council would insist that they draw another name from the lottery entrants. If not, they'd have a chance to bring another crew member. If it was prudent to appoint two navigators, why not a second chemist in case something befell the first?

Ivo went on to describe the machinery he wished to commission from the instrument builders, to equip the *Gnat* with hands of air should it need them. Ulfa quibbled over some details, but eventually agreed that he could take his sketches to Marzio and have prototypes made.

When the meeting was over, Tamara caught up with Ada in the corridor.

"I can't believe I frightened off our passenger," Tamara lamented.

"It's not your fault," Ada replied. "She made her own judgment."

"So how's your co taking this?" Tamara asked her.

"He's a little jealous," Ada admitted. "But he'll survive."

"He's not worried about you?"

Ada thought for a while as they dragged themselves along the ropes. "Maybe he is. But he knows I won't get another chance like this. I mean, I'm not going to be guiding the *Peerless* home, am I? And I'm never going to spot anything in the sky that really matters."

Tamara buzzed admonishingly. "You have more years as an observer ahead of you than I do!"

"Maybe. But what could surpass the Object?"

"Something that surprises us completely," Tamara suggested. "We've barely started making use of infrared."

"At the launch of the *Peerless*," Ada mused, "everyone must have felt some pride to be bearing the world on their shoulders. And if we ever return, I expect the whole generation who make it back will be treated like heroes. But when you've been born into this mess halfway, with no say in it, what can you do? If you're vain enough you could spend your life imagining you're going to discover the Eternal Flame. As for the rest of us... we get to starve ourselves as best we can, make some tiny contribution to the Great Project, and try to remain contented while we pass the time until we have children."

Tamara thought that was putting it rather bleakly. "Except for the starving, would things have been so different if we'd been born back home, before the Hurtlers?"

Ada tipped her head, conceding the point. "The big cities had many more people than the *Peerless*, but how many people can you meet in a lifetime? And if I was traveling from town to town by truck or train, instead of reveling in my freedom I might have spent the journey gazing up at the sky, wishing I could go flying in a rocket instead."

"And you'll be traveling from town to town soon enough," Tamara joked. The Object was unlikely to be populated, but the latest measurements suggested that it was comparable in size to the *Peerless*. "You have the best of both worlds."

"I know!" Ada said. "Believe me, I realize how lucky I am. Not only will I escape this prison for a while, the journey might even turn out to be useful. Addo understands that, which is why he'd never ask me to give it up."

Tamara was silent. They'd reached the junction where they'd have to go their separate ways.

Ada said, "So your co's not the same?"

"I'm working on it," Tamara said. "Right now all he can see is the danger, but I'm sure I'll bring him round in the end."

12

Carla was reaching behind the textbooks for her stash of groundnuts when she heard someone moving on the ropes near the entrance to the classroom. She closed the cupboard quickly, embarrassed. She should have been strong enough to deal with her hunger without playing these stupid games.

Patrizia appeared in the doorway. "Do you have a moment, Carla? I need to ask you about something."

"Of course." Carla's gut was squirming, cheated of the imaginary meal she'd promised it, but she kept her voice even and her face composed.

Patrizia dragged herself to the front of the room. "I know I made a fool of myself, with what I said about the tarnishing," she began.

"That's not true," Carla insisted. "I asked for wild ideas, and you were brave enough to offer one. Just because it didn't hold up doesn't make you foolish."

"Well, I've had another wild idea," Patrizia admitted. "But this time, I was wondering if you'd hear it in private."

"Of course."

"I hope I'm not wasting your time," Patrizia said. "Sometimes it's so hard to concentrate that I start making stupid mistakes. Things I ought to know just… go into hiding."

The misery in that last phrase was painful to hear, but Carla didn't know what she could do about it. It wasn't her place to tell the poor girl to put off the famine for another year or two—trading the risk that she'd face a much more arduous struggle, later, for a little more youthful energy and clarity when she really needed it.

"We all make mistakes," she said. "Tell me your idea, I'll be happy to hear it."

Patrizia began haltingly. "The first part is just elementary mechanics, really. But I wanted to check it with you before I go any further."

Carla did her best to hide her dismay. She'd been thinking of the groundnuts all through the lesson, but if she could survive her cravings for a whole bell she could remain polite for another few lapses.

She said, "Go ahead."

"Suppose you have a motionless particle, and it's struck by another particle that's about three times as heavy," Patrizia said. "I *think* their energy-momentum vectors before and after the collision would be something like this:"

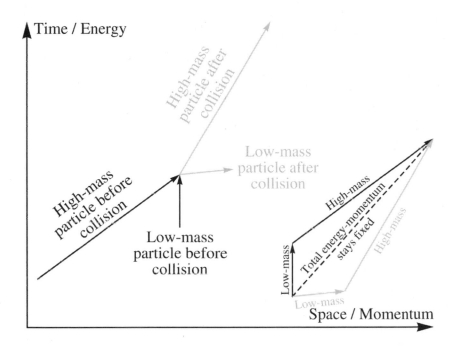

"That looks fine to me," Carla replied. The first diagram portrayed the history of the collision, while the second repositioned the same four vectors to make the geometrical rules that governed them visible at a glance. "You're just using the triangle law, right? The sum of the two energy-momentum vectors has to be conserved, and their individual lengths are just the masses of the particles, which don't change. So the vectors will form two sides of a triangle whose shape is left unchanged by the collision, and whose third side—the total energy-momentum—remains fixed."

Patrizia seemed relieved, but still far from confident. "And *all* the possibilities for a collision like this can be found by rotating that triangle around its third side?"

"Yes."

"That will give you the off-axis collisions as well? You just swing the triangle out...?" She sketched some examples, showing what happened to the particles' momenta if they glanced off each other during the impact, scattering to either side of the original axis, bringing in another dimension of space.

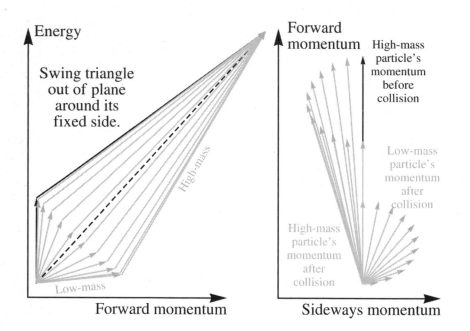

"That's all correct," Carla assured her, letting a hint of impatience into her voice. Wherever Patrizia was taking this, she had the basics right, she could move on.

Patrizia said, "On the same assumptions, I calculated the final energy for the heavy particle, for a few different starting energies." She opened a pocket, pulled out a sheet of paper and unrolled it.

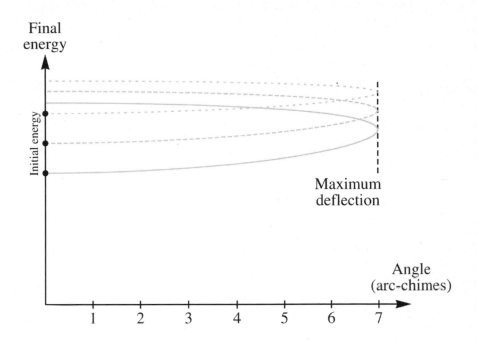

Carla hesitated now. Though she'd surely made a similar plot once herself—as part of some long-forgotten exercise when she'd first been studying mechanics—this had gone past the obvious-at-a-glance stage. "The angle here is measuring how far the heavier particle ends up off-axis?" she asked.

"Yes," Patrizia said. "The details of the collision itself—whether it's glancing or head-on—would determine that angle, but I'm just trying to be clear about the final outcome, about the possible combinations of angles and energies allowed by the conservation laws. The really striking thing about these curves is the way the greatest angle of deflection always turns out the same! So long as the lighter particle starts off at rest, there's a maximum angle at which the heavier particle can end up being knocked off course, and it only depends on the ratio of the masses—the energy of the collision doesn't come into it."

"Hmm." Carla couldn't recall ever being aware of that result, and she couldn't see any simple geometrical reason why it had to be true, so she worked through the algebra on her chest. The claim turned out to be perfectly correct: the maximum angle of deflection was the same, regardless of the energy.

Carla's impatience was tempered by curiosity now. Was Patrizia going to try to rescue her tarnishing theory by adding a second luxagen, three times heavier than the first?

Patrizia said, "I can put curves with exactly the same form as this through the data we measured in the light scattering experiment." She dug out a second plot.

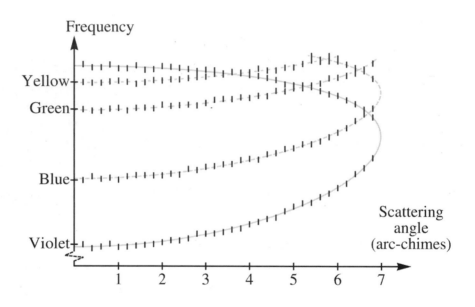

"All four curves use the same mass ratio, of about three to ten," Patrizia explained. "You can find that straight away, from the maximum scattering angle! And then the only parameter left to determine is the vertical scale."

Carla reached over and took the plot from her. With a judicious choice of just two numbers, Patrizia's model had nailed every point. A pattern like this didn't happen by chance. What these curves implied was that the light scattering off the luxagens was behaving exactly like a particle, about three times as heavy as the ones it was striking.

Except... this plot wasn't showing the energy of a particle, it was showing the frequency of a wave. What they'd actually measured for that vertical axis had been the scattered light's subsequent deflection through a prism, and then *that* had been converted to wavelengths and frequencies using the prism's calibration against a light comb. So how did energy come into it? The energy in a light wave depended on its brightness—something they hadn't even tried to measure.

"Tell me," Carla asked, "what do you think's going on here?"

Patrizia spoke tentatively. "Surely this means there's some kind of particle, moving at the speed of the light itself? Not trapped in the wavefronts, like a luxagen would be, but actually traveling *with the light.*"

"And the luxagens we released from the mirrorstone scattered this particle?"

"Yes."

"And then what?" Carla asked indignantly. "The light that had been pushing this mystery particle along decides to *follow it*? The laws of mechanics tell us how the particle alone should be moving after the collision... and the light wave accommodates that by adjusting its own speed, adjusting its frequency, to maintain the original relationship? Is the light supposed to be propelling this particle—or is the particle magically dragging the light around?"

Patrizia flinched. Carla hadn't realized how sarcastic her tone had become. "I'm sorry," she said. "I didn't mean to be dismissive. I'm just confused. I don't know how to make sense of this."

Patrizia looked up and met her gaze; they both knew exactly what was making the conversation so difficult. She said, "I've been trying to think how we could explain the tarnishing experiment, making use of this result. Suppose there's some reason why light waves *have to be* accompanied by these particles—let's call them 'luxites', just to give them a name."

Carla managed to stifle a derisive buzz. "Luxite" was the term that had been used by disciples of the ninth-age philosopher Meconio, the man who had first proposed—without a trace of evidence—that light was composed of "luminous corpuscles". Giorgio had buried that notion with his double-slit experiment, and Nereo and Yalda had built a whole mountain of wave theory on top of the grave. Patrizia wasn't to blame for Meconio's failings, but the name carried too much baggage.

"Let's call them 'photons'," Carla suggested. "Different root, same meaning."

"If the light-makers are called luxagens, shouldn't the particles that accompany light share the same root?"

"People might confuse the two," Carla said. "This will be clearer, trust me."

Patrizia nodded, indifferent. "The rule is, the photon moves at the speed of the light pulse," she continued. "But for that to be true, to create light of a certain frequency means creating photons with a certain *energy*. So if a process generates a particular frequency of light, that imposes a peculiar constraint on the amount of energy involved: you can create one photon, or two, or three... but your choices are confined to whole numbers. You don't get to make half a photon."

"Wait!" Carla interjected. "What about the energy in the light wave itself? How is that connected to the energy of these particles?"

Patrizia gave an apologetic hum. "I'm not sure. For now, can we just say that it's very small? That most of the energy in the light actually belongs to the photons?"

"It's your theory," Carla said. "Go ahead."

Patrizia shifted anxiously on the guide rope. "Suppose the energy valleys for the luxagens in mirrorstone all have a certain depth. The luxagens would have a bit of thermal energy as well, raising them off the floor of the valley, but if that doesn't vary too much there'll still be a particular amount of energy that a luxagen would need to gain in order to climb out of the valley and into the void—leaving behind a tarnished surface."

"That's a reasonable starting point," Carla agreed. Nereo's theory implied that the luxagens should have climbed out of the valley on their own, eons ago—as their thermal vibrations generated light and ever more kinetic energy—but since nobody else had managed to solve the stability problem it would hardly be fair to expect Patrizia to deal with it.

"When you hit the mirrorstone with light of a single frequency," Patrizia said, "the luxagens vibrate in time with the light, and create light of their own. But creating light means creating photons. Suppose a luxagen creates one photon; that will give it a certain amount of kinetic energy, but it might not be enough to get it out of the valley. Two might not be enough either, or three, but suppose four is sufficient. So once it's made four photons, the luxagen escapes, the mirrorstone gets tarnished."

Carla was following her now. "But if the light striking the mirrorstone has a lower frequency, that corresponds to a smaller energy for each photon, and there'll come a point where it suddenly takes *five* to do the job. So that's the first transition point we see in the tarnishing pattern: on one side four photons bridge the energy gap, on the other side you need five."

Patrizia said, "Yes. All the nonsense I came up with before about the luxagens in the valleys being struck by different numbers of 'wandering luxagens' pushed around by the light… that's all gone! The *four* and the *five* in the frequency ratio are just *the numbers of photons* that have to be created by the luxagens in order to escape from the valley."

A stint ago, Carla would have called this new version twice as nonsensical as the first. If you could ping a rope as hard or as gently as you liked, making waves in it as strong or as weak as you liked, why should waves in the light field be so different, burdened with these strange restrictions and appurtenances? But if you were willing to treat the frequency of light as a surrogate for the energy of a particle moving at the same speed, Patrizia's plot through the scattering data brought this hypothetical "photon" to life, showing it behaving in precisely the manner you'd expect when one particle collided with another.

Carla said, "Before we begin praising the genius of Meconio, can you think of any way we can test this idea?"

"I haven't been able to come up with any wholly new experiment," Patrizia admitted. "But there's something in the original experiment that we haven't measured yet."

"Go on."

"The time it takes for each part of the tarnishing pattern to appear."

Carla could see the merit in looking at that more closely. "If it takes a certain amount of time to create each photon, then the extra time required for successive tiers to reach a given tarnishing density should be the same. We'd need to push it to a longer exposure, though, and get another tier at frequencies so low that it takes six photons to leave a mark."

Patrizia said, "It might not take the same time to produce a photon at different frequencies. What if the light that's driving the process has to go through a certain number of cycles?"

"Like… cranking the handle on those mechanical loaf-makers? It's the number of turns, not the time you spend turning." Carla had no idea what was required to crank out a photon, so there was no obvious way to decide between the two criteria. "The period of violet light is only one and a half times that of red light; we can make a long enough exposure to test both possibilities, and see if either of them fits the results."

Patrizia emitted a chirp of delight. "So we're really going to test this theory?"

"Of course," Carla replied. "Isn't that what we're here for?"

When Patrizia had left, Carla took the groundnuts from the cupboard and went through her ritual. As she savored the odor, she realized that she'd rushed through the discussion too quickly, leaving too many problems unchallenged.

How could a luxagen "know" how long it had been exposed to light? Whether it was meant to be counting cycles of the light or simply recording the passage of time, what physical quantity could play the role of timer? Not the luxagen's energy, or the jumps in the tarnishing pattern would have been smoothed away. The success of Patrizia's theory relied on the axiom that you couldn't make half a photon, but unless something was keeping track of the process—if it could not, in some sense, be *half done*—then why should it take any particular amount of time to create one of these particles?

The scattering curves were beautiful. The link between energy and frequency was beautiful. But the whole theory still made no sense.

Carla put the groundnuts away, wondering how she was going to persuade Assunto—who doubted the existence of particles of matter—to give her six times as much sunstone as before so she could now go hunting for particles of light.

13

Silvano had an announcement for his friends. "I've decided to run for the Council."

Carlo was caught unprepared. By the time it occurred to him that it would be polite to offer a few words of encouragement, he also knew that he'd left it too late to sound sincere.

"What's in it for us?" Carla joked.

"Ah, that would depend on how much help I get with the campaign." Silvano reached out and grabbed his son Flavio, who had drifted away from the guide ropes and started to flail around in midair. The family's new apartment had weaker gravity than the last one, but Carlo could understand why Silvano had felt compelled to move.

Carla said, "I'll tout for you six days a stint if you can take the pressure off my department's sunstone allocations."

"Hmm." Silvano wasn't willing to make rash promises, even in jest. "Wait and see what they find with the *Gnat*. If it turns out that we can run the engines on orthogonal rock, you'll have all the sunstone you could wish for."

Carlo said, "What will you be campaigning on?"

"Farm expansion," Silvano replied.

"Expansion?" Carlo was bemused. "Do you think you can find a structural engineer willing to gamble on squeezing in another layer of fields?"

"No, no! Everyone agrees that's reached its limit; we have to look for other opportunities." Flavio was starting to squirm out of his father's grip; he wanted to get back on the rope with his co. Silvano released him and let him drag himself clumsily away.

"Such as...?" Carla pressed him.

Silvano said, "When the *Gnat* visits the Object, what might it find? Either the Object will be made of something violently reactive, which we can use as part of a new kind of fuel, or it will turn out to be nothing but ordinary rock."

Carlo exchanged a glance with Carla. She didn't accept this list as exhaustive, but she was willing to let it pass for the moment.

"If it's the first case," Silvano continued, "we'll be rebuilding the engines completely to make use of the new reaction, which should give us a chance to reclaim some of the feed chambers for agriculture. But the second case would be even more promising: we won't have solved the fuel problem… but we'll certainly have a lot more space."

Carla caught his meaning first, and it forced a chirp of admiration from her. "You want to turn the Object into a *farm*?"

"Why not?" Silvano replied. "We should be prepared to make the best of whatever the *Gnat* finds. If the Object turns out to be ordinary rock, there'll be nothing to stop us cutting into it, making some chambers, spinning it up—"

Carlo said, "But if it's ordinary rock, the *Gnat* won't be able to halt it." The whole idea that they could capture the Object was based on the assumption that it was made of a substance that would react with calmstone as dramatically as the specks that had once lit up the *Peerless*'s slopes.

"That's true," Silvano agreed. "We'd need to follow up quickly with a second expedition, carrying enough fuel to do the job with a conventional engine. But think what it would mean: in the long run, we could easily quadruple the harvest."

Carlo didn't reply. He couldn't declare that this plan was impossible. But the workforce that had carried out the same kind of transformation on Mount Peerless itself—with all the benefits of air and gravity, and a planet's worth of resources behind them—had vastly outnumbered its present population.

Carla said, "No one could accuse you of thinking small."

"We need something like this," Silvano replied. "A big project of our own, in the service of a common goal that might actually be achieved in our lifetimes."

"A project of *our own*?" Carla's tone remained friendly, but she made no attempt to hide her irritation. "So now everything gets classified that way? Is it for *us*, or is it for *them*?"

"You know what I mean," Silvano said, impatient with her umbrage. "Even if we all had the skills to work on some ingenious scheme for rescuing the ancestors, none of us has the slightest chance of living to see the pay-off. Maybe you're happy pondering the deep reasons why mirrors get tarnished—and maybe that will lead somewhere, in an age or two—but the only way that most of us can stay sane is to think about doing something for our own children and grandchildren. The generations we can actually… empathize with." It sounded as if he'd been on the verge of invoking a closer connection than mere empathy, but then recalled just in time that his interlocutor would not be cuddling her own grandchildren.

"Just be careful what you promise," Carlo warned him. "The Object will give its own verdict on all of these plans, and if you've talked up the prospect of quadrupling the harvest you might have some disappointed voters to deal with."

Silvano was puzzled. "I told you: the whole point of my candidacy will be to ensure that people benefit regardless. If we can't farm the Object, solving the fuel problem would certainly be a big boost to morale—but we have to be prepared to find more space for agriculture, whatever the *Gnat* discovers."

"Rocket fuel or rock, you win either way?" Carla was finding the whole thing amusing. "I can see the posters already."

When they'd left the apartment, Carlo turned to her. "You think there's a chance we'll end up farming the Object?"

"Anything's possible," she said. "Though if the whole thing's as inert as calmstone and we end up relying on it, the fuel problem won't just be unsolved, it will be doubled."

"Yeah." As a child, when he'd first understood that the *Peerless* had been loaded up far beyond its capacity to return, Carlo had railed against the ancestors—and now here was Silvano, contemplating doing exactly the same thing. "Do you want to run for the Council on a No Expansion platform? 'Forget about a bigger harvest, people! There's no point getting used to a mountain of extra food, when we have no way to decelerate a mountain of extra rock!'"

Carla buzzed wryly. "Maybe not. I can't really blame Silvano, though.

He doesn't want his son to have to do what he did." When Carlo didn't reply she glanced across at him. "Your solution would be better, but it's harder for most of us to believe in. We all know that a flying mountain can be turned into a farm, but for well-fed women to start having two children sounds more like turning people into voles."

"Western shrub voles, to be precise," Carlo replied. "They're the biparous ones. But they have no males, so that doesn't really help—breeding still doubles their numbers. As far as anyone knows, there's never been an animal population that was stable in the absence of predation, famine or disease."

"Don't get discouraged," Carla said, reaching over and putting a hand on his shoulder. "That's just the history of life for the last few eons. It's not as if it's a law of physics."

14

Tamara woke in the clearing as the wheatlight was fading. She brushed the straw and petals off her body, then lay still for a while, luxuriating in the sensation of the soil against her skin. She was spoilt as a farmer's co, she decided; she didn't know how anyone could sleep in the near-weightlessness of the apartments. She'd never had any trouble doing her work in the observatory, and she often spent the whole day close to the axis, but having to be held in place by a tarpaulin every night, trying to cool yourself in an artificial bed's sterile sand, struck her as the most miserable recipe for insomnia imaginable.

She rose to her feet and looked around. Tamaro was standing a short distance away; her father was up, but she couldn't see him.

"Good morning," Tamaro said. He seemed distracted, the greeting no more than a formality.

"Good morning." Tamara stretched lazily and turned her face to the ceiling. Above them, the moss was waking; in the corridors the same species shone ceaselessly, but here it had learned to defer to the wheat. "Have you been up long?"

"A lapse or two," he replied.

"Oh." She'd half-woken much earlier and thought she'd sensed his absence—in the yielding of the scythe when she'd brushed an arm against it—but she hadn't opened her eyes to check. "I should get moving," she said. She had no urgent business to attend to, but when Tamaro was distant like this it usually meant that he was hoping she'd leave soon, allowing him to eat an early breakfast. That was probably what her father was doing right now.

He said, "Can I talk to you first?"

"Of course." Tamara walked over to him.

"I heard about Massima," he said.

"Yeah, that was a shame."

"You never mentioned it."

Tamara buzzed curtly. "It wasn't that much of a shame. I would have been happy to have her with us, but it won't affect the mission."

Tamaro said, "She must have decided that it wasn't worth the risk."

"Well, that was her right." Tamara was annoyed now. Did he really think he could compare her to Massima? "Since she was only ever going to be a spectator, I don't blame her for setting such a low threshold."

"Do I have to beg you not to go?" he asked her. He sounded hurt now. "Have you even thought about what it would mean to me, if something happened to you?"

Tamara reached down and squeezed his shoulder reassuringly. "Of course I have. But I'll be careful, I promise." She tried to think back to what Ada had said, the way of putting it that had won over her own co. "We were born too late to share the thrill of the launch, and too early to take part in the return. If I turn down an opportunity like this, what's my life for? Just waiting around until we have children?"

"Did I ever put pressure on you to have children?" Tamaro demanded indignantly.

"That's not what I meant."

"I've always been happy for you to work!" he said. "You won't hear a word of complaint from me, just so long as you do something safe."

Tamara struggled to be patient. "You're not listening. I need to do *this*. Part of it's the chance to help the chemists fix the fuel problem—and that in itself would be no small thing. But flying the *Gnat* is the perfect job for me: for my skills, my temperament, my passions. If I'd had to spend my life watching rocks like this pass by in the distance, I would have made the best of it. But *this* is a chance to do everything I'm capable of."

Tamaro said coldly, "And you'd risk our children, for that?"

"Oh…" Tamara was angry now; she'd never imagined he'd resort to anything so cheap. "If I die out there, you'll find yourself a nice widow soon enough. I know most of them have sold their own entitlements, but you'll have mine, won't you? You'll be the definition of an irresistible co-stead."

"You think this is a joke?" Tamaro was furious.

"How was I joking? It's the truth: if I die, you'll still get to be a father. So stop sulking about it, as if you have more at stake here than I do."

He stepped away from her, visibly revolted. "I'm not fathering children with someone else," he said. "The flesh of our mother is the flesh of my children; however long you might borrow it, it's not yours. Least of all yours to endanger."

Tamara buzzed with derision. "What age are you living in? I can't even look at you, you buffoon!" She pushed past him onto the path and headed out of the clearing, half expecting him to start following her and haranguing her, but each time she stole a glance with her rear gaze he was still standing motionless where she'd left him.

When he vanished from sight behind a bend in the path, Tamara felt a strange, vertiginous thrill. *Was she leaving him?* At the very least, she wouldn't be coming back to the farm until he sought her out and apologized. She could sleep in the office next to the observatory—in a bed without gravity, but she'd survive.

As she strode along between the dormant wheat-flowers, she began to feel a twinge of guilt. She wanted Tamaro to understand what the *Gnat* meant to her, but she didn't want to bludgeon him into acquiescence. If he was afraid of losing his chance to be a father, the threat of desertion would be even more distressing than the prospect of her death: her children, not his, would inherit the family's entitlement. What kind of fate was she prepared to force upon him? The choice between a lonely death and... what? Hiding the children he had with some widow? Stealing grain for them from his own crops, until the auditors finally caught him? He needed to grow up and accept her autonomy, but there were limits to how ruthless she was willing to be. She still loved him, she still wanted him to raise their children. Whatever they'd both said in the heat of the moment, she couldn't imagine anything changing that.

Tamara thought of turning back and trying to effect a speedy reconciliation, but then she stiffened her resolve. It would be painful for both of them to pass the day with this quarrel hanging over them, but she had to let Tamaro feel the sting of it. Maybe their father would talk some sense into him. As often as he'd taken Tamaro's side, Erminio knew how stubborn his daughter could be. If he'd overheard the morning's conversation, what counsel could he offer his son but acceptance?

She came to the farm's exit and seized the handle of the door in front of her without slowing her pace. The handle turned a fraction then stuck; she walked straight into the door, pinning her outstretched arm between the slab of calmstone and her advancing torso.

She cursed and stepped back, waited for the pain in her arm to subside, then tried the handle again. On the fourth attempt she understood: it wasn't stuck. The door was locked.

The last time she'd seen the key, she'd been a child. Her father had shown her where it was kept in one of the store-holes, a tool to be wielded against fanciful threats that sounded like stories out of the sagas: rampaging arborines who'd escaped from the forest to conquer the *Peerless*, or rampaging mobs driven mad by hunger, coming to strip the grain from the fields.

It was possible, just barely, that Tamaro had run ahead of her by another route. But he would have had to cut through the fields, and he could not have done it silently.

So either he'd locked the door before she'd even risen that morning, before they'd exchanged a word, or Erminio really had been listening to them—and far from resolving to plead her case with Tamaro, he'd decided that the way to fix this problem was to keep her on the farm by force.

"You arrogant pieces of shit!" Tamara hoped that at least one of them was lurking nearby to overhear her.

Angry as she was, she was struck by one ground for amusement and relief: *better that they try this stunt now than on the launch day.* If they'd caught her by surprise at the crucial time it would not have been hard to keep her confined for a few bells. Once she'd failed to show up, Ada and Ivo would have had no choice but to leave without her, and her idiot family would have got exactly what they'd wanted. But apparently they couldn't bear to defer the pleasure of punishing her.

Tamaro was coming down the path toward her.

"Where's the key?" she demanded.

"Our father's taken it." He nodded toward the door, implying that Erminio was outside, beyond her reach.

"So what's the plan?"

"I gave you chance after chance," he said. "But you wouldn't listen." He didn't sound angry; his voice was dull, resigned.

"What do you think is going to happen?" she asked. "Do you know how many people are expecting me to turn up for meetings in the next three days alone? Out of all those friends and colleagues, I promise you someone will come looking for me."

"Not after they hear the happy news."

Tamara stared at him. If Erminio was out there telling people that she'd given birth, this had gone beyond a private family matter. She couldn't just forgive her captors and walk away, promising her silence, when the very fact of her survival would show them up as liars.

"I've burned all your holin," Tamaro told her. "You know I'd never try to force myself on you, but what happens now is your choice."

She searched his face, looking for a hint of uncertainty—if not in the rightness of his goals, in his chance of achieving them. But the man she'd loved since her first memory of life seemed convinced that there were only two ways this could end.

Either she'd agree to let him trigger her, and she'd give birth to his children—taking comfort in the knowledge that he'd promised himself to them.

Or she'd stay here, without holin, until her own body betrayed her. She'd give birth alone, and her sole victory would be to have cheated her jailer and her children alike of the bond that would have allowed them to thrive.

15

The hiss from the sunstone lamp rose in pitch to an almost comical squeak. Carla could hear the remaining pellets of fuel ricocheting around the crucible, small enough now that the slightest asymmetry in the hot gas erupting from their surface turned them into tiny rockets. A moment later they'd burned away completely and the lamp was dark and silent.

Onesto walked over to the firestone lamp and turned it up, then went back to his desk.

The workshop looked drab in the ordinary light. Carla punctured the seal of the evacuated container, waited for the air to leak in, then tore away the seal and retrieved the mirror. After she'd inspected it herself she handed it to Patrizia, who surveyed it glumly.

It had been obvious for the last few days that the tarnishing wasn't proceeding in the manner they'd predicted. The first tier had matched the reference card placed beside the mirror after a mere two chimes' exposure; the second tier had taken two days. That alone showed that the time to create each photon couldn't be the same in each case. But Patrizia's idea that the time might be proportional to the period of the light couldn't explain what they were seeing, either. For two near-identical hues on either side of the border between the second and third tiers, the period of the light was virtually the same—but while the fifth photon needed to complete the tarnishing reaction in the second tier had only taken two days to appear, after waiting more than twice as long for one more photon, the third tier remained pristine.

Carla sketched the results on her chest. "The photon theory can explain the frequencies where we switch from one tier to the next. But how do we make sense of the timing?"

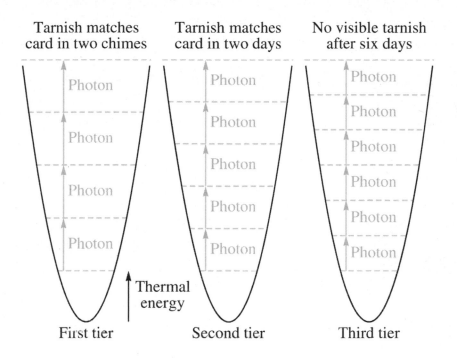

"Maybe some energy leaks out of these valleys as heat," Patrizia suggested. "Then it takes time to make up for that."

"Make up for it how?"

"With a longer exposure."

"But all you can *do* with a longer exposure is create more photons!" Carla protested. "And if the numbers of photons aren't what I've drawn here, where does the five-to-four ratio in the frequencies come from?"

Patrizia hummed in self-reproach. "Of course. I'm not thinking straight."

Carla saw Onesto glance up from his papers. He'd endured the jarring lighting for six days, and now he had to listen to the two of them stumbling around trying to make sense of their non-result. "I'm sorry if we're disturbing you," she said.

"You're not disturbing me," Onesto replied. "But to be honest, I haven't been able to get much work done for the last two bells."

"Why not?"

"Something's been puzzling me about your theory," he said, "and the more I see you puzzled yourselves, the more I'm tempted to break my silence. So if it's not too discourteous, I hope you'll let me speak my mind."

Carla said, "Of course."

Onesto approached. "Nereo posited a particle, the luxagen, to act as a source for Yalda's light field. If I've understood what you're saying, you're now positing an entirely new particle that plays a very different role: traveling with the waves in the field itself, carrying their energy for them."

Carla turned to Patrizia; the theory was hers to define and defend. Patrizia said, "That's right."

"Then why not complete the pattern?" Onesto suggested. "If you have reason to believe that the light field can manifest as a particle, why should Nereo's own particle be different? Shouldn't *the luxagen* be associated with waves in a field of its own?"

Patrizia looked confused, so Carla stepped in.

"There would be an appealing symmetry to that," she said. "To every wave, its particle; to every particle, its wave. But I think it would complicate the theory unnecessarily. Without any evidence for a 'luxagen field', it's hard to see what could be gained by including it."

Onesto inclined his head politely. "Thank you for listening. I'll leave you in peace now."

He was halfway to his desk when Patrizia said, "You want us to treat the luxagen as a standing wave?"

Onesto turned. "I wasn't thinking of anything so specific," he admitted. "It just seems odd to treat the two particles so differently."

At this response Patrizia's confidence wavered, but then she persisted with her line of thought. "Suppose the luxagen follows the same kind of rules as the photon," she said. "It has its own waves—and just like light waves, their frequency is proportional to the particle's energy."

Carla said, "All right. But…"

"If the luxagen is trapped in an energy valley," Patrizia said, "its wave must be trapped as well. A trapped wave, a standing wave, can only take on certain shapes—each one with a different number of peaks."

Carla felt the scowl vanish from her face. Unlike Patrizia's last suggestion, this wasn't hunger-addled nonsense. Onesto's proposal had sounded naïve—but now Carla could see where her infuriating, erratically brilliant student was taking it.

For each shape it could adopt, the luxagen's standing wave would oscillate with a specific frequency. The same kind of principle governed the harmonics of a drum: the geometry of the resonant modes of the drumhead dictated the particular sounds it could make, each one with its characteristic pitch.

But Patrizia's rule linked frequencies to energies—so a trapped luxagen would only be able to possess certain *energies*. The energy closest to the top of the valley would set the gap that needed to be jumped in order for tarnishing to occur, and there would be no doing it by halves: a luxagen couldn't accumulate five photons' worth of energy and then wait around for a sixth. Once you reached the highest energy level there were no more resting places; it was an all-or-nothing trip. You either made the total number of photons you needed, *all at once*, and escaped the valley... or you didn't.

As they talked it over, Patrizia sketched the general idea. Onesto looked on, pleased that his suggestion had proved helpful but a little daunted by the strange outcome.

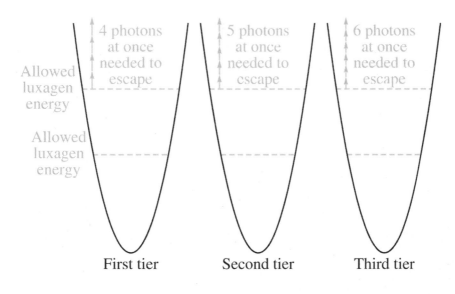

"I still don't understand the details of the timing," Carla confessed, "but if you don't get to make the photons separately, one by one, there's no reason to expect the time it takes to be proportional to the number of photons."

"Can we quantify any of this?" Patrizia asked.

Carla said, "We could try to write an equation for the luxagen wave. Whatever we know about the luxagen's energy, we translate into the wave's frequency; whatever we know about the luxagen's momentum, we translate into the wave's *spatial frequency*."

The idea seemed straightforward, but they struck a problem almost at once. Taking the rate of change of an oscillating wave multiplied it by a factor proportional to its frequency, but also shifted the wave by a quarter-cycle: at every peak of the original wave the rate of change crossed zero, heading downwards, while at every such zero of the original wave the rate of change was at a minimum, the bottom of a trough. When Yalda had devised her light equation she had been able to go one step further: the *second* rate of change was shifted by another quarter-cycle, putting it a half-cycle away from the original—yielding the original wave turned upside down and multiplied by the frequency squared.

Multiples of the original wave were easy to combine. The geometrical relationship Yalda had sought to express—that the sum of the squares of the wave's frequencies in all four dimensions was a constant—could be encoded in the wave equation simply by multiplying every term in that relationship by the strength of the wave, then re-expressing the squared frequencies as second rates of change.

But with a luxagen in a solid, the relationship between its energy and momentum included its potential energy, which depended on its position in the energy valley. It was impossible to write this relationship purely in terms of the energy *squared*—so it was impossible to talk only of frequencies *squared*. To go halfway and include the frequency itself meant taking the square root of the operation that turned the wave upside down—putting the square root of minus one into the wave equation.

"It looks as if we're stuck with complex numbers," Carla declared. "What does *that* mean? That our premises are wrong?"

Patrizia seemed to share her sense of trepidation, but she wasn't ready to give up. "Let's follow the mathematics," she suggested. "We should see what the final answers are before deciding whether or not it all makes sense."

To make the calculations easier they chose a field described by a single number—albeit complex—rather than a vector like light, with its different polarizations. They also assumed that the luxagen would be moving slowly. For a parabolic energy valley—the easiest idealization to work with—it was possible to solve the equation exactly.

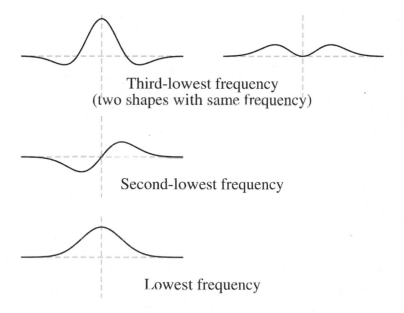

Shapes of luxagen waves in parabolic energy valley

Third-lowest frequency
(two shapes with same frequency)

Second-lowest frequency

Lowest frequency

As Patrizia had guessed from the start, there was a sequence of solutions with distinct shapes. Those shapes could be described with real numbers alone, though the wave's variation over time swept out a circle in the complex number plane with a frequency corresponding to its energy.

Some solutions shared the same energy, though that was just a consequence of the idealized shape of the valley. Carla pushed on further and managed to calculate the effect of switching to a more realistic valley, closer to the kind that was actually produced by Nereo's force in a solid.

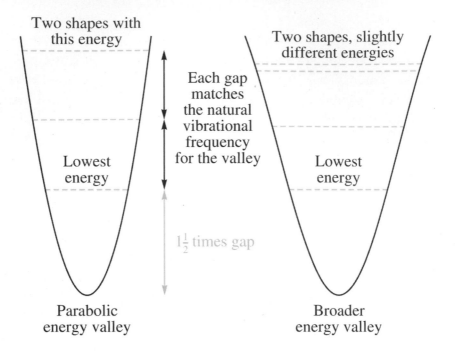

Two shapes with this energy

Two shapes, slightly different energies

Each gap matches the natural vibrational frequency for the valley

Lowest energy

Lowest energy

$1\frac{1}{2}$ times gap

Parabolic energy valley

Broader energy valley

For the parabolic case all the energies were governed by the natural frequency at which a luxagen—as a particle—would be expected to vibrate in such a valley. The gaps between the allowed energies all corresponded precisely to that frequency, while the lowest energy sat one and a half times higher above the valley floor. For a more realistic valley, all the energies were reduced slightly, and the perfect agreement between the multiple higher-energy solutions broke down, splitting the idealized single energy levels into closely spaced sets.

Onesto said, "Suppose the natural frequency for the valley is greater than the maximum frequency of light. That's the assumption at the core of the original theory of solids. But what does it mean, in your terms?"

Carla thought for a moment. "It means the energy gap exceeds the mass of a photon—so creating a single photon can never give you enough energy to jump the gap."

"And if the valley's not a perfect parabola," Onesto observed, "that doesn't really change the significance of the main energy gaps, does it? There'll be smaller gaps as well, but if the main ones are large enough there'll still be energy levels where you need to make more than one photon in order to rise any higher."

"Right," Carla said. "And if the valley is deep enough, those gaps could end up so large that you'd need to make six or seven photons to cross them."

Patrizia turned to Carla. "Doesn't that... solve the stability problem?"

Carla considered the question seriously. In the old way of looking at the problem, even if the walls of the energy valley were so steep that the luxagen rolled back and forth at a rate dozens of times greater than the maximum frequency of light, the tiniest deviation from a parabolic shape would introduce lower-frequency components into its motion—some of them low enough to produce light. And however feeble the radiation emitted that way, the luxagen would slowly gain energy and creep up the valley, until it finally escaped.

But that was in a world where energies could take on any value at all. In the new theory of luxagens as waves, a steep enough valley would have gaps between its energy levels that were insurmountable—and the inevitable imperfections in the shape of the valley would merely split some of those levels. As Onesto had pointed out, if the rungs of the original energy ladder were spaced sufficiently widely, adding a few extra rungs close to the originals wouldn't suddenly make the whole thing traversable. The valley's imperfection no longer undermined its stability.

"We still don't know how long it takes to create a given number of photons," Carla said cautiously. "But we do know that it takes much longer to make five than four, and a great deal longer to make six—even with the beam from a sunstone lamp to help. If we could understand what was going on there, I think we'd be getting close to explaining how some solids can be stable."

Patrizia sketched the shapes of the first few luxagen waves on her own chest. "What happens if I add two of these solutions together—two waves with different energies? The sum will still solve the same equation... so what does the combined wave represent? Two luxagens, one with each energy?"

Carla said, "That doesn't sound right. We found the wave equation by translating the energy-momentum relationship for a single particle. And what if I add two solutions in unequal proportions? Say, one quarter the first solution and three quarters the other?"

"Couldn't that be… one particle with the first energy, and three with the second?" Patrizia didn't sound too persuaded herself; she could probably see where this numbers game was heading.

"*Irrational* proportions, then," Carla replied. "Multiply the second solution by the square root of two, then add it to the first. It's still just one particle."

Patrizia hummed with frustration. "You can multiply these waves by any number you like!" she said. "It doesn't change their frequency, so it won't change their energy—I mean the luxagen's energy. Unless the wave has some energy of its own, separate from the particle's energy, what does it actually mean if you double the size of the wave, or triple it?"

Carla was worried now. If the luxagen wave *did* have an energy of its own that depended on its amplitude, the discrete energy steps that were the theory's great virtue would be erased. "What if we ignore the overall size of the wave?" she suggested. "Or better yet, we *standardize* the size of each solution, by some measure. Then we could still ask what it means to combine two solutions in a certain proportion. If we start with a wave with the lowest energy, and combine it with the next one, say at one part in twelve… what would that mean, physically? It can't describe a particle with an energy lying one twelfth of the way between the two values." That route would lead them back to continuous energies again, rendering the whole thing useless.

Patrizia spread her arms in a gesture of defeat; she'd run out of guesses.

"Part one energy, part another," Carla muttered. "We could even have a luxagen that was part trapped in the valley, part free!"

Nothing was making sense any more. The exhilaration she'd felt when they'd found the energy levels had vanished now. Why should they take the luxagen equation seriously, if they couldn't say what its solutions meant in all but a few special cases? If she tried to peddle this nonsense to Assunto as the answer to the stability problem, he'd have her teaching the wavelength-velocity relationship to three-year-olds for the rest of her life.

Then she heard her own words as if someone else had spoken them: *Part trapped in the valley, part free.* Two solutions you could combine, in any proportion. That *proportion* could be the missing timer—the means by which a luxagen in the tarnishing experiment kept track of how long it had been sitting in the light. Its energy couldn't creep up over time... but the ratio between the two solutions could. The luxagen could start out as a trapped wave, but then gradually take on more and more of the free solution.

Carla didn't know what this hunch was worth, but they had all the tools they'd need to test it. She said, "If we want to know how long it takes to get a luxagen out of the valley by blasting it with light... why don't we just add the energy due to the light itself to the energy of the valley, and calculate exactly what that does to the luxagen wave over time?"

Patrizia quailed slightly. "That sounds like a long calculation."

"Oh, it will be," Carla promised her. "So before we even start, we should break for a meal." She turned to Onesto. "Will you join us? Loaves for everyone, out of my entitlement. Let's celebrate, replenish our strength—then start dragging some real predictions out of this equation."

16

As she checked the link to the light recorder, Amanda leaned close to Carlo and whispered, "If this works, you should take it to the Variety Hall. They haven't had an act that drew a crowd like this for years."

There did seem to be about twice as many people gathered around the bench where they'd set up the signaling experiment than were usually present in the entire animal physiology workshop. Carlo didn't know who'd invited them all, but he was feeling apprehensive enough without adding a layer of stage fright. He needed to keep both arms still or risk shifting the probes skewering his wrists, but he managed to roll his shoulders without the motion reaching below his elbows as he tried to unknot the tense flesh in his back.

Both probes had been aligned to pick up the signal to one finger of each hand. Amanda started the light recorder, then Carlo executed a sequence of moves with the chosen finger of his left hand, following the instructions on a sheet of paper clipped to the bench in front of him. Each individual action was simple enough, but they were arranged in an arbitrary progression that he could only adhere to by paying close attention, and he had deliberately refrained from any rehearsal. The eye-catching periodicity of his first, repetitive experiment had had its advantages, but this time he didn't want his flesh to sense a pattern and pursue it on its own.

When this first stage of the performance was over, Amanda took the spool of paper out of the recorder, slipped it onto a shaft mounted on the bench, then wound the whole strip across onto another spool—the simplest way to inspect it without risking it getting tangled or damaged.

To Carlo's relief, there was a strong signal darkening the paper from start to finish; they wouldn't need to dig around in his flesh any more to improve on it.

"Do you want to use this?" Amanda checked with him.

"Please." Carlo wasn't in great pain, but his body kept drawing his attention to the probes' unnatural presence, refusing to let him feel at ease.

Amanda loaded the spool into the inverter, inspected the contact rollers for any grit or paper-fluff that could do mischief, then threaded the two leader tapes—from the recording itself, and from a second spool of unexposed light paper—together through the core of the mechanism and onto their respective receiving spools. Then she lit the lamp, closed the device, wound the spring, and engaged the drive. The spectators waited patiently as the machine whirred—better behaved than the usual crowd at any magic show.

Tosco said, "Have you checked that you're not saturating the light paper's response? Outside a limited range of intensities, that coating just flattens any variation in brightness."

"We've checked," Carlo replied tersely. Amanda added, "Everything's been calibrated so it lies within a suitable exposure range. We won't get the original light curve back, but any distortion should be comparable to the natural range of variation in the signal." If the brain itself didn't send out identical sequences for the same action every time, the flesh ought to be as forgiving with this artificial version as it needed to be with the biological messages it received every day.

The inverter gave a soft thud as its tension arm detected the end of the spool, halting the drive. Amanda retrieved the duplicate tape and rewound it slowly so Carlo could scrutinize it. The darkest paper in the original recording had protected the second strip from the lamplight in the inverter, allowing it to remain almost translucent, while the most translucent parts of the original—those exposed to the weakest signal from the probe—would have offered far less protection, allowing the duplicate to darken almost to opacity.

Carlo could see no sudden shifts in the tone of the paper that would indicate a surge or deficit of the sensitizing gas, and no stretches of flattened contrast that would imply that they'd saturated the coating. Light recording was a finicky art, but their experience was beginning to pay off.

"What do you think?" Amanda must have reached her own conclusion, but she kept her voice neutral. If Carlo wanted to declare the tape unusable—giving him an excuse to back out of the experiment—that was up to him.

"It's fine," he declared. As he spoke, he felt his left forearm twitch in dissent: a needle of hardstone driven through his wrist wasn't *fine* at all, and every scrag of his flesh knew that there was a stranger incursion yet to come.

Amanda loaded the duplicate tape into the light player, running the leader through onto the receiving spool. She gently tugged the connecting arm from the left-hand probe out of its socket in the light recorder and swung it around toward the new machine. When it was in place, there was one more adjustment to make: she reached down and took hold of the probe itself, and turned the ring attached to the mirror at the bottom of the needle. Before, it had faced back up along his arm, to catch some of the light arriving from his brain. Now it was angled toward that light's destination, down the motor pathway into his hand.

"Why doesn't he just use a vole?" one of Tosco's students whispered to another.

"That needle's too big."

"So why not make it smaller?"

"Be quiet, or you'll be playing vole next time."

Carlo said, "A smaller needle wouldn't capture enough light. We'll need to develop more sensitive paper before we can shrink the probes."

"Are you ready?" Amanda asked him. She'd wound the player's spring and lit the lamp while he'd been distracted by the students.

Carlo started to relax his left arm—doing his best to surrender control, to prepare himself not to fight what was coming—but then he felt the slight change in muscle tone threaten to shift the probe. He didn't really need to disown the whole limb, though, so long as he could hold back the urge to intervene when the ghost of his earlier self started taking liberties with his body.

"I'm ready," he replied.

Amanda engaged the drive on the player. Carlo gazed down his arm at his finger, which was moving without his bidding.

Cold nausea churned through his gut and esophagus, loosening food tubules from mouth to anus; he fought it and managed to hold onto his breakfast. There was nothing painful in the sensations coming from his finger—but a part of his brain was insisting that some kind of parasite had invaded the flesh, and its alarming twitches could only presage the likelihood of it burrowing even deeper. As he struggled to understand precisely where this revulsion was coming from—focusing his attention on the stretching of the skin, the tension in the muscles, the disposition of the joints—he couldn't identify any one thing he hadn't felt when he'd performed the same movements willingly. But he couldn't separate that raw sensation from the context and declare that it was as innocent as before. Flesh that moved of its own accord simply could not be treated with equanimity.

When the playback stopped, Carlo shuddered with relief. The illusory parasite lingered for a moment, a fat dead thing trapped under his skin, but when he crooked his finger a few times it vanished. He realized that he hadn't had the presence of mind to check his movements against the original script; he looked to Amanda for her verdict.

"The mimicry was pretty close," she said. "A few gestures were dropped or ambiguous, but most were repeated accurately."

Some of the onlookers offered congratulatory cheers. Carlo felt drained, but as his nausea faded he managed a chirp of satisfaction. As primitive and unpleasant as the whole demonstration had been, it had established an important principle. All the more so if they could repeat it with one more twist.

Amanda had already started rewinding the tape. "Give me a lapse or two," he told her.

"You don't have to do the second stage today," she replied.

"I'm not wasting that spike in my wrist." Carlo turned from her and saw Tosco watching him in silence, then he shifted his gaze slightly and addressed the man's students. "You can mark this day as the birth of a new field," he proclaimed. "The light recorder will revolutionize the study of the brain's signals—and *light puppetry* will be the best way to compare those signals in different species." Once they refined the equipment, they could replay the instructions from one vole's brain in a distant cousin's body and see which parts of the signal were interpreted the same way in both species. Not every nuance would be the same, but flesh was flesh, it all shared a common ancestor. With time and patience, they could take this language apart and uncover all its subtleties, as surely as scholars of ancient writing had decoded old engravings by their own process of comparison.

He nodded to Amanda to proceed. She uncoupled the connecting arm from the first probe, and swung it over toward his right hand. Carlo resisted the urge to pluck the needle out of his left wrist immediately; sometimes the extraction went horribly wrong, and he didn't want to vocalize that much pain in front of an audience.

With the player connected to the right-hand probe, Carlo spent a moment preparing himself. It hadn't been so bad the first time, and now he knew exactly what to expect. His gut had settled, he wouldn't disgrace himself.

"I'm ready," he said.

Amanda engaged the drive.

The finger they'd targeted with the probe remained motionless. "What?" Frustrated, Carlo moved his forearm slightly, just enough to feel the bite of stone against his flesh. Suddenly his whole right hand sprung to life: all six fingers flexing and waggling, turning and twitching, wriggling like worms with their heads in a trap.

With one word he could have had the signal shut off, but Carlo wanted to see this final stage play out; even with the probe misaligned it could tell them something useful. His sense of violation was more acute than before, but he could tolerate it for a couple of lapses. He glanced at Amanda; she was diligently observing his contortions, trying to judge how well they conformed to the script. Carlo could only be sure of one detail: some of his fingers were moving differently than others, so they couldn't all be doing the right thing.

He heard the gentle thud from the player as it halted. His relief was short-lived; his fingers kept squirming. "All right," he muttered. If his first recording of a twirling finger had revealed the potential for fleshly autonomy, this shouldn't be entirely surprising or alarming. He just needed to tell his wayward hand to stop, firmly and clearly.

He commanded his fingers to be still—but this edict was completely ineffectual.

Carlo let out a hum of frustration, hoping to convince himself as much as the onlookers that he was more irritated than afraid. He tried to clench his fist, but his body had news for him: the burrowing parasites owned that flesh, and they weren't taking instructions from him.

"I think his hand's giving birth," someone joked from the back of the crowd.

"Could you take off the connector, please?" Carlo instructed Amanda, each polite syllable a proof that he remained unflustered. When she'd complied, he swung his arm away from the bench, mapping out the degrees of freedom he still controlled. He could move his arm at the shoulder, at will. He could flex and extend the limb at the elbow joint. He pictured the vast territory subject to his rule, pictured the tiny rebellious province, pictured the inevitable reconquest. But all of this stirring martial imagery remained nothing more than a fantasy. Beyond the wrist, he might as well have had a brood of angry lizards grafted to his flesh.

He drew his arm back and slapped the bench, trying to bash some sense into his hand. Again, harder. The third blow drove the probe's needle deeper into his wrist; the pain was excruciating, but it felt right, it felt necessary.

"Carlo?" Amanda wasn't panicking yet, but she wanted him to tell her how she could help.

"I haven't lost control of my arm," he assured her, struggling to get the words out. His actions were entirely voluntary—at least by the standards his rogue hand had set—even if the urge to damage the thing was becoming increasingly compelling.

But the blows weren't helping, they weren't changing anything. His battered hand was squirming as energetically as ever.

"Just cut it off," he said.

"Are you sure?" Amanda looked to Tosco.

"Cut it off!" Carlo repeated angrily.

"Can't you resorb it?"

The suggestion made him recoil in disgust. *Bring these squirming parasites into his torso, into the depths of his body to go where they pleased?*

But there were no parasites. His hand was merely damaged and dysfunctional. It needed to be reorganized, the way he would have dealt with any other injury.

Carlo began drawing the flesh in at his shoulder. He managed to shorten his arm by about a third before his body rebelled and halted the process. The prospect of bringing the afflicted hand any closer felt like ingesting something rotting and poisoned. And for all he knew, his body was right. What if it *couldn't* reorganize this flesh, any more than it could subdue a virulent parasite?

"I can't do it," he said finally. "It has to come off."

Amanda said, "All right."

Tosco sent someone to fetch a knife. Carlo rested his forearm on the bench, resigned now. *So this was the way to make biparity safe and easy? Even if he found the right signals… how many years, how many generations of refinements would it take before any sane woman would let a machine like this near her body?*

The knife was passed through the crowd until it ended up with Tosco. As he approached the bench, Carlo said, "Amanda's my assistant."

"As you wish." Tosco handed her the knife.

"Where exactly?" she asked Carlo. He gestured to a point a couple of scants above the probe.

Someone behind Carlo whispered sardonically, "Welcome to the age of light."

Amanda rearranged her harness to allow her to exert more force against the bench. With one hand she pinned Carlo's forearm in place, then she quickly brought the knife down.

Carlo contracted the skin over the fresh wound, almost sealing it, then he drew the remainder of his arm into his torso as rapidly as he could. By the time the full force of the pain hit him, it belonged to a phantom limb. The loose, punctured skin around his shoulder still stung, but his severed wrist no longer existed, and the message of searing agony it had sent to his brain dissipated into irrelevance.

On the bench, though, his lost fingers were still twitching.

17

For the eighth night in a row, Tamara made her bed beside the door to the farm, close enough to ensure that no one could come or go without waking her. If Erminio had the only key he would have to return eventually. She couldn't think of any way for Tamaro to get a message to him—to summon him for assistance, or even just to tell him that his grandchildren were born—so surely her father would soon feel compelled to come and see for himself what was happening.

She slept fitfully, disturbed by every small sound. But even half-awake she could classify the noises around her: the faint creaking of the stone walls, air rustling through the crops, a lizard dashing across the ground. When she woke to the fading wheat-light she did not feel rested, but she knew that if she'd tried to eschew sleep entirely that would have left her completely dysfunctional.

She hadn't eaten for two days now, having finished the stock of loaves she'd brought with her from the clearing, but she decided not to risk leaving the door unguarded; she could go without food for at least another day. She could not rule out Tamaro having his own key hidden somewhere, but even so she did not believe that her father could wait patiently for however long it took for Tamaro to emerge. Too many things could go wrong with the plan—and the more he'd been expecting a swift resolution, the more the long silence would come to weigh on him.

Tamara sat slumped against the door, gazing up into the moss-light, trying to decide if Erminio really would have risked telling people that she'd already given birth. With women starving themselves to varying degrees there was no such thing as a normal birth mass any more, and by the time the children went to school a few stints' difference between their real and reported age wouldn't be obvious on developmental grounds, so it was far from inevitable that the deception would be uncovered. But while her friends from the observatory might not expect to see the children until they were old enough to be brought to them, people from the neighboring farms would normally have visited within days of the birth. So the balance there was shifted: her father's best bet would have been to say nothing to them. Though she ran into the neighbors often enough as she came and went from the farm, if by chance their paths failed to cross for a stint or two, no one would think twice about it.

The greatest risk that remained, then, was that word of her supposed fate would spread beyond her colleagues and their immediate circle. It was not a preposterous vanity to think that the leader of the expedition to the Object abandoning that coveted role would be an event widely remarked upon, and that news of her surprising choice—or entertaining mishap—would diffuse faster and farther than if she'd been a farmer or a maintenance worker.

If Erminio's lie collided with his inexplicable silence to the neighbors, people would start asking awkward questions. He could make excuses, he could invoke his family's privacy, but that would only get him so far. If she could outlast his luck and outlive his bluster, there was a chance that someone would come looking for her.

Halfway through the morning, Tamaro came down the path toward her.

"I'm still here," she said. "Just the one of me."

"I brought you some loaves."

"Why? Do you think you can stupefy me with wormbane, and then do what you like?"

Tamaro looked every bit as hurt by this suggestion as if it had come out of nowhere, a gratuitous slur against an innocent man. He said, "If I really were the kind of monster who'd treat you that way, don't you think it would have happened without warning, a long time ago?"

"You were probably just worried that it might affect the children, but now you're willing to take that risk."

He stopped a few strides from Tamara and tossed the loaves on the ground in front of her. "And you're willing to risk them being fatherless?"

"That makes no difference to me," Tamara replied coolly. "I won't be here to deal with it. And why should it bother me if my children despise you? I doubt you'd go so far as to kill them out of spite—you'd be much too afraid of Erminio to do that. You'll just get out of the way and let him raise his grandchildren."

"You should hear yourself," Tamaro said sadly. It was surreal just how sincerely he clung to his right to express disappointment in her.

"It was his plan though, wasn't it?" Tamara needled him. "You just spluttered with helpless indignation, day after day, but he was the one who goaded you into this heroic rescue of the family's legacy."

"Neither of us wanted to do this," Tamaro said. "It's no one else's fault that you wouldn't listen to reason."

"So that's what this is about? *Reason?*"

"You could have found an old man to take your place," Tamaro insisted. "Can you name one benefit that the *Gnat* would not have been able to bring us, if you'd done that?"

"Who is this mysterious 'us'?" Tamara wondered. "I hear the word a lot from you, but whatever the usual rules of grammar might imply I never actually seem to be a part of it."

"If that's true, it's because you cut yourself out."

"Ah, my fault again."

Tamaro tipped his head in agreement, not so much oblivious to her sarcasm as indifferent.

"Am I even a person to you any more?" she asked.

"I've never stopped loving you for one moment," he replied.

"Really? Me, or the children?"

Tamaro scowled. "You want me to choose?"

"No. I just want you to separate the two."

"Why?"

"Because if you can't," she said, "we might as well be animals. Just bundles of reproductive instincts."

Tamaro contemplated this claim. "And if I were just a friend, a neighbor, what would *you* feel for *me*? If I weren't destined to raise your children, would you ever have cared if I lived or died?"

"Prior to this obnoxious stunt," she said, "I'm sure I wouldn't have tried to turn you into worm feed just because that's nature's plan for you in the long run."

"So if I try to stop you risking your life, you equate that with murder?"

"Not at all," Tamara said. "I don't blame you for wanting to dissuade me from flying on the *Gnat*. If our places had been swapped, I probably would have argued just as hard for you to stay. It's only what you're doing now that amounts to murder."

Tamaro was silent for a lapse. Then he said, "How many years do you think you would have waited? If not for the scythe in our bed, are you telling me you were never as likely to have woken me in the night as I was you?"

"I don't know," Tamara replied truthfully. "But once I found the Object, I would never have let you take the scythe away until I'd made that trip."

He spread his arms. "So what now?"

"Let me leave."

"I don't have the key," Tamaro declared. "I couldn't open the door if I wanted to."

"I don't believe that. Either you have a key, or you have some way to summon Erminio."

"Believe what you like."

Tamara said, "If there's no trust left between us, we should just part. If you want me to tell all your friends that I'm to blame for the separation, I'll do that."

Tamaro was offended. "You think I'm clinging to you out of pride? Or worse than that: I'm just fretting about what people will say?"

"No," she conceded. "I think you're worried about feeding your children. Which is why I'm willing to sign over the entitlement to you."

Tamaro stared at her. It was the first time she'd seen him truly shocked since the whole thing had begun.

"Why would I believe that?" he said. "Why would you honor an agreement like that?"

"Signed and witnessed, what choice would I have? Fetch as many of our neighbors as you like and I'll sign the transfer in front of them."

"But then what would you do for your own children?"

Tamara said, "I'd find a widower with an entitlement of his own. But

I know, there's no guarantee of that. So I'd have to be ready to go the way of men."

She could see him thinking it over. That in itself gave her hope: if he'd had no way to release her, what point would there have been in weighing up the pros and cons?

"You know I'm prepared to risk death," she said. "If you didn't believe that, we would never have ended up in this standoff."

Her words seemed to push him toward a decision, but not in the direction she'd been hoping. "Why should I take the entitlement away from my own family?" Tamaro demanded angrily. "Even if you deny me the chance to be the father of your children, they'll still be my own mother's flesh."

Oh, the mother thing again. If only Erminia had had the foresight to leave a few written instructions for her mama-smitten son.

Tamara was tired. She bent down and picked up one of the loaves. "All right, then. I'll give you an easier decision. It's better that I stay hungry, but I can only hold out if we finish this now."

"What are you talking about?"

"I'm sick of fighting you," she said wearily. "This isn't what I wanted, but I have no other choice left."

Tamaro stood motionless, confused. "You're serious? You're ready right now?"

"My body's been ready for days," she declared. "I keep waking in the night, thinking you're beside me." She gazed at him imploringly. "Can't we make peace, for this? Can't you show some mercy and let me feel loved at the end?"

Tamaro lowered his gaze, ashamed. "I'm sorry I've been so hard on you," he said. "I never wanted it to be like that."

When he looked up again Tamara buzzed happily. She threw the loaf away and gestured to him to approach.

She forced herself to wait until he was a little closer than arm's reach, lest he slip away and lead her on a chase she might be too famished to win. But before he could embrace her, she grabbed him by the neck and forced his body around. Then she kicked his legs from under him, and knelt forward, pinning him face-down on the ground.

His rear eyes stared up at her angrily. She put a hand over them and sprouted two more arms; he'd already extruded an extra pair himself in the hope of struggling free, but they were short and feeble, of little more than nuisance value.

"Where's the key?" she asked him softly. Tamaro didn't answer. "Wherever it is, I'm going to find it." She ran her new hands over his body, starting just below his tympanum, keeping her fingertips sharp and sensitive as she searched for the tell-tale crease of a pocket.

Touching his skin made the scent of his body stronger than she'd known it for years, forcing her back to memories of the two of them wrestling as children. She'd never hesitated to take advantage of her size to overpower him then, though when she'd done it in anger and hurt him it had always left her ashamed. But she couldn't afford to be sentimental now. He wasn't her co any more, he was just her jailer, with a secret she needed if she wanted to live.

Tamara searched every scant of him; he had no pockets. "Where is it?" she demanded. He wouldn't have buried it in any of the store-holes she knew about, and it would take her a year to dig up the whole farm.

He said, "I told you: Erminio has the only key."

"Open your mouth," she suggested, twisting him onto his side.

"Get off me!"

Tamara gripped his lower jaw tightly and pulled it down. Tamaro sharpened his own fingertips and began stabbing at her hand, but she hardened the skin and persisted. She was dizzy from hunger now, and doubted she was thinking clearly, but her strength hadn't deserted her.

She managed to get his mouth open, wide enough to see inside. She stretched out two fingers on either side, braced them against his cheek-bones, and ossified their joints so she wouldn't have to struggle to keep them from bending. Then she extruded a fifth limb from her chest, long and narrow with a circle of small fingers reaching out on all sides, like the petals of a flower.

She checked the roof of his mouth first, then forced his tongue aside and felt beneath it.

"You're going to give birth here," he proclaimed gleefully. "It doesn't matter what you do. And I'm going to love the children as if they were my own. They'll never even know that I'm not their father."

Tamara pushed her new hand down into his esophagus and spread her fingers, fighting her revulsion and the contractions of the muscular tubules branching out from the main passage. She rummaged through the chewed food and digestive resin, waiting to strike something unyielding. The key wasn't small, so there was a limit to how far it could have penetrated these side channels. But there was no real limit to how deep it might be.

Tamaro was humming, so softly she could barely feel his tympanum moving, unwillingly revealing his distress. Did she honestly believe he would have swallowed the key, or was she just trying to humiliate him? What did she do next—force a limb into his anus? Cut him open from end to end?

She pulled her hand out of his throat and resorbed the soiled arm, leaving the mush that had adhered to it sliding down her chest.

"Take the entitlement," she begged him. "That's all I can give you."

"Why should I compromise?" Tamaro replied.

"This is my life," she said. "What is it you don't understand about that?"

Tamaro said nothing. Even if she took him by the legs and bashed his skull against the ground, he'd die without conceding any parallel between their fates. And what would that gain her? The opportunity to search the farm for the key, with nobody to interfere, or to move it.

It would be easy enough. She could make it quick. She would mourn and wail afterward, for sure, but the satisfaction of the act itself would be incomparable. *Can you understand my stubbornness, now? Can you finally see the downside of having your brain split in two?*

She kept the glorious vision spinning in her head, promising herself the giddy dance of retribution even as she forced her grip to weaken. Tamaro broke free and crawled across the ground, spitting up traces of loose food. Then he rose to his feet and jogged away down the path.

Tamara closed her eyes. If she'd had no other hope, she might have done anything. But Erminio's lies would catch up with him, and someone would come looking for her.

18

Carla waited quietly at the entrance to Assunto's office until he looked up from his work and gestured for her to enter. "There's good news and there's bad news," she announced as she dragged herself toward his desk. "But best of all, there's a chance to make the bad news good."

Assunto managed a weary buzz. "Why can't things ever be simple with you?"

"I make them as simple as possible," Carla replied. "But no simpler."

"So tell me the good news."

Carla took a sheet of paper from her pocket and handed it to him.

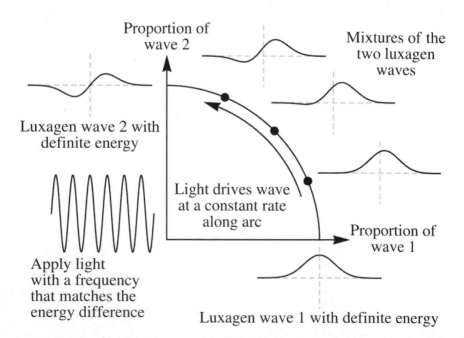

"This is what happens when you take a luxagen with access to just two energy levels and hit it with a beam of light at a frequency tuned to the difference between those levels."

Assunto stopped her. "What does that mean? 'Tuned to the difference'?"

"Ah." Carla realized that it had become second nature to her to think of energies and frequencies as interchangeable. She had to make a conscious effort now to unpack the details behind the instinctive translation. "If you imagine a particle and a wave moving at the same speed, the energy of the particle will be proportional to the frequency of the wave—with the ratio unchanged as you vary their common speed. If you set the speed to zero, the ratio is the mass of the particle divided by the maximum frequency of the wave—and that's what it remains for every other speed."

"That's just geometry!" Assunto said. "The wave's propagation vector will be parallel to the particle's energy-momentum vector. That locks all of their components into a fixed ratio with each other."

Carla said, "Yes—but now go a step further and suppose that *the same ratio* holds for every wave and its corresponding particle, whether it's a luxagen wave and a luxagen or a light wave and a photon. None of the physics makes sense unless this ratio is a universal constant; I think of it as 'Patrizia's constant', because the whole idea started with her. It's as if these particle masses really *are* the maximum frequencies of the corresponding waves... just measured in different units."

Assunto looked pained for a moment, but then he said, "You mean like times and distances?"

"Perhaps." Carla didn't want to over-reach with the comparison: one was a fundamental truth about the cosmos that the *Peerless* itself had helped to prove beyond doubt; the other was an appealing, but still untested, speculation.

Assunto said, "So let's take it for granted that we can turn any frequency into an energy, and vice versa. You have a luxagen trapped in some energy valley, and the corresponding wave equation has two solutions with definite frequencies."

"Yes," Carla replied. "What I've drawn for the two waves is their variation in space, but while maintaining that shape they're oscillating in time, each one with its own pure frequency."

"Then you add a light wave whose frequency matches the *difference* between the luxagen frequencies—and it drives the low-frequency luxagen wave up to the higher frequency?"

"Yes."

"Well, that much makes sense," Assunto said. "You can do something similar with waves on a string, if you vary the tension periodically at a frequency equal to the difference between the frequencies of two resonant modes."

"What's more surprising, though," Carla said, "is the simple rule that this wave follows along the way. Where I've plotted the proportion of each of the waves, the arc that links the point that's 'purely wave one' to the point that's 'purely wave two' isn't an artistic flourish: the dynamics really does follow a perfect circular arc. The sum of the squares of the two proportions remains equal to one, throughout the process."

"I see." Assunto was prepared to take her word for this, even if the significance of it escaped him.

Carla said, "Hold on to that thought."

She produced the second sheet.

Proportion of free waves

Free luxagen waves

Light *never* drives the wave entirely to a free wave.

Mixture of free and trapped luxagen waves

At first, the *square* of the free-wave proportion grows linearly with time.

Proportion of wave 1

Apply light with a frequency at least a quarter of the energy gap

Luxagen wave 1

"I take it that this is the bad news." Assunto examined the diagram. "The light never frees the luxagen? So... that's the end of your theory of tarnishing?"

"Wait!" Carla pleaded. "When there are just two waves, two energy levels, you'd *expect* the dynamics to take you all the way from one pure wave to the other. Where else are you going to go? But here, there are a multitude of free waves whose frequencies are almost identical—what I'm showing on the vertical axis covers them all. So there are ways you can wander around in this space of possibilities—keeping the sum of the squares of the proportions equal to one, as before—without the trapped-wave proportion ever falling to zero."

"Without it ever falling very far at all," Assunto noted, pointing to the modest arc that showed the limits of the process. "Which I can well believe, given your assumptions. But why isn't it fatal? How can this be a description of light knocking a luxagen out of its valley, if the wave barely changes no matter how long you expose it to the light?"

Carla braced herself. She had managed to convince Patrizia and Onesto that her hypothesis wasn't entirely deranged, but Assunto would be the real test.

"The thing is," she said, "there's always more than one luxagen and a light wave to consider. There's the whole slab of mirrorstone as well. We can sum up *most* of its influence in terms of a simple 'energy valley', but the reality is more complicated than that. With all the luxagen waves reaching part-way out of their own valleys, every luxagen is interacting with its neighbors—and to some degree with its neighbors' neighbors, and so on."

"So your model's inadequate?" Assunto suggested.

"Yes," Carla conceded. "But a model of the entire solid would just be intractable. The only way we can get anywhere is to try to find a rule of thumb that lets us extract useful predictions from the things we *can* model."

Assunto was skeptical. "What kind of rule?"

"We start with two reasonable assumptions," Carla said. "If a wave that is purely trapped interacts with the rest of the solid, it remains trapped. If a wave that is purely free interacts with the rest of the solid, it stays free."

Assunto said, "I can live with that. But what happens to a mixture of the two?"

"I doubt we could ever predict that with certainty," Carla admitted. "Not without knowing exactly what's going on with every single luxagen in the solid. But maybe we can still predict what will happen *on average*. If we treat the square of the proportion of the wave that's trapped as the *probability* that the luxagen will remain trapped when it interacts with the rest of the solid, everything makes sense—because the squared proportions always add up to one, just as the probabilities for any set of alternatives always add up to one. I know it sounds too simple to be true—but the mathematics seems to be offering us the perfect number to use as a probability when we can't make an exact prediction."

Assunto raised a hand for silence, and Carla let him think the whole thing over. Finally he said, "When, exactly, does this probability get turned into a fact? You have the luxagen wave changing shape under the influence of the light alone, but then at some point it's supposed to interact with the rest of the solid, which finally determines its fate. But the probability keeps changing, as the wave changes shape. So what probability do you use?"

Carla said, "It makes no difference exactly when the interaction happens, so long as it happens often enough, and so long as the probability grows in direct proportion to the time. Suppose the probability is one in a gross after one pause, two in a gross after two pauses, and so on. If the rest of the solid only interacts with each luxagen once every pause, the rate of tarnishing will be one luxagen per gross per pause. But even if the interaction takes place far more frequently than that, each time it happens the probability will have risen to a much smaller value than it would have reached if the luxagen had been left undisturbed for longer. The two effects—the lower probability and the greater number of interactions—almost cancel each other out, and you end up with a simple exponential decay curve."

She sketched the result.

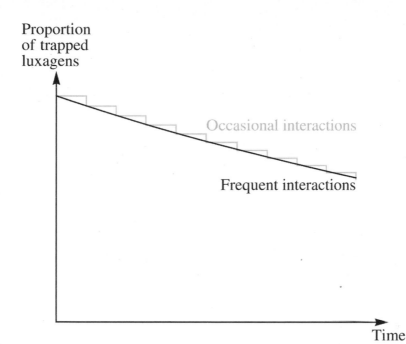

Assunto was not impressed. "Almost every process looks linear on a short enough time scale, so whatever's going on with the tarnishing the net result could end up looking like exponential decay. If I gave you the sunstone for one more experiment, and you came back to me with a curve like that, what would it prove? Nothing."

"One curve would be meaningless," Carla agreed. "But this is where the bad news finally redeems itself. When the energy gap is small enough for a light wave to bridge the two frequencies, the rate at which the probability grows is just proportional to the intensity of the light. But the tiers we found with the mirrorstone suggest that the energy gap is four times too big for that—and for lower frequencies of light, five times too big. In which case, the rate is no longer proportional to the intensity itself: it's proportional to the fourth or fifth power."

Assunto grasped the significance of this immediately. "So it's a higher-order effect," he said. "The light wave creates a small disturbance in the energy valley, and the effect of that isn't perfectly linear—so a complete description would have to include ever-smaller terms that depend on the square of the wave, the cube, the fourth power…"

"And the fourth power of the wave," Carla added, "contains a frequency *four times higher* than that of the wave itself. There is no *light* with a frequency high enough to bridge the energy gap in a stable solid—but the fourth power of the same disturbance oscillates four times faster."

"So how are you proposing to test all this?" Assunto pressed her.

"In the past, I've wasted sunstone," Carla admitted. "There were things I could have measured that I didn't even try to record. This time I'll do it properly, once and for all. With a system of apertures and shutters, in a single run I can expose different parts of the same slab of mirrorstone to different intensities of light, for different lengths of time. The variation in the tarnishing over time should give us the exponential decay curves—and the variation with intensity should confirm the fourth-power rule in the first tier, and the fifth-power rule in the next. If we do find those power rules, surely that will be a sign that we're on the right track."

Assunto said, "Last time, the tiers were meant to mark the number of 'photons' each luxagen needed to make in order to break free."

"They still do!" Carla replied. "These powers of the light's intensity are the only way I know to calculate the tarnishing rates, but that doesn't mean photons are out of the picture. When a luxagen changes its energy level, it still has to add a whole number of photons to the light: four or five, just as before."

"But what drives the luxagen from one level to another in the first place?" Assunto answered the question himself. "Not a bombardment with particles, but the shaking of a wave."

Carla couldn't deny that. Patrizia's interpretation of the scattering experiment in terms of colliding particles seemed irrefutable, but as yet there was no way to describe the tarnishing in the same language. They were still groping their way toward the truth, and the argument everyone had once thought settled in the days of Giorgio and Yalda was refusing to lie quietly in its grave.

Assunto said, "I'll give you the sunstone for one more experiment, but that's it. No more tinkering with the theory and trying again. If you don't find the power rules you've predicted, you'll have to accept that your ideas have been refuted and move on. Agreed?"

Carla had known that they were approaching this point, but to hear it put so starkly gave her pause. She could return to her collaborators and work through everything one more time: checking their calculations, revisiting their assumptions. Maybe they'd missed something crucial that would lead them to change their predictions—or something that could sweep away the lingering confusion and provide them with a surer bet.

But in less than two stints, Assunto would be answering to an entirely new Council, and there was no guarantee that he'd still have the power to offer her any sunstone at all. If they ended up losing the chance to perform this last experiment, there were no calculations that could tell them whether or not they'd been wasting their time. They needed to know the result itself, even more than they needed to be right.

Carla said, "Agreed."

19

Carlo abandoned the voles a bell earlier than usual to join the celebration in the hall below the main physics workshop. The corridors along the way were lined with posters for Silvano's next election rally, promising voters the chance to MAKE YOUR CHILDREN PROUD.

Carla had urged him to invite all his colleagues and their families, but as far as he could see only Amanda and her co had turned up. The whole chamber was festooned with chains of small lamps, and—rather cruelly for the women, Carlo thought—there were baskets of seasoned loaves attached to every cross-rope, putting out an aroma that made it hard even for a moderately well-fed man to focus on anything else.

Patrizia, Carla's young student, clung to a rope near the center of the hall, fending off an endless barrage of congratulations. "It took the three of us to get this far," she kept saying. "And I didn't solve the stability problem, that was Carla." Her modesty appeared entirely sincere, but when Carlo moved among the clusters of physicists orbiting this star all he heard was talk of the urgent need to start applying "Patrizia's principle" to some new problem or other.

He tried not to begrudge the girl her share of acclaim, but it undercut his sense that he ought to join in the rejoicing out of simple loyalty. What was there to celebrate, really, in this minuscule advance in the theory of solids? It had made Carla happy, and no doubt it would have some kind of payoff eventually, but what urgent need had it fulfilled? The ancestors would be oblivious to however long it took to find the cure to their woes. The travelers didn't have that luxury.

Carla caught up with him. "Are you enjoying yourself?" she asked.

"Of course."

"You don't seem to be talking to anyone."

Carlo said, "I get all the luxagen-speak I need from you."

She feigned a punch at his shoulder. "Actually, it's not all physicists here. Don't you want to meet the woman who'll be flying the *Gnat*?"

"That astronomer who found the Object?"

Carla emitted an exasperated hum. "Where have you been hiding for the last stint? Tamara gave birth. This is her replacement, Ada."

Reluctantly, Carlo followed her across the hall. Ada was surrounded by her own circle of admirers, but they parted for Carla and she made the introductions.

"You're a biologist, aren't you?" Ada asked Carlo.

"That's right." There was an awkward silence, and Carlo realized that he was expected to say something more about his work, but he knew how that was likely to end. Everyone had heard the story of his amputation, and he was tired of being the butt of that joke.

Ada said, "Maybe you can answer this for me. Why should lizard skin be sensitive to infrared light?"

Carlo was about to deny that any such thing was true, when he realized what she was talking about: one of the chemists had extracted a component of the skin that fluoresced in visible light when it was illuminated with IR. "I'm not sure that it's actually *sensitive*, in that the animal would know when it's being exposed to infrared. As far as I'm aware it's just a fluke, a chemical property with no biological significance."

"Fair enough," Ada said. "I was just curious, it seemed so strange."

Carlo wasn't really in the mood for small talk, but he didn't want to embarrass his co. What did he know about this woman? "You must have been surprised when your colleague stepped down," he ventured.

"It wasn't that formal," Ada replied. "She didn't resign, we just got word from her family."

"Ah." That was shocking in its own way, but it made a lot more sense. No one in their right mind would give up the chance to fly the *Gnat*, but it wasn't unheard of for couples with other plans entirely to wake in the night and let instinct take over.

"I wanted to see the children," Ada said sadly. "But her co's a farmer, and they're quarantine with blight."

"Quarantined?" Carlo had no reason to doubt her word, but he was taken aback. "I worked with wheat myself, not long ago. Wheat blight's not usually that hard to control."

"Her father said it was something new," Ada explained.

Carlo felt a twinge of anxiety; he'd met half a dozen of his agronomist friends a few days earlier, and they hadn't mentioned a new strain of blight. Had his defection so offended them that they were shutting him out of the loop? Or maybe they'd just been too busy teasing him about his mutinous fingers.

"Well, good luck with the journey," he said. He started to back away along the rope when he caught Ada casting a quizzical glance at Carla, as if she'd expected something more from the exchange. Carlo paused, wondering which further nicety would be most appropriate: congratulations on her promotion, or commiserations on the fate of her friend.

Carla said, "Ada's offered me a place on the *Gnat*."

Carlo turned to Ada; her expression made it clear that this was the subject she'd been waiting to discuss. "I thought that was all down to the lottery," he said.

"When the winner pulled out we asked the Council to reconsider," Ada explained. "They agreed to let us choose a new crew member on the basis of their expertise. Tamara had talked about picking another chemist—but orthogonal matter isn't something that chemists have actually worked with. Since Carla seems to have solved Yalda's First Problem… I thought she might stand the best chance of also solving the Third."

Carlo felt sick. Carla seemed excited, but he could tell that she was fearful too. A moment ago he'd told himself that no sane person could give up a chance like this, but his perspective had undergone a wrenching shift.

"She didn't solve the stability problem overnight," he said. "Do you really expect a once-in-a-generation breakthrough to be repeated on demand? Under pressure, in that tiny vehicle…?"

Ada raised a hand reassuringly. "That's not what I was thinking at all. I don't expect the mysteries of orthogonal matter to be resolved on the spot. I just want someone with us who's familiar with the new ideas, and who'll have a chance of applying them if the opportunity arises. Ivo's a brilliant chemist with a vast amount of experience, but there's no point telling him to start thinking of luxagens as waves. And frankly, there's no point telling me either; I have no idea what it implies."

Carla said, "We'll have a few days to decide. But Ada wants to take the final crew list to the new Council for approval at their first meeting, so this is the time to ask her any questions."

"Right." Carlo struggled to clear his head. The mere thought of his co inside the *Gnat* as it receded to invisibility was painful enough, but now he had to face up to the purpose of the mission: capturing a mountain-sized mass of fuel by setting it alight. Orthogonal rocks that no one understood sprouting flame wasn't the worst-case scenario—it was the whole plan.

He looked to Carla again. As anxious as she was, it was plain that this was what she wanted. And after all her work with the tarnishing experiments, all the false starts and blind alleys, all the grief Assunto had given her… didn't she have the right to this moment of glory? He wasn't going to tell her to be content that she'd done her bit for the ancestors.

What he owed her now was encouragement. That, and whatever he could do to ensure that she remained safe.

Carlo dragged himself closer to Ada.

He said, "Tell me what you'll do if you start a wildfire on the Object. I want to know where the *Gnat* would be, relative to the point of ignition, and how you can be sure you'll be able to get clear in time."

20

The night before the election, Tamara walked to the clearing and checked the clock there, just in case she'd lost track of the date. She hadn't. For the fourth time in her life the inhabitants of the *Peerless* were about to vote for a new Council.

Weeds were sprouting in the flower bed. It looked as if Tamaro hadn't slept there for days. Did that mean that he was afraid of her now? Or was he spending his time even closer to her, hiding in the fields, watching and waiting for her children to arrive? Perhaps he believed that merely being present when they opened their eyes would be enough for him to form a bond with them, closing the rift he'd made and restoring the family to normalcy.

Tamara wound the clock, but left the weeds as she'd found them. She milled some flour and made a dozen loaves, then took them back to her camp beside the door. When she'd eaten three loaves she buried the rest in the store-hole, then lay down in her bed. She did not expect to sleep now, but the soil was blissfully cool.

In the morning, vote collectors would come to every farm. They would accept no excuse for neglecting this duty—however busy someone might be, however sick, however indifferent to the outcome. Erminio would have had Tamara's name struck from the roll, but how could he keep the collectors away from his son? He might claim that Tamaro had business elsewhere and would cast his vote in another location—but then, by the end of the day the missing vote would be noted, the announcement of the tally would be delayed, and locating the miserable shirker would become everyone's business. On the home world people had paid to become Councilors—and if the historians could be trusted, not one woman had ever attained that office. Tamara had trouble believing that, and the even more surreal corollary: when the *Peerless* returned, in the four years of its absence the situation was unlikely to have changed. True or not, though, the very idea was sufficiently affronting to imbue each election with added gravitas. To fail to vote would be seen as a declaration that the old ways had been just fine.

Tamara closed her eyes, willing the night to pass more quickly. Her fellow prisoner had no hope of sneaking past her, and his shameful dereliction would soon bring both of them all the attention she could have wished for. In a day or two her ordeal would be over.

Unless someone forged Tamaro's signature. The local vote collectors would be neighbors who'd recognize him by sight, but it could be done in a remote part of the *Peerless* where neither Tamaro nor the impostor was known. The fake Tamaro could then travel back to his usual haunts to cast his own vote, so the tally would add up perfectly. Erminio couldn't perform the fraud himself, the disparity in age would be too obvious. But if he could bribe a younger accomplice and teach him to mimic his son's signature, the plan would not be too difficult to execute.

Tamara rose to her feet, shivering. Her long vigil by the door had been for nothing. No one was coming for her; she was dead to her friends, dead to the vote collectors, dead to the whole mountain. She should have been digging up every square stride of the farm from the first day of her captivity, looking for Tamaro's buried key—or some tool misplaced by her grandfather, or some secret hatch left by the construction crew. Anything would have been better than squandering her time on this fantasy.

She walked over to the door and ran her hand across the cool hardstone surface. For the dozenth time she extruded a narrow finger and tried to force it into the keyhole, but the spring-loaded guards between the tumblers were too sharp. It wasn't a matter of bearing the pain; if she persisted the guards would simply slice her flesh off, ossified or not. The right tool might have enabled her to pick the lock, but with her body alone it was impossible.

Apart from this one entrance the farm was hermetically sealed. Even the air from the cooling system ran in closed channels deep within the floor rather than moving through the chamber itself, lest it spread blight from crop to crop. She couldn't burn her way through the walls with a lamp, she couldn't cut her way out with a scythe. And the stone around her was far too thick for any cry for help to reach her neighbors.

Erminio wasn't going to creep back in to be ambushed. Ada and Roberto weren't coming to the rescue with a construction team wielding air-powered grinders. The only way out was with the key. The only way to get the key was from Tamaro.

It took her until morning to find him. As the red wheat-flowers began closing across the fields, she saw Tamaro rise from a hiding spot beneath their spread blooms and look around for better cover.

He heard her approaching and disappeared between the stalks, but she dropped to all fours to match his height and pursued him in the gloom of the moss-light. The crops rustled at every touch, making stealth impossible for both of them, but Tamara was faster. She wondered why he didn't halt and grant himself the advantage of silence; perhaps he thought he needed more distance between them before he had any real chance of her losing him.

As she pushed on through the stalks their relentless susurration might have deafened her to anything similar, but Tamaro was weaving back and forth, sending out his own distinctive rhythm. She could hear every change of direction he made, the slight hesitation as he swerved. They'd played this game before, she realized. More than a dozen years ago. He had never learned to escape her then; it had never been important enough.

Tamara could almost see him now—or at least she could see the rebounding wheat stalks ahead of her, darkened by their momentary clustering, brightening as the gaps re-opened to admit the moss-light. She knew when he'd zigzag next, and she sprinted straight for the point where she could intercept him.

Pain flared in her left front leg. She recoiled and brought herself to a halt as an arc of neatly sliced stalks fell to the ground ahead of her.

"Stay where you are," Tamaro warned her.

"I only want to talk," she said. In the silence she could hear him shivering. "What's the plan now? Are you going to hack me to pieces?"

"If I have to," he replied. "Don't think I won't defend myself."

He was terrified. She'd thought she'd done him very little harm the last time she'd got her hands on him, but he must have sensed how close she'd come to something worse. Tamara wanted to buzz with mirth, but she found herself humming with grief and shame. *They were both in fear of their lives from each other. How had it come to this?*

She got control of herself. "I'm not going to hurt you," she said. "We need to talk. We need to fix this." She caught a red glint as he raised the scythe, holding it ready in case she advanced on him. "Please, Tamaro."

"I can't let you out," he said. "They'll lock me up. They'll lock up Erminio."

"That's true," she admitted. There was no point pretending that any lie she could tell would be enough to exonerate them. "But it's up to you how bad it is. If they catch you out after I'm gone, you know they'll throw away the key. If you turn yourself in right now and I ask the Council for leniency, it could just be a year or so."

"I can't do that to him. I can't betray *my own father!*"

Tamara shivered wearily. Mother, father… why was his co always last on the list?

"What do you want from your life?" she asked him. "Do you want to raise children?"

"Of course," he said.

"Then find a way to do it. Find a co-stead and raise your own. If I give birth here you can be sure it won't be your doing, and you'll have lost all hope of having children of your own. If you give me the key, I'll keep my promise: I'll sign the entitlement over to you as soon as we have paper and a witness."

The wheat rustled; he was moving the scythe again. "How can I trust you?"

"You're my co," she said. "I still love you, I still want you to have a good life. You can't expect us to have children together after what you've done, but I don't care about the entitlement—just let me fly the *Gnat*, let me have a few moments of happiness. Let me be what I am, and I'll grant you the same."

The silence stretched on for more than a lapse. Tamara forced herself to wait it out; one misjudged word now could cost her everything.

She heard Tamaro put down the scythe.

"I'll show you where the key is," he said.

He led her to a nondescript part of the field, far from any store-hole old or new, and dug into the soil beside one of the plants. When he plucked the key out from between the roots she knew she would never have found it herself if she'd searched for a year.

He handed it to her.

"Come with me," Tamara said. "I'm not going to lie to people, but I won't make it hard for you."

"I should wait here for Erminio," Tamaro decided. "I should talk to him first."

"All right." Tamara reached over and touched his shoulder, trying to reassure him that she wasn't going to renege on any of her promises. He wouldn't look her in the eye. Was he ashamed of what he'd done to her, or just ashamed that he hadn't been able to follow through on his father's plan?

She left him in the field and ran to the doorway. The key fitted neatly, forcing the guards apart, but when she tried to turn it the lock wouldn't yield. Panicking, she pulled it out and scoured it clean with her fingers, then she tapped it against the door until a tiny clump of soil fell from one of its intricate slots.

She inserted it again and twisted it gently; she could hear the faint clicks as one by one the cylinders in the lock engaged. She tried the handle and the door swung open as if nothing had ever been awry.

A few stretches down the corridor she turned a corner and ran into her neighbor, Calogero. He was carrying a ballot box and a stack of voting papers.

"Tamara?" He stared at her. "So… the blight's under control now?"

"It certainly is." *Blight.* What else could keep every prying neighbor away until the deed was done? Tamara stood a moment, marveling at Erminio's cunning. The worse he claimed the infestation to be, the keener the agronomists would be to investigate the aftermath—but it would only take a few burned patches in the fields to make it look as if Tamaro had eradicated the menace entirely.

Calogero was still confused, though if he'd been told that children had already been sighted he wasn't letting on. "Is Tamaro coming out to vote?"

"He didn't say. But there's nothing in the farm for you to worry about," she said.

"You're sure of that?"

"Absolutely. The election probably slipped his mind. You should go in and get his vote."

"All right." Calogero put down the ballot box and offered her a paper. He said, "I know there'll be other places on your way, but since we're here you might as well get it over with."

21

"**C**arla! I thought we'd lost you to the astronomers!"

Patrizia looked alarmingly gaunt, but she seemed to be in good spirits. Carla dragged herself across the small meeting room toward her. With all the preparations for the trip it had been more than six stints since they'd last spoken. "If Tamara had her way I'd be doing another safety drill right now," Carla replied. "I've spent more time inside their fake *Gnat* than I ever will inside the real one."

"Better than being unprepared," Patrizia suggested.

"True." Every member of the crew had made mistakes in the tethered mock-up that might well have been fatal if they'd taken place on the real flight. "But I wasn't going to miss this for anything. 'Demoting the Photon'? Assunto agreed that our experiments were conclusive. I can't believe he'd turn around and attack us like this."

"Does demotion count as an attack?" Patrizia wondered. "At least he didn't call it 'Forget About the Photon.'"

"You're much too forgiving," Carla complained. "It'll ruin your career."

Patrizia said, "Don't you think we should hear him out before deciding if there's anything to forgive?"

Carla spotted Onesto and raised a hand in greeting. As he approached she called out, "Here for more punishment?" As enchanted as Onesto was by the grand narrative of physics, he wasn't always keen to dirty his hands with the real thing. When he'd sat in on her power series calculations for the tarnishing experiment he'd ended up moaning and clutching his head.

"Duty compels me," he said. "Someone has to document this revolution."

"Including every petty little backlash?" Carla replied.

Onesto was amused. "So you're taking the title of this talk personally?"

"How else should I take it? I have to defend my one claim to immortality."

"Wasn't it Patrizia who posited the photon?"

"Yes, but I chose the name."

By the time Assunto arrived the room was crowded. He placed a stack of copies of his paper in a dispenser by the doorway. Carla was hurt that he hadn't shown it to her earlier, giving her a chance to respond. She hadn't had the time to engage in any serious collaboration since she'd agreed to join the crew of the *Gnat*, but she wasn't—yet—literally unreachable.

Assunto began, without ceremony. "The tarnishing experiments carried out by Carla and her team have given us compelling evidence that the luxagens in a solid can only occupy certain definite energy levels. These levels can be explained by treating the luxagens as standing waves, spread out across the width of their energy valleys, rather than particles with a single, definite position at every moment in time.

"Yet once they're freed from the solid, the same luxagens scatter light in a manner suggesting that they really are particles—and that the light they scatter also consists of particles, some three times heavier than the luxagens.

"But light, undeniably, is a wave. Giorgio and Nereo showed us how to measure its wavelength from the interference pattern it makes when it passes through two or more slits. Carla and Patrizia have never sought to deny that, but they do ask us to accept that this wave is always accompanied by a suitable entourage of particles—not so much driven along with the wave by any explicable force, as bound to it by an axiom too profound and opaque to yield to any further reflection or inquiry."

Carla tried not to grow angry; in truth, this was the weakest part of their theory. But no amount of sarcasm directed at that awkward hybrid ontology could change the evidence: light's granular nature was every bit as plain as its wavelike properties.

"What are we to make of this?" Assunto continued. "I propose a solution that builds on the success of Patrizia's principle. The equation governing a particle trapped in an energy valley is transformed, by that principle, into an equation for a standing wave in the same valley. Such a wave can only take on certain distinct shapes, each with its own characteristic energy.

"But if our ideas about the mechanics of a simple particle require such a radical new approach, surely we shouldn't apply it in a piecemeal fashion?

Suppose we can identify *another system* that appears to be governed by the very same equations that we once thought adequate to account for the motion of a particle in a valley. Shouldn't that system be treated in exactly the same way?"

Carla had no idea what example he had in mind, but on the face of it this sounded like a reasonable proposal.

Assunto said, "Consider a light wave with a single, pure frequency, traveling in a certain direction and possessing a definite polarization. In the real world we never encounter anything so simple—but the actual waves we *do* find traveling through the void can always be constructed by adding together a multitude of those idealized waves.

"Because this wave has a single frequency, we can capture everything about the way it changes over time by picking one location and measuring the strength, the amplitude, of the light field at that point. This amplitude behaves very simply: it oscillates back and forth at the frequency shared by the entire wave.

"Does that remind you of anything? Such as… a particle rolling back and forth in an energy valley?"

Assunto paused, as if expecting objections, but the room was silent. Carla wanted to leap ahead of him—to complete the analogy, grasp its implications and find some fatal flaw that he had missed—but her mind seized up and the opportunity passed.

"The parallels can be made precise," Assunto claimed. "The amplitude of our idealized light wave corresponds to the distance of a particle from the center of a one-dimensional, infinitely high, parabolic energy valley. The energy of the light wave can be broken down into two parts: one analogous to the particle's potential energy, due only to its position in the valley, and the other analogous to its kinetic energy, which depends only on its speed.

"Carla and her team have already shown us what happens when you apply Patrizia's principle to a particle trapped in an energy valley in a solid. Our system is actually simpler, since the valley in a solid is three-dimensional, and it's not exactly parabolic. The simpler version of all the same calculations yields an infinite sequence of energy levels, all spaced the same distance apart.

"What determines the spacing of those energy levels? In a solid, it comes from the natural frequency of a particle rolling in the valley—so in our case, it comes from the frequency at which the amplitude of the light field oscillates back and forth. So the light wave must have an energy that belongs to a set of discrete values, and the *gap* between each level and the next will be equal to Patrizia's constant times the frequency of the light."

Carla knew exactly where he was going now—and exactly what his belittling title meant.

"But that gap is precisely the energy attributed to each *photon* associated with this light wave!" he proclaimed. "So the fact that the wave can only change its energy in discrete steps no longer requires the peculiar fiction of a swarm of particles following the wave around, like mites caught on a breeze."

Assunto sketched two examples on his chest.

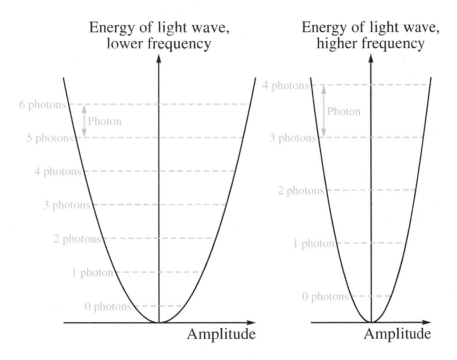

"Are there particles of light in this picture?" he mused. "Not if you think a 'particle of light' is something like a tiny grain of sand. The number of photons associated with each wave is really just a label for its energy level, found by counting the steps up from the lowest level. It's *not* a count of things you could hold in your hand."

"The lowest level, with zero photons, doesn't have zero energy," Carla protested. "That's…"

"Strange?" Assunto suggested. "I agree. But the same kind of thing is true of your luxagen in a solid: you can't make it lie still at the bottom of the valley."

"Yes, but at least there's something there in the valley," Carla replied. "You're claiming that *the void itself* has energy—with a contribution from every possible mode of the light field!" Every frequency, every direction, every polarization that any light wave could possess would each leave the vacuum with a trace of energy—without the need for the light waves themselves to be present at all.

Assunto said, "Only changes in energy are detectable. The actual value is a meaningless concept: if you redefine every energy level by adding or subtracting the same amount, that won't change anything you can measure. So it doesn't bother me at all if a theory gives a non-zero value for empty space… but if you prefer to subtract that value from everything in sight, bringing the vacuum energy down to zero, go ahead and do that. It won't make any difference."

Carla fell silent. The result still struck her as preposterous, but she couldn't yet see how to argue against it.

"Where has this taken us?" Assunto continued. "We started with Yalda's light field, which has a precise value at every point in space and every moment in time. But now Patrizia's principle has given us a theory where we can no longer think that way. Just as a luxagen in a solid lacks a precise location and is spread out across its valley, *the amplitude of a light wave* must also be spread out across a range of values. In a strong enough light wave, the spread of values can be much less than the peak amplitude of the light, so this need not contradict the way we use waves in conventional optics. But when a single luxagen 'scatters a photon'—when it lowers by one the photon count for light of a certain frequency and direction, and then raises by one the photon count for light of a different frequency and direction—we should neither expect conventional optics to apply, nor assume that the failure of the old laws means that we're describing something akin to colliding grains of sand."

Assunto spread his arms in a gesture of finality. There'd be more details in the paper itself, but his presentation was finished. "Questions?"

Most people in the room looked as if they were still struggling to absorb what they'd heard, but Onesto responded immediately.

"What about luxagens?" he asked Assunto.

"What about them?"

"Can they fit into the same framework? If photons are really just steps in the energy levels of a light wave, can you account for luxagens the same way?"

Assunto said, "When a luxagen wave in a solid rises to a higher energy level, that doesn't amount to making a new luxagen. It just means the original luxagen has more energy than before."

"I understand that," Onesto replied. "But I'm not talking about the energy levels in a solid. You took a light wave traveling through empty space, and showed that the energy levels of each mode amounted to what Carla and Patrizia would have called the number of photons in the wave. So why can't you do the same thing with a luxagen wave in empty space, finding energy levels for each mode of *that* wave that correspond to the number of luxagens?"

"Because they're completely different kinds of waves!" Assunto said. "A light wave isn't all that different from a wave on a string: the higher its peaks, the more energy it carries. Given that relationship between energy and wave size, we can come along and apply Patrizia's principle, which forces the energy to take on discrete values.

"But to get luxagen waves in the first place, we've *already* applied Patrizia's principle to the energy of a single particle. A luxagen wave's energy has nothing to do with the size of the wave; its overall size is meaningless, only its shape and its frequency matter. How could you apply Patrizia's principle for a second time, to a wave like that? It would make no sense."

"I see." Onesto clearly wasn't satisfied—but his personal sense of nature's symmetry would have to defer to these annoying technicalities for now.

Patrizia turned to Carla. "You should be happy! Assunto wasn't trying to dispute our results; he just found a better way to think about photons."

"It's an interesting theory," Carla admitted begrudgingly. The truth was, it still felt like trespass to her: Assunto had snuck into her room and rearranged the guide ropes, and it didn't matter whether or not he'd left them tidier than he'd found them. "We should have spotted the same pattern ourselves," she said. The formula for the energy in a light wave was elementary optics, generations old. If she and Patrizia hadn't been half-dazed by hunger when they'd come up with the whole idea of energy levels, they might have noticed the analogy and pursued it, long before Assunto had paid the slightest attention to their results.

"So what now?" Patrizia asked eagerly. "Maybe we could write a new paper together, re-analyzing the scattering experiment with the photons treated Assunto's way."

"Maybe when I get back," Carla replied.

"Oh, of course." In her excitement, Patrizia had forgotten about the *Gnat*. "In six days you'll be—"

"Traveling through the void," Carla said. She watched the other physicists filing out of the room, reverently collecting their copies of Assunto's paper. "So I'll let you know if empty space turns out to be full of some mysterious, ineradicable energy."

22

arlo woke so abruptly that for a moment he was sure he must
have sensed some imminent danger. That idea quickly faded, but
the urgency remained. He could feel the tautness of the tarpaulin
above him, trapping grit against his skin, and the coolness of the bed
below, the resin-caked sand clumping in places. Between these familiar,
superficial sensations a third occupied the whole space of his body, a
solid presence coexistent with his flesh, agitating every muscle and bone.

Eyes still shut, he reached over toward Carla, but then he stopped
himself before his hand touched her shoulder. There was no point acting
only to be rebuffed. He dug his fingers into his chest, trying to assuage
the ache long enough to make a plan.

You've done enough, he could say. *You've lit the fire with your theories;
you can leave it to others to nurture the flames. Why put up with another
day's hunger? Why risk dying out there in the void? This is the time to make
yourself immortal: not just loved and remembered, but living on in the flesh
of your children. On and on forever, down the generations. The ancestors
will hear of your discoveries, your descendants will share in your fame.*

What more do you want? This is the time.

Carlo opened his eyes. He reached up and took hold of the nearest rope
and pulled himself out from beneath the tarp. He stared at the clock in
the moss-light until the dials became clear. It was too early to light a
lamp and pretend that the day had begun.

He dragged himself out of the bedroom, then released his hold on the
rope and let himself drift. The ache in his chest was as strong as ever, and
the voice that spoke for it refused to be silenced. *What did he have to be
ashamed of? Had he locked up his co, like Tamaro? Had he contemplated a*

single act that went against her will? If Carla listened—if his words made sense to her—how would he have wronged her?

His skin brushed the cool stone of the floor. He scrabbled about for a suitable rope, then pulled himself into a corner. If he wasn't going back to bed, he should at least be touching something solid that could draw away the heat.

It had been his suggestion that they sleep together, on this last night before the trip. He'd argued that the signal to her body from his presence—the reminder that she hadn't been widowed or abandoned—would help protect her during their separation. The logic of that was impeccable, but it proved nothing about his real intentions. A different message seemed to have reached his own flesh: his co was heading into danger, and she might never return.

Carlo spread his fingers against the stone. How many times had he silently cursed Silvano's weakness? *You really couldn't stop yourself? You really couldn't wait?* But what was his own great strength, then—being divided against himself? Despising the one act that would complete his life?

His father had died young. What if he died, himself, before his children were grown? Before they were even born?

His father's death had been down to chance, though, brought on by a harmful influence, not some heritable disposition. He had no reason to expect the same fate. In a year or two—or three, or four—when Carla's work was done, they'd make the decision. She wasn't spurning him, she wasn't leaving him, and she wasn't going to let herself die in the void.

Let herself? As if she'd have a choice about it, when the Object lit up like a star and engulfed the *Gnat* in its flames.

Carlo reached up and hooked his arm around the rope, then moved his hand through a full circle; the helix of rope bit into his forearm, but he locked his hands together and let the pain drive a spike of clarity into his thoughts. If they'd woken together—side by side, eyes still closed, oblivious to the plans of their waking lives—anything might have happened. He hoped that danger was past now, but at the very least there was still a chance that he might spew out some idiotic plea to Carla to change her mind.

He would wait here until morning. Wait a bell, then light a lamp, then wake his co to wish her a safe trip and a speedy return.

The great workshop where the *Gnat* and the beacons that had gone before it had been built was all but empty now. From the entrance, nothing could be seen rising from the once-crowded floor but a mound of half-disassembled scaffolding. When Marzio called out a greeting from afar, the echoes were so disorienting that Carlo couldn't stop himself looking around for accomplices in some kind of aural prank. Carla raised a hand, and held off her reply until they were closer.

"Are we early?" she asked Marzio. No one else was in sight.

"Everyone's early," he said. "The others are down near the airlock."

The three of them headed off together. Carlo was glad they had a guide; in the dim light from the ceiling's moss, this part of the workshop looked as featureless as empty space.

"Viviana and Viviano spent the last three bells conducting final checks," Marzio offered reassuringly. "Everything's in good order, cleaned and calibrated."

"Thank you," Carla replied. Carlo took some comfort in the record of the beacons: of the gross that had been launched, only three had failed to light up after their long periods of dormancy. Marzio and his team knew how to build machinery that could function in the void, and Carlo trusted the astronomers to guide the *Gnat* to its destination. It was only the behavior of the Object itself that lay beyond anyone's experience.

As they approached the airlock, Carlo could see some of the people gathered there, their bodies emerging feet-first from behind the horizon of the convex ceiling. A little nearer, he understood why there were a few more legs than he'd been expecting. The crew had decreed that only their families should see them off, but three Councilors had decided to put in an appearance, regardless.

Silvano stepped forward to greet Carla effusively. There was no throng of constituents to witness the gesture, no crowd on whose behalf he could claim the Object, but this moment could still feature in later speeches. By the time the next election rolled around, whatever good had come from that lump of rock might well be seen by half the *Peerless* as Silvano's personal benison.

Councilors Prospero and Giusta didn't hang back for long, either.

Carlo was impressed that a full nine of their colleagues had deferred to the crew's request for a private departure, but then, as incumbents when the *Gnat*'s construction was approved they probably felt secure already in their ownership of the mission.

With Carla monopolized by the other Councilors, Silvano turned to Carlo. "You must be feeling proud."

Carlo struggled to suppress his irritation. "You make it sound like she's a child who just won a school prize. Today I'm more concerned with her safety."

"Everything will be fine," Silvano assured him.

"Really? How would you know?"

"I know that a lot of good people have done their best."

Carlo gave up on the conversation. He knew that he should have been willing to tolerate a few platitudes from a well-meaning friend, but all he could hear in Silvano's words these days was Councilor-speak.

Ivo was off to one side with his son and grandchildren, but he raised a hand in greeting to the new arrivals. Carla dragged Carlo past the politicians to join Ada and Addo, their father Pio, and Tamara.

"We should meet up at the observatory, just before the rendezvous," Addo suggested enthusiastically. "Roberto was telling me that we might be able to see some signs of the first experiments." Carlo listened with an awful fascination. Did he want to watch for those flares of light, and try to judge their significance from a distance? A sequence of orderly, isolated flashes would prove that the crew were still in control, but what would he make of a sustained light, or prolonged darkness? He watched Addo talking and talking, and wondered how peaceful his night had been.

Tamara said, "We should start boarding now." The words were like a knife against Carlo's skin, but there was nothing to be done about it.

He embraced Carla briefly. "Safe voyage," he said.

"Stay happy," she replied. "I'll see you soon."

As he stepped away, Tamara caught Carlo's eye. "I'll bring her back," she said. Carlo nodded in acknowledgment, but he felt uneasy before her gaze, as if her ordeal might have left her with the power to judge exactly how close other men had come to repeating the sins of her co.

The crew separated from the onlookers. Carlo watched as the four fitted their cooling bags with practiced movements. Once they'd donned the bulky helmets it was hard to tell the women apart. The airlock was big enough for two people at a time; Ada and Tamara went through first. When it was Carla's turn she raised a cloth-covered arm in farewell, then stepped through the door with Ivo.

Marzio touched Carlo's shoulder. "Come and watch the launch."

Everyone gathered around the observation window, an octagonal slab of clearstone a couple of strides wide set in the floor beside the airlock. When Carlo looked down he could see all four travelers still on the ladder, the white fabric that enclosed their bodies catching the starlight. The *Gnat* itself was directly below the window, a dark silhouette hanging from a dozen thick support ropes. As he watched, Ada or Tamara stepped from the ladder through the vehicle's open hatch, and a moment later a small lamp lit up inside the cabin.

Pio said, "Imagine the farewells at the launch of the *Peerless*. This is nothing." Carlo wanted to thump him, but he did have a point. Not one traveler who'd marched into the mountain, not one father or child or co left behind, had had the slightest hope of a reunion when the voyage was over. His own generation's troubles weren't small, but no one had lived without sorrows.

As Carla reached the end of the ladder she looked up and waved, sweeping her arm across a wide arc. Her exuberance was unmistakable, and Carlo felt a sudden rush of happiness. *This was what she wanted.* She had balanced everything against the dangers and wanted it still. Whatever had passed in the night, he hadn't robbed her of this chance. He was tired of feeling ashamed and fearful. Why couldn't he just rejoice?

Carla climbed through the hatch. As Ivo followed her, Carlo leaned back and let Silvano, behind him, get a better look.

Marzio said, "They'll pressurize the cabin, but keep their cooling bags on just in case."

In case the vehicle itself sprung a leak, or worse. In case the *Gnat* fell apart, and the crew had to try to make their way back with air rockets.

Carlo stepped away from the window and checked the clock beside the airlock, its dials specially calibrated for the launch. A little more than a chime remained.

"What if they're not ready?" he asked Marzio.

"They can delay for a revolution or two," Marzio replied. "Or a dozen, if it comes to that. The orientation of the *Peerless* has to be just right, or the boost they get from the spin will be wasted, but they have more than enough fuel to cope with a variation in the timing."

"Good." Carlo made his way back to the window. Everyone in the crew had performed endless safety drills. The two navigators were equally proficient; Ada had been prepared to fly the *Gnat* herself. And the ancestors had managed to launch a whole mountain into the void; this modest expedition should not be beyond their descendants.

When Carlo looked down the whole vehicle was dark again. That was a good sign, he remembered: Carla had told him that they'd extinguish the lamps once everything was in place and they were ready for the launch. Ada and Tamara were astronomers, used to working by touch and starlight.

Marzio counted. "Five. Four. Three. Two. One."

Inside the *Gnat*, the clockwork released the clamps that had been gripping the support ropes. Carlo's skin tingled with fear and awe as the dark shape fell away into the void. He staggered slightly; Silvano put a hand on his shoulder.

The silhouette shrank against the star trails, dropping straight toward the bright, gaudy circle that marked the division of the sky. But the rendezvous point didn't lie in that plane, the *Gnat* couldn't simply be flung toward its destination. Marzio began counting again. Carlo braced himself.

The tiny dark point erupted with light as the *Gnat*'s sunstone engines burst into life. "We can still do it," Pio said softly. The skills that had lofted the *Peerless* from the home world hadn't been lost.

The dazzling speck of radiance stretched into a blinding streak of light, then the *Gnat* disappeared from view. Carlo looked up; at the opposite edge of the window, Ivo's grandchildren were still gazing down from their father's arms.

"That looked like a clean burn to me," Addo opined, as if he'd spent his life watching events just like this.

Marzio said, "It won't be long now."

"I don't think the relay clerks will be slacking off today," Silvano joked.

The paper-tape writer clanged. Marzio walked over to it and read out the message from the observatory. "Intact and on course." He let the tape fall from his hand. "Roberto is seeing light of the right size and brightness, from the right direction, heading the right way."

Carlo wanted that to be enough, but he couldn't keep silent. "And if the engines were damaged, we'd know? If anything had burned too fast or too slowly…"

"Everything is fine," Marzio declared. "The launch was perfect. The *Gnat* is on its way."

23

When the glare of the exhaust had vanished from the windows and her weight had died away with the shuddering of the engines, Tamara relaxed her tympanum and unhooked her harness. The starlit cabin was dark to her dazzled front eyes, and the only sound she could discern was the soft rhythmic ticking of the nearest clock.

She pulled off her helmet, which remained attached to her cooling bag on the end of a short cord. "Is everyone all right?" she asked. Ada, Carla and Ivo responded in turn, their hesitation sounding more like diligence than a lack of confidence: the answer was too important to be given without a pause or two of mental and physical self-inventory.

Tamara took hold of the guide rope beside her couch and dragged herself toward the center of the cabin, where the three mutually orthogonal ropes, offset slightly, didn't quite meet. She opened her dark-adapted rear eyes; the view they added was so much crisper than the gray shadows in front of her that it felt as if she had a lantern strapped to the back of her head. She could see her fellow crew members clearly now; Ada had taken off her helmet, and Carla was in the process of doing so. The bright horizon line of the home cluster's stars shone through the windows, its hoop tilted satisfyingly against the *Gnat*'s axis. That small geometric hint alone told her that they were not wildly off-course: it was unlikely that any serious mishap with the engines could have left the craft so close to its expected orientation.

"No pain, no dizziness, no hearing problems?" she asked.

"I'm fine," Ada replied, propelling herself with her legs from the couch. She drifted across the cabin before grabbing one of the transverse guide ropes.

"I am too," Carla said. Ivo took off his helmet before responding, "My right shoulder's a bit sore. I think my arm got pinned in an awkward position when the engines fired. It's not even worth resorbing though; a short rest will fix it."

Tamara wasn't too worried; Ivo's age left him more vulnerable than the rest of them, but this sounded no more serious than the twinges he'd owned up to after the most strenuous of the safety drills. Resorbing and re-extruding a limb was difficult without removing your cooling bag, and though the cabin's air was cooling them perfectly well, the ideal was to keep the bags on at all times in case there was an unexpected breach.

She said, "Ivo, I want you resting for the next six bells, but when Carla's checked her own equipment you should talk her through the checks on your own."

"Right," Ivo agreed.

Tamara dragged herself away from the center of the cabin and took her place beside one set of theodolites, mounted within the polyhedral dome of a window. Ada, at the opposite window, had her own duplicate instruments, including a separate clock. Tamara began with some star measurements, establishing the *Gnat*'s orientation precisely, then she aimed the theodolite with the widest field in the direction where she expected to sight the next scheduled flash from a beacon.

"If we had sufficiently accurate clocks," Carla mused, "we could find our distance from each beacon using the time it takes for the light to reach us."

Tamara buzzed with mirth. "Accurate to what, a piccolo-pause? While you're at it, why not use the geometric frequency shift to compute our velocity?"

"Who knows?" Ada interjected. "If people end up shuttling back and forth between the *Peerless* and the Object, do you think they'll still be navigating like this after a dozen generations?"

"There's only so much you can do to make a clock keep better time," Tamara replied. "We're already close to the limits of engineering."

"But nature's full of systems with their own rapid, regular cycles," Carla countered. "Light itself, among others."

"Very practical," Tamara retorted. "Once you filter out a single pure hue from a lamp, the beam will still be made up of lots of short wave trains: a few cycles at a time, all with random phases compared to each other. Even if you had some way to count the cycles, it would be like listening for the ticking from a vast heap of clocks that started up at random moments, ran for a few pauses and then died."

"That's true," Carla said. "But why not look for better ways to use the same clocks? The light given off by tarnishing mirrorstone as it spits out each luxagen ought to be in phase with the light that stimulated the emission in the first place. If you bounced that emitted light back onto the mirrorstone, looping the whole process around, you might be able to build a source that remained in phase over much longer periods than any kind of natural light."

"Light that elicits light that elicits still more light?" Ada joked. "That's starting to sound like the Eternal Flame."

"Not so eternal," Carla said ruefully. "The tarnishing would use up the mirrorstone just as surely as any flame consumes its fuel."

"And you count the cycles... how?" Tamara pressed her.

Carla said, "I'll have to get back to you on that."

Tamara felt the dials at her fingertips reach the configuration she'd been waiting for. The beacon's flash came a moment later—almost certainly from her own clock running slightly fast. But this wasn't Carla's brave new world yet, and it was the position of the beacon against the stars that mattered most, not the timing. She recorded the angles on her forearm, then turned the theodolite toward her second target.

"First sighting acquired," she announced. "Well within the expected region."

Ivo hummed with pain. "I'm sorry, I'm going to have to take the bag off. Just partly, along the right side."

Tamara said, "Carla, can you assist him?"

"Of course."

Tamara watched them without leaving her post. It was a simple enough maneuver, and even if the *Gnat* chose this moment to split apart and spill them all into the void, Ivo would still have his bag, helmet and two air cylinders with him like the rest of them.

Ivo chirped with relief as he resorbed his right arm, then he spent a lapse rearranging the flesh internally before extruding a new limb. Carla helped him refit it to the bag, running some air through as a test.

"Thank you," Ivo said. "I think I can check the equipment myself now."

"There's no pain at all?" Tamara asked him.

"None. The new arm's perfect."

"All right." With anyone else she wouldn't have fretted over such a minor injury, but Ivo's dexterity would soon be crucial.

Tamara turned back to the theodolite in time to catch the flash of another beacon. "Second sighting acquired," she said. "Within the expected region." Each flash, observed against the background of the stars, placed the *Gnat* on a line that passed through the beacon in question. Had the craft been stationary it could have been pinned down at the intersection of two such lines, but even in motion three sightings would be enough to determine its trajectory, and any more would improve the accuracy of the solution. That was assuming that all the errors in the measurements were random, but she and Ada could compare their results as a check against any systematic bias.

"Still nothing?" Tamara asked Ada, puzzled that her co-navigator had yet to report a single sighting. Each beacon only flashed once a bell, but the times were staggered so that one beacon or another was visible every lapse.

"Either my first target's died, or something on the window obscured it," Ada explained.

"Why didn't you tell me?" Tamara was confused. They needed to communicate everything clearly, but Ada knew that perfectly well. In all of the drills, she'd been scrupulous.

"Ivo was telling us about his injuries, I didn't want to interrupt him."

"But once he'd stopped—"

"I know," Ada said. "I apologize." Her tone was even, with no trace of resentment, but Tamara still felt awkward to be reprimanding her.

There were contingency plans for all the observations to be performed out on the hull if there was serious damage to the windows from an encounter with orthogonal dust, but that was an extreme measure that would make the whole procedure much more arduous. Stray particles from the *Gnat*'s own exhaust might have left a smattering of subtle defects in the clearstone, but Tamara had never really thought through the proper response to such a minor vitiation.

"Once we've finished with the beacons, we should do a systematic check for pitting," she decided.

"Good idea," Ada said. A moment later she added, "Ah, first sighting acquired! Within the expected region." ·

An ache in Ivo's arm. A few flaws on a window pane. Tamara had no intention of becoming complacent, but these were the kind of problems she could live with. In the drills, they'd rehearsed the complete disintegration of the *Gnat's* cabin, flailing around the mock-up in their cooling bags until they'd learned to use their air cylinders as rockets to bring themselves together on the engine module, ready to make the flight home without a single wall to protect them. She should not be unsettled by anything less.

When they'd both computed their estimates of the *Gnat's* trajectory, Tamara's agreed with Ada's to within the error bounds. The results implied that they would need to fire the engines again, briefly, in order to aim the *Gnat* squarely at the rendezvous point, but they could refine their measurements even further by waiting a few bells before repeating them.

To quantify the pitting on the windows, they each made observations of two gross stars that should have been visible from their respective posts, checking for any images that were obscured or distorted. Tamara found two cases where she could see a faint, blurred oval of light in place of a portion of one of the star trails—and by shifting the theodolite sideways while retaining its direction, she could move this aberration across the field, a sure sign that the flaw was in the window itself.

Ada found three. It was not a bad rate. And when the beacon Ada had missed was due to repeat, they were able to use the trajectory data to anticipate its location in the sky much more precisely. This time it did show up, in the dead center of the targeted star field. Whatever the original problem had been, the navigational procedure itself was proving to be as robust as Tamara had hoped.

Carla fetched four loaves from the storage cupboard and the whole crew ate together. The women had agreed to double their usual food intake; they could return to fasting once the mission was over, but for now nothing mattered more than a clear head.

"I've been thinking about your luxagen waves," Ivo told Carla. "They're not confined entirely to the energy valleys, are they?"

"Not entirely," Carla agreed. "The bulk of the wave lies in the part of the valley where a particle with the same energy would be rolling back and forth—but at the point where the particle would come to a halt and move back toward the center, the wave doesn't instantly drop to zero. It just becomes weaker as you follow it out past that point."

She sketched an illustration, but no one could see it clearly in the starlight so Tamara lit a small lantern and aimed the beam at Carla's chest.

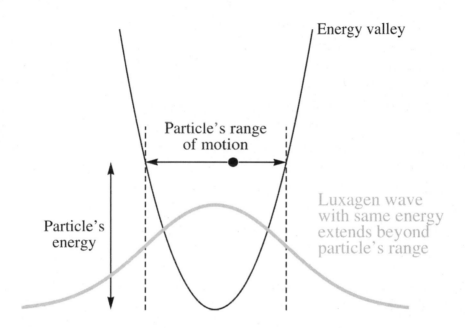

"And the same is true for a luxagen outside the valley, trying to get in?" Ivo wondered. "The energy ridge around the top of the valley won't keep out a luxagen wave entirely—even if that ridge would be insurmountable to a particle with the same energy?"

"Right," Carla said. "Energy barriers aren't absolute for these waves, the way they are for particles."

Ivo chewed on his loaf for a while, thinking this over. "Then why are solids stable under pressure?"

"Under pressure?"

"You've solved the original stability problem," Ivo said. "You've explained why luxagens in a solid don't gain energy by radiating, which would blow the whole structure apart. But there's another problem now: if you squeeze a solid hard enough, why doesn't it collapse? With the old particle mechanics you could expect the energy ridge between two valleys to keep the neighboring luxagens out. But if a luxagen wave has some probability of getting past that ridge, then over time, under pressure, shouldn't the luxagens be squeezed together into fewer and fewer valleys? Shouldn't the rock at the center of every world end up as a tiny, dense core too small to see?"

Carla said, "If you pack more luxagens into each valley, the ridges grow higher, making it harder for the waves to get past them. But the valleys do grow deeper as well, which will help to draw the waves in. I'm not sure if those two effects balance out..."

"And the gravitational pressure grows stronger, as the rock becomes more dense," Ivo added.

"Yes. So it's complicated. Let me do some calculations when we get back to the *Peerless*."

"Hmm." Ivo seemed pleased that Carla had no immediate answer to his puzzle. "And in spite of all these new ideas, the power of orthogonal matter to act as a liberator remains as mysterious as ever."

"It does." Carla was beginning to sound a bit besieged. "An ordinary, plant-derived liberator must have a distinctive shape that allows it to bind to a particular solid and modify its energy levels—rearranging the rungs on the ladder so a luxagen can climb all the way to freedom, radiating just one photon at a time. A rare fifth- or sixth-order phenomenon becomes a first-order event; a faint trickle of light over eons becomes an instantaneous avalanche.

"But what are the chances that the orthogonal dust that fell on the *Peerless* before the spin-up had just the right geometry needed to modify the energy levels of calmstone? If you pick some mineral at random, that certainly won't do the job. If you swap its positive luxagens for negative ones, its structure will be exactly the same as the original. It might interact with ordinary calmstone a bit differently—each will see the other's energy valleys as peaks, and vice versa, so grains of the two minerals might stick together half a wavelength closer than usual—but that would still be a weak and distant bond. So I don't see how it could

compare to the kind of chemical tricks that plants took eons to learn…
and in fact, no plant ever gave us a liberator for calmstone."

Ada said, "How elusive can the answer be, once we have a mountain
of orthogonal matter to play with?"

"We've been playing with ordinary matter for generations," Tamara
pointed out. "And we don't have all the answers there."

"If the Object turns out to be inert," Carla argued, "that could mean
that we do understand both kinds of matter reasonably well. We'll just
be left with the historical curiosity of the dust that threatened to light
up the *Peerless*… and I suppose that could turn out to have been some
kind of freakish bad luck."

Tamara wasn't inclined to argue when she had no better ideas herself.
But she did not believe in that kind of luck.

Tamara gathered six new beacon sightings, then merged them with Ada's
to sharpen their estimate of the *Gnat*'s trajectory. A few brief squirts of
air from the attitude-control jets reoriented the craft so the engines could
deliver a small push in the required direction. She set the parameters
of the burn into the controlling clockwork, then the crew donned their
helmets and strapped themselves into their couches again.

The glare from the exhaust through the windows was as bright as it had
been at the launch, but Tamara had barely registered her weight against
the couch when the burn was over. She'd been worried that using the
engines again might exacerbate Ivo's problem, but he assured her that
he was completely unharmed this time.

A bell later, the observations showed their modified trajectory to be as
good as they could have wished for. There was no point trying to aim the
Gnat down to the last saunter yet, when they still hadn't pinned down the
rock they were aspiring to reach with the same precision. The infrared
color trails taken from the *Peerless* could only tell them so much—but
they'd soon be able to make a fresh determination of the Object's trajectory, with the aid of some decent parallax at last.

Looking out at the familiar stars, Tamara realized that she'd never even
searched the sky for the *Peerless*. It would have been invisible to the naked eye,
but she'd felt no urge to hunt for it, no pang of separation at its disappearance.

And why should she have felt lost? The light from the beacons and the stars formed a grid of intangible guide ropes, transforming the void around the mountain into a solid, traversable realm.

If they could find a way to hold this ground, building a permanent framework of beacons and observatories, the sky from the *Peerless* need never be flat again—need never revert to the kind of painted dome that befitted a pre-scientific culture. Whatever triumphs or disappointments the Object had in store, if they could just retain the hard-won benefits of parallax, at least her generation would have that much to its name.

"Four different kinds of rock, at least!" Ada declared excitedly. "Different hues, different textures, different albedos."

Tamara hung back and let Carla and Ivo take their turns at the telescope first. She didn't mind waiting, listening to their descriptions before she saw the image; it was like savoring the odor of a seasoned loaf for as long as possible before finally taking a bite.

"The more variegated the better," Ivo said, squinting through the eyepiece. "Ah… wouldn't it be perfect if just one of these minerals set calmstone on fire, and the others were inert? Then Silvano could have his new farms out here, alongside the liberator mines."

He moved aside, and Tamara prepared to take his place. From the *Peerless*, the best view of the Object had given them its rough dimensions but little else. For two days now, she and Ada had been tracking it through their theodolites, treating successive locations of the blurred ellipse as one more set of navigational data, their sightings building up to a family of lines that would complete the elegant geometrical construction that made the rendezvous possible. But now they were close enough for the *Gnat*'s largest telescope—barely the size of Tamara's own body—to show her the whole point of the exercise.

Tamara closed three eyes and pressed the fourth to the instrument. The ellipse was now a crisply rendered, idiosyncratic oval with a pinched and tilted waist. About a third of one lobe was as red as firestone, but the rest bore patches of brown, of gray and of white. Everything was pale and subdued in the starlight—and any comparisons she made with the sight of mineral samples in a well-lit workshop or storeroom would be unreliable—but the brown outcrops more or less matched the calmstone slopes of the *Peerless*, viewed under similar conditions. There was a sprinkling of small impact craters everywhere—structures Tamara had only ever seen before as sketches in astronomy books, recorded by the ancestors when they'd observed the inner planet Pio.

"We finally have our own sister world," she said.

"Sister or co?" Ada replied.

"It almost matches us in size," Carla pointed out. "A co should be smaller."

Ivo said, "It's what happens when the two come together that counts."

"Either way," Tamara said, "it doesn't look like a stranger." After three generations alone in the void, the travelers could hardly dismiss any companion as mundane. But these rocks did appear to be ordinary rocks, old and pitted as they were after a long journey. If their origins really could be traced all the way around the history of the cosmos, back to the primal world's past-directed disintegration, that only made their similarity to the stuff of the *Peerless* all the more striking. Matter was matter, shaped by the same rules and forces everywhere—and it looked no different even when you encountered it backward.

Two small burns nudged the *Gnat*'s trajectory toward the rendezvous point. The crew kept returning to the telescope as the Object's slow spin revealed its whole surface: more of the same minerals, more small craters.

"The only thing missing is life," Carla said. "Not one patch of weed, not one speck of moss."

"Pio, Gemma and Gemmo were dead worlds too," Tamara reminded her. "Chemistry might be universal, but life must still be rare."

Ivo took his turn at the eyepiece. "Forget life," he said. "I'd be happy with any sign of rubble."

Tamara felt the same. If the Object had been nothing but a loose pile of stones then they would have had no hope of altering its trajectory—but enough fragmentation to save Ivo from having to chip off samples himself would be a huge advantage. The Object's spin was slow enough that even its weak gravity could, in theory, maintain a tenuous grip on pebbles scattered across its surface, but the creation and persistence of such things would depend on the whole detailed history of the body. Over time, the radiation pressure of starlight should have pushed away the very tiniest dust grains, but that was no loss: anything too small to see and avoid would only have posed a hazard.

While Tamara had been locked away on the farm, Ivo had been working on his sampling techniques. By now he was able to get decent results with powderstone as the target and pure air as the blade, and with calmstone as the target and traces of hardstone in the airflow to act as an abrasive. The first was easy enough, but the second could take more than a day.

He had also tried to carve firestone using air flecked with its liberator. Burning furrows into the firestone hadn't been a problem, but getting an intact sample free of the main body had proved impossible.

People had been studying firestone since antiquity. But if Ivo had to hack a piece of the Object loose using its own kind of fire as his only cutting tool, he would need to learn to do it in a matter of days.

The deceleration was planned to take place in three stages. Tamara put aside every distraction and devoted herself to the navigator's arts. She didn't care about the jagged beauty of their companion world any more; all that mattered was the geometry and timing of the encounter.

The first and longest burn rid the *Gnat* of most of its velocity relative to the Object—but it was impossible to aim the engines perfectly, and observations soon revealed that in slowing the craft they'd also pushed it slightly off course.

Tamara tweaked the second burn to compensate. It would add its own errors, but the thrust would be less and the consequences smaller.

Before the third burn, she and Ada spent half a day sighting and re-sighting beacons and following the Object's slow drift against the stars. Their target was growing visibly larger by the bell now, and though they were aiming for a suitable offset a small mistake could see them slam right into the rock. Tamara was duly meticulous—but it was hard to resist a kind of sneaking pride in the thought that it wouldn't be the worst way to go. For the *Gnat* to become lost in the void would have been humiliating—quite apart from the unpleasantness of hyperthermia—but if they actually hit this lonely speck after crossing such a vast distance, their demise would at least be a testament to their almost perfect navigation.

Tamara set the clockwork for the burn, and when Ada had checked the dials she checked them again herself. She strapped herself into her couch and, for the first time, closed her front eyes.

The couch pushed against her back, the shuddering of the engines penetrated her bones. The glare of the exhaust came through her eyelids, two giant gray stars blossoming in the darkness where the windows would have been.

The gray stars faded. Tamara opened her eyes, took off her helmet and unstrapped herself from the couch. As she crossed the cabin, the Object's now familiar terrain filled the view through the window on the left—neither approaching nor retreating, giving every appearance of perfect stillness.

That was impossible, but inasmuch as any one moment could be called an arrival, this was it. Trying to steer the *Gnat* into a well-defined orbit once and for all would have been too ambitious; the tug of the Object was so weak that orbital velocity and escape velocity were just two different kinds of brisk walking pace. But with careful observations and the odd gentle push from the air jets, they ought to be able to weave back and forth between a safe altitude and an unintended departure.

It was Carla who rose first to join her, chirping with delight at the land-scape suspended below. "Well done!" she said, turning to include Ada.

Ada said, "Now that we're here… why not just rest for a while, then go back and break the news that the Object was inert?"

She was joking, but the proposal did have a certain mischievous appeal. "We could probably get away with it," Tamara replied. "Silvano might try to send a follow-up mission, but I doubt he could persuade the Council to back it. Dragging some giant self-contained engine, big enough to capture *this* by brute force…?" She swept an arm across the alarming arc the Object now subtended.

Ivo said, "They'd never do it, you can be sure of that. Our own plans are quite insane enough."

24

Carla helped Ivo attach his spectrograph to the telescope, then watched him load the first sample into the catapult beside the window: the first small irritant with which they hoped to goad the Object into a revelatory response. The *Gnat* had no airlock as such—nothing large enough for the crew to come and go without depressurising the whole cabin—but Marzio had designed a miniature version, equipped with lever-operated scoops and pincers, that allowed them to move these tiny samples the short distance through the hull and into the catapult's launch tube.

Back when the surface of the *Peerless* had been suffering the sporadic flashes attributed to orthogonal dust, no one had ever managed to observe—let alone record—the light's spectrum. Before the centrifugal force of the mountain's spin put an end to those displays, people had proposed spectrographs with such a wide angle of view that the inability to know precisely where the light would be coming from would cease to matter. The problem they'd never solved, though, had been the question of timing: no one could react quickly enough to open a shutter just as the flash occurred, and a prolonged wide angle exposure, even if it encompassed one of the rare events, would bury any signal from the flash itself in the accumulated background of reflected starlight.

No one had managed to find so much as a single tiny crater or other blemish left behind by the strange ignitions. With no more empirical clues, three generations of travelers had been left to speculate about the collisions. That the modest spin of the *Peerless* had been enough to brush the encroaching specks of dust aside ruled out sheer speed of impact as an explanation for the flashes, in favor of some kind of chemical reaction with the rock of the mountain itself. But no theory of chemical luminescence, no theory of fuels and liberators, no theory of light and luxagens, had ever offered a believable account of the events.

Ivo said, "One scrag of calmstone, delivered to the northern gray flats." He released the catapult.

Carla glanced across the cabin at Ada, who was resting a hand on the emergency lever that would fire the engines immediately to propel the *Gnat* out of harm's way if the Object did a Gemma and began to transform itself into a star. Tamara, clinging to the rope beside Ada, was wearing a heavy blindfold. If the Object burned so fiercely that its radiance became injurious, this macabre precaution might at least spare the sight of one of their navigators.

Carla bent down and peered through the theodolite in front of her—willingly putting one eye at risk in order to cover the opposite contingency, that the flash might be too weak to see any other way—while her fingertips brushed the dials of the adjacent clock. They believed they knew how long it would take the speck of calmstone to reach the surface, but if the reaction itself was delayed the exact timing would be a valuable further datum.

"Opening the shutter," Ivo said softly.

Carla stared at the starlit gray surface, expecting an anticlimax. The secret that had eluded generations couldn't give itself up with the first grain of sand they tossed. She felt the dials reach the estimated impact time and move on: one pause beyond, two, three—

A dazzling point of light blossomed against the grayness, like a sunstone lamp seen through a pin-hole. Carla dutifully transcribed the precise time of the event onto her thigh even as she waited for the pin-hole to burst open, for the barrier between the realms to be torn apart and chaos to come spilling through.

The light faded and died. Carla quickly turned around and put an undazzled rear eye to the theodolite. There was no wildfire spreading from the impact site. The surface appeared completely unchanged.

Ivo said, "Tell me I didn't hallucinate that."

"Hallucinate what?" Tamara asked impatiently.

"It was bright but… contained," Carla managed. "Just as they described it in the old fire-watch reports!" Just as Yalda herself had first seen it—

looking back on the *Peerless* from the void, when a construction accident during the building of the spin engines had almost sent her to her death.

Ivo pulled the strip of paper out of the spectrograph. Carla lit a lamp so they could examine it properly. The paper had been darkened across the entire range of frequencies, showing a spectrum similar to that of the light from any burning fuel. But superimposed on this was a feature so sharp that Carla at first mistook it for a calibration mark on the paper—a line Ivo might have drawn for the purpose of alignment. It was no such thing. The paper had been blackened by the flash itself, along a narrow band corresponding to an ultraviolet wavelength of one gross, eight dozen and two piccolo-scants.

Tamara was keeping her blindfold on, so Carla explained the results to her.

"What could produce that?" Tamara asked. "A single, sharp ultraviolet line?"

"I've never seen anything like it," Ivo declared. "No ordinary rock burns with a narrow peak brighter than all the other light from the flame."

"Let alone *just one peak*," Carla added. "The total amount of energy a luxagen needs to gain in order to escape from calmstone would be something like two dozen times greater than the jump corresponding to that ultraviolet line. You'd expect a liberator for calmstone to modify the energy levels so the total gap was bridged in a lot of small steps—but there's no reason why all of those steps should turn out to be identical in height!"

Ada said, "And yet, there it is: one lonely peak."

Ivo launched a second scrag of calmstone, this time at the red-tinged portion of the Object's southern lobe. The terrain here looked as if it was covered in firestone; watching through the theodolite, Carla braced herself for the sight of a wildfire, if not a full-blown Gemma event.

Three pauses and five flickers after the impact, there was a single, brief pinprick of radiance.

When Ivo extracted the paper from the spectrograph, there were some minor differences across the visible frequencies but the spectrum was dominated by exactly the same ultraviolet peak as before.

Ivo repeated the experiment, choosing two more regions of the Object with their own distinctive appearance. Then he switched the projectile from calmstone to hardstone, then powderstone, clearstone, mirrorstone, firestone and sunstone. In two dozen and four variations, the delay before the flash was sometimes a little longer or shorter, and the visible part of the spectrum showed clear differences that depended on the particular area being targeted on the surface. But in every case, a single ultraviolet line blackened the paper at exactly the same position.

Carla could offer no explanation, and Ivo was equally perplexed. Ivo went so far as to aim the spectrograph at a lamp inside the cabin, to see if the ubiquitous line was really just the product of some bizarre flaw in the optics. It wasn't.

"Take away the ultraviolet line from this spectrum," he said, holding up a strip of paper he'd exposed to a flash from the red rock of the southern lobe, "and take away the liberator lines from *this one*." He grabbed the test strip he'd made from the lamp. "Apart from those features, they both look the same: burning firestone."

"So firestone is firestone, luxagen-swapped or not," Ada said. "Once it's actually burning, the light is identical, just as Nereo's theory would predict."

Carla said, "But the *process* by which the Object's firestone is being set alight looks nothing like the way a liberator acts on ordinary firestone. And it's completely indiscriminate: it acts the same way with every mineral. It doesn't care about the detailed structure of any of these solids—their geometry, their energy levels. It just does its magic trick and pfft…"

Tamara finally took off her blindfold. "Whether or not we understand the ignition process, surely this is an answer to the fuel problem? Every scrag of the Object can be made to burn! A little too easily for comfort… but if we can slow this thing down enough to keep it in reach, the next generation can deal with the practicalities."

"Or the next generation could catch up with it and fetch it back," Ada suggested. "They'll have had time to think deeply about the results we've seen, and work out what's really going on. We know the Object's trajectory with very high precision now. We can't lose track of it."

Tamara almost seemed swayed, but then Ivo interjected angrily, "We came here to capture the Object! That was the mission the Council approved: to take samples, to do calorimetry, then to trigger a blast that would leave this thing motionless. If we give up now, all we'll be bequeathing our descendants is a longer journey and a more difficult version of the task we should have done ourselves. We've had three generations of theorizing about orthogonal dust, and that's left us none the wiser. The only way to understand this material is by experiment."

Ada said, "You've just completed a whole set of experiments! Do you really want to get any closer to something that can set every tool and container you have on fire?"

"I have the air tools," Ivo insisted.

"Which can only carve powderstone," Ada replied.

Ivo rummaged through the spectra, then pulled out one strip. "Here! The gray mineral, in the north. As you said, luxagen-swapped or not, the basic properties of a substance are the same. Except for the ultraviolet line, this spectrum is the spectrum of powderstone! To the eye, this rock *looks like* powderstone! Physically, there is no reason why it shouldn't be every bit as soft as powderstone."

Ada and Tamara looked to Carla. "I can't argue with that," she said. "It ought to have the same mechanical properties as the ordinary mineral. But from what we've just seen, if a speck of it touches *anything*—"

Ivo said, "There'll be air flowing out of my cooling bag, constantly. The *Mite* has an air shield around it too. I've practiced this: I know I can take a sample of powderstone without touching it."

Tamara was silent for a while. "All right," she said reluctantly. "If you're still confident that you can do this, I'm not going to stand in your way."

She reeled in one of the guide ropes to make some room, then Carla helped Ivo slide the *Mite* out of its storage bay and bring it to the middle of the cabin. It was less a vehicle in its own right than a kind of chemistry workbench fitted out for the void, with air jets attached. As Ivo's understudy, Carla had had her own rehearsals with a mock-up of the thing, maneuvering it around the *Peerless* and practicing the descent from orbit. After a few days she'd become quite comfortable with the way it moved—but she'd lost count of the number of gentle collisions she'd had with the mountain.

She moved aside to let Ivo run through his equipment checks. Ada watched the process with an expression of contained disapproval, though Carla suspected that what she most resented was Tamara ignoring her advice. Ada had prepared herself to lead the mission, to bear the final responsibility for everything they did. However much she'd rejoiced to learn that her friend was alive after all, it must have been difficult to relinquish that commanding role.

Tamara told Ivo, "I want you to limit yourself to the powderstone outcrop. Trying to get samples anywhere else will be too difficult; that one mineral will have to serve as a surrogate for all of them."

"I can live with that," he replied. He was testing the recoil balance for his air blades, hovering beside one of the remaining guide ropes, proving that he could maintain a fixed separation from it even as he waved the invisible cutting jets about. "Whatever's responsible for that ultraviolet line looks like the strongest reaction in every case. So if we can quantify the energy release for powderstone—"

Ada said, "What's wrong with your right arm?"

"Nothing." Ivo shut off the cutting jets and held up the accused arm for inspection. "Why would you even—?"

"You're favoring the left one," Ada said flatly.

"That's not true," he protested. "This is a whole new limb! Since I re-extruded it there's been no pain at all."

Tamara said, "Hold onto the rope and give the *Mite* some spin around a vertical axis, using your right hand."

Ivo buzzed, offended. "Why would I ever need to do that? If I need to adjust the orientation, that's what the air jets are for."

"I know," Tamara said quietly. "I just want to see how strong that arm is."

Ivo gripped the rope beside him as she'd asked, and reached for the edge of the *Mite* with his right hand. He managed to get it spinning, but his struggle to ignore the pain was obvious now.

Carla understood: the flesh from his battered right arm hadn't recovered, because he hadn't actually managed to resorb it. He had gone through the motions of drawing it into his torso and making it appear that he was extruding an entirely new limb, but the injury had kept the damaged tissue stuck at its original site.

Ada said, "You can't go out there with an injury."

Caught out in his deception, Ivo had no reply. Carla couldn't help feeling some relief that he had been spared the risk of the excursion—but Ada seemed altogether too pleased with the outcome. Ada had had the chance to revel in her own skills, as no navigator had for generations; why should Ivo be cheated of the same kind of fulfillment? What satisfaction was there in tossing sand at the Object, watching the fireworks, then running away? He was a chemist, and he'd come here to do chemistry: he needed to get as close to dirtying his hands as possible, without actually going up in flames in the process.

Carla heard herself saying, "I'll go with him. I'll be his right hand."

"There's no provision for two operators in the mission plan," Ada replied, as if that settled it.

"I know how to use the *Mite*," Carla said, stubbornness winning out over fear. "If Ivo had had to stay behind for some reason, I'd be the one charged with doing his job. But with a mild injury like this… he's got too much experience to be replaced. We can add a second harness to the *Mite*, go out together, and I'll be there to back him up if he needs it."

Ada turned to Tamara, scowling. "You can't possibly countenance this!"

Tamara said, "Ivo?"

"We can make it work," he said, glancing at Carla with an expression of newfound respect. "I'm sure we can."

"Let's just try some rehearsals first," Tamara said cautiously. "Each of you operating the *Mite* up here in orbit, with the other in harness as a passenger. If you strike any problems, the whole thing is off."

"Of course," Carla agreed. "That sounds fair." She could feel her whole body growing charged with excitement, even as the voice of prudence in her head began howling in disbelief.

Ivo reached over and placed his palm against Carla's, their skin making contact through the small apertures they'd cut into the cooling bags.

Ready? he wrote.

As I'll ever be, Carla replied.

She glanced up at the *Gnat*, a dozen strides above them; Ada and Tamara were looking out through the window, their forms visible in the starlight but their faces impossible to read.

Carla rested the exposed fingertips of her lower right hand against the dials of the clock on the underside of the *Mite*, and wriggled a little to make herself more comfortable. She and Ivo were harnessed to a long flat plate that ran beside the main structure, held apart from it by six narrow struts. Struts and plate alike were hollow, and covered in fine holes; just as air flowed out through the fabric of her cooling bag, every part of the *Mite* was leaking, sending a thin breeze wafting out into the void in the hope of warding off danger. For all the sense this made, Carla still felt almost comically exposed—as if a solid hull like the *Gnat's* might have offered them greater protection.

Ivo reached down and opened the valve on the air jet to his left. In itself, the kick of acceleration was barely noticeable; Carla merely felt as if one side of her harness had been drawn a little tighter. But when she looked up again the *Gnat* was receding—outpacing them in its orbit now, as the blast of air acted as a gentle brake on the *Mite*.

Ivo shut off the jet. They were separating from the *Gnat* so slowly that Carla could imagine Tamara stepping out through the hatch onto a fanciful sky-road, catching up with them effortlessly and handing them some item they'd neglected to pack. As for their rate of descent, that was too slight to discern at all. But the tiny reduction in their orbital velocity had reshaped their trajectory from a circle into an ellipse; in six bells, their altitude would be less by a factor of ten.

The whole flight plan they'd prepared relied on the assumption that the usual principles of celestial mechanics would keep working in the Object's environs. Given the spectacular failure of traditional chemistry Carla wasn't willing to take anything for granted, but all the evidence so far was that the orthogonal rock beneath them was producing the same kind of gravitational field as a comparable body made from ordinary matter. From the *Gnat's* orbital period Tamara had estimated the Object's total mass, and her figure was consistent with the kind of minerals Ivo's spectra had identified on the surface. Rock couldn't magically change into something entirely new just because you encountered it at a different angle in four-space. Indeed, one faction among the chemists maintained that ordinary matter ought to contain both positive and negative luxagens—in equal numbers, symmetrically arranged—and that the swapped rock in the Object would thus be literally identical to ordinary rock. Carla had had some sympathy for the notion on purely esthetic grounds—and it certainly would have made Silvano happy if it had turned out to be true—but the fate of Ivo's projectiles had demolished that idea.

Comfortable? Ivo asked her.

She turned to him. **Sure.** Ivo looked composed, as far as she could judge from the sight of his face through his helmet. If all went well, for the next six bells they'd have nothing to do but watch the stars and the scenery. All the danger would be down on the surface—and the trick to staying sane until then was to accept that they couldn't speed up their descent and get the whole thing over any sooner.

Carla gazed down at the gray plain directly below the *Mite*; though they were leaving this region behind, it was precisely where their spiral journey would finally deposit them. The craters here were wider and more numerous than elsewhere on the surface, bolstering the hope that the gray rock really would turn out to be as soft as powderstone.

As the plain slipped away she tried to imagine the collisions that had left these craters. The strange reaction with ordinary matter was probably not to blame; they looked too much like Pio's craters, the product of nothing but like crashing into like at planetary speeds. The astronomers believed that the Object had started out deep within the orthogonal cluster a dozen light years away, then spent eons drifting alone through the void. Once, though, it must have been part of something larger.

What had torn that mother world apart? Perhaps a wildfire deep within it. A wildfire ignited how? By the tiny probability for every luxagen in every rock to break free from its energy valley—with the chance of escape mounting up over cosmic time. Some solids would be resilient, succumbing to nothing more than an inevitable slow corrosion, but others would suffer a kind of avalanche, with the change at one site shrinking the gaps between the energy levels for its neighbors, accelerating the process.

In the end, everything in the cosmos wanted to make light and blow itself to pieces. The only thing that differed was the time scale, set by the number of photons required to make the leap from solidity to chaos. But if the luxagens in most kinds of rock needed to make six or seven photons at a time in order to decay—six or seven far-infrared photons, each with the highest possible energy—what could possibly shrink that gap down to the single ultraviolet photon that Ivo's spectra had revealed?

Carla's gut tightened. She hadn't been hungry since the journey began, but she found herself longing for the comforting aroma of groundnuts.

Other hands feeling steady? she asked Ivo.

Very, he assured her.

She wanted to see this reaction close up; the more she pondered the mystery, the more she ached to understand it. She just didn't want to end up partaking in it herself.

Gyroscopes kept the *Mite*'s orientation locked against the stars, so as its orbit carried it around the Object, the Object in turn moved across the sky. Carla hardly needed to check the clock to know when they'd made half a revolution: the terrain that now stretched out above her head, its wide horizon upside down but level, rendered the whole configuration obvious.

It was her side of the *Mite* that was leading now, so it was her turn to brake the vehicle. She opened her air jet, counting the flickers beneath her fingertips, delivering a blast a little longer than Ivo's. Their new orbit would be much rounder than the last one, but still sufficiently elliptical for its closest approach to bring them almost to the surface. Skimming above the powderstone plains, they could choose the most promising site and then kill their velocity entirely. Once they had fallen to within arm's reach of the surface, resisting any further motion would require only the gentlest vertical thrust.

The ceiling of rock began tipping down toward Ivo's side of the *Mite*, their descent propelling them around the Object ever faster. Carla found the sense of momentum more empowering than alarming; she'd had enough of waiting. She wanted to see a plain of orthogonal matter spread out beneath her, near enough to touch. This fragment of the primal world had traveled backward around the history of the cosmos; the world that had given birth to her ancestors had taken the opposite course. For a child of one to encounter the other would close that vast, magnificent loop—and the meeting that the Hurtlers offered with violence could here be made serene. With caution, serene.

Ivo took her hand. **Did you see that?**

What?

The flash, he replied.

Carla looked past him at the jagged brown rock, unchanging in the starlight. Perhaps the Object collided with specks of ordinary dust now and then. It was even possible that some fleck of material from the hull of the *Gnat*, or a particle of unburnt sunstone from their final burn, had just made its way to the surface.

She saw the next flash herself. It was less fierce than the ones they'd provoked from the *Gnat*, and much more diffuse—less a blazing pinprick than a brilliant daub of light. An ignition as dispersed as that wasn't due to a *fleck* of anything.

What's doing this? she asked Ivo. He didn't have time to reply before the surface lit up again, a burst of blue-tinged flame spreading out across the rock, then quickly dissipating.

Us? he suggested.

Carla felt her muscles grow tense with fear, but his theory made no sense. How could they still be shedding anything, after the air had flowed over them for so long? Any loose material in their equipment or on their bodies should have been carried away into the void long ago by the relentless breeze.

What, exactly? she replied.

Ivo thought for a lapse or two, while another flash erupted on his left.

Contaminant in the air, he concluded.

Carla couldn't see his face, which was turned toward the Object, but his posture was hunched in shame. Ivo had been responsible for filtering all the air they'd packed, ensuring that it contained no particulate matter. She couldn't imagine him treating the task with anything but scrupulous attention.

But he wasn't taking the blame for no reason; the symptoms lent his verdict a horrible plausibility. If the *Mite*'s would-be air shield was actually spraying traces of fine dust in all directions, that would explain why these ignitions were so much more dispersed than the ones brought on by the projectiles.

The flashes were coming every pause or two now, and the wall of rock was drawing closer. Carla struggled not to panic; the single worst thing they could do would be to aim an air jet straight at the surface in the hope of a swift ascent. All their tanks had to be treated as equally suspect: the contents of any of them touching the surface could engulf the *Mite* in a conflagration.

She made some quick calculations on her thigh. **Jet four, six flickers**, she suggested. Jet four was pointing back along their orbit; though the burst of air would be aimed horizontally, it would raise their velocity and reduce the curvature of their trajectory enough to cause them to ascend.

What about spillage? Ivo protested.

Can't be helped. The jet's nozzle would send out a wide spray, some of which was sure to reach the surface. But if they did nothing they'd remain on their original orbit, passing within a few dozen strides of the rock. The flames were probably reaching at least that high already, and with the source of contamination even closer the eruptions could only become more intense.

Shut off all air? Ivo replied.

Carla hesitated. Would that be wiser than risking the jet? The air shield was clearly more of a liability than a source of protection, but she couldn't say the same about their cooling bags.

Hyperthermia? she countered.

Shield is worst thing, Ivo pointed out. **Bags later, not for long**.

He didn't wait for a reply for the first step; he reached into the center of the *Mite* and closed the outlet valve on the air tank feeding the shield.

The blue flares persisted, undiminished, for so long that Carla came close to proclaiming that Ivo's dismal hypothesis was wrong, and that they could use the air jet to retreat with impunity. Then, abruptly, the rock became dark.

Once it had actually happened, it was hard to think of this respite from the encroaching flames as a bad thing. But the fact that Ivo had been right about the cause didn't mean his minimal air scenario really was the *Mite*'s best chance. If they did use the jet, how much spillage would there be? How high would the explosion reach? Would it spread out from the ignition site fast enough to catch them?

The truth was, Carla didn't know. She couldn't quantify any of these things.

How long, then, could they survive without air drawing heat from their bodies? People who'd lived through accidents in the void rarely had a chance to consult a clock, but Carla had heard claims that the limit was a couple of chimes.

The Object filled half the sky. Her irresolution had settled the matter: they were too close now to risk using the jet. All they could do was follow the orbit down.

Carla could see the plains of gray powderstone approaching, below her to the left but swinging toward her right, the wall of rock tilting and coming full circle. The scale was impossible to judge; she checked the clock. The lowest point on the orbit was still seven chimes away.

A wide, shallow crater slid by, its ancient walls broken like the ruined desert fortress her father had described to her as he recited a story from the sagas. As it passed, flames erupted along part of its rim and spilt across the ground. *This was it: the meeting of worlds she'd longed for.* With a pang of grief she thought of sweet Carlo, fighting so hard to keep her alive, poring over census records to plan their every meeting.

A trail of blue fire pursued the *Mite*, streaking across the pitted landscape. The light from it was dazzling, almost painful, but Carla couldn't look away. Ivo reached up to the tank on his chest and shut off the air to his cooling bag. Moments later the flames subsided, but they did not die completely.

She squeezed Ivo's hand, lost for words but trying to let him know that she didn't blame him. He hadn't forced her to join him. The ground was so close now that Carla could see the structure of the rock, the surface of coarse lumps and concavities about the size of her fist. It looked exactly like powderstone. Ivo's bold plan to grab a sample here might even have worked, if not for the blunder that had rendered his air blades as suicidal as any hardstone chisel.

The flames were rising again, and gaining on the *Mite*. Carla checked the clock; the low point was still four chimes away. She turned down her cooling air as far as she could while still sensing some flow across her skin, but the effect on the height of the flames was slight, and soon overtaken by the *Mite*'s descent. She could feel the heat coming off the blazing ground now, worse than anything her own body could inflict on her.

She shut off the air completely.

The flames faltered, then winked out, leaving the *Mite* gliding over the starlit landscape. Carla felt a rush of euphoria, but time and geometry were not on her side. Once she and Ivo had both lost consciousness, their deaths would be guaranteed. Even if they were still alive at the point where it was safe to turn on the air again, they'd be oblivious to the chance to save themselves.

She stared at the useless air blades atop the workbench, angry now. Ivo had seen his grandchildren; maybe the folk saying was right after all. That sense of completion had made him careless with his own life, and now his sloppiness was going to kill her too. She thought of grabbing the stupid tools and aiming them at the ground, going out in a blaze of glory that would carve her own name into the sagas.

She saw the whole scene from outside her body: she was silhouetted against the inferno she'd made, one blade in each upper hand, the tubes that fed them running down into the *Mite*. It was a striking image, no doubt about that—but there'd be no witness to record her defiant pose.

The tubes.

She turned to Ivo; he was slumped in his harness, eyes closed. What was she waiting for—his permission to tear the device apart? Carla wrenched the tube off the right-hand blade, then reached down and pulled the other end free from the outlet of its air tank. With her lower hands she groped inside the bottom of the *Mite*, finding the clock whose dials she'd been checking. The mechanism was completely exposed; Marzio, bless him, hadn't sealed it away behind decorative panels that would only have made repairs more difficult.

She could feel the shafts that led out to the dials: she was disoriented for a moment, but the one for counting flickers was easy to distinguish by its speed, and the one for pauses not much harder. Once she had those two fixed in her mind, the shaft she wanted—the shaft that turned once every chime—was easy to find.

She probed the space between the back of the clock face and the gear at the base of the shaft. The separation was more than the thickness of the air tube. Better more than less—but the fit would not be tight enough to keep the tube in place by friction alone.

She felt her way deeper into the flying workbench and found a rack of vials, a stock of reagents that Ivo had intended to use in his calorimetry experiments. Each vial was sealed with a thick blob of resin. Carla sharpened her fingertips and sliced the top half off one of the seals, then daubed the sticky resin over the shaft. She did the same with a second seal, using it to coat the center of the gear. Her body was starting to protest against the heat now; mites were crawling beneath her skin, and some pointless instinct was trying to tempt her with visions of a cooling bed of sand.

She bent the air tube, bringing the two halves together so the corner was crimped to an impassably narrow fold—probably not air tight, but the flow it allowed would be a tiny fraction of the flow through the unobstructed width. Then she passed the tube down to her lower hands and pressed the folded end against the resin-coated shaft.

Laboriously, she began wrapping the tube into a spiral, threading the long tails in and out of the narrow spaces of the clock. The tube fought against the curvature and broke free. She sliced off more resin from two more vials and spread it over the gear and the tube. Her skin was stinging all over now, and points of light were moving across her vision.

The tube stayed in place, curled five times around the slowly turning shaft. Carla pulled apart the join between her cooling bag and its supply tank, and interposed the crude timer.

She opened the valve on the air tank slowly, afraid that too much pressure would tear the tube free. She stopped at the point she remembered by touch—well short of fully open, but where she'd last felt enough air flowing across her skin to make some difference. Nothing was coming through the pinch, and there'd been no tell-tale bounce of the tube unraveling.

She was dizzy now, too disoriented to trust herself to check anything she'd done, let alone try to change it. The lights behind her eyelids swarmed and chittered. She tried to picture Carlo, his body pressed against her, but then part of her refused to be fooled or comforted and the image of him spun away into the whiteness.

25

Carla shuddered and vomited a thin sludge into her helmet. She felt as if every scant of her flesh had been pounded with a mallet. She opened her rear eyes and looked down to see blue flames flickering over the gray rocks beneath her. *Again?* She was about to start buzzing hysterically, before her mind cleared enough for her to realize that the fire didn't have to be a bad sign at all.

She reached for the clock, afraid that the tube might have become caught in the mechanism and jammed it, but far from being stuck the dials showed a later time than she'd dared to hope for. The *Mite* had passed its lowest point. She was alive, and she was moving away from danger.

She quickly turned Ivo's air back on. The flames rose up in response, but she persisted until the heat became threatening, then she cut the flow back a fraction.

Ivo didn't move. He'd shut off his air long before she had. Carla shivered but refused to start mourning him. A few lapses later the flames went out completely, so she set his cooling bag to full strength. The tube that had saved her life had broken away from the clock shaft and was floating around in front of her in an irritating loop, so she reconnected her tank directly to her bag and stowed the tube inside one of the *Mite*'s small storage compartments.

Ivo stirred and began rolling his head, as if trying to unkink his neck muscles. Carla let him be until he opened his eyes and appraised the situation for himself.

He reached for her hand. **We're ascending?**

Yes.

He didn't ask her to explain what had happened. After a while, he took his hand away and began loosening his harness.

Carla's first instinct was not to intervene; if he'd been injured by the ordeal he might need to move to make himself more comfortable. It was only when he was entirely free of the harness and on the verge of pushing away from the *Mite* that she understood and grabbed hold of his arm. She was not at her strongest, but he was in no condition to resist her.

She took his hand again.

Better that I die, he wrote.

Carla didn't know what to say to that, but she resisted the urge to slap him across the head. He'd made an honest mistake that had put them in danger, but they'd both survived. He'd undermined the *Gnat*'s chances of capturing the Object, but a future mission could always try again, better prepared. And though his reputation would be marred by this débâcle, he'd still been instrumental in the fact that the *Gnat* had flown at all.

The contamination was an uncharacteristic lapse. Carla had seen Ivo inspecting the air filters with a microscope, to ensure that there were no tears in them. But if the problem hadn't arisen through carelessness, what had been its root? A misunderstanding of some kind. Which process was better understood, though: the filtering of dust from air… or the behavior of air in the presence of orthogonal matter?

What if the air is pure? she wrote.

Ivo didn't dignify that with a reply. There was no better established fact in all of chemistry than the inertness of air. Nobody had a perfect explanation for this, but it had long been conjectured that each particle of the gas was a spherical cluster of luxagens, arranged in such a way that Nereo's force canceled almost perfectly outside the cluster.

Still, when air bounced against rock it was Nereo's force that made it bounce. Once an air particle actually made contact with something, the luxagens within couldn't hide themselves completely. So it wasn't *inconceivable* that orthogonal rock could react differently to air built from positive luxagens than it would to its own, presumably innocuous, swapped version. Let everyone on the *Gnat* and the *Peerless* share the blame, then, for failing to imagine that possibility.

Carla hadn't thought to try to get a spectrum of the flames their spilt air had summoned, but she'd have bet anything that the same dominant spectral line as they'd seen before would have been present. Every mineral's structure was complicated in a different way, and even a particle of air had its own elaborate geometry, but that one line screamed simplicity.

What was the UV frequency? she wrote.

Ivo gave her the wavelength.

No, the frequency.

I have no idea, he replied. His spectrograph was calibrated for wavelengths; it was the convention among chemists to express all their results in those terms.

You can't work it out? Carla wasn't so rattled that she couldn't do it herself, but she wanted to keep Ivo engaged.

He humored her, carrying out the calculations on the patch of skin they shared. The spectral line's wavelength wasn't much greater than the minimum wavelength of light. Yalda's formula put the frequency at near enough to three tenths the maximum; Ivo dutifully multiplied this out to get roughly a dozen and three generoso-cycles per pause.

Carla didn't care about the final number; it must have been nice for the ancestors that a "pause" was a convenient fraction of the rotational period of the home world, but it had no bearing on anything else in the cosmos. All the real physics was in the pure ratios of numbers, untouched by the whims of history and convention.

The UV line they'd seen in every fire on the Object was three tenths the maximum frequency of light. Every photon of that frequency was traveling at a speed that tilted its energy-momentum vector steeply enough to make it lie at three tenths its original height.

But *three to ten* was the ratio Patrizia had found, when she'd fitted her curves for colliding particles to the data for light scattering off luxagens. A luxagen's mass was three tenths the mass of a photon. So every photon in this ultraviolet line possessed the same energy as a stationary luxagen.

What if a luxagen became a photon? Carla wrote.

She could feel Ivo's body shaking as he buzzed with mirth. **Source strength?** he replied.

He was right to object; a luxagen carried one unit of source strength, a photon had none. And from Nereo's equation you could prove with mathematical certainty that source strength could never simply vanish.

Mathematically, though… it could cancel.

One positive luxagen, one negative, Carla suggested. Strictly speaking, the only quantity that had to remain unchanged was the *total* source strength: the count of positive particles minus the count of negative ones. The individual numbers didn't need to stay fixed.

Ivo didn't respond. Carla looked to his face; he appeared to be mulling it over.

She tried to imagine the process. Two luxagens came together, one of each sign… but instead of them simply bouncing off each other, the original particles were destroyed and two photons emerged.

It sounded absurd, but what principle did it violate? Source strength would be conserved, since the total was zero both before and after. Energy would be conserved, so long as each photon had the energy of a single luxagen. Momentum would be conserved if the photons were traveling in opposite directions, making the total zero before and after.

Is this charity? Ivo asked her.

Carla was taken aback. He thought she'd concocted the whole theory just to get him off the hook with Ada and Tamara. **Of course not!**

Luxagens vanish? Ivo's face made it clear that he found this no more plausible than a conjuror's claim to make a vole disappear from a sealed box.

Only in pairs, Carla replied, as if that were enough to make the idea respectable.

But no wonder it sounded preposterous: where else could they have seen positive and negative luxagens come together, with any hope of understanding the result? Not in the fleeting, uncontrollable events on the hull of the *Peerless*. Not in the light from the Hurtlers that menaced the ancestors; they hadn't even known the luxagen's mass or grasped the link between energies and frequencies.

Only here. Wherever this beautiful new physics carried them, it could only have begun here.

By the time the *Gnat* was fully re-pressurized and Carla had removed her cooling bag, she'd given Ada and Tamara a version of the *Mite*'s misadventures that never even raised the possibility of contamination in the air tanks.

"Air sets orthogonal rock on fire?" Tamara sounded every bit as skeptical as Ivo had been. "Are you sure there wasn't some other—?"

"Air is made of positive luxagens," Carla interjected. "Just like any other ordinary matter. That's all it takes to set orthogonal matter on fire." She offered an illustration.

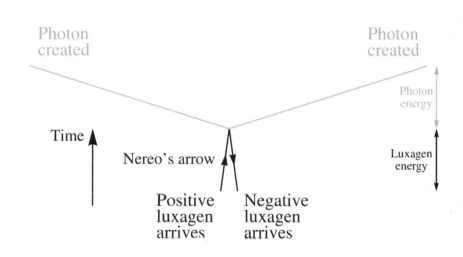

"The length of each line is the mass of the particle, and its height is the particle's energy. Nereo's arrow agrees with our time axis for positive luxagens, and opposes it for negative ones."

Ada said, "Doesn't a positive luxagen repel a negative one, close up?"

"It does," Carla agreed.

"And the force pushing them apart goes to infinity as they get closer," Ada added. "So how do they ever get to touch?"

"Luxagen waves don't respect energy barriers absolutely," Carla replied. "The wave for two luxagens with opposite signs will lie *mostly* in the energy valley where they're far enough apart for Nereo's force to become attractive—but it won't be entirely confined to that valley, and it will allow some probability for the two luxagens to make contact. The fact that the probability is so small is why the process is relatively slow—why we had measurable delays before the flashes when we dropped the projectiles. But slow or not, once it happens, it happens."

Ada looked dubious. Carla said, "Let me show you another process that's worth thinking about."

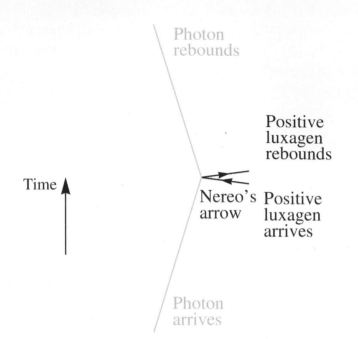

Ada stared at the new diagram. "A photon comes in from the left, a positive luxagen comes in from the right. They collide and bounce off each other."

"Nothing too strange in that?"

"No," Ada conceded.

"This picture is the same as the last one," Carla said. "I just rotated it by a quarter of a turn. If a photon and a luxagen can bounce off each other like this, the version of events where two luxagens turn into two photons must be possible as well. It's exactly the same thing, seen from a different viewpoint."

Ada looked annoyed, but Tamara gave a chirp of delight.

"It's an audacious theory," Tamara said. "But where does it leave us? If we can't even touch orthogonal rock with air, how are we going to get a sample to calibrate the reaction?"

"We can't get a sample," Carla replied. "But if these pictures are right, they tell us most of what we need to know. The UV line outshines everything else in the spectra, and if we dump a few hefts of calmstone onto the Object almost every luxagen in that heap of gravel will end up suffering the fate I've drawn. We know the energy and momentum produced by that reaction, so we can calibrate everything using that as our first guess."

Tamara turned to Ivo. "What do you think?"

Ivo had been quiet since they'd returned to the *Gnat*, letting Carla give her version of events without comment.

"I don't know what to make of this hypothesis," he said. "But if we drop enough material to have a measurable effect on the Object's trajectory—by Carla's calculations—then we'll have a chance to see how well her prediction bears out. If we're going to be forced to work by trial and error, we might as well make the first trial count for something."

Carla computed the total mass that needed to be flung onto the surface, but left the details of the orbit that would deliver it to Ada and Tamara. When Ivo had checked her arithmetic—and had her justify every assumption behind the numbers—she took on the purely physical task of winding the large catapult. Whatever damage the hyperthermia had wrought on her body, as she struggled against the wheel the pain and tenderness began to leave her.

Ivo loaded the catapult's chamber, working the levers inside the hull that shifted measured scoops from the calmstone store. Compared to the tiny pellets they'd dropped before, this new bombardment was like a declaration of war. Carla had tried to balance the likelihood that some proportion of the material would be blown clear of the surface, unconsumed, against the possibility of an unanticipated process amplifying the whole effect. Though she'd never set eyes on Gemma, she'd heard the tale of the dark world that became a star repeated endlessly since childhood.

But Gemma had been ignited by a Hurtler, traveling at an infinite velocity relative to the rock of the planet. Sheer momentum would have carried the Hurtler deep below the surface before the annihilation began, trapping much of the heat produced and rendering it far more damaging. She did not believe that an explosion that was open to the void would start a wildfire.

Ada wore the blindfold this time, but she followed a clock with her fingertips and called out the command to launch. When Ivo released the catapult, Carla could see the pile of brown rubble tumbling away in the starlight, receding almost as slowly as the *Mite* when it began its journey. But in five bells' time the rubble would take a tighter curve around the Object than she and Ivo had done, and find a wall of orthogonal rock in its way. By then, the *Gnat* would be diametrically opposite the point of impact, shielded from the blast.

The wait was as tense as the *Mite*'s descent, but at least they could converse normally. "Who wants to break the news to Silvano?" Ada joked. "I don't think he'll be farming much wheat here."

"Or mining much fuel," Tamara added, "unless we can think of a way to handle it." She turned to Ivo. "Is orthogonal rock a fuel, or a liberator?"

"There is no right word for it," Ivo said. "Chemistry is about the rearrangement of matter. If matter disappears, that's something else entirely."

Half a bell before the impact, Carla handed out loaves, trying not to think about the fast she'd have to go through when she needed to return to her old mass. What mattered now was that they kept themselves alert, prepared to respond to any more surprises.

With one tap of her hand, Tamara deftly reversed the trajectories of the last crumbs that had been floating away from her mouth, then she took hold of the drive's emergency start lever. If the reaction they provoked made a mockery of Carla's guesses and blew the Object apart, the very alignment that had been intended to provide them with the most shielding from the blast would see the bulk of the flaming remnants propelled in the direction of the *Gnat*.

"One lapse to impact," Ada announced.

Carla turned to the window. The powderstone plains were below the *Gnat* again; the rubble would strike an outcrop of calmstone on the opposite side. Calmstone meeting calmstone, putting paid to its name.

A soft blue halo appeared at the limb of the Object. *A wildfire, come this far already?* But then the halo expanded, creeping no closer as it slowly faded, and Carla understood: a plume of incandescent debris must have risen so high above the impact site and spread so widely as it soared into the void that its edges had become visible over the Object's horizon.

Two bells later they'd moved far enough around the Object to see the plume clearly: a faintly glowing streak of gas and dust stretched out against the stars. Their trajectory was aimed right into it, so Tamara shifted the *Gnat* to a new orbit, its plane orthogonal to the axis of the plume.

Ada and Tamara began making observations, sighting beacons and timing the moments that various stars vanished behind the Object's edge. Carla tried to catch up on her sleep as she waited for the verdict. When she closed her eyes she saw herself back on the *Mite*, descending into flames, but she was tired enough that it made no difference.

Two days later, the navigators had their first estimate of the change the calmstone rocket had produced. "We've removed three quarters of the Object's velocity relative to the *Peerless*," Tamara announced. "A couple of scaled-down corrections should be enough to meet the target." A perfect result was unattainable, but the target velocity would see the Object remain within reach for generations.

They waited one more day to be sure that the plume posed no danger, then Tamara tilted the *Gnat*'s orbit enough to let them see the impact site. The crater was like nothing else on the Object: a flat bowl nearly a stroll wide, its floor a smooth black ellipsoid. The original terrain had been jagged, but the fireball that carved this shape had been oblivious to the varied heights of the boulders that stood in its way.

"So *this* is what our engines will do to the antipodal apartments when we use the new wonder fuel," Ada said.

Carla buzzed, but the joke stung. "I'd better swap mine before word gets out."

A few more blasts and the Object would be captured. They could return to the *Gnat* in triumph, their mission complete.

But what was the Object, right now? A vast new repository of energy—in a form that nobody knew how to handle, let alone safely exploit.

The fuel problem hadn't been solved. Everything that made this new power source promising rendered it equally terrifying. And the fate of the *Peerless*, as ever, remained hostage to discoveries yet to be made.

26

arlo looked on with a growing sense of dread as Ada and Tamara emerged from the airlock. Tamara was the leader; shouldn't she have been the last to leave the *Gnat*? He watched the navigators' faces as they removed their helmets, bracing himself for confirmation of his fears.

They both looked tired, but happy. They did not look like bearers of bad news.

Addo ran forward to embrace his co, with Pio close behind. Tamara approached the rest of the welcoming party: Marzio, Carlo and Ivo's son Delfino. "They'll be up soon," she said. "There were some records they'd packed away for the return journey that they suddenly decided they couldn't leave for the decommissioning team to bring up."

"Thank you," Delfino said, his voice strained with relief. Carlo could understand why he hadn't brought his children to the disembarkation; out of all the crew, Ivo had faced the greatest risk of not coming back.

"So what's the news about the Object?" Carlo asked Tamara. Addo had spoken to the astronomers who'd seen it light up three times, but Carlo didn't trust any remote interpretation of the events. "Rocket fuel or just rock?"

Tamara said, "Your co would murder me if I spoiled her chance to tell you the whole story. You'll have to be patient."

"But everyone's fine?"

"Absolutely," Tamara promised.

As Tamara spoke with Marzio, Carlo surveyed her appraisingly, looking for any sign that the journey might have done her harm. The most striking thing, though, was how much mass she'd gained. He'd been expecting that, but he was glad of the reminder; he didn't want Carla to catch him noticing the change, forcing her to think about the struggle she'd be facing when they were meant to be celebrating her return.

Ivo climbed into view inside the airlock, a bundle of papers under one arm. Carla followed, similarly encumbered. "If they drop them they'll be sorry," Marzio said, bemused. "I don't know why they couldn't wait." The papers began to flutter alarmingly as the airlock refilled, but with the entrance hatch closed any danger of losing them had passed.

Carlo approached the airlock. When Carla stepped through the doorway he took the papers so she could remove her helmet; the cooling bags made it impossible to extrude new limbs at will. Carlo noticed a neatly cut hole in the fabric over her left palm.

"Welcome back," he said.

"I missed you," she replied. Her words were strangely charged, like a threat or a confession.

The bag between them made a crinkling sound as they embraced. Carlo buzzed at the tickle of the creases.

"I managed to keep the Councilors away," he said. "You won't have to face any of them until the official reception."

"Ha." Carla relaxed slightly. "Poor Silvano isn't going to be happy. Let me get this off, then we can go and talk."

They stood together on the empty workshop floor, far enough from the others for a modicum of privacy. Carlo listened, entranced, to the results of the first experiments, but when Carla began describing her decision to join Ivo on the *Mite* it was hard to keep the horror from showing on his face. As the story went on he could feel himself losing the struggle.

"You almost died," he said.

"But I didn't."

He tried to balance his anger against his gratitude that she'd survived, but the scales refused to lie still.

"Ivo could have gone down alone."

"He was injured," Carla replied. "I was the one who should have gone down alone. It was my job to replace him if he wasn't in perfect health."

Carlo didn't reply. *What could he do about this recklessness?* Nothing. The whole thing was past.

He dragged his attention back to Carla's words as she described her theory of luxagen annihilation; he even managed to ask half-intelligent questions as she summoned diagrams of the process onto her chest.

"When you turn everything sideways," he said, "one of the photons that these annihilations 'produce' has to be there from the start?"

"Yes."

"But that's the ancestors' reference frame, isn't it?" Carlo realized. "So if they could watch all this, they'd claim that something emitted that photon in a completely separate process—to explain the fact that it came along just in time to bounce off the luxagen?"

Carla said, "That's what you'd expect, though I wouldn't swear to anything like that without a way to test it."

"But doesn't that mean that if the ancestors managed to ensure that there *were no* suitable photons… we wouldn't see the luxagens annihilate each other?"

"What happens, happens," Carla offered gnomically. "Everything in the cosmos has to be consistent. All we get to do is talk about it in a way that makes sense to us."

"Unless we can't," he replied. "Where's the guarantee that we can even do that much?"

Carla buzzed softly. "We don't seem to have lost the ability just yet. I'd save the angst about free will for the return journey."

Everyone else had started moving toward the exit. "The reception's tomorrow, at the third bell," Carlo said. "Are you up to that?"

"I'll survive," Carla replied. "Where am I sleeping tonight? I've lost track of the system."

Carlo hesitated; he'd planned on the two of them going to his apartment. And it wasn't just the system, it was what he longed for: to see her lying safely beside him, to reassure himself that the danger of losing her had passed.

But he could already hear the arguments he'd make to himself if he woke in the night. *The danger's passed, for now—so now is the time to forestall any chance of it returning.* And to Carla: *You've solved another of Yalda's puzzles: you've explained the reaction with orthogonal matter! What more do you want? That part of your life is complete.*

"We should meet at the reception," he said.

"Are you sure?"

Carlo thought she sounded disappointed, almost hurt by his rejection. But why couldn't he just speak plainly? They were trailing the others, out of hearing.

"It's too hard for me right now," he said. "I almost lost you; all I can think about now is keeping you."

Carla looked stunned. He'd said too much, she'd never trust him again.

But then she reached down and squeezed his shoulder. "Me too," she said, shivering a little. "We should stay apart for a few more days, until it passes for both of us."

Amanda caught Carlo's eye; she flicked her head slightly to point to Tosco, dragging himself across the workshop toward them.

"I'd like to see you both in my office," Tosco said. "At the next chime, if you can get away from what you're doing."

Amanda had her hand in a cage, poised to inject an immobilized vole on the verge of reproducing, but she said, "That's no problem."

Carlo said, "We'll be there."

When Tosco was gone, Amanda shot Carlo a questioning glance. "I have no idea," he said. Their work had been progressing far more slowly than any of them wished, but Tosco was the one who'd counselled Carlo to be patient.

As they approached the office at the appointed time, Carlo saw one of their colleagues, Macaria, waiting on the rope outside the doorway. Carlo had no idea what she'd been doing lately; he'd seen her coming and going from the main workshop, using the centrifuges and other equipment, but she'd been spending most of her time elsewhere.

Tosco emerged and called the three of them inside. When they were settled, he addressed Carlo and Amanda.

"I've brought you here for a briefing on Macaria's experiments," he said. "She'll be publishing the results shortly, but I wanted you to hear them first."

Carlo was relieved; this didn't sound like a preamble to the termination of his own project. "What's the work about?"

Macaria said, "I'm in the early stages of an investigation into infrared communication in lizards."

"*Communication?*" Amanda had worked with lizards for years; she was entitled to express some skepticism at the claim.

"'Signaling' might be a better word," Tosco suggested. "We're not talking about a language, in the conventional sense."

"Ivo found an infrared-sensitive component in lizard skin," Macaria explained. "So I wondered if it had a specific role—maybe supplementing ordinary vision in some way. But I thought the easiest starting point would be to look for a complementary substance: one that would *emit* IR to the environment in response to an internal signal. And I found one."

"Triggered chemically?" Amanda asked.

Macaria said, "No. It responds directly to illumination from pathways in the flesh at the usual wavelengths, but it's shielded from external visible light by a layer that's only transparent in infrared."

"Ah." Amanda sounded as if she was starting to be won over, but Carlo was still unconvinced; demonstrating an interesting physical property in some goo you'd centrifuged out of lizard skin didn't prove that that property served a biological function.

"I set up an infrared camera and took exposures of small lizard populations in various circumstances, to see if I could catch the signal being used," Macaria continued. "Most of the experiments came up blank. A new food source and the appearance of a predator—things that elicit audible calls—didn't trigger any infrared chatter."

Carlo said, "But…?"

"When I took two groups that had been bred apart and brought them together for the first time, the paper turned black." Macaria swept a hand back and forth, as if slathering dye onto a sheet. "I'd been expecting a few gray streaks across the image, but in a two-lapse exposure there was complete saturation wherever a lizard had been in view."

Carlo understood now what the meeting was about. "So you think this is what carries an influence?"

Tosco said, "We don't want to rush to any conclusions."

"No." But it was a tantalizing possibility. When two unrelated groups of animals came together, they almost always managed to exchange some traits. Lizards had no males, so there was no question of cross-breeding, but in other species even when the groups were kept from making physical contact the next generation of young ended up with traits that could not be explained by ordinary inheritance. The mechanism remained so obscure that biologists still used the vocabulary of folklore: an "influence" passed between the groups. When you had no idea how the traits had actually been disseminated, what else could you say?

"I'm going to test that hypothesis, of course," Macaria said. "Block the IR or interfere with it, and see if that affects the exchange of traits. But it's going to take several generations of animals to get meaningful results."

"In the meantime," Tosco said, "I think this calls for a collaboration. Carlo and Amanda have experience with their light recorder, capturing the time sequence of internal signals. So I want the three of you to work together, to analyze the structure of these IR signals in the same way."

Carlo felt a twinge of anxiety returning; Macaria's discovery was important, but he didn't want his own work slowed down. "You're not scaling back our project?"

"No." Tosco was annoyed by this petty response. "All I'm asking you to do is to find the time to help Macaria become familiar with your techniques. Anything more is up to you—though I would have thought you'd be grateful for the chance to become involved in this work and learn from it yourself."

Carlo was duly chastened. "Of course."

And Tosco had a point. The messages that moved within the flesh had proved harder to manipulate than he'd imagined, whereas the signals Macaria had found were out in the open, there for the taking. This might be a chance to watch some kind of concise description of traits moving from group to group, instead of trying to take apart the detailed mechanics of the same traits unfolding within each animal's body.

He didn't know whether quadraparous voles were ever *influenced* by biparous cousins to follow their example. But if they were—and if he could record the transaction that made it happen—how far might that take him?

"I'd be happy to help Macaria," he said. "And happy to learn from her."

27

Tamara waited in the visiting room, harnessed to a bench, fidgeting with the three seasoned loaves she'd brought. Patches of red moss glowed from the walls, but the hue looked strange to her, as if it belonged to a different species than the one she was accustomed to. The prison had been built in the middle of a disused engine feed; for most of her life she'd been aware of its existence without ever knowing exactly where it was.

The guard brought Erminio into the room, then withdrew. "Has he gone to fetch Tamaro?" she asked her father.

"Tamaro isn't coming. He doesn't need to see you."

Need? "It's his choice," she said. "I thought it would be so boring here that he'd welcome a visit from anyone, but if he's found a better way to pass the time, good for him."

She offered one of the loaves to Erminio. He hesitated, then accepted it.

"How Tamaro spends his time isn't your concern," Erminio said. "He has someone else to visit him."

Tamara understood what he was implying. The news took her by surprise, but she did her best not to show it. "As I said, good for him."

Erminio finished the loaf, then leaned back in his harness and stretched his arms languidly. "I hope you haven't come to beg for your entitlement back. There's no chance of that now: it's well and truly spoken for."

Tamara buzzed with derision. "What, she's given birth already?"

Erminio said, "Hardly. But Tamaro's made a formal agreement. With a co-stead and future children involved, you'll never get the transfer rescinded."

"I never expected to," Tamara said angrily. "I keep my promises."

"You'll still be looked after," Erminio declared magnanimously, as if this were somehow his doing.

Tamara said, "I know the terms of the transfer; I dictated them myself. If Tamaro was here I expect he'd be thanking me for them, but I don't know why you've raised the subject. You'll be *looked after*, too."

"So why did you come here?" Erminio asked coolly. "You survived your trip, so you've come to gloat?"

"I'm not sure why I bothered," Tamara replied. "You're still my family, I thought I owed you something."

"There is no *family*," Erminio said. "You've destroyed it. Tamaro has done the only honorable thing he can, in the circumstances: he'll salvage the life of a blameless woman who's lost her co. But the flesh you inherited was wasted on you. You think you're vindicated, because you gambled with your life and won. But who'll raise your children now? It would have been better if you'd died in the void."

"I think I should go. Give Tamaro my regards." She took hold of the rope behind her and began to pull herself out of the harness.

"Don't bother coming back," Erminio said. "I have more than enough visitors to keep me entertained. A lot of people want to show their support. They know our punishment was an injustice."

Tamara dragged herself out of the room. "That was quick," the guard said.

"My father's a great communicator," Tamara replied. "It never takes him long to get his message across."

The guard regarded her with weary amusement. "It took him a bell and a half yesterday."

On her way back to the summit she couldn't stop thinking about Erminio's claim to have supporters. When she'd asked for leniency for her kidnappers, she'd hoped that would deprive them of any trace of sympathy. One year *an injustice?* The Council took autonomy seriously; the sentence could have been six times longer, if she'd called for that.

Imprisoned and disgraced, Tamaro had still found a co-stead in no time at all. The Council had judged her father to be the instigator of the crime, but apparently he still had friends. Everyone she knew had told her to her face that they were outraged by what had happened to her, but she understood that she'd be fooling herself if she took that sentiment to be universal. Three generations away from the old world and its barbarities, there were still people who believed that a woman's life was a kind of *tenancy*, devoted to protecting—and in due course, meekly vacating—a body that was never really her own.

28

arla threw the tarpaulin aside and dragged herself out of bed. Still half asleep, she approached the food cupboard and tugged on the handle, but the door refused to budge. She recalled sliding the bolt into place the night before: her reminder that this was meant to be a fast day.

Had it really been three days since the last one? Her gut squirmed in disbelief; it had learned to follow a daily cycle, but these calendrical variations were too arcane to be internalized. She ran a finger over the cross-bar at the side of the bolt, pondering excuses for breaking the rigid pattern. Today was her first appearance before the Council; any day without food was hard enough, but short of her life-or-death encounter with the Object she had never needed her wits about her more. She could eat today and fast tomorrow.

She tugged at the cross-bar and began guiding it through the little maze of obstructions she'd built that made it impossible to disengage the bolt unless she was fully awake. Halfway through, she paused. Breaking the pattern would set a precedent, inviting her to treat every fast day as a potential exception. Once the behavior that she was trying to make routine and automatic had to be questioned over and over again, the whole scheme would become a kind of torture, a dozen times harder to follow than it was already.

She returned the cross-bar to its starting position and dragged herself away from the cupboard. Once she was back to her old mass, she could resume the old routine: one loaf every morning, like clockwork.

Carla stepped forward and faced the assembled Councilors across the brightly lit chamber. Behind them, portraits of Yalda, Frido, and the dozens who'd followed them crowded the wall. That her old friend Silvano was among the *Peerless*'s twelve current leaders did nothing to put her at ease; it just made the encounter more complicated. Addressing an audience whose personal histories were uniformly opaque to her would at least have made it easier to stop fretting about these people's individual agendas and just put the merits of her own case as best she could.

Assunto had warned her that if she wanted to be taken seriously she needed to quell any instinct for deference and resist averting her eyes. She followed his advice—but to stop herself feeling intimidated she focused her attention on the fellow crew members gathered behind her.

"So far as we understand it," she began, "every solid and every gas in the cosmos is built from luxagens. From a cosmic perspective all luxagens are identical, but because their histories through four-space are marked with a kind of arrow—Nereo's arrow—we can distinguish between those luxagens whose arrows point toward our future and those whose arrows point toward our past. By convention, we call the first kind 'positive' and the second 'negative'.

"The peculiar histories of the Object and the *Peerless* have led to a curious disjunction: although our thermodynamic arrows of time agree, the arrows on our luxagens do not. The *Peerless* and everything it carries is built entirely from positive luxagens, the Object entirely from negative ones. And as the *Gnat*'s experiments showed us, if positive and negative luxagens are brought together they will annihilate each other. The purely *chemical* variation of the materials available to us is of no help here: no rock or resin, no plant material or animal product, no gas or smoke or dust will be immune to this effect."

Carla allowed herself a quick glance at Silvano. His expression was grim, but she believed she was about to improve his mood considerably.

"There is one thing, though, that can safely interact with the material of the Object: light. Light does not itself produce light, so its history isn't marked with Nereo's arrow: there is no 'positive' light and 'negative' light. The starlight from ordinary and orthogonal stars falls on both us and the Object alike, causing no damage to either. So if we hope to make tools that will allow us to acquire and manipulate samples of the Object,

I believe that will require a new source of light."

Councilor Giusta interjected, "So you want to drill into the Object with the beam from a giant sunstone lamp?"

"No," Carla replied. "Brute force like that wouldn't get us very far. What we need is a light source whose output is more *orderly* than the beam from any kind of lamp."

She summoned a sketch onto her chest.

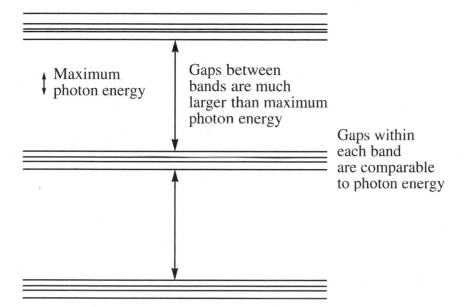

"The luxagens in every solid are restricted to certain energy levels," she said. "These levels are arranged in bands. The bands themselves are so widely spaced that a luxagen can only jump between them by creating several photons at once. That's a very slow, inefficient process—which is what makes solids stable in the first place.

"Within each band, though, the levels are close enough for luxagens to move between them by emitting or absorbing single photons. Left to themselves, most luxagens will occupy the highest possible levels in their bands, because those at lower levels will spontaneously emit a photon and move up." Carla hesitated, half expecting someone to challenge her on these events without a cause, but either the Councilors had heard of

Assunto's strange "zero-photon" light that filled the cosmos and shook every luxagen at every imaginable frequency… or they were simply willing to accept that there would always be some kind of disturbance pushing luxagens from the most precarious states into more stable positions.

"When a photon enters a solid, it can affect the luxagens in two different ways," she continued. "If there are luxagens in a high energy level, they can absorb the photon and move down to a lower level. And if there are luxagens in a low energy level, they can emit another photon exactly like the first, and move up to a higher level. For either of these things to happen, the energy of the photon must match the difference in energy between the two levels."

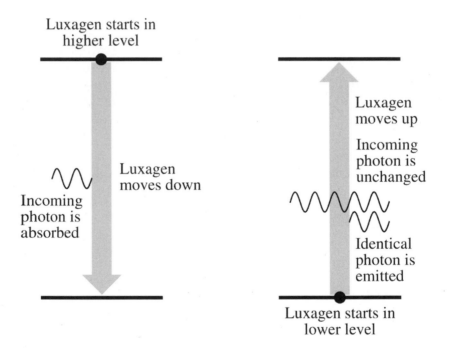

"The two processes push the luxagens in opposite directions, and all things being equal they'd both take place at exactly the same rate. But with luck, it might be possible to find a solid where things can be kept very far from equal. Suppose we have *four* different energy levels, and we illuminate the solid with light of the right frequency to push luxagens from the highest level down to the very lowest."

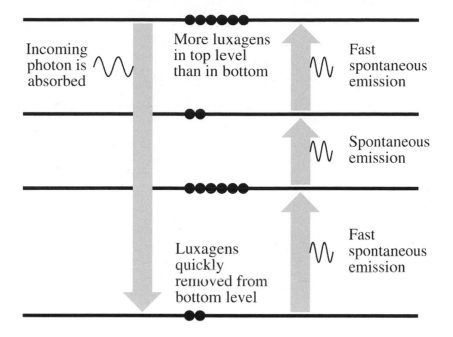

"If nothing else was going on, the same light would also give rise to the opposite process: stimulating luxagens in the bottom level to jump back up to the top. But suppose the *spontaneous* jump from the bottom level to the one just above happens very quickly—so quickly that most luxagens end up at that second lowest level instead. From there, the luxagens will spontaneously jump up one more level, and then one more again. Once they reach the top, our light will push them to the bottom again.

"Now, the photons that are emitted spontaneously will have random phases and directions, just like the light from a lamp. But suppose we put this solid between a pair of mirrors that send the light from the middle transition back and forth through the material."

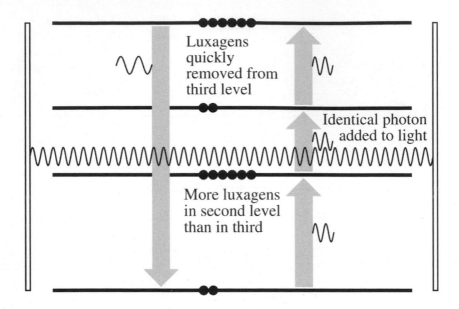

"Each time the light is reflected back through the solid, it will prompt more luxagens from the second lowest level to jump up one step, emitting photons of the same phase and in the same direction as the one passing through. But we can avoid the unwanted reverse process—where the photons we send back get absorbed, instead of duplicated—if the transition from the third level to the top one happens fast enough. If that third level is kept almost empty, there'll be almost no luxagens in a position to absorb the light.

"By separating the mirrors by an exact multiple of the wavelength of the light we're trying to multiply, we can reinforce a mode that is entirely parallel and in phase. If we make one of the mirrors only partially reflective, the beam that emerges from this device should be aligned like nothing we've seen before. A lens will focus it down to a spot whose size is limited only by the laws of optics—allowing all the power in the beam to be concentrated on a target a fraction of a scant across. What's more, the light itself will be comprised of an orderly series of wave fronts, maintaining a regular pattern over vastly longer times and distances than the jumble of waves that we get from a lamp. So instead of the light field changing direction at random, partly canceling out its own effects, the full strength of the field can be brought to bear at the focal point.

"The stronger the light field, the greater the pressure it exerts. So I believe there's a chance that this 'coherent light' could be used in much the same way as we originally hoped to use air jets: to manipulate small samples of orthogonal matter without touching them."

Carla spread her arms: she was finished. For a pause or two all the Councilors were silent, then Silvano asked, "How far does this take us toward a new engine design?"

Carla forced herself to meet his gaze. *Engine design?* She thought she'd just offered him a chance to salvage some dignity after his overblown claims for the Object, but apparently he wouldn't be satisfied with anything less than an instant answer to the fuel problem. "If we can build this tool it might let us conduct preliminary experiments," she said. "We could study the annihilation reaction between very small samples, under controlled conditions. But any talk about a new engine design would be premature, until we've done those experiments."

Councilor Massimo said, "Would you ever seriously envision bringing orthogonal matter into the *Peerless* at all?"

"Not unless we'd developed an extremely reliable technology for handling it," Carla replied.

"Reliable?" Massimo buzzed softly. "You're holding a universal liberator in place *using nothing but light*. What happens when your light source fails?"

"If the sample was kept under weightless conditions in an evacuated container, there could be days to recover safely from the failure," Carla said.

"But the whole point would be to use this in our engines!" Massimo reminded her. "When we're firing the engines, we're not weightless, are we?"

Hadn't she just said that any talk of engine design would be premature? Carla struggled to find an answer that wouldn't sound discourteous or uncooperative. "I can imagine an arrangement where a failure to contain the orthogonal matter would see it vented behind us—falling straight out of the engines into the void. But for now, all I'm talking about is a research program to try to build a coherent light source."

"For argument's sake," Councilor Prospero said, "let's suppose that we do find a way to fuel the *Peerless* with orthogonal matter. Where would that get us? If we could bring the unused portion of the Object back to the home world, would that be fuel enough to move the planet itself?"

"No."

"Or enough to power a swarm of rockets that could evacuate every one of the ancestors?"

"I very much doubt it," Carla replied.

"So what use is any of this?" Prospero asked bluntly.

"What use was there in launching the *Peerless* in the first place?" Carla snapped back. "All I'm proposing is the best means I can think of to improve our understanding of orthogonal matter. I can't tell you where that might lead us—except to a much-needed reduction in our ignorance on the subject."

Giusta said, "And we thank you for you proposal, Carla. I think it's time we heard from the next witness."

Carla retreated and stood beside Ivo. "Don't let them get to you," he said quietly. "They can't help acting out their own internal squabbles, even when they have company."

It was Tamara's turn to address the Council. "If we do hope to exploit the Object," she said, "or to conduct even the most modest experiments there, we're going to need to establish some permanent means to navigate safely between the Object and the *Peerless*. Many of the beacons we launched for the first flight of the *Gnat* are running out of sunstone or failing in other ways—and they're all spreading out too far to remain useful for much longer.

"What I propose is a new system of beacons, arranged in a grid that remains fixed relative to the *Peerless*. That will require manual supervision of each beacon's deceleration; there's no other way that we'd be able to get the final velocities low enough. But even if the Council chooses to take no further interest in the Object, I propose that we launch these beacons regardless. We ought to be able to navigate the void around the *Peerless* at will, whenever the need arises. Suppose another body like the Object is sighted. Consider how much easier it would be to deal with, if we could send observers out to get a fix on its location immediately."

Councilor Dino said, "You want to keep another gross of beacons out there in the sky, stocked up with sunstone, flashing once a bell... just in case we need them?"

"That was my original plan," Tamara confessed. "But after listening to my colleague here, I've had a much better idea." She turned to face Carla. "Don't worry, I'm not going to take you up on that 'light clock' nonsense you were feeding me on the *Gnat*."

Dino was bemused. "It's reassuring to hear that we'll be spared nonsense, but—"

Tamara said, "We won't need to put lamps in these beacons, or clockwork. Just optics! If Carla can build the light source she's described, the beam it produces would only spread out a little as it traveled across the void. We could light the beacons from home: illuminate them all from the *Peerless*, keeping them simple and sparing us the need to refuel them or make repairs."

Carla listened, delighted, as Tamara fleshed out her new scheme on the spot. Carla hadn't given much thought to the infrastructure needed to make travel to the Object routine, but if she'd conspired with the navigators from the start they could not have made the case for her light source any stronger.

Ivo spoke next, then Ada. Though they all had different priorities, nobody was proposing a method of their own for manipulating luxagen-swapped rock. It would be light or nothing.

Giusta announced a recess in the hearing. Carla paced the chamber, wishing she'd brought her groundnuts along for comfort. Light or nothing—but most of the people she'd spoken to since the voyage had recoiled in horror when she explained just how dangerous orthogonal matter had turned out to be. And though Massimo's line of questioning had been irritating, there was no denying that any attempt to exploit the stuff as fuel would carry enormous risks. Massimo and Prospero would not be alone in preferring to leave the Object sitting in the void, untouched.

Ivo approached her. "How would you identify the material for your light source?" he asked. "Just trial and error, or could you narrow down the candidates from their absorption spectra?"

"In principle the spectra should help," Carla replied. "But to be honest, I've never been able to take a spectrum and turn it into a map of energy levels."

Ivo was surprised. "It's that difficult?"

Carla hummed softly. "Think of all the ways you can distribute luxagens among the energy levels. The only clear rule is that when the solid is in darkness, you'd expect all the luxagens in a given band to end up in that band's highest level."

Ivo pondered this. "Can't you predict the number of luxagens per band? Or the number per valley?"

Carla said, "Remember the stability puzzle you posed, on the *Gnat*?"

"Why don't solids implode under pressure?"

"I did the calculations," she said, "and the problem didn't go away: I can't explain why there should be *any* limit on the number of luxagens you can squeeze into each valley. So here I am rattling on about new ways to exploit the energy levels in solids… but I can't actually tell you why every planet in the cosmos doesn't shrink down to the size of a grain of sand."

"Hmm." Ivo tried not to sound too pleased. "I'm glad I wasn't just imagining the problem, but I'd be a lot happier if I knew how to fix it."

"I think we've all missed something," Carla admitted. "The wave model can't be completely wrong, but there must be some detail, some innocent-sounding premise that we rely on without thinking—" She realized belatedly that her gut had started spasming from hunger, the deep muscular twitches sending visible waves across her chest. Ivo politely looked away while she regained control.

The Councilors filed back into the chamber. Carla couldn't read the decision from their faces; Silvano did not look happy, but then neither did Massimo and Prospero.

Giusta spoke on the Council's behalf. "We thank all the witnesses for their testimony, and assure them that we've carefully considered their proposals. The judgment of this Council is that we must develop technology to allow a program of cautious experimentation into the nature and potential uses of orthogonal matter. For the time being, we require all such experiments to be conducted either in the vicinity of the Object or at similar remove in the void, with a strict moratorium on the transport of orthogonal matter into the *Peerless*.

"The only practical means to advance this program known to the Council is Carla's proposal to develop a coherent light source. Accordingly, we ask her to submit a detailed schedule of resources and personnel for approval."

"Congratulations," Ivo whispered.

"Since the other proposals put to us today are all contingent on the same technology," Giusta continued, "we will defer any decision in those cases until Carla's team are able to report on the success or failure of their efforts."

Carla was ecstatic. As the Councilors departed she stood swaying, listening to the good wishes of Ada and Tamara but unable to respond.

The lights of the chamber flared, becoming painfully bright. Carla tried to close her eyes but if she succeeded it made no difference. A voice addressed her from the whiteness. "Are you all right? Carla?" Someone put a hand on her shoulder, shaking her gently.

The lights faded. Tamara's face was in front of her.

"I'm fine," Carla managed. "Things just took me by surprise, that's all."

29

Carlo checked the viewfinder on the infrared recorder; the subject had moved a little off-center, but it remained in sight. Amanda had done her best to confine the lizard without alarming it, leading it with a series of treats into a twig-lined nook in its cage and then inserting a slender branch across the only easy exit. With a mound of freshly killed mites in front of it, discouraged from scampering away but not literally trapped, there was nothing compelling it to respond to the events that followed in anything but a natural manner.

"Ready?" Macaria called from the corridor.

"Ready," Carlo replied.

Macaria dragged herself slowly into the room, three hands on two guide ropes and the fourth holding out a cage. A sufficiently timid passenger could be unsettled by any mode of transport, but Macaria was advancing as smoothly as possible, and the animal had been given a chance to grow accustomed to the process, having been moved from room to room this way every few days for the last two stints.

Carlo started his recorder. Amanda waited for Macaria to clamp the second cage onto the guide rope, less than a stride from the first, then she aimed her own recorder squarely at the new arrival before starting the paper whirring through. There was a clear line of sight between the lizards now; Carlo couldn't swear that his subject's single pair of darting eyes had turned far enough away from its food to take in its distant cousin, but preoccupied or not it could probably smell the other animal. In any case, the infrared channel alone might be enough: Macaria had proposed that the lizards regularly sent out faint kin-group identifiers, too weak and sporadic to show up on her images but enough to initiate a more vigorous exchange once they were detected.

They let the recorders run for six lapses, exposing as much paper as the spools could contain.

"It looked as if they barely noticed each other," Carlo said.

"What were you expecting?" Macaria replied. "This species doesn't show much aggression unless they're jostling for the same scrap of food, and they're not potential mates in any conventional sense."

Carlo began rewinding his spool. "Doesn't it seem strange, though? Sharing notes about the future of your offspring without even looking up from your meal?"

Amanda said, "Were people on the home world ever conscious of the fact that they were exchanging influences?"

"It's hard to say," Carlo admitted. "The history of the subject is so vague."

Amanda mounted her own spool on the bench. "We might still be doing it ourselves. Even without geographical isolation, it's not as if everyone on the *Peerless* mixes daily with everyone else. We can still encounter strangers."

"Hmm." Carlo pondered the unsettling notion that his own children might be *altered* somehow if Carla bumped into a reclusive herb gardener—perhaps lured from his cave by rumors of an unusually well regarded variety show.

The paper from his recorder was still blank so far, apart from the metronomic time codes along the edge; either the exchange had been over when he'd stopped the recorder, or it had never begun. Macaria's original experiments had involved two large groups, but she'd decided to try capturing the time sequence from pairs of individuals, both for the sake of simplicity and to avoid squandering future opportunities. Once two lizards had been exposed to each other the infrared traffic between them was expected to die away, quite possibly for the rest of their lives.

"Ah, here it is!" Carlo's tape was marked now, with a complex series of dark bands. The pattern itself did not look familiar, but the general time scale, revealed in the typical length of each feature, was comparable to that of the internal signals he'd recorded from his own body.

Amanda kept winding until she reached her lizard's contribution. They'd made less effort to keep the second animal confined, so the bands were fainter and the pattern sometimes faded out completely.

Macaria didn't seem to care; she just turned excitedly from spool to spool, giddy at the sheer surfeit of information. "What do they *do* with all this?" she wondered. "If it really does encode a set of traits, they can't just give their offspring every trait that lands on their skin."

Amanda said, "Maybe there's some kind of counting going on. If a trait's being sent out by a majority of the strangers you meet, and they seem to be in good shape, maybe that makes it worth adopting. If all these other animals have used it and thrived, why not take advantage of their experience?"

"That sounds like a great way to kill off your rivals," Carlo suggested. "Live your own life, construct your own body one way, but send out the code for something else entirely. Gang up with your cousins so you all repeat the same lie, pretending you're offering the newcomers the secret to good health when you're really spreading something that will poison their children."

"But then the code won't spread far," Amanda countered. "I mean, the lizards aren't consciously planning any of this. A code that kills rivals might give some benefit to the animals who send it out, but a code for a genuinely useful trait would end up being copied far more widely."

"The way direct inheritance selects useful traits," Macaria said. "Only these ones spread horizontally, ignoring the family tree and leaping between branches that separated before the trait was invented."

"So can an influence make you sick or not?" Carlo wondered. "Is that real or just folklore?" He thought for a while. "What if a code isn't necessarily fatal, but it forces you to send out copies of itself? That would divert resources from other things your body should be doing—so it could certainly weaken you—but so long as you spewed out enough copies in a form that other people would absorb and act on, the code would spread like wildfire."

"Maybe there are both kinds," Amanda conceded. "Good and bad influences, just like the folk belief."

"I always thought bad influences would turn out to be like plant blights," Carlo admitted. "Something solid spreading through the air, not messages encoded in invisible light."

"We haven't actually shown that infrared signals can carry disease," Macaria pointed out.

Amanda said, "So we should find some sick voles and see for ourselves if they're putting out bad influences."

"Voles?" Carlo was confused. "Why change species? We don't know if voles use this kind of signal at all."

"Lizards hardly ever get sick," Macaria explained. "Or if they do, it's impossible to tell."

At the breeding center, Sabina was happy to oblige them. "I've got five families of voles in quarantine. Take your pick."

"Can we take three?" Amanda asked. "We'll bring them all back in a couple of bells."

"Bring them back?" Sabina was confused. "Who's going to want them for a second experiment?"

"We're not going to lay a hand on them," Macaria explained. "We just want to observe them."

They carried three cages back to the workshop, a male and four children in each. Carlo felt sorry for the listless animals, though he'd done much worse to their relatives than disturb a convalescent's rest.

The recordings from all three families were blank. Carlo was ready to give up, but Amanda said, "They've been sitting in quarantine together for days. They've already influenced each other. Why keep sending out the code for no reason?"

Carlo said, "What about us? We're not worth infecting?"

"Maybe the influence doesn't bother trying to cross species," Macaria suggested. "Or maybe it did try early on, when we picked out the cages."

Amanda said, "Load the recorder again. I'll go and get a healthy vole."

She returned a chime later with the bait, almost re-enacting Macaria's entrance for the lizard experiment. These voles had not been bred apart, though; they'd all been raised together until the sick ones were removed, so any signal they exchanged now would not be due to a lack of familiarity.

When Carlo rewound the tape it was covered in dark bands. His skin crawled. This was it, right in front of him: a disease that could leap through the air from victim to victim as infrared light. The voles had merely been weakened, but there was a chance that the very same kind of pattern had pushed his father to the point of death.

"Why not ignore every code?" he asked. "Why would our bodies risk harming themselves?"

"The trade-off must be worth it," Macaria said. "There must be beneficial traits circulating as well. The catch is, how do you know which is which without trying them out?"

Carlo said, "So… some traits we pick up don't get expressed until the next generation. We come across a healthy-looking group of strangers, exchange advice with them in infrared, and try some of it out on our children. If everyone's being honest, there's a good chance that everyone benefits."

"But then the system was hijacked," Macaria conjectured. "Someone sent out a code that acted immediately on the recipient, forcing them to send out copies of itself. And maybe we developed some defenses against that… but it turned out to be advantageous *not* to shut off the process completely. We hijacked the hijacked system, at least enough to make it useful sometimes."

"And all of it by chance." Amanda buzzed softly. "No malice in it, or beneficence. Just accidental success."

Carlo wound the tape back further, looking for the start of the sequence. If he could identify the part of the code that made an animal accept that the whole thing was worth trying, then cut that out and splice it onto instructions to the body to give birth to exactly two children… would that work? No one had ever reported an influence like that, but then, even if such a sequence had come into existence there'd be no reason to expect it to persist. What could be found in nature would be a tiny subset of what was biologically possible.

He reached the start, and examined the innocent-looking stripes. *Do whatever follows*—was it as simple as that? No doubt some voles had learned to ignore this particular directive, but for those who had succumbed it was apparently as hard to resist as the patterns passed down through their own flesh.

Carlo said, "We need to keep studying this process in voles, but their biology is still too distant from our own. We should use them whenever we need a short breeding cycle, but their bodies are so small that the internal signals are always going to be hard to collect."

Amanda said, "Lizards don't grow much larger, and we have even less in common with them."

"I know." Carlo glanced at the vole she'd brought in; it was already looking subdued as its body followed the instructions imposed on it. "We need to scale things up, and move closer on the family tree. We need to go and capture some arborines."

30

"Mirror balls," Tamara told Marzio, unrolling the plans across his desk. "Take a sphere, and cover it with small, planar mirrors. That's it: no fuel to replace, no moving parts, nothing to align or orient. All we need to do is get enough of these in position while the old beacons are still visible, then we can set up the whole grid using nothing but the *Gnat*."

Marzio looked over the sketches. "You do recall that mirrors tarnish faster in the void?"

"We haven't forgotten," Ada replied. "But we'll only be illuminating these things for a tiny fraction of the time they're out there. When they're in use we can limit it to periodic flashes—longer than the old sunstone ignitions, so they're harder to miss, but pulsed, so the total exposure time for the mirrors is less. And when nobody's flying we'll just shut down the beams completely."

"What's more," Tamara added, "if Carla gives us a choice of frequencies we can opt for something at the blue end of the spectrum. That will cut the tarnishing rate even more. If we can get the drift speed low enough, these things could be in service for generations."

"Hmm." Marzio still didn't seem happy. Tamara suspected that he found the new design almost insultingly simple; the old beacons had been triumphs of precision engineering, but now she was asking him to supervise the gluing of reflective shards onto a gross of identical spheres.

"The real challenge will be keeping the beams on target," Tamara reminded him. If the beacons themselves looked like toys, the machinery required to illuminate them would still demand the skills of a master instrument builder. "But we can't make much progress on that until we have a prototype of the light source."

"No." Marzio smoothed the sheet and pointed to the core of the sphere that Tamara had drawn in the dissected view. "The choice of materials here is going to be crucial, if you want the mirrors to survive a couple of generations without air cooling."

"Right." Despite their lack of moving parts, the beacons would gradually gain thermal energy from purely optical effects. But it would be better to give the spheres enough heat capacity to slow their rise in temperature than to add the unwelcome complication of an active cooling system.

Marzio said, "Leave this with me, let me think about it."

Halfway back to the observatory, Ada turned to Tamara. "If you've got time, we should make a detour here. There's someone I'd like you to meet."

Tamara understood her meaning immediately. "You could have warned me," she protested.

"And given you the chance to think up an excuse?" Ada teased her. "You didn't object when my father offered to make enquiries for you. You can't say this has come as a surprise."

"I was only being polite to Pio," Tamara said. "I never thought he'd actually find someone."

"Your father found Tamaro a co-stead, and they're both in prison."

"Tamaro has an entitlement."

"And Livio has an entitlement," Ada replied. "Not all widowers give up and sell them."

"No—the smart ones find widows with entitlements of their own, then they sell the spare one when the children are born." Ada was already leading them down a side corridor; escape was looking increasingly unlikely. "What does this Livio do?"

"Masonry. Construction and repairs. Actually, he was in the crew that built the airlock for the *Gnat*." Ada hesitated, then added jokingly, "So he's hardly a stranger. You already have that connection."

Tamara didn't reply. She and Tamaro had been raised side by side from birth, expecting to remain together to the end. No arrangement of convenience with a co-stead could replace that. Whether or not Tamaro's betrayal proved that she'd been fooling herself all along about the nature of their bond, she would never feel as close to anyone again.

Ada navigated the way to the masonry workshop, far enough from the axis for gravity to keep the dust under control. Tamara was relieved to find that her suitor hadn't contrived to meet her on his own; half a dozen people were busy in the workshop, shaping and polishing blocks of calmstone.

Ada approached one of them, a short, robust-looking man. He shut off his grinding wheel and removed his safety visor.

"Tamara, Livio." At least Ada's introduction was discreet.

"Pleased to meet you," he said.

"Likewise." Tamara faltered. Forewarned, she might have had a chance to think up a suitable topic of conversation, but after Ada's minimal briefing what could she ask this man about? The death of his wife?

Livio said, "It must have been exciting, going out there in the *Gnat*." His enthusiasm seemed genuine, and Tamara was grateful that his opening gambit hadn't been to offer his commiserations on more infamous events.

"It was glorious," she said. "The experience of a lifetime." She glanced at Ada, willing her equally experienced co-navigator to chime in with some anecdote from the journey and take the pressure off her. "I'm hoping to do some more flights soon—but I doubt I'll ever see anything to compare with the first big explosion we raised on the Object. There was so much burning smoke stretching out from the impact site that it was visible from the opposite side."

"I've worked out on the slopes a bit," Livio said. "It's beautiful, just looking down into the stars. But I hope my children get a chance to cross the void. We can't stay cooped up in this rock all the time."

"No." Tamara didn't want to believe that he'd feign these sentiments merely to put her at ease. "It was just dumb luck that I saw the Object first," she admitted. "That's the only reason I ended up on the *Gnat*. But what I'm trying to do now is make travel away from the *Peerless* as easy as possible. Maybe for the next generation, instead of the lotteries it will simply be a birth right: everyone gets to make at least one trip."

Livio chirped approvingly. "I like that idea."

Tamara said, "I should let you get on with your work."

"All right." Livio hesitated. "Can we meet up again? Share a meal, perhaps?"

He didn't suggest a time, knowing she'd have her own schedule for eating. "Tomorrow, around the sixth bell?" Tamara proposed.

"That would be good. You know the food hall, about halfway to the summit from here—?"

"Yes."

"Can we meet there?"

"That would be fine."

"I'll see you then," Livio said. He tipped his head in thanks to Ada, then returned to his workbench.

Tamara was silent most of the way to the observatory. Livio seemed charming, civilized and enlightened. He would send their children out across the void, reveling in the starlight. Even if it was all an act, it was a more appealing performance than Tamaro's endless lectures on her familial obligations.

But she couldn't help feeling a twinge of claustrophobia at the thought of where she was being led. However genuine Livio's virtues might be, the ultimate purpose of their alliance would be the same: one day, they would come together to end her life. This charming man might never coerce her—but she would still be expected to make the choice herself before her co-stead grew too old to raise children, and before any other fate befell her own borrowed flesh.

31

Carla looked up from her desk to see Romolo approaching, dragging himself across the workshop. Shafts of light escaping from the sunstone lamps crisscrossed his path, bright enough to be delineated clearly by the dust in the air, flaring into dazzling patches of radiance as they fell on his skin. She had been told to stay alert for warning signs, defects in her vision that might presage a relapse, but how would she tell? Everyone working in this maze of light was blinded momentarily a dozen times a day.

"I think I might have found something," Romolo said cautiously. He offered her a strip of paper from his spectrograph.

The single dark line standing out against the background was in the far ultraviolet. For an instant Carla came close to panic: if this was the signature of annihilating luxagens, whatever was behind it could kill them all. But the line's position against the calibration marks made its wavelength even shorter than the UV Ivo had recorded on the *Gnat*—and the notion that Romolo might have shaken some dormant cache of negative luxagens out of a lump of clearstone would have been fanciful at any frequency. Sharp, monochromatic UV didn't have to come from the destruction of matter. All it would take would be stimulated emission between two closely spaced energy levels.

Carla freed herself from her harness and followed Romolo back along the guide rope. Across the workshop, five other students were working on their own samples. The ancestors who'd stocked the warehouses of the *Peerless* had made an effort to be comprehensive; more than three gross varieties of tinted clearstone were represented. Under the microscope about half of these had turned out to be variegated, with the hue they presented to the naked eye just a blend of the colors of various inclusions, but the remainder, the apparently pure specimens, would still take years to test.

Romolo's current candidate was a dark green cylinder the size of Carla's thumb, carefully polished so the ends were flat and parallel, held in place between one full mirror and one thin enough to be partially transparent. Making the search even more laborious was the need to try out each sample of clearstone with a dozen different pairs of mirrors. The lowest grades of mirrorstone produced small but measurable alterations in the hue of the light they reflected, but the same effect had the potential to ruin a coherent light source even when it was too small to measure. For now, the only solution was sheer force of numbers, with the hope that random variations among the highest quality mirrors would produce a few that were good enough to allow the device to function.

Romolo had shut off the sunstone lamp before coming to fetch her, but at her urging he lit it again, then quickly pulled the housing closed around the apparatus, leaving most of the lamplight to fall upon the sides of the clearstone. If they really had stumbled on a substance with just the right pattern of energy levels, this light would be pumping luxagens from their natural state in the highest level, down to one from which three separate jumps would take them back to their starting point, completing the cycle.

From the end of the cylinder, a diffuse, wan green disk fell onto the screen at the entrance to the spectrograph. To the naked eye, there was certainly no sign here of a perfectly aligned coherent beam. "Why couldn't it be a longer wavelength?" Romolo lamented.

"Ha! Don't be ungrateful." An invisible light source wouldn't please the navigators, but Carla would accept vindication of the underlying theory in any form. "The spectrum shows a strong, monochromatic signal," she said. "Stronger than the UV of the same frequency in the sunstone's light. So at the very least, you're shifting energy into that line somehow. What we need to check next is the coherence length."

She reached into the cupboard below the bench top and found a suitable double-slitted screen. It was a nuisance not being able to see the results immediately, but Carla mounted the slitted screen and a UV-sensitive camera in the path of the beam.

The image from the camera showed a clear pattern of interference stripes, as expected from any monochromatic light source—even a single hue filtered from the chaotic mixture emitted by a lamp. So long as the tiny difference in travel time that arose when the wave passed through one slit or the other didn't exceed the lifetime of each wave train, the light from the two slits would interfere this way.

"Now, what would clinch it?" Carla waited for Romolo; she hadn't spelt out every possible confirmatory step in the protocol the students were following, but she was sure he could think of something.

"We delay one of the paths," he suggested.

"Yes!"

He took a small rectangular slab of clearstone from the cupboard, its faces polished to optical flatness, and mounted it against the screen so that it covered just one slit. This setup would leave the geometry of the light paths much the same, but the extra travel time through the clearstone would be more than enough to destroy the interference pattern from any ordinary source.

Romolo loaded the camera and made the exposure. When he retrieved the paper, Carla's skin tingled with excitement. The interference pattern was shifted off-center, but the stripes were almost as sharp as before. The wave's oscillations were following a regular sequence of peaks and troughs that persisted for so long that the delay couldn't scramble the smooth variation of phase shifts responsible for the pattern.

"Coherent light," she said. "Invisible or not, the principle's the same. Congratulations!"

Romolo seemed unsure what to make of his achievement. Carla said, "In all of history, no one's seen light like this before."

He managed a self-deprecating chirp. "But do I get to tell my grandchildren that I helped to solve the fuel problem?"

"Maybe. Let's see where this takes us."

Carla gathered the whole team to watch the next test, checking the beam's collimation. A truly parallel beam was impossible, but images of the UV light emerging from the end of the green cylinder showed a disk with no detectable change in size across the entire width of the workshop.

"The wavefront speed of this beam will be tiny!" Patrizia enthused. "Trap some luxagens in the valleys, and we might even have time to watch them jump levels."

Carla said, "Slow down. Anything trapped in these beams will only be confined in one direction. That's not enough to force the luxagen waves to take on discrete energies."

Patrizia hesitated. Romolo said, "Couldn't you use three beams, for the three dimensions?" He gestured with his hand, sketching three orthogonal planes in the air. "Combine three waves, and you can hem the luxagens in on all sides."

"Perhaps," Carla conceded. If the wave trains from all three beams were long enough, the pattern they formed together could persist for a significant time. And as Patrizia had said, the wavefronts themselves would be moving relatively slowly. This weird array of hills and valleys—like the energy landscape of a solid, but floating ethereally in the void—would drift backward through the beams that created it, carrying any cargo they managed to load into it.

Carla set Romolo to work testing all the mirrors in the workshop with the same slab of clearstone. Seeing whether the device still worked after the substitution would finally reveal which of the mirrors were good enough for their purpose—sparing his colleagues years of wasted effort.

At the end of the day she took Patrizia and Romolo aside. "I think the beam trap is an idea worth trying," she said. "If we can arrange things so the majority of the valleys end up containing at most one luxagen, that would be the simplest possible system to study—maybe even simple enough for us to map out a direct connection between its spectrum and its energy levels."

Romolo looked daunted. "How will we know what energy state the luxagens are in to start with? I don't see how we can control that."

"I don't think we can," Carla agreed.

Patrizia said, "Suppose we feed the luxagens in at one end—we don't just scatter them into the valleys everywhere. Then we can sample the light that's emitted at various distances from that starting point, which will tell us what's happening at various times after the luxagens are dropped in. Every transition will take place at a different rate, so at least that should spread things out, making it easier to untangle what's going on."

The three of them worked together, sketching a preliminary design for the apparatus they'd need. The new project would not be simple, but Carla hoped the detour would prove to be worthwhile. Luck had delivered them a coherent light source that nobody could see, but if they could leverage that into a deeper understanding of the rules that dictated the behavior of every solid, they'd have a chance to make the rest of the search far more systematic.

32

Carlo gazed down at the forest canopy, the light from the giant violet flowers beneath him struggling through the murk of dust, loose petals and dead worms.

"Don't panic!" Amanda called up to him. "Once I see where you are, I'll throw you the rope."

"You can't see me? I can see you!" They were both peering through the same detritus—but if the sight of her was easy enough for Carlo to fix against the variegated glow of the treetops, from her point of view he'd be drifting through a formless clutter, back-lit by the ceiling's uniform red moss. Breezes stirred the airborne litter around him, each small gust creating a flurry of petals, and not even the worms remained undisturbed. If she caught a glimpse of him, then glanced away, there'd be nothing to guide her back.

"Ah, I've got you now!" Amanda replied. "Get ready."

Carlo saw her fling the end of the rope up from the canopy. It was a good throw, and she managed the uncoiling well, leaving the hook following an almost straight trajectory as it ascended. He reached out hopefully, but the rope passed half a stride beyond his fingertips as it extended past him. A moment later it was fully uncoiled, and he strained toward it on the chance that it might yet come his way as the hook rebounded, but instead it whipped sideways before folding messily and drifting back toward the thrower.

"Sorry!"

"That was close," Carlo called back encouragingly. He was ascending, though; they'd probably only get one more try. It was not as if he could be stranded here forever, like some fire-watcher lost in the void, but if

Amanda had to come back with a rescue team the humiliation would take years to live down. No adult on the *Peerless*—save the most reclusive farmer, accustomed to living entirely under gravity—would misjudge a leap from a guide rope or a solid wall. But Carlo hadn't been in the forest since he was a boy, and he'd lost the instinctive feel he'd once had for the complicated way a slender tree branch could recoil.

"Hey! I can see an arborine!" He regretted the words as soon as he'd spoken them; this was not the time to offer Amanda distractions. But their quarry was maddeningly close: the female was clinging to the very same branch from which he'd inadvertently launched himself above the forest. She was about his own size and slightly built, but if her physique was not intimidating her behavior was disconcerting. Lizards and voles mostly stared right through him, but this animal was gazing up at him attentively, and she seemed to have had no difficulty spotting him amongst the litter.

"Tell me later," Amanda replied sensibly. She had gathered up the rope again, and now luck had granted them clear sight of each other through the forest's detritus. She tossed the hook directly at him.

Carlo drifted aside as it ascended, but not so far that the rope went out of reach. He seized it before it was taut, then waited anxiously for the forces to be distributed, afraid that the far end might whip itself out of Amanda's grip—or worse, that the struggle to hold on to it might dislodge her from her branch. But she held firm to both the rope and the tree.

Carlo dared fate with a cheer of jubilation. The arborine was still watching him. He wondered if it was worth trying to get a dart into her from his present vantage; all the crud in the air wouldn't help, but he'd never get a clearer shot in the maze of the canopy. He reached into the belted pouch he'd made and retrieved the slingshot, but when he felt around for the darts his fingers instead found a tear in the material. One small item did remain: a sheath from one of the darts. He was lucky he hadn't ended up paralyzed himself.

Amanda saw the slingshot in his hands. "Leave it!" she shouted. "We can come back tomorrow with an expert."

Carlo's pride was wounded, but she was the only one with any darts left. "You're right," he replied. He began dragging himself along the rope, back toward the canopy. He looked around for the arborine, but she had vanished into the forest.

Carlo had expected Lucia's workshop to be full of lizards, but it seemed all her captives went straight to the breeding center. On the walls there were dozens of sketches of the creatures, along with botanical drawings, all keenly observed and skillfully rendered.

Lucia's family had been supplying biologists with animals from the forest for three generations. She'd been a young girl the last time anyone had requested an arborine, but she claimed that her father had let her come with him to watch the procedure. "It's pointless trying to pursue them," she explained. "You might entertain them for days that way, but you'll never catch them. All you can do is pick a good spot and wait."

Carlo couldn't see how that would work. "If they're smart enough to stay ahead of a pursuer, aren't they going to be smart enough to avoid a stationary threat?"

"They won't come close," Lucia replied, "but they won't stay as far away as they need to. They won't go near a net trap—they'll smell it, even if they didn't see you set it. But they don't understand darts; people have only used them a couple of times since the launch, and arborines can't pass knowledge like that on to their children."

Amanda said, "We need a breeding pair, if that's possible. Do you think you can recognize a pair of cos?"

"Not from appearance alone," Lucia said. "But with luck, we'll be able to tell from their behavior."

The three of them met in the forest the next day. After they'd penetrated a short way into the undergrowth, Lucia told the biologists to wait and she clambered up into the trees.

Carlo clung to one of the guide ropes they'd tied between trunks on their last incursion. "We're lucky these species are so long-lived," he said, gesturing toward the tree roots that penetrated the netted soil and found purchase in the rock beneath. "That's never going to happen again without gravity: no seedling is going to establish itself here. And no one's going to give up their farms to make way for a new forest out on the rim."

"You don't believe they're going to free up space from the engine feeds?" Amanda asked.

"Not in our lifetimes."

Amanda looked around, puzzled by something. "The lizards haven't exactly vanished, have they?"

"No." Carlo had seen two or three the day before.

"If the lizard population hasn't crashed," Amanda reasoned, "the arborines shouldn't be starving. But when you look at the surveys of their numbers it's pretty clear that they've mostly switched to biparity."

Nobody had had the patience to try to observe any actual births among the arborines, but Carlo had seen the numbers too, and they were compelling. "Maybe the threshold is set differently for them," he suggested. "They just don't have to be as hungry as we do."

"Maybe." Amanda wasn't convinced. "Or maybe it's the fact that the males are struggling to feed themselves as much as the females."

Carlo buzzed dismissively. "I hate to break the facts of life to a biologist, but it's the female's body that provides all the flesh." Quaint folk tales notwithstanding, even the ancestors had weighed male animals before and after breeding and established that they made no measurable contribution to the blastula.

Amanda ignored the jibe. "Breeding is an exchange of information. The female has certain physical resources at her disposal in creating the offspring, but why wouldn't she also make use of every available fact? Surely the male's state of nutrition says as much about the scarcity of the food supply as the female's own mass?"

Lucia called down to them, "I've found the right place! Come on up!"

When they reached her, Carlo could see what she'd been looking for. They were still below the canopy, but the branches protruded into an open space about six stretches wide. If the arborines were sufficiently curious, there was no reason they wouldn't feel safe watching the intruders from across the gap. Carlo's aim with a slingshot wouldn't pose much of a threat at that distance, but Lucia had brought a dart gun powered by compressed air. It would have been insane to try to carry a bulky machine like that on a long chase through the treetops, but as a stationary weapon it wasn't so impractical.

"Is there any behavior we need to avoid?" Amanda asked. Lucia had made no effort to keep them quiet; they were here to be noticed and attract a few onlookers.

"Don't light fires," Lucia replied. They'd brought no lamps in any case. "And don't do anything ostentatiously belligerent."

"We shouldn't beat each other up?"

"Not if you can help it. There's a risk that might spook them."

They secured their equipment, tied their harnesses to some robust branches and settled in for a long wait.

"Are you hoping to start raising a captive population?" Lucia asked Carlo.

"We'll see how far we get," he replied. "If we manage to collect data from even one fission I'll be happy." He explained his plan to record some of the internal signals during the event.

"And the ultimate goal of this is biparity on demand?" Lucia must have heard rumors about his work—probably as a postscript to the story of his hand.

"That's what I'm hoping for," he admitted.

"Good luck." Lucia sounded skeptical about his chances, but not disapproving. "It would make life easier for most people. But I sold my entitlement when my co died, so I'm going the way of men regardless."

"You never looked for a co-stead?" Amanda asked. The thought of a woman choosing death over childbirth seemed to unsettle her.

"I didn't want to replace Lucio. It didn't feel right." Lucia buzzed and gestured at her body. "Besides, there are compensations: if I'm going to the soil, at least I'm not obliged to be fanatical."

Carlo looked away. No woman could plan her future with certainty, but if the holin failed her the children would all be killed, so it made no sense for her to torture herself. With universal biparity, there'd be no need for a market in entitlements and no need for orphans to be slaughtered.

He felt his gut tightening. If his efforts with this came to nothing—like his work on the crops—would he have emboldened a successor, or just frightened everyone away from the field for another generation? Maybe the whole project had come too late to be of any use to Carla, but the prospect of his daughter trapped in the same cycle was unbearable.

Lucia misread his expression. "Don't worry, it's early yet. You have to expect them to be wary at first, but they'll come gawping at us soon enough."

Carlo hadn't brought a clock, but the forest flowers shone in staggered shifts that still echoed the rhythms of the home world. In the absence of sunlight to tell them when to rest, the plants had settled on a kind of mutual deception, with half of them treating the onset of light from the others as if it were dawn, and the roles exchanged six bells later.

Sunlessness must have been disorienting for the first generation of animals brought into the mountain, and Carlo suspected that their current descendants still weren't entirely at ease in this endless, violet-tinged night. When his own turn to sleep arrived, it did not come easily. The forest air was kept cool enough to make it safe to skip a few nights in a sand bed, and once he closed his eyes being weightless in his harness wasn't all that different from being weightless anywhere else, but even with two companions standing guard it was hard not to feel vulnerable. No wonder the arborines of folklore didn't sleep: a lifetime of wakefulness was easier to imagine than a creature, apparently so much like a person, slumbering contentedly in the treetops.

Halfway through their second day in the forest, Lucia spotted an arborine watching them across the gap. She passed her spyglass to Carlo for a better look. The male was stretched out in front of a clump of brightly glowing yellow flowers, gripping two protruding branches with all four limbs. It was the clearest view Carlo had ever had of an arborine in the flesh. All the sketches he'd studied in his comparative anatomy class had been in old books from the home world, predating any changes adopted by the local population—and the one thing that struck him most now was the uncanny similarity between the hands the creature had formed on its lower limbs and those the travelers themselves made when they were weightless.

"I could shoot him right now," Lucia said, "but if there are others watching you'd probably lose the chance to get his co."

Amanda said, "One male is useless. If we have to make do with a single animal it had better be a female, but I'm happy to wait as long as it takes to get a breeding pair."

The male freed one hand to swat mites from its eyes. Like the female who'd watched Carlo drifting above the canopy, he did not seem agitated or afraid, merely curious.

"How much time do the cos usually spend together?" Carlo asked Lucia.

"From what I've seen, they tend to forage separately, but they do meet up to share food."

"So if this male's co is foraging elsewhere, we'll have no way to identify her?"

"Not if we take him before we've seen them together," Lucia replied.

Carlo handed the spyglass back, unable to suppress a low hum of impatience. He was used to grabbing a cage full of voles from the breeding center, with all the cos bearing matching tags.

"If this turns out to be too difficult," Amanda said, "there is one alternative."

"Really?" Carlo gave her his full attention.

"All the other animals are too small to tolerate the light probes," she said. "But you could always ask for people to volunteer to be recorded in the act."

The three of them took shifts with the spyglass, scrutinizing the arborines that came to watch them. Carlo saw the first male grow bored and disappear, but a second male replaced him a bell or so later. Amanda reported the return of the first male, briefly accompanied by a female, but she saw nothing to prove that the two were cos. Lucia saw nothing at all, but the timing alone suggested an explanation: the arborines weren't going to lose sleep over the intruders.

"At least we can guess now which flower-cycle they're treating as night," Lucia said wearily, preparing to rest herself.

"If we'd been smarter we would have been prepared for this," Amanda suggested. "We should have had full time observers in the forest, people who'd know the whole arborine society inside out."

"That's easy to say with hindsight," Carlo retorted. "But if I was going to rewrite history I'd start with a captive breeding program."

"No one ever managed that on the home world."

"Isn't that what the *Peerless* is for? Anything too difficult for the home world?"

Over the next two days they saw the same four arborines coming and going: two males and two females. Carlo was fairly sure that the second female was the one he'd seen in the canopy. None of them would have been alive when Lucia's father took one of their ancestors, to deliver to an enthusiastic anatomy teacher for dissection. They couldn't know what Carlo was planning for them. But while they were curious enough, and organized enough, to take turns making their own observations, they were also sufficiently wary to ensure that they were never all in harm's way at the same time.

On the sixth day in the forest the expedition ran out of food. Carlo sent Amanda to fetch provisions. He couldn't blame Lucia for their lack of success, but he was beginning to wonder if he'd simply asked for the impossible.

Lucia was asleep when Carlo saw the first male joined in his lookout by the first female. This was not unprecedented, and she rarely stayed for long. Were they cos? Friends? Brother and sister from some quadraparous mating? Carlo swept the mites away from his face. He expected to die without learning the answer.

The female handed the male a dead lizard, and stayed to watch him chew on it.

"Wake up," Carlo called softly to Lucia. She hummed irritably and stirred in her harness. "They're sharing food."

Lucia pulled herself over to Carlo and he handed her the spyglass.

"I can't promise you anything from one incident," she said. "But they probably are cos."

"That will have to be good enough," Carlo decided. "We have to take them."

Lucia returned the spyglass, then scrambled back to the fork in the branches where she'd tied up her equipment. She left the compressed air cylinder where it was and began unreeling the hose with the gun. Her safety rope was beginning to get tangled; Carlo moved to another branch to give her room. "Quickly!" he urged her. The male was almost finished with the lizard. The dart gun had its own small sighting telescope; Carlo watched Lucia take aim, then turned his attention to her targets.

The gun could shoot a dozen darts in rapid succession. Two struck the male in the back; the female barely had time to look around before Lucia planted three in her chest. The arborines' posture slackened, but they clung on to their branches. They might manage to drag themselves a few strides back into the trees before they were completely paralyzed, but once the toxin took full effect they wouldn't be going anywhere for six or seven bells. Carlo considered waiting for Amanda to return before trying to retrieve the animals; the three of them working together would make the job easier.

A slender gray arm reached out from behind a clump of yellow flowers, grabbed the male by a lower wrist and yanked him out of sight.

Carlo was dumbfounded. "Did you see—?" Before he could finish speaking, the paralyzed female had gone the same way.

Lucia said, "It looks as if their friends are trying to hide them. We should—"

Carlo turned to her; she was struggling to untangle her safety rope. "Can you push me across first?" he begged her. She'd spent half her life in the forest, so she'd have no trouble following him unaided, but after his last misjudged leap he didn't trust himself to aim his own body across the gap.

"All right."

Carlo unhitched his own rope from the tree, tucked its coils into his harness, then crawled onto the branch in front of her. She took his lower hands in her upper pair, and they both bent their elbows, making a catapult of their arms. Carlo hadn't done this with anyone since childhood, playing with Carla in some ancient weightless stairwell.

Lucia gripped the branch tightly with her lower hands, sighted their quarry and maneuvered Carlo's body into alignment. They unlinked their fingers, leaving their hands flat, palm against palm.

"Now!" she said. Carlo pushed against her and she reciprocated, propelling him away from the tree.

His progress through the air felt painfully slow. Flurries of dead petals swirled out of his path; even inanimate matter could outrace him. But as he drew closer to the far side of the gap the onrushing branches began to look threatening. He reached out and grabbed them, twigs scraping his palms and his shoulder muscles jarring as he brought himself to an ungainly halt.

Carlo looked around to orient himself. He was clinging to a pair of jutting branches, and he recognized the yellow flowers in front of him; Lucia had sent him to exactly the right spot. He could see her preparing to launch herself, but he decided not to wait for her; there were twigs rebounding just a stretch or so ahead of him, and if he delayed giving chase he risked losing the trail. The arborines were agile, but their paralyzed companions would make unwieldy cargo. If he could pursue them closely enough to put them in fear of ending up in the same condition then they'd have no choice but to abandon their friends.

Carlo dragged himself toward the retreating animals, moving as fast as he could, dislodging whole bright blossoms and snapping small twigs as he advanced. The tree's less yielding parts pummeled and lacerated him in revenge, but he persisted. It didn't take long for him to lose all sense of his location, but he kept catching glimpses of the arborines, near-silhouettes against the floral light, deftly pushing branches aside and swinging their passengers this way and that to spare them the kind of punishment Carlo was receiving. Their gracefulness was as humbling as it was infuriating, impossible not to admire even as it mocked his own brutish efforts. If the animals had been unencumbered he would not have had the slightest chance of staying close to them, and as it was they were going to make him suffer.

"Carlo!" Lucia wasn't far behind him.

"I still have them in sight," he called back to her. "Just follow me!"

"Take it easy, or you'll make yourself sick," she warned him. "You haven't been in a proper bed for days."

The arborines hadn't been in a bed, ever, but their smaller size made air cooling more effective. Then again, they were carrying twice their usual mass—and it was his ancestors who'd developed a way to store heat and discharge it later, letting them grow larger than their air-cooled cousins. The question was, had he already saturated that heat store?

Carlo pushed on, maintaining his pace, sure the gap was narrowing.

He couldn't tell how much of the stinging sensation in his skin was due to hyperthermia and how much to the thrashing he was getting from the obstacles in his path, but the arborines had to be tiring too.

He forced his way through a tangle of vines sprouting brilliant green flowers and almost collided with the paralyzed male, drifting alone between the branches. Carlo chirped in triumph. They'd made a hard choice and abandoned one friend, but the female they were still carrying was larger. And though they'd lightened their collective load, he couldn't see it being much help to them: trying to share the burden as they moved through this painfully narrow labyrinth would only complicate the task.

"Lucia!" he called out. "They've left the male! Can you watch him? I'm going on." He would not have put it past the arborines for one of them to double back and spirit the male away if he was left unattended.

"All right," Lucia replied reluctantly.

Carlo couldn't see his quarry. He waited, surveying the luminous forest around him, ignoring the mites that were starting to insinuate themselves into his broken skin. Then he caught the tell-tale twitch of a branch in the distance, and set off in pursuit once more.

The arborines had changed direction. Carlo had been more or less lost from the start, but at least he'd recognized when he'd been traveling from the outer tips of branches in toward the trunk. Now he was being led in some kind of arc, or possibly a helix, crossing from branch to branch around the axis of the tree.

It was exhausting work, propelling himself across these treacherous gaps full of fine twigs that scraped against him—sometimes snapping, sometimes rebounding, deflecting him unpredictably. But it had to be less punishing than penetrating deeper into the thicket of branches. His skin tingled, no doubt from trapped heat as much as every other insult, but whatever failures he might yet be forced to swallow he was not going to abandon this chase out of sheer lack of stamina.

Carlo could see the three arborines clearly now, framed between thick branches bearing radiant blue flowers. The ambulatory female gripped the paralyzed one with her right hands, while the male kept pace beside them, offering occasional nudges whose purpose and efficacy were hard to judge. The darkness behind them was tinged with the red moss-light of the cavern's ceiling. They were heading straight for the canopy, Carlo realized. The female had seen him stranded there; she knew that if they leaped through the air to another tree he'd either be afraid to follow them, or his aim would be so bad that he'd never catch up with them.

Carlo quickened his pace, pushing off harder from each branch, trying to maintain momentum, fighting a powerful urge to be more cautious. Weightless or not, now that he had it fixed in his mind that he was moving *vertically* the idea had become imbued with a sense of danger. He had never been in a forest under gravity, but perhaps he'd inherited instincts attuned to his deep ancestors' life in the trees—or attuned to the time when they'd begun to abandon them. A strong aversion to arboreal heights might have kept his forebears from dashing their skulls against the ground once they'd lost their cousins' more graceful anatomy. But he couldn't let his cousins win this race, least of all out of some misguided fear of falling. He shut out the warnings and kept climbing.

More and more moss-light was penetrating the canopy, but Carlo had the arborines fixed in his sight, and he could see that he was gaining on them. Their coordination as they swung between the branches was a marvel, and the male seemed to have taken on a kind of shock-absorbing role—pushing back on the paralyzed female when she threatened to tear herself out of her friend's grip through sheer momentum—but all this heroic effort had a cost. They were flagging. They were not going to escape.

The male leaped off to one side, shrieking noisily, as if he imagined he could serve as a decoy. Carlo ignored him and forced himself onward; his own strength was dwindling rapidly, but he was sure he still had the edge. All he needed to do now was scare off the female, then he could rest for a few lapses and think through the logistics of joining up with Lucia and extracting their two specimens from the forest.

The female halted, clinging to a branch just a stretch or so ahead of him. Carlo stopped too, waiting for his adversary to flee, but instead she turned and defiantly wrapped three arms around her insensate friend.

Carlo swung onto a closer branch. The female glared at him balefully, her eyes glinting violet. Surely she was intelligent enough to understand that she risked paralysis herself? He opened his slingshot pouch and checked the contents; despite everything it had been through, the sturdier version Lucia had given him hadn't spilt any darts.

As he took out the slingshot he caught a blur of motion in his rear gaze, but before he could react there were arms encircling his chest, a hand tugging on the slingshot, a fist pounding his tympanum and teeth buried in the side of his neck. The worst pain by far was in his tympanum; he stiffened the membrane and managed to seize hold of the offending fist. The male tried to pull free, without success, then redirected all his effort into his jaws.

Carlo retained just enough presence of mind not to start cursing aloud. His upper hands were already fully occupied and his lower hands couldn't reach the jaw clamped to his neck. There was an urgent, combative tension keeping his whole body rigid, and his first attempts to change his form faltered from the sense that any relaxation would mean surrender. He kept trying. Finally his lower limbs softened, and he extruded enough flesh into them to let them stretch up to the arborine's mouth. He forced his fingers between the creature's teeth, hardening his fingertips into wedges, and tried to prise the jaws apart.

Gradually the arborine yielded, but while Carlo was focused on that battle the thing pulled the slingshot out of his hand and tossed it away. Carlo quickly plunged his hand into the pouch again and got hold of a dart; with a flick of the thumb he unsheathed it. The arborine grabbed his wrist and refused to let him take his hand from the pouch.

Carlo's skin was feverish, but the animal's flesh against him felt hotter. The scent of it was overpowering, but horribly familiar: it reminded him of the smell of his father before he'd died. He still had his hands in the arborine's jaws; he pulled them further apart and twisted the head back sharply. This felt satisfying, but however much pain he was inflicting it didn't weaken the arborine's grip on him.

Carlo tried to extrude a fifth limb, but nothing happened. He let go of the fist that he'd stayed from battering his tympanum, sharpened the fingertips of his newly freed hand and plunged them into the arborine's forearm just above the pouch. He felt the muscles below twitch and slacken; he'd disrupted some of the motor pathways.

The arborine appeared confused; it didn't bother resuming its assault on Carlo's tympanum, but before it could make up its mind what to do Carlo tore his hand free from the pouch and plunged the dart into the arborine's shoulder. He felt the body grow limp immediately, but he still had to prise the lower arms from around his chest and shake the thing off him.

The females were gone.

Carlo looked around; his slingshot was caught on a branch nearby. He dragged himself over and grabbed it, then set off toward the canopy as fast as he could.

As he ascended, the light from the flowers above him thinned and faded and was gone. Suddenly he was in open air, in the murk again, with nothing but the forest's decaying litter between him and the cavern's red ceiling. He searched for the females, hoping the one who'd carried her friend so far might have needed one last rest before launching the pair to safety, but then he saw them. They were in the air, a couple of stretches away, drifting straight toward the safety of a neighboring tree.

Carlo loaded his slingshot, took aim and released the dart. A breeze stirred the dust and obscured his view, but when he had clear sight again the projectile was nowhere to be seen.

He tried again. His second dart sliced through the detritus and miraculously struck flesh—but he'd hit the female that Lucia had already paralyzed.

"No, no, no!" he pleaded. The arborines vanished into the murk; he waited helplessly, and when they appeared again they'd almost reached their sanctuary. Carlo reloaded and released, reloaded and released, aiming through the grit and swirling dead petals by memory and extrapolation until a single dart remained.

He couldn't bring himself to use the last one blindly. He waited for the air to clear. Lucia knew the forest better than anyone living, but she'd been a child the last time an arborine had been captured. There were no experts at this. How many people would he need to beg from Tosco in order to succeed at this task by force of numbers alone?

He finally caught sight of the arborines, silhouetted against the light of the adjacent tree. They had separated; their outlines were distinct. Carlo waited for his indefatigable nemesis to reach out and drag her friend to safety, but both animals remained motionless. She wasn't just weary. He had hit her.

They hadn't drifted far in among the branches, but they'd be within reach of any determined allies. If he descended to the floor of the cavern, crossed through the undergrowth and climbed up the neighboring tree, there'd be no guarantee that the arborines would still be waiting for him.

Carlo looked up toward the ceiling, wondering if he should go back and fetch Lucia. But even that might take too long.

He dragged himself out along the branch he was holding, then grabbed another one and pulled the two together to the test the way they flexed. They were loose and springy; maybe an arborine could judge exactly how they'd recoil, but the task was beyond him.

Then again, if he aimed low he might face a long climb to his target, but he probably wouldn't find himself stranded.

Carlo glanced down at his torn skin. He'd come too far to give up on the chase now. He crawled to the end of the swaying branch, holding it only with his lower hands, then pushed himself away into the air.

33

"We've hit a dead end," Romolo confessed. "Just when the Rule of Two was starting to look plausible, we checked it against the second set of spectra and it fell apart."

Carla glanced at Patrizia, but she appeared equally dispirited. They had been toiling over the spectra from the optical solid for more than a stint, but the last time they'd reported to her they had seemed to be close to a breakthrough.

"Don't give up now!" Carla urged them. "It's almost making sense." She had hoped that the problem would yield to a mixture of focus, persistence and brute-force arithmetic—and it was easier to free her two best students from other commitments than to achieve that state herself. Someone had to supervise the experiments the Council had actually approved.

"Making sense?" Patrizia hummed softly and pressed a fist into her gut, giving Carla a pang of empathetic hunger. When things were going well there was no better distraction than work, but the frustration of reaching an impasse had the opposite effect.

"Why should the Rule of Two depend on the polarization of the beams?" Romolo demanded.

"And why the Rule of Two in the first place?" Patrizia added. "Why not the Rule of Three, or the Rule of One?"

Carla tried to take a step back from the problem. "The first set of spectra *does* make sense if every energy level can only hold two luxagens. Right?"

"Yes," Romolo agreed. "But why? Once they're this close together, luxagens simply attract each other. So how does a pair of luxagens get the power to push any newcomers away?"

"I don't know," Carla admitted. "But it would solve Ivo's stability problem." If each energy level could hold at most two luxagens, then beyond a certain point it would be impossible to squeeze more of the particles into each energy valley. That would be enough to prevent every world in the cosmos from collapsing down to the size of a dust grain.

Patrizia said, "For the first set of spectra, we made the field in the optical solid as simple as possible—using light polarized in the direction of travel for all three beams. With that kind of field, each luxagen's energy only depends on its position in the valley. For the second set, we changed the polarization of one of the beams, so the luxagen's energy depends on the way it's moving as well as its position. But the strangest thing is that it looks as if there are more energy levels than there are solutions to the wave equation!"

Carla said, "I don't see how that's possible." Two solutions—two different shapes for the luxagen wave—might turn out to have the same energy, but the converse was nonsensical. The luxagen's energy couldn't change without changing the shape of its wave.

Patrizia pulled a roll of paper from a pocket and spread it across Carla's desk. The depth of the valleys in the optical solid had been chosen to ensure that they only had ten energy levels—limiting the possible transitions between them to a manageable number. But the data showed clearly that when one of the three beams was polarized so its field pointed at right angles to the direction of the light, the spectra split into so many lines that it took more than ten levels to explain them all.

"What if the luxagen has its own polarization?" Carla suggested. She'd ignored that possibility when first deriving the wave equation, largely for the sake of simplicity. "Depending on the precise geometry of the light field, the *luxagen's* polarization could start affecting the energy—adding new levels."

"Then it's a shame we didn't find a Rule of Three!" Romolo replied. "We could have said that the *true* rule was the Rule of One: in every valley, you can have at most one luxagen with a given energy *and* a given polarization. The Rule of Three would only hold for the simplest fields—where you couldn't tell that the three luxagens were different, because their polarization had no effect on their energy."

Patrizia turned to him. "But what if luxagens could only have two polarizations?"

Romolo was bemused. "Isn't that like asking for space to have one less dimension?"

Carla wasn't so sure; it could be subtler than that. She said, "Let's make a list. If we've been working from false assumptions, what exactly would we need to have been wrong about in order to make things right?"

Patrizia warmed to the idea. "Luxagens have no polarization—wrong! Polarizations only come in threes—wrong! Any number of luxagens can share the same state—wrong again! I think that would cover it."

Carla said, "The first one's just an empirical question, but the second one's going to take some thought." She glanced at the clock on the wall; she'd told Carlo she'd meet him in his apartment by the sixth bell, but he knew better than to expect her to be on time. "Why do we assume that polarizations come in threes? For light, you have two vectors in four-space: the direction of the light field itself, and the direction of the light's future. If I see a bit of light over here, and you see a bit of light over there, then I ought to be able to grab the two vectors that describe my light and rotate them together in four-space so they agree with those describing your light. That's the absolute core of rotational physics: if we couldn't do that, your light and my light wouldn't deserve to be called by the same name."

Patrizia said, "If the vectors are constrained to be perpendicular, they'll look perpendicular to everyone. Fix the direction of the light's history through four-space, and that leaves you with three perpendicular choices for the field—three polarizations."

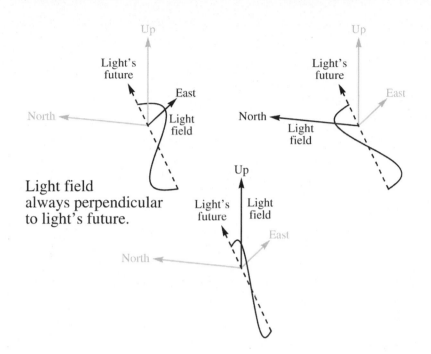

Light field always perpendicular to light's future.

"You can imagine a case where they're parallel instead," she added. "Everyone would agree on that too. But you could never rotate one kind of light into the other, so there'd be no reason to classify them as the same thing at all."

"So what are the choices?" Romolo said. "Light has three polarizations, but the alternative where the vectors are parallel only has one."

"A luxagen wave takes complex values," Carla reminded him. "So it has a kind of two-dimensional character to it already, if you think of real and imaginary numbers as pointing in perpendicular directions. But that doesn't double the possibilities for polarization. You can rotate a luxagen wave by any angle at all in the complex plane without changing the physical state it describes."

"So it *halves* the possibilities," Patrizia said. "A complex wave looks two dimensional, but it really only has one dimension."

"Half four is two," Romolo noted. "Half the size of an ordinary four-vector gives us the number of polarizations we're seeing. Does that help?"

Carla wasn't sure, but it was worth checking. "Suppose a luxagen wave consists of *two* complex numbers, for the two polarizations," she said.

"Each one has a real part and an imaginary part, so all in all that's four dimensions."

"So you just think of the usual four dimensions as two complex planes?" Romolo suggested.

"Maybe," Carla replied. "But what happens when you rotate something? If you've got two complex numbers that describe a luxagen's polarization, and I come along and physically turn that luxagen upside-down… what happens to the complex numbers?"

Romolo said, "Wouldn't you just take their real and imaginary parts, and apply the usual rules for rotating a vector?"

"That's the logical thing to try," Carla agreed. "So let's see if we can make it work."

The simplest way to describe rotations in four-space was with vector multiplication and division, so Carla brought the tables onto her chest as a reminder.

Vector multiplication table

×	*East*	*North*	*Up*	*Future*
East	Past	Up	South	East
North	Down	Past	East	North
Up	North	West	Past	Up
Future	East	North	Up	Future

Vector division table

÷	*East*	*North*	*Up*	*Future*
East	Future	Down	North	East
North	Up	Future	West	North
Up	South	East	Future	Up
Future	West	South	Down	Future

Any rotation could be achieved by multiplying on the left with one vector and dividing on the right by another; the choice of those two vectors determined the overall rotation. Romolo worked through an example, choosing Up for both operations.

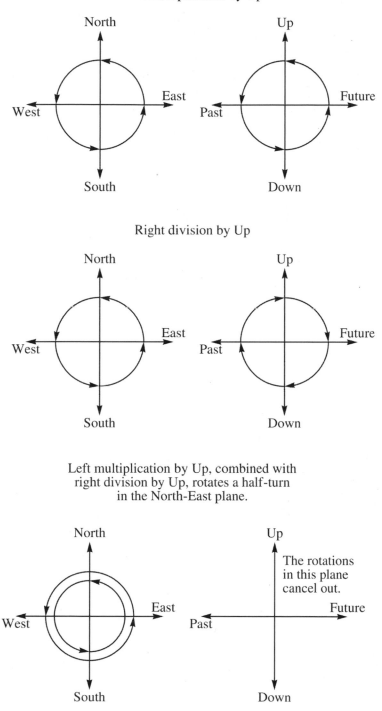

Left multiplication by Up

Right division by Up

Left multiplication by Up, combined with
right division by Up, rotates a half-turn
in the North-East plane.

The rotations
in this plane
cancel out.

"There's one thing we'll need to get right if we're going to make this work," Carla realized. "Given a pair of complex numbers, if you multiply them both by the square root of minus one that will affect each number separately. It doesn't mix them up in any way—it just rotates each complex plane by a quarter-turn, making real numbers imaginary and imaginary numbers real. So if we're going to treat two planes in four-space as complex number planes, we'll need some equivalent operation."

"But I just drew that!" Romolo replied. "Multiplication on the left by Up rotates everything in the Future-Up plane by a quarter turn, and everything in the North-East plane by a quarter turn. Vectors in one plane aren't moved to the other. Do it twice—square it—and you get a half turn in both planes, which multiplies everything by minus one. So we could treat those two planes as the two complex numbers, and use left-multiplication by Up as the square root of minus one!"

Carla wasn't satisfied yet. "All right, that works perfectly on its own. But what happens when you physically rotate the luxagen as well? If I rotate an ordinary vector and then double it, or double it first and then rotate it, the end result has to be the same, right?"

"Of course." Romolo was puzzled, but then he saw what she was getting at. "So whatever we use to multiply by the square root of minus one has to give the same result whether we rotate first and then multiply, or vice versa."

"Exactly."

Patrizia looked dubious. "I don't think that's going to be possible," she said. "What about the rotation you get by multiplying on the left with East and dividing on the right by Future? Future acts like one, it has no effect, so you get:"

$$\text{Rotated vector} \quad = \quad \text{East} \times \text{Old vector} \div \text{Future}$$
$$= \quad \text{East} \times \text{Old vector}$$

"Romolo's definition of multiplying by the square root of minus one is:"

$$\sqrt{-1} \text{ vector} \quad = \quad \text{Up} \times \text{Old vector}$$

"Follow that with the rotation:"

$$\text{Rotated } \sqrt{-1} \text{ vector} \quad = \quad \text{East} \times \text{Up} \times \text{Old vector}$$
$$= \quad \text{South} \times \text{Old vector}$$

"But now do the rotation first, and then multiply by the square root of minus one:"

$$\sqrt{-1} \text{ Rotated vector} \quad = \quad \text{Up} \times \text{East} \times \text{Old vector}$$
$$= \quad \text{North} \times \text{Old vector}$$

"The end result depends on the order," Patrizia concluded. "Since you can't reverse the order when you multiply two vectors together, that's always going to show up here and spoil things."

She was right. There were other choices besides Romolo's for the square root of minus one, but they all had similar problems. You could multiply on the left or on the right by Up or Down, East or West, North or South; they would all produce quarter turns in two distinct planes. But in every single case, you could find a rotation that wrecked the scheme.

Romolo took the defeat with good humor. "Two plus two equals four, but all nature cares about is non-commutative multiplication."

Patrizia smoothed the calculations off her chest, but Carla could see her turning something over in her mind. "What if the luxagen wave follows a different rule?" she suggested. "It's still a pair of complex numbers, and you can still join them together to make something four-dimensional—but when you rotate the luxagen, that four-dimensional object doesn't change the way a vector does."

"What law would it follow, then?" Carla asked.

"Suppose we choose *right*-multiplication by Up as the square root of minus one," Patrizia replied. "Then multiplying on the *left* will always commute with that: it makes no difference which one you do first."

"Sure," Carla agreed. "But what's your law of rotation?"

"Multiplying on the left, nothing more," Patrizia said. "Whenever an ordinary vector gets rotated by being multiplied on the left and divided on the right, this new thing—call it a 'leftor'—only gets the first operation. Forget about dividing it." She scrawled two equations on her chest:

| Rotated vector | = | Left vector × Old vector ÷ Right vector |
| Rotated leftor | = | Left vector × Old leftor |

Carla was uneasy. "So you only use half the description of the rotation? The rest is thrown away?"

"Why not?" Patrizia challenged her. "Doesn't it leave you free to multiply on the right—letting the square root of minus one commute with the rotation?"

Rotated leftor	=	Left vector × Old leftor
$\sqrt{-1}$ leftor	=	Old leftor × Up
Rotated $\sqrt{-1}$ leftor	=	Left vector × Old leftor × Up
$\sqrt{-1}$ Rotated leftor	=	Left vector × Old leftor × Up

"Yes, but that's not the only thing that has to work!" Carla could hear the impatience in her voice; she forced herself to be calm. She was ravenous, and she was late to meet Carlo—but she couldn't eat until morning anyway, and if she cut this short now she'd only resent it.

"What else has to work?" Romolo asked.

Carla thought for a while. "Suppose you perform two rotations in succession," she said. "Patrizia's rule tells you how this new kind of object changes with each rotation. But then, what if you combine the two rotations into a single operation—one rotation with the same overall effect. Do the rules still match up, every step of the way?"

Patrizia said, "However many rotations you perform, you just end up multiplying all of their left vectors together. Whether it's for a vector or a leftor, you're combining them in exactly the same way!"

That argument sounded impeccable, but Carla still couldn't accept it; throwing out the right vector had to have *some* effect. "Ah. What if you do two half-turns in the same plane?"

"You get a full turn, of course," Patrizia replied. "Which has no effect at all."

"But not from your rule!" Carla wrote the equations for each step, obtaining a half-turn in the North-East plane by multiplying on the left by Up and dividing by Up on the right.

First rotated vector	=	Up × Old vector ÷ Up
Second rotated vector	=	Up × Up × Old vector ÷ Up ÷ Up
	=	Past × Old vector ÷ Past
	=	(−Future) × Old vector ÷ (−Future)
	=	Future × Old vector ÷ Future
	=	Old vector
First rotated leftor	=	Up × Old leftor
Second rotated leftor	=	Up × Up × Old leftor
	=	Past × Old leftor
	=	(−Future) × Old leftor
	=	Future × (− Old leftor)
	=	− Old leftor

Patrizia kept rereading the calculation, as if hoping she might spot some flaw in it. Finally she said, "You're right—but it makes no difference. Didn't you tell us a lapse or two ago that rotating a luxagen wave in the complex plane has no effect on the physics?"

"Yes." Carla looked down at her final result again. Two half-turns left a vector unchanged; two half-turns left a leftor multiplied by minus one. But the probabilities that could be extracted from a luxagen wave involved *the square of the absolute value* of some component of the wave. Multiplying the entire wave by minus one wouldn't change any of those probabilities.

Romolo said, "So when you rotate this system all the way back to its starting point, the wave changes sign. But we can't actually measure that... so it doesn't matter?"

"It's strange," Carla agreed. "But what troubles me more is treating the rotation's left vector differently from the right. All it takes to swap the role of those two vectors is to view the system in a mirror. Should physics look different, viewed in a mirror? Have we seen any evidence of that?"

Patrizia took the criticism seriously. "What if we tried to balance it, then? Could we throw in a 'rightor' as well as a leftor, for symmetry's sake?" She wrote the transformation rule for this new geometrical object, a mirror image of her previous invention.

$$\text{Rotated vector} \quad = \quad \text{Left vector} \times \text{Old vector} \div \text{Right vector}$$
$$\text{Rotated rightor} \quad = \quad \text{Right vector} \times \text{Old rightor}$$

"Throw it in where?" Romolo asked.

"Into the luxagen wave," Patrizia replied. "Two more complex numbers, but these ones transform by the rightor rule. If you look at the system in a mirror, the leftor and rightor change places."

"That sounds very elegant," Romolo said, "but haven't you just doubled the number of polarizations from two to four?"

"Hmm." Patrizia grimaced. "That would defeat the whole point."

Carla pondered the new proposal. "The light field is a four-dimensional vector—but we don't get four polarizations, because of the relationship between the field vector and the energy-momentum vector. What if there's a relationship between the luxagen field—the leftor and the rightor—and the luxagen's energy-momentum vector? Something that brings the number of polarizations back down to two."

Romolo said, "What kind of relationship? Setting a leftor or a rightor perpendicular to an ordinary vector won't work—when you rotate all three of them, they'll change in different ways, so the relationship won't be maintained."

"That's true," Patrizia conceded. She drove her fist into her gut; the glorious distraction was losing its power again. "Maybe we should tear this up and start again."

Carla said, "No. The relationship's simple."

She wrote:

$$\text{Vector} \quad = \quad \text{Leftor} \div \text{Rightor}$$

"That's it," she said. "Just look at how these three things transform when we rotate them."

$$\text{Rotated leftor} \quad = \quad \text{Left vector} \times \text{Old leftor}$$
$$\text{Rotated rightor} \quad = \quad \text{Right vector} \times \text{Old rightor}$$
$$\text{Rotated leftor} \div \text{Rotated rightor} =$$
$$\text{Left vector} \times (\text{Old leftor} \div \text{Old rightor}) \div \text{Right vector}$$

"A leftor divided by a rightor changes in exactly the same way as an ordinary vector. So if we demand that the energy-momentum vector of a luxagen wave is proportional to the wave's leftor divided by its rightor, rotation won't break the relationship—and any free luxagen wave that meets this condition could be rotated into agreement with any other."

Romolo said, "And the rightor is completely fixed by the leftor and the energy-momentum vector. There are no extra polarizations."

Patrizia looked dazed. She said, "Follow the geometry and everything falls into place." She exchanged a glance with Carla; this was not the first time they'd seen it happen, but the sheer power of the approach was indisputable now. "Two polarizations, to fit the Rule of Two. But what do they mean, physically?"

Carla said, "Let's work with a stationary luxagen, to keep things simple. Then its energy-momentum vector points straight into our future. Suppose the luxagen field has a leftor of Up; its rightor will be the same, because Up divided by Up is Future.

"Suppose we rotate this luxagen in the horizontal plane: the North-East plane. Any such rotation will come from multiplying on the left and dividing on the right by a vector in the Future-Up plane—which will move our leftor and rightor from Up to some new position in the Future-Up plane. But the Future-Up plane is one we're treating as a single complex number, so if the luxagen field *remains* within that plane, it hasn't really undergone any physical change. And if you can rotate a luxagen in the horizontal plane without changing it, it must be vertically polarized."

"So how do the same rotations affect the other polarization?" Patrizia wondered. "Pick any leftor in the other complex plane: the North-East plane. Say we choose North. If you multiply North on the left by a vector in the Future-Up plane, the result still lies in the North-East plane. So again, rotating the luxagen in the horizontal plane won't change anything."

"*Two* vertical polarizations?" Romolo hummed softly in confusion, but then he tried to work through the contradiction. "It's meaningless to talk about two vertical polarizations of light—'up' as opposed to 'down'—because the wave changes sign as it oscillates; if the light field points up at one instant it will point down a moment later. But when a *leftor* is multiplied by a complex number that oscillates over time, that oscillation will never move it from one complex plane to the other. So these two vertical polarizations really are separate possibilities."

Effect of luxagen wave's oscillations over time

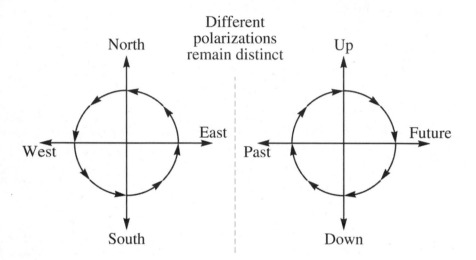

"But how could we turn one polarization into the other?" Carla pressed him. "Say, turn a leftor of North into a leftor of Up?"

"East times North is Up," Romolo replied. "That's the leftor, getting a quarter-turn. But the rotation of *vectors* that involves left-multiplication by East is a *half-turn* in the North-Up plane—which exchanges Up and Down. So when you flip a luxagen upside down, you swap the two vertical polarizations. That means they really do deserve to be called 'up' and 'down': the whole Future-Up plane for leftors describes a vertical polarization of 'up', and the whole North-East plane describes a vertical polarization of 'down.'" He sketched the details, to satisfy himself that the rotation really did swap the planes as he'd claimed.

Effect *on leftors* of a rotation
that swaps Up and Down *as vectors*

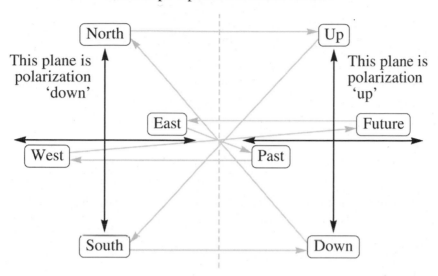

Patrizia said, "So the luxagen has a kind of axis in space that you can distinguish from its opposite. Like the two ways an object can spin around the same axis."

Carla had been struggling to think of a suitable analogy herself, but Patrizia's choice was weirdly evocative. "We should see if the new wave equation conserves the direction of this axis—if it really does stay fixed like the axis of a gyroscope."

She converted the relationship between the field's leftor and rightor and the energy-momentum vector into a more traditional form, where the energy and momentum came from the rates of change of the wave in time and in space. From there, they could work out the rate of change of the polarization axis—and it wasn't necessarily zero. For some luxagen waves, the axis would shift over time.

"So it's not like a gyroscope," Patrizia said.

"Hmm." Carla puzzled over the results. "The axis of a rotating object won't always stay fixed. If the object is in motion—like a planet orbiting a star—and there's some mechanism that allows angular momentum to flow back and forth between orbital motion and spin, you wouldn't expect either one to be conserved individually. Only the *total* angular momentum will stay the same."

Patrizia said warily, "So if we give the luxagen some angular momentum in its own right—as if it really were spinning around its polarization axis—then any change in *that* should be balanced by an equal and opposite change in orbital angular momentum?"

"Yes. If the analogy really does hold up that far." Carla was exhausted, but she couldn't leave the idea untested. As she ploughed on through the calculations she kept making small, stupid mistakes, but Romolo soon lost his shyness about correcting her.

The final result showed that the luxagen's orbital angular momentum would not be conserved on its own. But by attributing half a unit of angular momentum to the luxagen itself—fixing the amount, but allowing its direction to vary with the polarization axis—the rate of change of the two combined came out to zero, and total angular momentum was conserved.

Patrizia's chirp was half disbelief, half delight. "What would Nereo say? First his particles have spread out into waves, and now they're spinning at the same time."

Romolo gazed down at the spectra he'd brought. "So when we arrange the light field in the optical solid so the luxagen's energy depends on its motion… it makes sense that it also depends on its *spin*." The mystery that had spurred the night's calculations had all but yielded. He looked up at Carla. "We can quantify the way the energy depends on the spin now, can't we? The new wave equation will let us do that!"

Carla said, "Tomorrow."

The three of them left the office together. The corridors of the precinct were empty, the rooms they passed dimmed to moss-light. "Your cos don't mind how late you work?" Carla inquired.

"I moved out a few stints ago," Patrizia said. "It's easier."

"I'll probably do the same," Romolo decided. "I don't want to end up with children in the middle of this project!" He spoke without a trace of self-consciousness, but then added, "My co's not ready either. We'll both be happier without the risk."

They parted, and Carla made her way up the axis to Carlo's apartment. He was still awake, waiting for her in the front room.

"You're looking better," she said, gesturing to him to turn around so she could check that he wasn't just relocating his wounds.

"I'm fine now," Carlo assured her.

"So have the arborines bred yet?" Carla found the new project grotesque, but she didn't want his ordeal in the forest to have been for nothing.

"Give them time."

"How's the influence peddling?" she asked.

"Some progress," Carlo said cautiously. "We've managed to get tapes from a few people with infectious conditions—and they're definitely putting out infrared."

"And you let that tainted light fall on your own skin?"

"We make the recordings from behind a screen," Carlo assured her. "We're as careful as we can be. But these things are probably all over the mountain; I'm sure you've been exposed to all the same influences without even knowing it."

"And now you need a volunteer who'll let you play these tapes back to them, to see if they catch the disease?" It sounded like one of the tales from the sagas, where tracing the words of a forbidden poem on someone's skin could strike them dead.

"We're still working on the player," he said. "But that would be the next step."

Carlo extinguished the lamp and they moved into the bedroom. "You're not skipping meals again, are you?" he asked sternly.

"No!" Carla helped him straighten the tarpaulin. "I'll wait a few more stints, to be sure I'm having no more problems with my vision." He didn't reply, but she could see that he wasn't happy. "It has to be done," she said. "I'll take it more slowly this time, but I can't put it off forever."

Carlo said, "I want you to wait another year before you risk your sight again. Wait and see what your choices are."

"Another year?" Carla drew herself into the bed and lay in the resin-coated sand. He really thought he had a chance to compose his magic light poem by then, to spare her from Silvana's fate? "But what if something happens first?" She looked up at him in the moss-light. "Before I'm ready?"

Carlo reached across her and pulled an object out of a storage nook on her side of the bed. It was a long, triangular hardstone blade, with three sharp edges tapering to a point.

"If I ever wake you in the night and start trying to change our plans," he said, "show me this. That should bring me to my senses."

Carla examined his face. He was serious. "And what if I'm the one who wakes you?"

He returned the knife to its hiding place and produced a second one from the other side of the bed.

34

Carlo arrived a few chimes early to take over from Macaria. Having done the arborine night shift himself for a stint he knew how tiring it was: the less active the animals were, the harder it had been to keep watching them closely without his mind wandering. It was only by constantly reminding himself of what a few lapses of inattentiveness might cost him that he'd managed to stay awake to the end of each shift.

"Anything unusual?" he asked.

"Zosimo was up for about a bell, leaping around the cage," Macaria recounted. "At one point he woke his co; I was sure something was going to happen. But in the end all they did was exchange a few calls. Benigna and Benigno slept through all the drama."

"Hmm." Carlo had read old reports, written on the home world, claiming that arborines in the forests had been seen waking at night in order to breed. But he had doubts about the veracity of those accounts, let alone their relevance to these captives twice removed from their ancestors' original habitat.

"There ought to be something we can do to encourage them," Macaria said wearily. "Both couples are reproductively mature, so what are they waiting for? There must be some environmental change that would clinch it. Maybe a dietary signal—"

"If we increase the food supply any more, we risk them becoming quadraparous," Carlo replied.

"Would that be so terrible? If you really want to understand the signaling during fission, aren't you going to need to compare biparous and quadraparous versions at some point?"

That might have been a reasonable attitude if they'd had an unlimited supply of experimental subjects, and as many lifetimes as they needed to achieve the project's goal. Carlo said, "If we don't get a tape of biparous fission from this lot, you can volunteer to catch the next four arborines."

Macaria left him to it.

Carlo positioned himself on the guide rope midway between the two cages, at a point where he could see Benigna and Benigno in his rear gaze and Zosima and Zosimo to the front. The flowers adorning the scaffolding of amputated branches that crisscrossed each cage were still putting out light, more or less following their original alternating cycles, but over the last few days he'd begun to notice a decline in their luminance. As the imitation forest faded the moss-light took over, and the whole place began to look more like a prison of bare rock decorated with a few wan twigs.

The observers' shifts were synchronized to the arborines' activity, and he'd arrived just in time to watch all four animals waking. The females, pinned to their heavy plinths, had long ago ceased making vigorous attempts to detach themselves, but their posture and movements changed completely once they were conscious, with the uncoordinated twitches and flailing of sleep replaced by an eerily disciplined-looking series of muscular stretches and rearrangements of the flesh. Benigna and Zosima in their separate cages performed an almost identical set of exercises, which suggested that they were instinctive responses to their lack of mobility—perhaps as a way of maintaining health while recovering from an injury. But it was possible that there was a component of mimicry as well; from their plinths, they could see each other clearly enough. Mimicry? Encouragement? Solidarity? Zosima had carried Benigna's limp body through the forest unflaggingly while Carlo pursued her. It was hard not to think of the two of them as fellow prisoners, aware of each other's plight, striving to keep up each other's morale.

For their part, the males did not remain still for long either: every few lapses either Zosimo or Benigno made a sudden leap from one branch to another. Though the cages were currently empty of lizards, to Carlo these moves looked similar to ones the arborines used when ambushing prey. He wasn't sure if they had failed to grasp the unfamiliar rules governing the presence of the lizards and had started jumping at shadows in the hope that it might be food, or, like the females, they were merely intent on staying active.

In the light of Macaria's report Carlo paid special attention to Zosimo. The male was certainly more agitated than usual, swaying restlessly on each branch before flinging himself onto the next. The cage was just a couple of stretches across, so Zosimo couldn't help revisiting the same locations—but far from executing a tight, repetitive cycle, he crisscrossed the miniature forest in an elaborate sequence of permutations of departure points and destinations, as if intent on squeezing as much novelty out of his impoverished surroundings as he could.

When feeding time came, Carlo fetched two lizards from the storeroom; they squirmed in protest for a while, then went limp in his hands as if they could save themselves by playing dead. The arborines must have learned the routine by now, but they didn't hang around like supplicants as he approached. Benigno clung, aloof, to a distant branch while Carlo tossed the lizard through the bars of his cage. Zosimo was positively disdainful, baring his teeth at Carlo threateningly, but he too kept his distance.

Carlo returned to his observation post. He'd seen these hunts too many times now to remain enthralled from start to finish, but it was impossible to ignore them completely. The cages were small, but every branch held a dozen hiding places, and the lizards always vanished from sight long before the arborines showed any interest in them. Today the pursuit seemed unhurried at first, almost desultory: Zosimo crossed from branch to branch purposefully a few times, then appeared to grow distracted, while Benigno's bounces, more playful than stealthy, sent luminous petals wafting through the air.

Carlo's thoughts wandered, but he was aware of the two arborines gradually narrowing the search: jumping to a new branch, looking about for a moment, then feigning indifference and pretending to be more concerned with swatting at mites. It was nearly a chime later when things sped up, rapidly; Carlo could hear one lizard's panicked claws as it fled along a branch before Zosimo reached out and snatched at it. The lizard must have jumped to another branch, because the hand came back empty, but then Zosimo leaped after it and moments later he had it in his mouth and was biting it in two.

Zosimo chewed on half the lizard, chirping softly with pleasure. There was a flurry of activity in the rear of Benigno's cage, but Carlo couldn't see what was happening so he stayed focused on Zosimo. The arborine swallowed his share of the meal, then swung down to the branch closest to his trapped co. He handed Zosima the remainder of the lizard; as she raised it to her mouth he reached across and ran a hand over the side of her face.

Carlo watched her eating, Zosimo beside her. For the first few days both of the males had tried to help their cos work the light probes out of their flesh, but the tubes were hardstone, impossible to bend or break, and Carlo had melded the females' skin together around half a dozen loops set into the plinth. No ordinary deformation of the flesh could free them, and even if they'd grown desperate enough to bite or scratch themselves loose there was no access for teeth or claws.

The females had been unconscious for the surgery, and the aftermath should not have been painful, but Carlo still felt a twinge of revulsion at the fate he'd imposed on them. They would divide, or they would stay trapped: that was the verdict he'd written in stone.

Zosima had finished eating. She called out with an elaborate sequence of chirps, and when she received no reply she repeated herself; the pattern was almost identical, but some notes now rose more emphatically above the rest. After a moment Zosimo responded.

The exchange continued, longer and more elaborate than any Carlo had heard before. He'd been taught that the arborines lacked a true language, but he doubted that anyone was in a position to know. In the old reports there had been a crude attempt to classify the cries, but no systematic annotation of their structure. If the day ever came when future biologists were free of more desperate concerns, it might be worth someone's time to spend a year in the forest, just watching these animals and listening to their calls.

Zosima stretched a hand up from the plinth; her co took it and she drew him toward her. Carlo hesitated, afraid for a moment that he was deceiving himself and misinterpreting the encounter. But Zosimo had released his hold on the branch and the two were maneuvering into a tight embrace. Carlo scrambled quickly along the cross rope and reached the lever under the front of the cage.

He tugged on it; it stuck. Trying not to panic, he pushed back on the lever and worked it past the obstruction, then he succeeded in disengaging the brake. The sudden clatter of the six light recorders was so loud that he feared it would startle the arborines into changing their minds, but when he looked up they were undeterred, oblivious to the machinery.

As Carlo watched them he was unable to dismiss a shameful sense of voyeurism, though it was doubly absurd when the recorders were capturing far greater intimacies than his gaze. But the arborines' posture had never looked more like their cousins', and the shape they made together was disturbingly close to the vision of Carla and himself that years of anticipation had burned into his brain. This was not like breeding voles.

Zosima grew still, but Zosimo continued to stroke her face as if to comfort her. A yellow glow shone out from the skin where they were joined: the male's promise in light, committing him to care for the children. Carlo couldn't untangle how much of his discomfort at the sight was guilt at forcing the arborines' choice and how much was a rebuke from the part of his mind that would judge his own life worthless until he'd made the same promise himself.

Abruptly, the noise from the recorders took on a new component: the sound of paper being shredded. "No, no, no!" Carlo dragged himself under the cage into the dimly lit equipment hatch. As he approached the offending machine the tearing was replaced by a rhythmic thwack; the tape had broken completely and the loose end from the driven reel was whipping against the chassis. He shut off the motor and quickly removed both reels, but it took him another few lapses to tug all the fragments of damaged tape from between the capstans, then load a fresh reel and restart the machine.

As he emerged from the hatch and climbed toward the observation post, he saw that Zosimo had broken free of his co and moved back to the branch that overhung the plinth. Zosima was limbless now, and Carlo watched, disquieted, as her anatomy began to surrender features that no conscious effort could have changed. The ridges of her tympanum sunk into the membrane, then the whole glorious structure merged with the top of her chest, resorbed as easily as an impromptu arm. Her closed mouth, the dark lips already strangely flattened, lost its usual contrast with the skin of her face until it faded entirely from view. Her eyelids were the last aspect to go, the pale slitted ovals rotated and stretched out vertically, distorted like the remnants of insignificant wounds as the head itself began to reform. It was as if an unseen sculptor, having crafted this body in resin years ago, had returned to swipe her thumbs across the remains of the ruined face before squeezing the entire figurine into an undifferentiated lump, mere material now, ready to be reused.

Zosimo emitted a long, mournful hum. Carlo looked up at him, struggling to retain a sense of distance, but then the arborine's whole body began to shake with anguish. Nature had bribed both participants in this metamorphosis, imbuing the act with an incomparable sense of joy, but while a vole could pass untroubled from the raw pleasure of triggering fission to the compelling obligations of nurturing his young, this arborine understood what he had lost. The companion who had loved and protected him all his life had just been erased before his eyes. What else should that elicit but grief?

Carlo averted his gaze and tried to regain his composure. *How had he imagined it would feel, when he and Carla finally brought her life to an end?* Had he ever really fooled himself into believing that he'd be borne through it all in a daze, anesthetized by the biological imperative, untouched by the gravity of what he'd done? No man ever told his children anything but anodyne lies, but if he could forgive his father for sparing him as a boy he could not forgive his own cowardice since. All his training, all his animal experiments, had only helped him bury the truth under a mountain of facts. He had to accept that his life's greatest purpose, the one role that would make him complete, *could never be right, could never be bearable, could never be forgiven.* It wouldn't matter how long they waited, it wouldn't matter what plans they'd made, it wouldn't matter how willingly they took the final step. In the end he would know exactly what he'd done, with only the children to keep him sane.

And that only if their number was right.

Carlo looked up. Zosimo was huddled against the branch, swaying, his upper arms wrapped around his head. He had fallen silent, but now Benigno and Benigna were howling in reply. But through all the arborine sorrow, Carlo finally had something to celebrate himself.

The surface of the blastula was marked with its first partition—and it was transverse, not longitudinal. Zosima would divide into just two children, and there was a chance that the light recorders had captured the signals underlying this result.

35

"It's working!" Romolo announced gleefully. He held a mirror in the beam and wiggled it, sending a dazzling red spot careering across the walls of the workshop. "Visible at last!"

Everyone gathered around to play with the new device. Carla watched, delighted by the spectacle, but she hung back herself and let the rest of the team enjoy it.

It would take some effort to scale up this humble red spot into a light for the beacons, but in time the navigators would have what they needed. Ivo was already working on a machine for capturing samples of orthogonal matter with a coherent UV source. It was beginning to look as if the *Gnat*'s successor could be flying to the Object within a couple of years.

"We should use these for our engines," Eulalia enthused. "No more exploding sunstone, just a photon rocket with an exhaust of pure light!"

"Er—" Romolo pointed to the lamp that was powering the device. "This beam's only carrying a tiny amount of the energy from the sunstone. The rest is being wasted. If we tried to drive the *Peerless* using something like this, we'd need to burn sunstone so much faster than the original engines that it would vaporize the whole mountain with waste heat."

"And the light source would stop working," Patrizia added.

"Why?" Eulalia demanded. "From the heat?"

"No. From the acceleration."

Romolo turned to Patrizia. "What do you mean, from the acceleration?"

"The light source only works at a particular frequency," Patrizia replied. "If the *Peerless* is accelerating, then while the light's traveling from one end of the source to the other, the clearstone will end up moving faster than it was when it emitted the light. Any change in the relative velocity between the light and the clearstone will change the apparent frequency of the light—so it won't be at the right frequency to stimulate any more transitions."

Romolo was at a loss for words, so Carla intervened. "She's joking! Any frequency shift would be extremely small. Even at one gravity there's no chance at all it could stop the light source from operating."

"I was joking," Patrizia admitted. "But maybe we could design a system that's deliberately sensitive to the shift, and use it as an accelerometer—as a kind of navigational aid."

Carla couldn't think of any objection to that in principle. "Why not?" she said. "Another project for our grandchildren."

Romolo angled the reflected beam onto Patrizia's chest. The red disk looked like a hole in her skin, revealing the realm of light within.

Carla woke, her gut in spasms. She turned to the clock by the bed and waited for her vision to come into focus. Breakfast was still more than two bells away.

She lay beneath the tarpaulin, humming softly. She wondered if it would help if she made some kind of promise to herself, to end her hunger if it became too much to bear. But end it how? She couldn't take Silvana's way out, even if she'd wanted to: Carlo was so convinced that he could rescue her from the famine that he'd rather fend her off with his ridiculous knife than cure her of her misery. She wasn't going to go off holin, or step out of an airlock. There was nothing to be done but to endure it.

She tried to sleep again, but it was impossible. She pulled herself out of bed and left the apartment. If she followed the corridor around in a circle until she was too weary to continue, she could drag herself back to bed with some hope of losing consciousness.

The precinct was quiet, the moss-lit corridor deserted. What did other women do, she wondered, when their hunger became unbearable? Did they lie beside their cos and fantasize about the day it would finally end, until one by one they abandoned all the plans they'd made for their lives and gave in to that glorious vision?

Carla searched for something cheerier to occupy her thoughts. Romolo's new light source was a striking vindication of the whole theory of energy levels... but when she thought about the journey the device would enable, the prospect filled her with dread. Without a deep understanding of the annihilation reaction, any plans for an engine that burned orthogonal matter would be nothing but whimsy. But was it really her duty to face the risk of becoming fuel for that fire herself, not just once, but over and over again?

If she refused, there would be plenty of volunteers to take her place. She could still work on the theory underlying the reaction, but she would probably slip behind the researchers with first-hand knowledge of the new results. If Patrizia flew on the second *Gnat* and returned with a triumphant discovery of her own, it would finally place her reputation unambiguously beyond Carla's.

Would that be so intolerable, though? Would it be unjust? They had both made contributions, but the most powerful ideas had been Patrizia's. Looking back, it seemed to Carla that the best thing she'd done had been to impose some discipline on Patrizia's wilder speculations and then tidy up the details of those that worked out. So perhaps she should reconcile herself to that role. If it was to be her legacy, better to value it than resent it.

What was left for her, then? More tidying up? Turning throwaway lines about accelerometers into real devices? If she could come up with a design for a light-based accelerometer that actually worked, there'd be nothing dishonorable in that. On the scale of a small craft like the *Gnat* it might be fanciful, but over greater distances there'd be more time for the acceleration to reveal its effect.

How long would it take the slowest detectable infrared light to run the full length of the *Peerless*, from the tip of the mountain to the base, and back? Still just a fraction of a flicker. In which time, at one gravity's acceleration, the velocity of the mountain would have changed by... a few parts in the fifth power of a gross.

Carla dragged herself faster along the guide rope, determined to complete her first circuit of the corridor and get past her apartment while she was still distracted. As she pondered the problem she realized that she'd been careless: it was reasonable to assume that the light's frequency would be unchanged when it bounced off the mirror that sent it back toward its source—that was the definition of a good mirror, after all—but she'd ignored the fact that the mirror would be accelerating along with the *Peerless*. On the finicky level of detail required to keep track of the tiny effects she was hoping to measure, that would be enough to change the result.

She worked through the geometry more carefully, sketching the history of the mountain's extremities and the light moving between them. The frequency measured for any given pulse of light depended solely on the relative velocity between the apparatus doing the measuring and the light pulse itself—which in turn came down to nothing more than the angle between their histories. Those angles were easy enough to find, and four of them told the whole story.

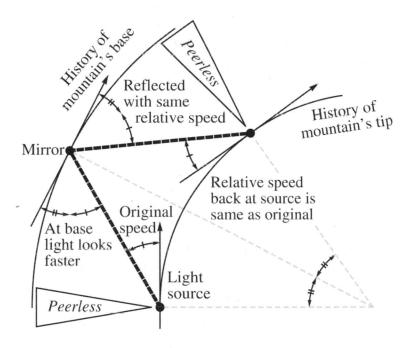

The mirror's acceleration into the oncoming light would mean that the light struck it a little faster than the speed with which it had left the source. But the light source, in turn, would be accelerating *away from* the reflected light. By the time the light came back to the source, the relative velocity between the two would be reversed but otherwise unchanged—and the net result would be that there was no frequency shift at all.

In principle the blue shift could be measured by comparing the light at the base of the mountain with a reference beam produced locally by a second light source. But the ideal method would involve a direct comparison between the shifted light and the *original* beam. Carla hunted for a way around the problem, but the geometry always led back to the same result: the beam would suffer a blue shift traveling down the mountain, and a red shift traveling back up. And so long as the light was reflected unchanged, on a round trip the two effects would cancel out. It was just a form of conservation of energy.

What about Eulalia's flight of fancy, then: a photon rocket? Would frequency shifts disrupt the light source there, or not? If a beam of light was powerful enough to be the *cause* of the mountain's acceleration, it would be imparting momentum to the mirrors it struck, and losing some of its own. It would no longer be reflected unchanged; it would have to experience a red shift.

How much, though?

That depended on the mass of the object each photon effectively bounced against. In the experiments with free luxagens, the light had been scattered back with a huge red shift; because the individual luxagens were less massive than the photons that struck them, their recoil had carried off a lot of momentum. In the inferior grades of mirrorstone that could ruin a coherent light source, the luxagens were still mobile enough to recoil significantly before they transferred their momentum to the bulk of the material. In the highest quality mirrors, the luxagens were bound so tightly to their neighbors that each photon was effectively colliding with a significant portion of the mirrorstone—a portion heavy enough to be unmoved. But there were limits to this collective inertia: a single photon could never bounce off an entire mountain, as if it were a rigid, indivisible whole. So it would be the material properties of the mirror itself, not the acceleration of the mountain, that determined the frequency of the reflected light.

Carla had lost track of her surroundings. She paused, clinging to the guide rope, and looked around the corridor at the doors ahead and behind her. She had passed her apartment twice, she realized, and she was now a short way into a third circuit. The reminder that her food cupboard was only a few stretches behind her was enough to make her gut start twitching again, but she resolved to complete a couple more circuits in the hope that it would be enough to let her sleep.

She took up the thread of her argument once more. A poor quality mirror would reflect light with a small red shift, bouncing back photons that were no longer tuned to the gap between the energy levels that produced them. And perhaps a beam intense enough to be part of a photon rocket would exacerbate the effect, with the stronger light fields effectively "softening" mirrors that were perfectly adequate at a lower power. Was there any way around that? A red shift meant an increase in true energy: each reflected photon would be carrying too much energy to stimulate the emission of another photon from the original transition. But then, why not give it a different task? If its energy matched another gap between levels, maybe the whole system could be made to do something useful nonetheless.

Carla tinkered for a while, and came up with one possibility.

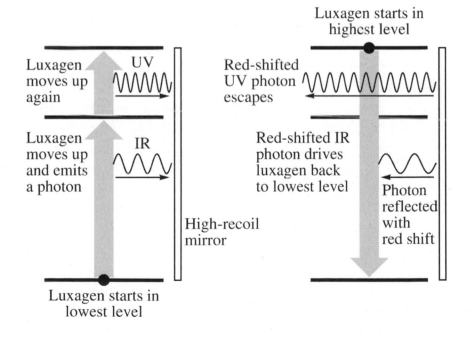

The luxagen started in the lowest of three levels; it would have to be pushed there by an external light source. From there, it jumped spontaneously to a higher level, emitting an infrared photon. Then it moved to a higher level still, emitting an ultraviolet photon.

Both photons were reflected back, red-shifted by their encounter with the mirror. But if the mirror's properties and the spacing of the energy levels were related in just the right manner, the reflected IR photon would be able to push the luxagen back to the lowest level: exactly where it had started.

And then the cycle could begin again.

In each cycle, two photons were created and one was never recaptured. To balance that photon's true energy, the clearstone and the mirrorstone would need to gain conventional energy; in principle, any mixture of kinetic, thermal and potential energy would do. But to balance the photon's *momentum*, the device as a whole would need to accelerate, so the energy gained couldn't be entirely in the form of heat. When a fuel met its liberator, the creation of light was accompanied by the creation of heat—and this device would certainly heat up to some degree. Over time, it might also suffer some degradation, some chemical change. But unlike burning fuel, it would not disintegrate in a flash, it would not turn to smoke.

To make light and not be consumed. These were the properties of an Eternal Flame.

Carla paused, amused by her absurd conclusion, wondering where the mistake lay. As things stood, the photons wouldn't really be produced all conveniently heading in the same direction, so the device would certainly need some refinements. Perhaps she could merge the recoiling mirror trick with her original design for a coherent source. But *this* source wouldn't squander most of the energy from a blazing sunstone lamp; the red-shifted reflection of the IR photons it emitted itself would act as the main pump. After an initial flash to get the process started, it would only need a small amount of ongoing illumination to compensate for its imperfections and inefficiencies—and the beam it produced would far outshine that modest input.

It would not violate the conservation of energy or momentum. It would not violate any thermodynamic law: creating photons and waste heat amounted to an increase in entropy. But a photon rocket based on this design could run on a tiny fraction of the sunstone needed by any conventional engine. If it worked, it would solve the fuel problem.

No—more than that. If it worked, the ancestors themselves might flee the home world in a swarm of photon rockets. If it worked, not only would the *Peerless* have gained the means to return home, it would have the right, it would have the reason. The purpose of its mission would have been fulfilled.

Carla moved slowly down the empty corridor, listening to the twang of the guide rope, waiting for the flaw she'd missed to reveal itself. When it finally hit her, she could buzz ruefully at her foolishness and drag herself back to bed. *What about cooling?* This rocket would still need a separate cooling system, burning fuel of its own… but there was no law that required the heat it generated to be as much as a conventional engine produced. And the right choices in the design could help: the faster the ultraviolet photons the device was able to emit, the less kinetic energy the mirror would need to remove from the other photons—which meant less energy ending up as heat.

Carla didn't need to search for a clock to know that it was still early, but the only person in the mountain there'd be any point in waking was also the only one who'd understand why she couldn't wait a few more bells to resolve this.

She reached the precinct easily enough, but she had to check the names on a dozen doors before she found the right one; she hadn't paid a visit since Patrizia had started living apart from her co. Carla knocked tentatively, wondering belatedly if her behavior would appear completely deranged. But the door opened before she had a chance to change her mind and retreat.

"Good morning Carla." Patrizia looked puzzled, but if she was annoyed at being woken she hid it well. "Come in, please!"

The apartment smelled of paper and fresh dye. There was a lamp burning in the front room, revealing walls stacked with books and tied bundles of notes. The gravity was very weak here, but Carla clung tightly to the guide rope.

"I won't waste your time," she said. "I've had a wild idea, and I need to hear your opinion."

She described the basic principle of the mirror trick, then went on to explain how it might be used in a real device. When she'd finished speaking she braced herself for a barrage of objections, but Patrizia remained silent, gazing thoughtfully into the middle distance.

"So have I lost my mind?" Carla pressed her. She'd gently put Patrizia straight when the girl had fallen prey to her own kind of nonsense; it was time for Patrizia to return the favor.

"I don't think so. Why would you even say that?"

"Because it can't be this easy! The Eternal Flame—from a few mirrors and a slab of clearstone?"

Patrizia buzzed softly. "In the sagas, the Eternal Flame doesn't *do* anything; it just sits there being cool and inscrutable. Your version would be more like the process plants perform every day: extracting energy from the production of light without incinerating themselves. Nature must have found a trick a lot like yours—shuffling luxagens around a closed cycle—even if it puts it to a very different use. Crossing the void with minimal fuel wasn't something a flower was ever going to find helpful, but that doesn't mean it's impossible."

Carla felt no sense of reassurance. If Patrizia had found a glaring flaw in the plan that would have settled the matter, but the fact that the idea had survived her brief scrutiny proved nothing. "And no one else thought of this? Not Yalda? Not Sabino? Not Nereo?"

"They all thought energy was continuous!" Patrizia protested. "Would this scheme work at all, without discrete energy levels?"

"I don't know," Carla admitted. Certainly the whole idea was easier to grasp when the luxagen could cycle repeatedly between a few fixed states.

"I think Yalda had hopes that we'd master the creation of light by studying plants," Patrizia said. "And maybe that will give us the best insights into the process, eventually. But someone had to be the first to spell out the kind of steps that would make this possible. You're the first, Carla. You're not losing your mind, I promise you."

"Thank you." Carla did trust her to give an honest opinion, and not to indulge in flattery. "But I won't believe I'm right until we've proved it."

"So where do we begin?" Patrizia asked. "We'll need to find varieties of clearstone with the right energy levels, but we'll also need to calibrate mirrors for their red shifts."

"This is going to be a whole new project," Carla said. "I'll have to go to the Council to get their approval for the change of plans."

"Hmm." Patrizia was impatient to get started. "Surely I can reanalyse a few absorption spectra without waiting for the Council? When Romolo and I went through them the last time, we were looking for very different properties."

"That's true." The search for the perfect clearstone would start all over again, and there was a chance that once again it would succeed. But even the navigators' modest needs would require the entire inventory of the clearstone Romolo had used in his visible light source. For this new application—

"It won't be enough," Carla realized. "Even if we can make this work in a demonstration rocket, there isn't the slightest chance that we'll have enough material to replace the engines." The mountain's stocks of exotically tinted minerals weren't miserly, but the ancestors had only intended them to provide representative samples to be studied for the sake of materials science. They had never anticipated the possibility that one particular variety would become more valuable than sunstone.

Carla buzzed with grim satisfaction, glad that she'd caught her own mistake before making a fool of herself in front of the Council. "What was I thinking? Anything less than a full replacement for the engines would be worthless. If we can't accelerate the *Peerless* at close to one gravity, it will take too much of the ancestors' time for us to get back to them." Returning to the home world a few years late—by the ancestors' clocks—would mean arriving just as collisions with the orthogonal cluster began in earnest.

Patrizia regarded her with bemusement. "Everything you say is true," she said.

"Then why didn't you tell me? That's what I came here for!" Carla dragged herself back along the guide rope, confused. "I needed to know where I'd gone wrong."

"There's nothing wrong with your plan," Patrizia insisted. "Not as far as I can tell. But as you say, the proof will be in the demonstration."

"*And then what?*" Carla hummed with frustration. "If we succeed, we'll have the satisfaction of knowing that *if* half the mountain had been made of exactly the right kind of clearstone, that would have solved the fuel problem? And that the ancestors are likely to have all the resources they'd need to evacuate the home world—with the only problem being the lack of any way to tell them how to do it?"

"If we succeed in making a photon rocket," Patrizia replied, "then it will be the start of an entirely new endeavor: working with the chemists to learn how to make the right kind of clearstone, in the quantities we need, from the materials we actually possess."

Carla was incredulous. "You want the chemists to make a mineral on demand, now? You mean the way they solved the fuel problem by transmuting all our spare calmstone into sunstone?"

Patrizia said, "*Now* you're being crazy. First, the quantities we'd need would be much, much smaller: we're talking about making engines that will run for years, not fuel that will be used up in an instant. Second, I suspect that different kinds of clearstone are chemically and energetically far more similar than calmstone is to sunstone. And third... if we can make your idea work, even on a modest scale, that will give us a new energy source. Burning sunstone to provide the energy to make sunstone would have been a losing proposition. But whether it's heat or photons the chemists need to nudge one kind of clearstone into another, if we can pull off your trick and make an Eternal Flame on our own—even once—then we ought to be able to supply that energy without *consuming* anything."

36

"Talk to your co!" Silvano pleaded. "I don't know what's got into her, but if she starts backing away from our plans to exploit the Object she'll lose all credibility with the Council."

Carlo had been puzzled when Silvano had invited him to visit without Carla, but he hadn't objected; he understood that there were matters that the two of them would be more comfortable discussing alone. It hadn't occurred to him, though, that Carla herself might be one of them.

"She's had an idea for something better," he said. "I'm not an expert in any of this, and I gather that the other physicists' opinions are divided. But what do you expect me to do? I can't tell her to ignore her own judgment."

"Wasn't the whole point of these new light sources to manipulate orthogonal matter?" Silvano seemed to think that everything came down to that: Carla had gained his support for her project on that basis, and any attempt to change course now made her guilty of acting under false pretences.

"The research has opened up another possibility," Carlo replied. "Why is that so terrible? The Object isn't going anywhere. If this new idea turns out to be a dead end, you'll still be able to resume the original project."

"*Resume?*" Silvano was appalled. "We won't get anywhere if we allow ourselves to be distracted every time someone's mind goes off on a tangent. We need to finish what we've started!"

"Finish it how?" Carlo shifted uncomfortably on the rope, then decided to be blunt. "Do you want to see people annihilated, before we even consider the alternatives?"

"You're saying the Object is so dangerous that we should forget about it completely? That wasn't Carla's attitude before."

"And it's probably not her attitude now," Carlo admitted. "I'm sure she still believes that the dangers could be managed, given enough time and effort. But if there's a chance to avoid those dangers altogether, why not look into that first?"

"Because it's a fantasy!" Silvano proclaimed derisively. "Believe me, I admire the courage Carla showed in what she did to capture the Object—and I don't blame her at all if she's reluctant to go back. She doesn't need to fly into the void again; she's already a hero to everyone on the *Peerless*. But that's no reason to sabotage the whole project, just to save face!"

Carlo said, "I have work to do." He stretched out an arm, pushing himself away from the rope so he could peer into the playroom. "Bye, Flavia! Bye, Flavio!" The children didn't turn away from the tent they were building, but they glanced toward him with their rear gazes and nodded in farewell.

Silvano tried to adopt a more conciliatory tone. "Look, if it were something easily settled then I'd be happy to support her. But it isn't that simple, Carlo. Even if her demonstration project works—and my advisers all tell me that's unlikely—there's this whole separate business about mass-producing new clearstone to order. Let the chemists loose on *that*, and orthogonal matter will start to look benign in comparison."

"So let them experiment out in the void," Carlo suggested. "Build a new workshop for the chemists and put it a severance or two away from the *Peerless*. That would deal with the safety issues, it would give the navigators another chance to exercise their skills—and if the clearstone thing doesn't work out, the same facility would be perfect for experiments with orthogonal matter." He tipped his head and began backing away along the rope.

"All I could do was warn you!" Silvano called after him. "It's up to you whether you listen."

In the corridor Carlo sped along the guide rope, trying to work off his agitation. Why had Silvano had to drag him into this dispute? It was possible that Carla was fooling herself and her scheme was too good to be true. It was possible, too, that Silvano was just clinging to his vision of the Object as the gift from fate that would solve all their problems.

Mercifully, there was no need for him to decide who he believed was right. He was neither a Councilor nor a physicist; no one would care about his opinion on these matters.

No one but Carla and Silvano themselves.

Carlo had transformed the storeroom beside the arborine cages into an office, so he wouldn't have to travel back and forth from the workshop Tosco had allocated for the original influence study. The room was cramped and it stank of the lizards awaiting their death as arborine food, but once he was in the harness beside the tape viewer he soon forgot his surroundings. The six reels sitting inert in their rack did not look like anything special, but in the viewer, illuminated and in motion, the strips' rhythmic shifts between translucence and opacity became something close to a recitation of the body instructing itself to reproduce.

A recitation and a transcript. He wound the sequence from Zosima's lower left probe past the lamp again slowly, pausing every few spans to glance down at his chest and check his notes. He had catalogued almost ten dozen recurring motifs in the recordings, and even those patterns were subject to further small variations—like words repeated with different inflections. Here it was, right in front of him: *the language of life*.

Now that they'd fed Benigna and Benigno to the point where quadraparity was all but assured, Macaria was pushing him to let them breed without any further interventions, in the hope that a comparison between the recordings of the two fissions would be illuminating. Carlo couldn't fault the idea in principle, but he was still reluctant to proceed. Going on the surveys, there were probably less than three dozen arborines on the *Peerless* in total—counting Zosimo and his children. Aside from any qualms he had about the cruelty of confining and manipulating still more of them, there simply weren't enough of the animals to grind through any exhaustive set of protocols, the way they'd all been trained to do with voles and lizards. If it was possible to learn more from Benigna than they could by conducting the single most obvious experiment—and losing another female of breeding age in the process—he owed it to all of them to find a way to do that.

Carlo worked on the tapes until his concentration began to falter. He checked the clock; it had been almost three bells. He pulled himself out of the room and went to check on the infrared recorders. A stack of four machines were monitoring Zosimo and his children, to see if they had acquired any of the influences the team had captured from sick people and played back into the cage. Carlo removed two exposed reels, then reloaded and reset the machines.

In the tape viewer, the reels were blank. The arborines appeared to be utterly unswayed by messages that had proved themselves capable of commandeering a person's body. Ultimately that might not matter; the goal was to influence people, not arborines. But the lack of a single message that could infect both species would make it much harder to test the whole scheme.

Carlo took a meal break, but the storeroom wasn't a pleasant place to spend it. Chewing on a loaf, he wandered back to the arborines' cages. Zosimo ignored him, but the children leaped to the bars and thrust their hands through, humming plaintively in the hope that he'd throw them a morsel. "You want me to spoil you?" he chided them. He'd resisted naming the children but that hadn't stopped him feeling a tug of affection for them, and he'd been weak enough to toss food to them before. "Your father will feed you soon. Be patient."

Carlo swallowed the last of the loaf quickly; Amanda sometimes came early for her shift, and it made him uncomfortable if she surprised him eating. He was about to return to the storeroom when a movement in the other cage caught his attention. He turned and pulled himself along the cross rope for a closer look.

Benigna remained attached to her plinth, but she was holding something in one of her hands. As Carlo approached she tried to conceal it, but it was too large to be hidden from view.

It was a stick, about half a stride long. One end tapered to a rough wedge; it must have been snapped off a slender branch. But Benigna's half of the cage had been emptied of branches, and Benigno hadn't breached the barred partition that separated him from his co. Carlo was stumped, but then he realized that Benigno must have thrown the improvised tool through a gap in the bars.

Carlo drew himself to the side for a better view. The skin on Benigna's back was torn, as if she'd been trying to force the stick between the stone surface and her body. "You want to be free?" he said dully. She couldn't reach her melded flesh with her fingers, however sharp she made the claws, but not only had she conceived of a better plan, she'd managed to communicate what she needed to her co.

Carlo fought to maintain his resolve. If he gave up now, where would that leave him? Watching Carla go blind? Murdering two of his own children? These animals had done nothing to deserve the hardship he was inflicting on them—but what had he or any of the travelers done to deserve their own plight?

"What's happening?" Amanda had arrived.

Carlo explained what he'd surmised. "You'd better tranquilize her and take it away," he said. They'd been entering the cage to put dead lizards within Benigna's reach, without drugging her first, but he didn't want anyone trying to wrest a sharpened stick out of her hand while she was conscious.

"So how will we stop them doing it again?"

"Build a proper wall, I suppose," Carlo replied. "I'll get a construction crew to put stone slabs across."

Amanda hesitated. "Wouldn't it be simpler just to let them breed?"

Carlo was tempted. "It would be simpler," he agreed. "But I have another plan."

He'd been turning it over in the back of his mind, unsure of its usefulness, but now Amanda had forced his hand. "I want to play Zosima's tapes back into Benigna's body," he said. "I want to see what each of those messages does."

"You mean... out of context? Without Benigno triggering her?" Amanda sounded skeptical.

"Yes."

"What do you expect will happen?"

"I don't know," Carlo admitted. "But there's no point trying to reconstruct the whole sequence—there was too much lost from one of the recordings. So I think it's better to go the other way, and see if any of the individual signals have an effect on their own."

"What if that just cripples her?" Amanda protested. "If it goes wrong the way your finger did, it's not going to be fixed by an amputation—and she certainly won't be able to breed."

"We have to take that chance," Carlo said. "How else are we going to decipher this language? We have to study something more complicated than a twirling finger—but we're never going to make sense of the fission process without breaking it down into smaller parts."

"It's your decision," Amanda said. "I'd better—" She gestured toward Benigna.

Carlo moved aside and let her into the equipment hatch so she could dispense a dose of tranquilizer through the plinth.

"Silvano's going to make trouble for you with the Council," Carlo said. "He was counting on your support, and now he thinks you've turned against him."

Carla hummed wearily. "Why does he have to take everything personally? If this works out, we'll have a better chance than ever of reclaiming the engine feeds. He wants space for new farms, doesn't he? I thought politics was all about the ends."

Carlo dragged himself over to the lamp and rescued the front room from its drab moss-light. "Politics is about people's feelings."

"And exploiting them for your own ends," Carla replied.

Carlo was still annoyed with Silvano, but he wasn't feeling quite so cynical. "For three generations, we've had to make do with what we carried with us from the home world," he said. "When the Object came along, everyone expected *something* from it. Silvano was hoping we could farm there, and he's already had to give up on that. A universal liberator sounds dangerous—but the idea of mastering it still makes us feel powerful. Now you want everyone to forget about the Object and just trust you to pull energy out of thin air."

"No one has to take this on trust," Carla replied. "If it works, it will work right in front of their eyes."

Carlo said, "But they still need to trust you that it's worth the resources to *build* this thing you want to put before their eyes."

"So do you believe there's any chance that it will work?" Carla didn't seem hurt by his lack of confidence; if anything, she sounded glad to have someone skeptical whom she could interrogate on the matter.

Carlo was honest with her. "I don't know. All this shuffling of luxagens between energy levels sounds a bit like sleight of hand."

"The light source we've already made was all about shuffling luxagens between energy levels," Carla protested. "The Council had no problem approving that idea."

"Because you shine a stonking great sunstone lamp on it!" Carlo replied. "It doesn't offend anyone's common sense to think that you can put light in and get light out."

"All right." Carla thought for a while. "Forget about the details of the device, then. Just look at what it claims to do."

She made a quick sketch on her chest.

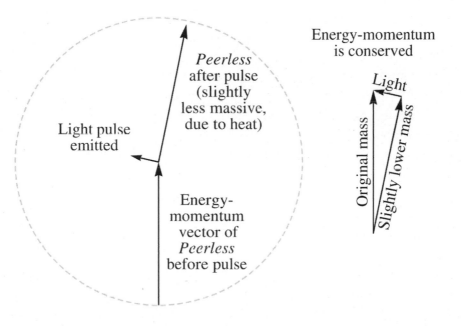

"The *Peerless* has a certain energy-momentum vector before we use this device," she said. "It's just an arrow whose length is the mass of the whole mountain, and we draw it vertically in a reference frame in which we start out at rest."

"Right." Carlo wasn't so tired that he couldn't follow that much.

"The photon rocket emits a pulse of light," Carla continued. "Ultraviolet, preferably, so it's moving rapidly and its energy-momentum vector is a long way from vertical. To obey the conservation laws, the total energy-momentum has to be the same, before and after that pulse is emitted. Before, there's just the original energy-momentum of the

Peerless: the vertical arrow. After the pulse is emitted, there's the light's vector, plus the new vector for the *Peerless*, whatever that might be. The sum of those last two vectors has to equal the first, so if you join up their arrows base to tip they form a closed triangle with the original vector."

She paused inquiringly. "I'm still with you," Carlo said.

"If the rocket had no effect on the mountain other than giving it a push," she continued, "the new vector would need to have exactly the same length as before: the same mass. That would be ideal—but I'm not even claiming to be able to do that! Instead, if we allow for some waste heat raising the temperature of the *Peerless*, the extra thermal energy lowers the mass of the mountain, very slightly. But even that doesn't ruin the geometry—there are still vectors for the light and the accelerated mountain that add up, exactly as they need to."

Carlo gazed at the closed triangle on her chest. "I can see that it's not physically impossible, in those terms," he conceded. "But everything else that makes light needs some kind of fuel, some kind of input." He gestured at the walls. "Even moss has to have rock to feed on."

"Because moss isn't *interested* in just making light! Its real concern is growth and repair; it can't do *that* without inputs."

"We need to make repairs, too."

"Of course," Carla agreed. "Even if this device works perfectly, it won't make us self-sufficient for eternity. We'll still be using up all our limited supplies, including sunstone for cooling and other purposes. It won't buy us another eon to contemplate the ancestors' plight. The most I'm hoping it can do is get us back to them—with an idea worth trying for the evacuation."

"So you're saying that our grandchildren might see the home world?" Carlo joked.

"Maybe our great-grandchildren," Carla replied. "We're not going to be firing up these engines tomorrow."

The note of caution only made her sound more serious. Carlo turned the idea over in his mind; it was shocking just how alien it felt. This would be their purpose, finally fulfilled. No one was prepared for that.

"If we could see ourselves returning within a few generations…" He faltered.

"You don't sound too happy about it," Carla complained.

"Because I don't know how people would take it," he replied. "Would it make it easier to keep the population stable, if we knew there was an end to the restraint in sight? Or would it be harder to stay disciplined, if we could tell ourselves that there won't be enough time for a little growth to do as much damage?"

"I don't know either," Carla said. "But as problems go, aren't these the kind worth having?"

Carlo reorganized the shifts so that Amanda and Macaria could work beside him on the playback experiments. The changes they'd be looking for might be subtle, so they'd need as many eyes on the subject as possible.

Eyes and hands. With Benigna tranquilized and locked to her plinth, he decided, they could palpate her body safely enough. How else would they be able to characterize small changes in the arborine's flesh?

Their record of the onset of Zosima's fission had been ruined by the torn tape, but Carlo had identified a subsequent pause in the activity and isolated the first unbroken set of instructions that followed. He had considered playing back the tapes from the individual probes one at a time, but when he wound the recordings from the three lower probes through the viewer together it was clear from all their shared, synchronized motifs that these signals were acting in concert. If he disregarded this, he risked unbalancing the light's effect to a point where it was merely pathological. He wouldn't have tried to decipher a piece of writing by throwing out two symbols in every three before offering it to a native speaker, and if his intuitive sense of the structure of this language meant anything, the three probes' recordings—over a period of about a lapse and half—constituted the smallest fragment with any chance of being intelligible to the arborine's body.

On the morning of the experiment Carlo arrived early and started administering the tranquilizer to Benigna. The drug he pumped into her gut through the plinth was far milder than the paralytic in the darts, and would not act anywhere near as quickly. Benigno didn't take long to notice the effects, though: he let out a series of low hums, and his co's steadily weakening replies did not reassure him.

"I'm sorry," Carlo muttered. He'd planned to put up curtains to block

Benigno's view of the procedure—and Zosimo's too, for good measure—but he hadn't thought to do it so early.

Macaria turned up as he was finishing the task. He tied the last corner of the fabric into place, then dragged himself over to Benigna. Her eyes were still open, but when he tugged on her arms the muscles were slack. Macaria joined him, and they set about establishing a baseline for the arborine's anatomy. Carlo had decided not to make any exploratory incisions; as informative as they might have been, there was too much risk of disrupting the very effects they were hoping to measure.

Amanda arrived and started setting up the light players in the equipment hatch. Carlo went down to help her, and to satisfy himself that nothing would get shredded this time. The tapes themselves were merely copies of the recordings, but a garbled message could wreak havoc on Benigna's flesh.

"Are you ready?" he asked Amanda.

"Yes." Though she'd shown no enthusiasm for the experiment, no one had more experience with the players.

"We can try for a breeding in a few days' time," Carlo promised her.

"You really think she'll still be fertile after this?" Amanda gestured at the tapes.

"Maybe not," he admitted. "Then again, maybe her body will just ignore these signals without the whole context they had for Zosima—then we'll have learned that much about the process, and we'll still have a chance to record her undergoing quadraparous fission."

Amanda didn't argue the point. "You know what we should be studying in the arborines?" she said.

"What?"

"The effect of the male's nutrition on biparity."

Carlo said, "That would take six years and dozens of animals. Let's finish what we've started first."

He clambered back up into the cage. Benigno was still humming anxiously, but Carlo shut out the sound. He dragged himself into place beside Macaria and put his palms against Benigna's skin.

"Start the playback," he called to Amanda.

As the clatter rose up from beneath the cage a tremor passed through the arborine's body, but it was probably just a vibration transmitted from the machines themselves. Carlo glanced at Macaria, who was moving her fingertips gently over the opposite side of Benigna's torso. "I think there's some rigidity," she said.

"Really?" He pressed a thumb against the skin; it was a little less yielding than before.

The players fell silent. Carlo tried not to be too disappointed by the unspectacular result. He'd chosen a short sequence in the hope that it would elicit a single, comprehensible effect, and if this hardening of the skin—a prerequisite for fission—could be attributed to the motifs they had sent in, that would be one modest step toward deciphering the entire language.

But the response to the tapes hadn't played itself out yet: the arborine's skin was still growing more rigid. As Carlo tested it, he saw a faint yellow flicker spreading through the flesh below, diffuse but unmistakable.

Macaria said, "I think we might have triggered something."

The body did its best to confine its signals, to keep them from spilling from one pathway to another; only the most intense activity shone through to the surface. These errant lights reminded Carlo of the sparks that tumbled out when he set a lamp spinning in weightlessness: each spark drifted away, fading, but there was always another close behind. The tapes, it seemed, hadn't issued a simple instruction to the arborine's flesh: *do this one thing and be done with it.* They'd provoked it into starting up its own internal conversation, sufficiently frenetic to be glimpsed from outside the skin.

Could they have pushed the body into fission? Carlo was confused; Benigna hadn't even resorbed her limbs, and all the optical activity he could see was confined to her lower torso. He reached up and touched her tympanum gently, then her face; the skin here was completely unaffected. "This is some minor reorganization," he suggested. "Some local rigidity and a few associated changes."

"Perhaps." Macaria ran a finger across Benigna's chest. "If by 'associated changes' you mean a partition forming."

Carlo prodded the place she'd just touched; not only was the surface hard, he could feel the inflexible wall extending beneath it. "You're right."

"Transverse or longitudinal?" Amanda asked. She'd left the equipment hatch and was dragging herself into the cage.

"Transverse," Carlo replied.

"You know what that means," Amanda said. "We recorded Zosima's body instructing itself to undergo biparous fission—and now we've fooled Benigna's body into thinking it's told itself exactly the same thing."

"This is *not* fission!" Carlo insisted. He summoned Amanda closer and let her feel Benigna's unchanged head and upper chest.

Macaria said, "We only replayed the signals from the three lower probes—and nothing from the very start of the process. If there's a single message that sets fission in train, I doubt we've reproduced it."

"So if this isn't fission," Amanda demanded, "when does it stop?" A prominent dark ridge had risen across the full width of the arborine's torso.

Carlo probed one end of the ridge, following it down toward the plinth. "It isn't encircling the body," he said. "It turns around and runs longitudinally." He prodded the fleshy wall, trying to get a sense of its deeper geometry. "I think it's avoiding the gut." During ordinary fission, in voles at least, the whole digestive tract closed up and disappeared well before any partitions formed. If that hadn't happened to Benigna, perhaps the process that was building the partition had steered away from the unexpected structure—guided as much by the details of its environment as any fixed notion as to its own proper shape.

"How much does the brain need to spell out, and how much does the flesh in the blastula manage for itself?" Macaria wondered.

"The brain's resorbed quite late," Carlo said.

"That doesn't mean it's controlling everything, right up to that moment," Macaria countered.

Amanda reached past Carlo and put a hand on Benigna's rigid belly. "If we've told half her body that it's undergoing fission, does it really need any more instructions? What if it's taken it upon itself to finish what it's started?"

Carlo felt sick. "Should we euthanize her?" he asked. He was not sentimental, but he wasn't going to torture this animal for no reason.

"Why?" Macaria replied, bemused. "Do you think she's in pain?"

Carlo examined Benigna's face. The muscles remained slack and her eyes did not respond when he moved his fingers; he had no reason to believe that she'd regained consciousness. But his father had told him stories from the sagas of men accidentally buried alive, and the mere thought of that still filled him with dread. What was fission, if not the female equivalent of death? Would it not be as horrifying—even for an arborine—to wake on the far side of a border whose crossing ought to have extinguished all thought?

Amanda looked torn, but she sided with Macaria. "Let her live, for as long as she's not suffering. We need to know if this will go to completion."

The misshapen partition was thickening. Carlo fought down his revulsion and explored its full extent. After crossing the torso then turning at the sides to follow the body's axis, the dark ridge closed up on itself at the back of the arborine's thighs, a few scants clear of the anus. The implied excision was potentially survivable; the blastula had not claimed any part of Benigna's flesh that would normally be immutable.

"It's lucky we fed her up," Macaria said. "Or there wouldn't be much to work with."

"Are the limbs included?" Amanda wondered.

"Good point." Macaria prodded each of Benigna's lower arms in turn. "Their skin hasn't hardened." She ran her fingers up toward the torso, searching for the boundary. "Oh!"

"What?" From the sound of her voice Carlo was reluctant to touch the spot himself.

"If I'm right we'll see it soon enough," Macaria replied.

Over the next few lapses, two more dark ridges appeared at the top of the thighs. For some reason the flesh beyond was as unacceptable to the blastula as the digestive tract.

"That seems wasteful," Amanda complained.

"It's avoiding the bifurcation," Carlo guessed. "At this stage there wouldn't usually *be* any maternal limbs around, so whatever follows probably requires a convex mass of flesh." If the partition had veered toward the front of the thighs in the first place the limbs could have been excluded with less drastic consequences—but this was a blind process, robbed of its ordinary context, not something nature had ever had a chance to hone for the sake of Benigna's welfare.

"Next time we should arrange for the subject to resorb them first," Macaria suggested.

The blastula—or half-blastula—had found its borders now. The volume it enclosed was small, but not absurdly so: perhaps a sixth of Benigna's flesh.

"Do you remember the story of Amata and Amato?" Macaria asked.

"Vaguely," Amanda replied. Carlo knew it well, but he wasn't in the mood to offer a recitation.

"The two of them are in the forest looking for food," Macaria synopsized, "when an arborine chases them and gobbles up Amato. But years later, Amata has her revenge. She catches the arborine and swallows it whole—and it turns out her co's been alive all the time, trapped inside the arborine. All she has to do to bring him back is separate him from her own body, the way she might extrude a new limb."

"The moral being that you should never try to learn biology from the sagas," Amanda concluded.

"A good rule in general," Macaria agreed. "But that story does make me wonder. If we could bring this on with just a fragment of the usual signaling, the same kind of thing might happen occasionally in nature."

"You think that story's about *a partially formed blastula*?" Carlo asked incredulously.

Macaria said, "If the ancestors ever did see such a thing, even if they understood what it was they might not have chosen to describe it that way. A female's body gives rise to a new life, without fission. What kind of incendiary nonsense is that? Better to make the new life an old one, and come up with a story about her swallowing the monster who swallowed her co."

Carlo wasn't interested in scouring the sagas for dubious cryptobiological clues. What mattered now was deciphering the language being spoken right in front of them.

"We've come close to enforcing biparity," he said. In his shock over Benigna's transformation he'd almost lost sight of that crucial point. "It was the signal from the tape that established the partition's geometry, not the female's mass. If we'd played back all six recordings, we might have triggered an ordinary biparous fission."

No one disputed his reasoning, but his colleagues did not seem as pleased by this conclusion as he was. The idea of inserting six hardstone tubes into a woman's body fell a long way short of the promise of splicing the signals into an influence that could be written painlessly on the skin in infrared—and in either case, it wasn't clear how the male could be integrated into the process. If fission was initiated by the co, could the signals from a light player still intervene to set the number of offspring?

Carlo glanced down at Benigna; the tops of her thighs were atrophying, the gray skin puckering as the flesh below parted from the blastula wall. He checked her ocular response, but she remained mercifully insensate. This was a more severe amputation than his own, but he hadn't been shielded from that ordeal by a tranquilizing drug. More than the injuries themselves it was the context that made him recoil from her plight.

But what would the context mean to Benigna? She might have formed a notion of childbirth after witnessing it among her friends; she might even have reached a clear-eyed expectation of sharing their fate. But would it actually distress her to find that she'd given birth with that expectation unfulfilled? However powerful the instincts that would have led her willingly to the usual outcome, it did not necessarily follow that she'd be troubled in the least by events taking a different course.

Carlo looked up. *And Amanda, Macaria?* For all the unease they'd shown about Benigna's condition, there'd been no sign that they shared his own visceral revulsion. *One child that separated from the body, formed from reserves of mutable flesh, leaving the mother with wounds she could survive.* That was not at all like being buried alive.

Benigna's right lower arm broke free and drifted away from her toward the bars of the cage; in the imperceptible gravity Carlo had almost forgotten which way was down. He could see the walls of the partition beginning to split.

The child inside squirmed and forced the hardened skin of its mother's belly to separate from her torso. Carlo backed away, overcome with panic. "Should we bring in the father? Give it to the father?"

"I'd be careful," Macaria warned him. "The co's just as likely to kill it as accept it."

The child would not stay still. Its body twitched and shuddered as it tried to separate itself from what would have been its siblings in any normal birth. It stretched its limbless form up from the dark encrusted wound it had made until everything that clung to it and impeded its motion began to crumble like powderstone.

Carlo could see its head now. Its eyes were closed but it was flexing its tympanum, clearing it of debris. If the birth of four children had become a tragedy in the unforgiving world of the *Peerless*, and two a blessing, what was this? It struck him that his horror was not entirely irrational: such an impoverished mode of reproduction could never have been the norm in any species. Each generation would have been at most the size of the last, with any fall in population irrecoverable. Unless the whole thing became even stranger, and the act could be repeated. Unless a mother could not only survive giving birth, she could do so more than once.

The child began to hum. Benigno heard it and responded in kind, the two of them wailing at each other in an unremitting chorus of distress.

Macaria took the tiny arborine in her arms and brushed it clean, her strokes brisk but tender. Carlo felt a mixture of disgust at the spectacle and relief that he hadn't been forced to take charge himself.

"She looks healthy," Macaria observed, holding the arborine out for inspection.

"She?" Carlo had no idea how to sex a newborn animal with no co beside it for comparison.

"If the fission had been complete this would have been the female half," Macaria argued. "Either the signals we recorded from Zosima's division specified the sex, or the location in Benigna's body would have done it."

Amanda said, "We'll need to test this again on another female and see if we can get the same result."

Macaria concurred, adding, "Half a dozen times at least." She thought for a moment. "It would be interesting to see if the tape is conveying any traits from the original parents—if it just captured a generic, universal signal, or if anything specific to Zosima and Zosimo has been transmitted."

Carlo wasn't ready to look that far ahead. He turned to Benigna's damaged body. The surface of the partition had broken up, and what remained was already separating from the skin along the edges, exposing the flesh beneath. It was the largest wound he'd ever seen, save that on a corpse he'd encountered as a student—a woman all but sliced in two in a chemical explosion, offered up for dissection by her grieving co. He said, "I should give her more tranquilizer and try to close this surgically." Whether or not an arborine could be disturbed by perceived violations of the natural order, if Benigna woke to see a gaping hole like this it would render her philosophical attitude to childbirth irrelevant.

The child had grown quiet in Macaria's hands, but Benigno was still calling out in confusion. Without the promise there was no predicting his behavior toward his not-quite-daughter, but across species it was not unknown for some cos to bond with the product of spontaneous fission. "We should at least show him," Carlo suggested. "We can observe his reaction without risking the child.

"All right." Macaria moved carefully out of the cage, dragging herself along the guide rope with her two lower hands. Carlo followed her.

When Benigno saw the child he fell silent, though he seemed more perplexed than mollified. Carlo wondered if he was capable of distinguishing the possibilities and acting accordingly. If Benigna had given birth with a co-stead, would he have known that at once from the scent of the child? And if the child had been fatherless, the natural consequence of their enforced separation, would he have recognized that too and made the best of it?

Macaria moved closer and held out the child. Benigno stared at her for a while, then he retreated back along the branch he was holding and leaped over to the side of the cage, where he started prodding angrily through the bars at the curtain that was hiding Benigna.

"I don't think it would calm him down if he saw her in that state," Carlo said.

"Probably not," Macaria agreed.

"I'd better get her stitched up." And then free her from the plinth, Carlo decided. She'd been through enough.

"You should put them together again," Amanda said.

"Yes." Carlo was struggling to contain his emotions; part of it was genuine sympathy for the arborines, though part of it was probably just shock. "Once she's healed, they can both go back to the forest."

There was an awkward silence, then Macaria said quietly, "I'm not sure that would be a good idea, Carlo."

"Why not? I know we should test the tape again, but we don't have to do it on her."

The tape-fathered arborine baby was starting to squirm; Macaria rearranged her hold on her.

Amanda said, "We need to know what this has done to her body. After this, can she still breed naturally? Or having given birth once, is she now infertile? We'll need to observe her with her co until that's settled."

"You're right, of course," Carlo conceded.

He headed for the equipment hatch.

As he pumped in the tranquilizer, out of sight of the women, Carlo found himself trembling. What the three of them had witnessed had been crude and brutal, but some of the problems could be addressed immediately now that they knew what to expect. They did not know yet if Benigna would recover completely, or if her child would thrive and live normally, but in time they would know. And in time what they had started here might be polished and refined into a procedure that any woman could undergo without danger or discomfort.

So it was conceivable that the famine would be banished, not with biparity on demand but with a single child born alongside a surviving mother. It was possible that after all the time he'd spent rehearsing his grief for her, Carla might bear a child and go on to outlive him. And it was not beyond imagining that the *Peerless* would return to the home world bearing among its greatest prizes the end of the early death of women.

Carlo moved away from the base of the plinth and tried to steady his hands for surgery. Having played his part in these transformations, there was a chance now that he would have no son, and that the time would come when everyone would follow him, and there would never again be a father in the world, never again a co. He would have ended the famine, the infanticides and the greatest blight on the lives of women—and extinguished his own kind entirely.

37

"You need to understand," Carla pleaded. "This kind of research is more like exploration than engineering. It doesn't always take you where you expected to go."

Silvano was unmoved. "We're grateful for your efforts, Carla, but with all due respect it's not your role to decide where the research is taking us." He turned and addressed his fellow Councilors. "*The Object* is as real and solid as this mountain. We've seen it, we've visited it, we've brought its trajectory into step with our own—and in doing so, we've proved beyond doubt that it's composed of a material that can serve as a powerful fuel. But now this petitioner wants us to divert resources away from the program to make use of this extraordinary boon and invest them in a new kind of matter made entirely of light!"

"Temporarily," Carla stressed. "And if you'll forgive me for correcting you, Councilor, an optical solid isn't made *entirely* of light; the light waves form the energy landscape, but we still put luxagens into the valleys. The point of using that kind of system is that it would let us vary the energy levels relatively easily, so we could see if a rebounder can be made to work, in principle. Once that's been established we'll know whether or not it's worth trying to manufacture an ordinary substance with similar properties. It might sound profligate to perform these experiments on a 'solid' that needs sunstone to be burned just to maintain its existence from moment to moment—but there is no practical alternative."

"Can you be certain there's nothing in the mountain already that would do the job?" Councilor Giusta asked.

"Very nearly," Carla replied. "We've gone through the spectra of every kind of clearstone, and tried to infer the energy levels. That's not a foolproof process, but to test all the same materials directly would take a generation, and it would use up far more sunstone than the protocols I'm actually proposing."

"You've asked for a very large amount," Giusta said, glancing down at Carla's application.

"We need to run the coherent light sources at a very high intensity, to make the energy valleys deep enough," Carla explained. "But once we've mastered this—and once we can reproduce the effect in an ordinary solid—it will act as a net energy source. If we can get to that stage, the project won't require any more sunstone at all."

Giusta looked to Silvano, then the rest of her colleagues, but no one had any more questions for Carla. Even Councilors Massimo and Prospero— who'd been as merciless with Assunto on the hazards of dealing with the Object as they'd been with Carla at the previous hearing—seemed embarrassed by the alternative she was offering. The rebounder was already tainted by the inevitable comparisons with pre-scientific myths, but to claim that she could conjure her own Eternal Flame from a crystal of light sounded like the hyperbole of a stage magician: not even an appeal to genuine credulity so much as an invitation to share a joke.

"We'll adjourn now," Giusta said. "Thank you for your testimony."

When the Councilors had left the chamber, Carla was alone with Assunto.

"If you change your mind, you'll always be welcome on the orthogonal matter team," he said.

"Thank you." Carla had no ill feeling toward him; someone was always going to take over the project after she abandoned it, and she couldn't blame Assunto for being a persuasive advocate for the cause. She'd benefited from his skills often enough, herself.

"I've had some thoughts about the Rule of One recently," Assunto confided. "I'd be interested to hear what you think."

"Of course." Since the night with Patrizia and Romolo when they'd split the Rule of Two in half, Carla had had no success in explaining the simpler but equally mysterious principle that remained: once you took spin into account, you never found more than one luxagen in the same state.

"When we have a system of two luxagens," Assunto began, "we need to think of it as a wave that depends on the positions of both particles. So if one particle is mostly *here* and another is mostly *there*, we need the

wave to have a bump where the combination of positions spells that out."
He sketched what he meant.

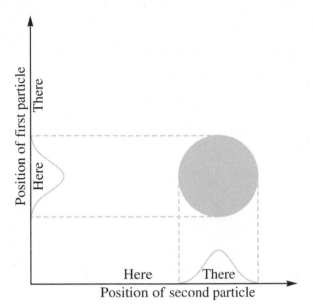

"Right," Carla said. "That's how I think of it too."

"But there's a problem," Assunto claimed. "Suppose we compare that with another wave, where we swap the two particles."

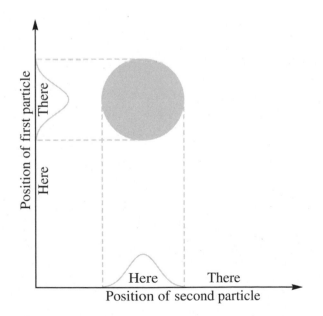

"That's really the same thing," Carla protested. "A luxagen is a luxagen; it makes no sense to say that it's the 'first luxagen' in one location and the 'second one' in the other. Unless they have different spins, and you're using that to tell them apart?"

Assunto said, "No, no. Forget about spins for the moment, or just assume the spins are identical. Take it as given that we really can't tell these luxagens apart."

"Then the two situations are exactly the same," Carla replied.

"So you're saying there are two different waves that can be used to describe the same physical situation?"

"Yes," Carla insisted. "It's just a convention, a naming scheme: you have to make a choice, but the choice itself makes no difference."

"All right," Assunto agreed, though his assent sounded distinctly provisional. "But now suppose I want to *compare* the wave for this pair of luxagens with the wave for another pair that are in roughly the same positions. How exactly should I make the comparison? Which of the two waves should I use in each case? There are four possibilities in all. Half those possibilities give the two pairs of luxagens very similar waves… while the other half give them very different waves!"

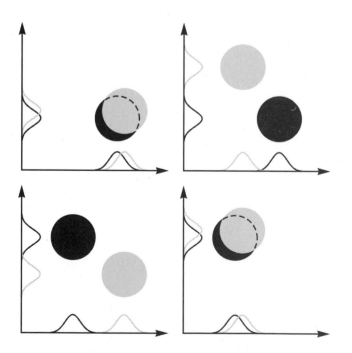

Carla thought for a while. "Surely you just need to use the same scheme for both? I mean, it's obvious that there ought to be some overlap between the two waves—and if you use different schemes there's no overlap at all."

"But if you can't tell the luxagens apart," Assunto pressed her, "how do you define 'the same scheme'? How do you actually *pick* which luxagen of the pair gets its position assigned to which axis?"

"Hmm." He'd forced her into a contradiction; she'd claimed the choice of schemes didn't matter, but now she'd starting talking about the importance of selecting the right one, case by case.

"Do you have to peek at their locations first, then make sure you give the same axis to whichever particles are closest together?" Assunto was gently mocking her now.

"Hardly." Carla stared at the four diagrams. She was starving, and she'd barely slept for the last three nights, but she wasn't going to let him make a fool of her with this problem.

"You use both schemes," she said finally. "Simultaneously. You *add* the wave where you use the first axis for the first particle to the wave where you use it for the second particle."

She sketched the idea.

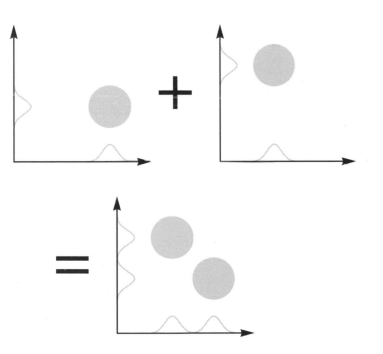

"The wave for the whole system is completely symmetrical," she said. "It makes no difference if you swap the axes, or swap the particles. And when you compare two situations with two particles in roughly the same two places, you're guaranteed to get a sensible result with some overlap between the waves."

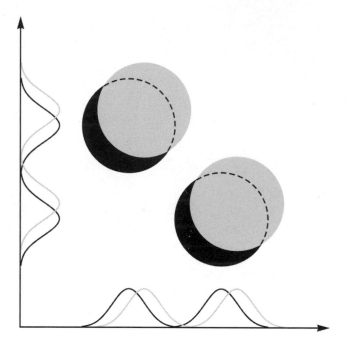

"I think you're right," Assunto said. He sounded pleased that they'd reached the same conclusion—but he wasn't yet finished with the subject. "That's one way of doing wave mechanics with identical particles."

"*One* way?"

"It looks like the most natural choice," he said. "But I don't believe it's the only one. What about this?"

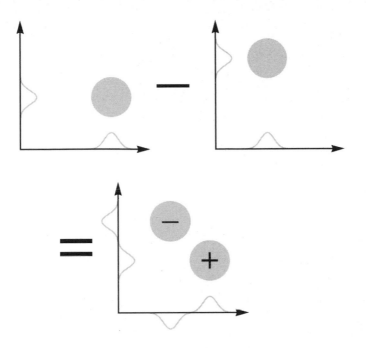

"You subtract the waves instead of adding them?" Carla was confused. "But subtract them in what order? Aren't you asking for the same problem again: which of two identical particles do you call the first?"

"No, because it *makes no difference*," Assunto replied. "If you change the order, you just turn the whole wave upside down—and an overall change of sign like that has no effect on the physics of the wave."

That was true. "But what's the point?" Carla asked. "You end up with a wave with two bumps of opposite sign, instead of two identical bumps. The mathematics becomes a bit more complicated, but the final answers all turn out the same."

"The final answers don't depend on putting the particles in any particular order," Assunto said. "But what makes you think they're the same when you subtract the schemes as when you add them?"

Carla examined the diagram again. "If the particles get close together, the two waves you're subtracting start to overlap."

"Yes."

"And if they're in *exactly the same state*," she realized, "you get nothing, zero."

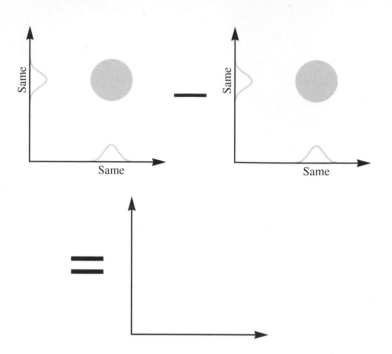

"Precisely." Assunto buzzed softly. "Does that remind you of anything?"

"The Rule of One," Carla said. "So you're saying that you can never have two luxagens in the same state, because they follow this subtraction scheme, where the total wave for the pair would vanish?"

"Yes!"

"But why? Why can't they follow the addition scheme?"

"It must be linked to the luxagen's spin somehow," Assunto said. "Think about the similarities! Take a luxagen, with spin of a half, and rotate it by a full turn: the rotation gives you the *opposite* of the original luxagen wave. A transformation that leaves most things unchanged leads to a change of sign. And now it turns out that we can get the Rule of One if we assume that *swapping two luxagens in a pair*—another transformation that might be expected to have no effect at all—also changes the sign of the overall wave."

Carla remained silent, but she didn't doubt his claim. These things could not be empty coincidences; Assunto was drawing close to a beautiful mystery.

He said, "I think we're on the verge of explaining all the different properties of luxagens and photons. Photons are simply jumps between the energy levels in the light field, but with this clue I think there's a chance we'll find a way to see luxagens in the same terms. I used to believe that that was absurd, that the two things were completely incomparable… but look at the difference we can get from one small change in the way the wave is constructed! With photons, you *add* the different ways you can arrange them, so there's no problem if a dozen photons are in the same state—it just means pushing one particular mode of the light field up a dozen energy levels. With luxagens, what we need to do is find the mathematical twist that *stops you* raising the energy of each mode once you've taken it to the first level—a way of guaranteeing that there's either a single luxagen in that state, or none at all. Once we've translated the Rule of One into the language of fields, everything will be unified into a single picture."

It was a glorious vision. And who with even a trace of curiosity in their soul wouldn't wish to follow it: to see the deepest, simplest rules that governed light and matter finally spelt out?

Carla said, "If I joined you, what would happen to the rebounder?"

"Why not let that wait until the politics is more favorable?" Assunto suggested. "Silvano won't be on the Council forever."

"No?"

"Do you think we'll see any real progress toward an engine based on orthogonal matter before the next election? Do you think we'll see the old feeds dismantled to make way for new farms?"

"Probably not." Carla regarded him with grudging admiration. "You're just playing them, aren't you? You don't think an engine like that can be made to work at all."

"Who knows what our descendants will achieve?" Assunto replied innocently. "But for now, this is the path of least resistance with the Council. So why not make the most of it? Whatever we can learn from experiments with orthogonal matter is sure to be worth knowing. If destroying two luxagens to make a pair of photons doesn't give us insight into both kinds of particles, I don't know what will. And you discovered that reaction, Carla! How can you not want to study it further?"

"I do," she said. "But if I put the rebounder aside in the hope that the

Council will eventually lose faith in the alternatives... I might not be around when they reach that position."

"None of us are going to be around forever." Assunto was probably six years older than her, which made his words a little less glib than they might have been. "Do you think either of us will live to see the *Peerless* decelerate, by any method?"

"Probably not," Carla admitted.

"You've published your idea," Assunto said. "It's exciting and provocative; it certainly won't be forgotten. If it can be made to work at all, you can be sure it will be put to use one day."

"And you expect me to leave it at that?" Carla knew better than to try to force him to give his own verdict on the rebounder's chances; the last time, all she'd managed to extract from him was an acknowledgment that it broke no laws in any obvious manner. "I know I'll never see the home world, but it would still be something to know before I die that we've found a way to turn the *Peerless* around."

"And what if you can't prove that? What if you can't make this thing work?" Assunto wasn't goading her; there were a dozen ways she could end up facing that result, even if the basic idea was sound. "To live on the *Peerless* means handing half-solved problems on to our descendants. The ancestors had to accept that at the launch, but it's no less true for this generation. There is no such thing for us as seeing an end to this. If you go looking for finality, you're only going to be disappointed."

The Councilors were returning. Carla didn't try to read their faces as they entered the chamber; she turned her gaze to the floor. What had she been thinking—talking up the promise of the Object one day, declaring it redundant the next? The science was what it was, but she should have sought a way to shift the political momentum gradually—instead of standing in the path of Silvano's blazing rocket, waving her arms and expecting him to change course.

Giusta announced the Council's decisions. Assunto's proposal had been accepted; the research into orthogonal matter would continue under his supervision.

"And Carla," Giusta continued, "as intriguing as your idea was to the Council, we owe it to our descendants not to be reckless in our use of their legacy. If it turns out at some time in the future that we have less need to keep sunstone in reserve—a position to which Assunto's project might well take us—then we would be prepared to reconsider your proposal. For now, though, we can't risk disposing of such a large quantity of fuel for such an uncertain outcome."

38

"Do you want to tell me what's going on here?"

Tosco was halfway along the guide rope that crossed the chamber between the arborines' cages; he must have entered while Carlo was in the storeroom. Carlo spent a moment contemplating his superior's demeanor before deciding that there was no point in lying to him. He would not have been so angry unless he already knew at least part of the answer.

"This female is doing well," Carlo said, pointing to Benigna asleep in the cage to his left. Almost hidden behind her, a smaller form clung to the same branch. "She's been feeding her child regularly, though her co is still ignoring it."

"*Her* child?" Tosco sounded neither amused by the claim nor incredulous, so it was unlikely he was hearing it for the first time. He must have had a chance to get used to the idea before coming to see the evidence with his own eyes.

"I don't expect she thinks of it that way," Carlo replied. "I believe she's treating it as she'd treat any orphaned relative; it's like the niece she never knew she had. And she's not such a stickler for logical niceties that it makes any difference that she never had a sister."

Tosco hadn't come here to discuss kinship-based altruism in arborines. "You've found a way to trigger the formation of a survivable blastula?"

"Survivable with surgical intervention," Carlo said. "I wouldn't put it more strongly than that."

"How many times have you done this?"

"Just three."

"Oh, is that all?" Tosco had finally found something funny in the

298

situation. "When were you going to tell me? After a dozen?"

"I wanted to be sure of the results before I made too much of them," Carlo explained. "If Benigna here was just an accident, it would hardly have been worth publishing."

"No? I think that sounds like exactly the right thing to publish."

"Well, that's not how it's turned out."

"Kill her," Tosco said bluntly. "Then the other two, after a suitable interval. When you dissect them, you need to find that all three bodies were riddled with malformations."

Carlo hesitated, trying to think of a way to phrase his reply that avoided a flat out refusal. "Amanda and Macaria aren't stupid," he said. "If I tried to fake something like that, they'd spot it—and who knows what kind of fuss they'd make?"

Tosco wasn't stupid either; if he knew that one of the women would make no fuss at all, he wasn't offering any hints. "How many copies of the light tapes are there?"

"A few."

"How many, exactly?" Tosco pressed him. "Where are they being stored?"

Carlo gave up on the idea that he could get through this without a confrontation. "There are dozens, and they're very widely scattered. You can forget about destroying them."

"You've lost your mind, Carlo," Tosco declared. "This was supposed to be about biparity."

"And it might yet be," Carlo replied. "In a stint or two, when Benigna's gained enough body mass I'm going to see if she can produce a second child the same way. Now there's a nice title for a paper: 'Light-induced facultative serial biparity in arborines'. We ought to start a competition, to find the phrase in reproductive biology that the ancestors would find maximally oxymoronic."

Tosco's curiosity got the better of him. "What about her co? Has he tried to breed with her?"

"Yes."

"And what? She fought him off?"

"No, she cooperated. But nothing happened. In that sense at least, she's infertile. It's possible that she's lost the ability for spontaneous division too, though we'll have to wait a year or two to be sure."

Tosco's interest in the biology vanished. "You can forget about another year or two. I want all the females dead within six days, and all the offspring. I want all the tapes destroyed—"

"That's not going to happen," Carlo said firmly.

Tosco dragged himself closer. "Have you forgotten who you're working for? Who got you permission to take these arborines from the forest in the first place?"

"Do you want to put this to the Council?" Carlo asked him. "I'll be happy to accept their decision."

"Maybe we should do that," Tosco replied. "There are five women on the Council, and seven men—and not all the women will see it your way."

"Nor all the men yours." In any case, Carlo was sure that he was bluffing. He wanted the possibility Benigna represented buried immediately, not debated throughout the *Peerless*.

Tosco turned to examine Benigna's cage. "That's the future you want to force on us? A world of women, reproducing by machine?"

"That doesn't have to be the end point," Carlo said. "It's possible that we can learn to trigger survivable male births as well. And in the long run it's possible that we could integrate the whole thing back into the body, via influences: no machines, just co mating with co again—leading to births without the death of the mother."

Tosco was unswayed. "That's generations away, if it can be done at all."

"You're probably right," Carlo conceded. "I'm just trying to be clear that we're not carving anything in stone. Nothing in this process can determine the way things happen for all time. Suppose a few children are born by this method. If they decide that they want to reproduce the old way, they'll be no worse off than solos are now: they'll be free to go and find a co-stead."

"Just 'a few'?" Tosco asked sardonically. "So are you going to help a few friends survive childbirth, and leave the rest of the women on the *Peerless* to follow their mothers?"

"Of course not. But as you said about the Councilors, not every woman will be in favor of this. No compulsion, no restrictions—we should just work to make this safe, then give people the choice."

"Most women can handle the fast," Tosco said. "Most births are already biparous. I'm sorry about the burdensome task you were given by your friend, but you have no right to destroy a whole society just to ease your conscience."

Carlo had never told him about Silvano's children. He wasn't surprised that word of it had spread, once Silvano became a Councilor and every aspect of his life gained new currency. But he'd never expected it to be thrown in his face.

"How many years is it now, since you murdered your co?" he asked. "Five? Six?"

Tosco buzzed derisively. "Murdered her? We made the choice together."

"What choice? Between slaughtering her then, or letting her starve for a few more years?"

"You're like an infant!" Tosco sneered. "Still humming at night about your poor lost momma and the terrible thing men do to their cos? Grow up and face the real world."

"I have," Carlo replied. "I faced it, and now I'm going to change it."

"This is finished," Tosco said. "It's over." He started dragging himself out of the chamber.

Carlo clung to the rope, shaking with anger, trying to decide what to do. Tosco wouldn't go to the Council; he'd round up a group of allies and come back to kill the arborines and smash the equipment.

Carlo wondered how long he had to prepare for that. A few bells? A few chimes? The news of what he'd done here might enrage many people, but it was a complicated message to get across; Tosco couldn't just shout a few slogans in a food hall and find himself the leader of a rampaging mob. He was more likely to start with fellow biologists, who'd understand the arborine experiments and their implications. But they wouldn't all share Tosco's view of the matter—and even those who did would take some persuading that violence was called for.

The biggest risk, Carlo decided, would arise if he panicked and went to summon help immediately, leaving the arborines unprotected. He needed to stay calm and wait for Amanda to start her shift.

When Amanda arrived, Carlo explained what had happened. "Are there people you can bring here?" he asked her. "People you'd trust to stand guard?"

Amanda regarded him with horror. "What do you want to do? Start some kind of siege here? Some kind of battle?"

"What choice do we have?" Carlo wasn't relishing the confrontation any more than she was, but he couldn't stand aside and let Tosco destroy their work.

"Let me think." Amanda swayed back and forth on the rope. "What if we released the arborines back into the forest?"

"They'll know we've done it."

"They'll guess that it's one possibility," she conceded. "But you know how hard it is to catch an arborine in the forest. And even Tosco's only seen the ones here briefly; do you think he can describe any of them reliably to an accomplice?"

Carlo wasn't happy, but her argument made sense. Taking a stand in this chamber would just offer their opponents a clear focus for their belligerence, and trying to hide an arborine anywhere else would be futile. The arborines weren't the ultimate repository of the technology anyway, so half a day in the forest would probably be enough to rob most people of their resolve to hunt them down.

"All right," he said. "But we'll need to tranquilize them as lightly as possible, or they could still be vulnerable if someone goes looking for them."

"That's true." Amanda hesitated. "You really couldn't finesse your way out of this with Tosco?" She made it sound as if it should have been easy.

"He already knew most of it!" Carlo protested. "Someone tipped him off."

Amanda said, "Don't look at me, I haven't told anyone."

"Not even someone you trusted to keep it to themselves?"

"I'm not an idiot, Carlo."

Amanda fetched the dart gun, and Carlo prepared darts with a quarter of the usual dose. The arborines were all still asleep, so most of them were easy targets, but Pia was hidden behind too many twigs and flowers for Carlo to get a clear shot. He entered the cage, dragged himself along a nearby branch, then plunged the dart into her chest. Her daughter, Rina, stirred and started humming; Carlo reached over and took her in his hands to soothe her. He'd held her at her birth, and she'd tolerated him ever since. Her mother's co was still in the forest, but if Benigno's behavior was any guide Pio would show her neither affection nor hostility.

"I'll take these two first," he called to Amanda.

It was only a short trip to the forest's entrance, and the corridor was empty. Rina clung to Carlo's shoulder as he dragged himself along the rope, lugging her limp mother beside him. Amanda followed with Benigna and her daughter Renata, the bewildered child squirming and humming in a net.

In the forest Carlo took Pia a short way up toward the canopy, maneuvering her laboriously past the snares of sharp twigs, impressed anew by Zosima's feat when she'd fled from him with Benigna in tow. Pia was already beginning to stir, so he released her and waited until she gripped the branch beside her; she was still weak, but she wasn't in danger of drifting away. Rina clambered onto her mother's chest, and Carlo headed back to the forest floor. Amanda had climbed a different trunk with her passengers, but she wasn't far behind him and she soon caught up.

"We need to know for sure that the children can breed normally," Carlo fretted. "That's more important than whether or not we can induce a second birth."

"We have two years until they're reproductively mature," Amanda replied. "Don't you think it's more important to keep them alive than to keep them under observation?"

"Of course." Carlo hesitated. "Do you think Macaria went to Tosco?"

Amanda said, "I doubt it. If she'd wanted to bury the work she could have poisoned the arborines herself, and damaged the tapes before we'd made any extra copies."

"That's true." *Who, then?* Since Benigna had given birth, one of the three of them had always been on duty in the facility, but Carlo often spent half his shifts in the adjacent storeroom. Tosco might have asked someone to look in on them, unannounced—and then he and his informant could have put most of the story together for themselves.

They shifted the remaining arborines to the forest, then began disconnecting the light players from the hatches below the cages. There was nothing here that couldn't be rebuilt, but Carlo wasn't going to surrender any of it while he still had a choice. The three researchers had each hidden three copies of the tapes without disclosing the locations to each other, so unless Tosco had had a small army of spies working around the clock it was unlikely that he'd be able to find them all.

When they'd packed the equipment, Amanda took hold of one box and surveyed the empty chamber. "What now?"

"I'll have to go to the Council," Carlo decided. "We're going to need their protection."

"And what if they back Tosco instead?"

Carlo scowled. "On what principle can they shut us down? Their job is to manage resources, keep us safe and honor the goals of the mission. Finding out if there's another way to give birth that would help stabilize the population—while improving women's productivity and longevity—is just good resource management."

Amanda said, "A few stints ago you weren't even interested in learning whether males could raise the chances of biparity by *eating less*. And now you expect people to stand on principle when there's a prospect of men being driven to extinction?"

"So which would you prefer?" Carlo retorted. "The satisfaction of seeing your co starving like a woman, or the chance to eat your fill and live as long as any man?"

"It's not about wanting to see anyone *starving*," Amanda replied. "The arborines aren't starving, but the effect must be stronger when both parents' bodies signal a lack of abundance."

Carlo was exasperated. "So now you want to quibble about what constitutes the best of all possible famines—when we're talking about surviving childbirth? Seriously, if we can prove that this is safe, which would you choose?"

"That's none of your business," Amanda said flatly.

Carlo caught himself. "You're right. I'm sorry." He'd spent the time since the first induced birth fighting against his own instinctive revulsion, telling himself that he owed it to the women of the *Peerless* to keep his resolve. But it would not be an easy decision for any woman, and he had no right to make the issue personal.

"But you do support the research?" he asked.

"Did I quit the project?" Amanda replied. "Why would I try to stop anyone having a child this way, if it's what they want? But a lot of people won't see this as a choice at all, they'll see it as a threat." She gestured at the other box. "Can you take that? I don't want to be here if Tosco does show up with a wrecking crew."

Carlo fetched the box and followed her out of the chamber.

"When I've stashed this somewhere safe I'd better go and see Macaria," she said. "Let her know what's happening."

"Thanks."

"I suppose we should all just lie low until you've been to the Council and we know their position."

"That sounds like the best idea." Carlo was beginning to feel more anxious now than when he'd pictured a mob coming for the arborines, waving flaming lamps like farmers burning out a wheat blight. Somehow he'd imagined the clash being over in a bell or two, leaving the whole thing resolved.

But however cathartic the idea of a battle seemed, it would not have settled anything. The victors would not have changed the minds of the vanquished, and whoever might have prevailed in that display of force, the ideas of their opponents would have lived on unchanged.

Carla listened patiently, as silent and attentive as when Carlo had first told her that he was giving up agronomy to work on animal reproduction. When he'd finished, she asked a few questions about the process itself: the range of signals he'd recorded from Zosima as she underwent fission, and the particular ones he'd used that had caused Benigna to give birth.

"It's interesting work," she said, as if he'd just described a study of heritable skin markings in shrub voles.

Carlo took her tone as a form of reproach. "I'm sorry I kept it from you. But the team agreed not to talk about it with anyone until we'd reproduced the results."

"I understand," Carla said.

Carlo examined her face in the lamplight. "So what do you think? Is this... a promising direction?" He didn't know how else to phrase the question, without asking her outright the one thing he knew she wasn't ready to answer.

She stiffened a little, but she didn't become angry. "It's always good to know what's possible," she said mildly. "Tosco's a fool; perhaps he was entitled to complain that he'd been kept in the dark, but shutting the whole thing down was an overreaction."

"I'm going to have to go directly to the Council," Carlo said. "I'll need your advice on that."

"Ha! After my last triumphant appearance?"

"You can tell me what mistakes to avoid."

Carla pondered that. "See how many allies you can get before the hearing itself. That's what I should have done."

"I only know one person on the Council," Carlo said. "Do you think Silvano's going to be in the mood to do me any favors?"

"You never know," Carla replied. "If you have a chance to talk to him before he's hemmed in by his fellow Councilors, he might decide that the issue itself is more important than paying you back for failing to drag me into line over the new engines."

"That's not impossible," Carlo conceded. "Silvano can be erratic, though. If it goes badly with him, it might be worse than having said nothing."

Later, as they climbed into bed together, Carlo felt a surge of anger. He was trying to build a road for her out of the famine. He'd risked his whole career for that—for her and their daughter. He'd understood when she hadn't dared to hope he would succeed, but even now, when he had the living proof that things could be different, why couldn't she offer him a single word of encouragement?

He lay beneath the tarpaulin, staring out into the moss-light. If he'd wanted unequivocal support from anyone—man or woman, friend or co—he'd stumbled upon the wrong revolution.

"I'll try to catch Silvano while he's still at home," Carlo said.

"Good idea," Carla replied, moving away from the food cupboard to let him pass. She was chewing her breakfast loaf slowly, stretching out each mouthful as if nothing had changed. But a lifetime's habits couldn't vanish overnight. Carlo tried to imagine her as plump as Benigna had been, all the old prohibitions reversed as she made herself ready to give birth to their first child. *Her child, their child?* He was not an arborine, bound by instinct; he was sure he could love any daughter of her flesh as his own.

"Keep the argument focused on the research," she suggested. "Don't make it personal. If you start trying to connect this to what happened to Silvana—"

"I'm not quite that crass," Carlo replied. "But thanks anyway." He dragged himself toward the door.

"Will you let me know how it went?" she asked.

He watched her for a moment in his rear gaze. She was not indifferent to what he was doing, just wary.

"Of course," he said. "I'll come by tonight."

Out in the corridor, Carlo glanced at passersby, wondering if any of them had yet heard the news about the living arborine mothers. With Amanda and Macaria released from their vow of secrecy and Tosco surely seeking allies of his own, it would not take long for word to reach every corner of the mountain. He might finally be known for something other than losing control of the fingers of one hand.

As he reached the corner and swung onto the cross-rope, two men who'd been coming in the other direction leaped onto the rope, one behind him and one in front.

They were wearing masks: bags of dark cloth with crude eye-holes.

"Do you mind?" Carlo was aware that this encounter wasn't actually a matter of clumsiness or discourtesy, but he was unable to think of any words that suited the reality.

The man behind him pulled a strip of cloth out of a pocket in his skin, then clambered onto Carlo's back and began trying to wind it around his tympanum. Carlo let go of the rope and concentrated on fighting him off; untethered, the two of them drifted sideways across the corridor. It was an ungainly struggle, but Carlo felt in no danger of being overpowered; he'd had a much harder time in the forest, wrestling with Zosimo.

The other man pushed off the rope and followed them, taking something small from an artificial pouch. Carlo abruptly changed his mind about his prospects and called out for help as loudly as he could. There had been other people in the corridor, before he'd taken the turn. Someone would hear him and come to his aid.

The man with the cloth lost interest in silencing him, but then in a sudden deft move twisted the fabric around the wrists of Carlo's upper hands. The constricted flesh was trapped, too rigid to reshape. With his lower hands Carlo tried to push the man off him, but the cloth kept the two of them joined. The accomplice had misjudged his move away from the rope, but having brushed the side of the corridor he was heading back toward them.

"Help me!" Carlo called again.

The man with the cloth pulled it tighter. "That's the thing about traitors," he said. "No one can hear them."

The second man reached out and seized the trailing end of the cloth, then used it to pull himself closer. Carlo could see him shifting the small object in his other upper hand, moving it into position. If they were working for Tosco it would probably be a tranquilizer. If they were working for themselves it might be anything at all.

Carlo extruded a fifth arm from his chest and reached out to grab the man's wrist, staying the dart. Instead of matching him limb for limb, the man released the cloth and brought his freed hand forward, but before it could join the fight Carlo pushed away hard, propelling the man backward.

The assailant behind him grabbed the end of the cloth and wound it around Carlo's fifth wrist. Carlo extruded a sixth limb and tore at his bonds, to no avail. The accomplice scraped the wall again and managed to reverse his velocity. The first man was blocking Carlo's rear view, but ahead the corridor was deserted.

Carlo had no flesh left for a seventh arm. "Who are you?" he demanded. The man with the dart was drawing closer.

"Nature won't be mocked," the other man said quietly. "What did you expect? You brought this on yourself."

39

"Can you spare a moment, Carla?" Patrizia clung to the rope at the entrance to the classroom. "I have a wild idea I'd like you to hear."

Carla regarded her with affectionate bemusement. "Why aren't you at the planning meeting for Assunto's team?"

"Assunto's team? Why would I be there?"

"The future's in orthogonal matter." Carla tried not to sound bitter. "All the new ideas, all the new technology—"

"All the new explosions and amputations," Patrizia replied, dragging herself toward the front of the room. "I thought the chemists had a bad reputation, but at least they never messed around with negative luxagens."

"You could always stay away from the experiments," Carla suggested. "Assunto's trying to build a field theory for luxagens. Don't you want to be a part of that?"

Patrizia said, "If there's a luxagen field permeating the cosmos, I expect it will still be around next year."

"That's true. But what's your big plan for the coming year?"

"What are you going to do?"

Carla spread her arms, taking in the empty classroom. "Was I such a bad teacher?"

"Never. But is that enough?"

"I'm too tired for anything else," Carla admitted. The news that Carlo's best attempts to end the famine now involved the prospect of inserting signals from a mating arborine into women's bodies had crushed whatever small hope she'd once had that she might free herself from the hunger daze. "Maybe someone will look at the rebounder again when the politics is right."

"Forget about the politics," Patrizia said blithely. "You won't need to go begging for sunstone if you can make this work in an ordinary solid."

"We've looked at every kind of clearstone in the mountain," Carla protested. "Are you going to try cooking up something new?"

"Not exactly," Patrizia replied. "But I just read Assunto's paper on multi-particle waves and the Rule of One."

Carla hesitated, turning the non sequitur over in her mind in the hope that a connection would become apparent.

It didn't.

"Go on," she said.

"According to Nereo's theory," Patrizia began, "if you take two tiny spheres with source strength and set them spinning, one beside the other, if the 'north poles' are sufficiently close they'll try to repel each other. That means the system will have its highest potential energy if you force those poles together. The circumstances in which that happens will depend on both the directions in which the spheres are spinning and their relative positions."

She sketched two examples.

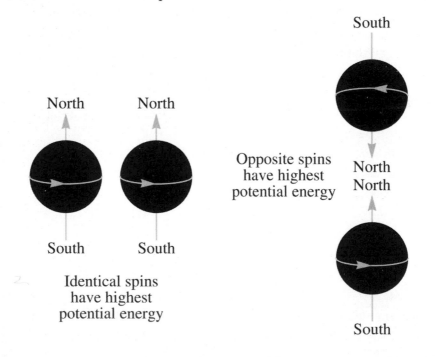

"It's an odd effect, isn't it?" Carla mused. "Two positive sources attract, close up, but the poles of these spheres work the other way: like repels like."

"It's strange," Patrizia agreed. "And I can't claim that it's ever been verified directly. Still, everything we know suggests that it's true—and that it ought to apply to spinning luxagens, in addition to the usual attractive force."

Carla said, "I wouldn't argue with that." They'd found that the energy of a single luxagen in a suitably polarized field depended on its spin, and there was no reason to think that the analogy would suddenly break down when it came to two spinning luxagens side by side.

Patrizia continued. "The Rule of One won't let you have two luxagens with identical waves and the same spin—but that still leaves open the question of what happens to the spin when the waves themselves are different. If you take this pole-to-pole repulsion into account for two luxagen waves in the energy valley of a solid, on average it gives a higher potential energy when the spins are identical. So if the spins start out being different the system will emit a photon and gain the energy to flip one of the spins and make them the same. In other words, though the paired luxagens with identically shaped waves *must* have opposite spins, the unpaired ones ought to end up with their spins aligned!"

Carla wasn't sure where this was heading. "The energy differences from these pole-to-pole interactions would be very small, and we probably don't have the wave shapes exactly right. Do you really think this is a robust conclusion?"

Patrizia said, "I don't, which is why I didn't raise it with you before. But then I read Assunto's explanation for the Rule of One, and that changes everything."

"It ruins the effect?"

"No," Patrizia replied. "It strengthens it enormously!"

Carla was bewildered. "How?"

Patrizia buzzed with delight. "This is the beautiful part. Assunto claims that for any pair of luxagens we need the overall description to *change sign* if we swap the particles. If the spins are identical, in order to satisfy that rule you need to subtract the swapped versions of the waves. But if the spins are different, you use the spins *instead of* the waves to do the job of changing the overall sign when you swap the particles. So in that case, you find the positions of the luxagens by *adding* the swapped versions of the waves."

She sketched an example.

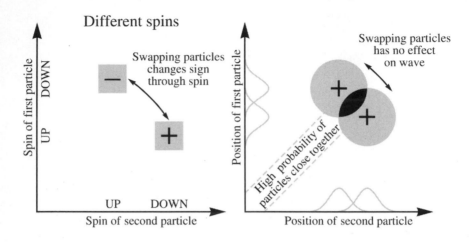

"By adding the waves," she said, "you end up with a high probability of the luxagens being close to each other. Now compare that with the case where the spins are the same and you need to subtract the waves to get the change of sign. There's a much lower probability of the luxagens coming close."

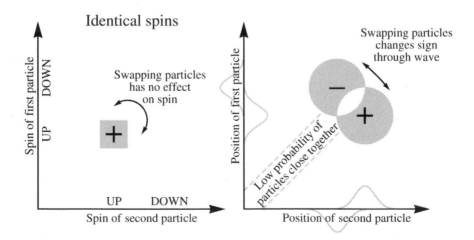

"All from the spins," Carla marveled. "And by changing the distance between the luxagens..."

"You change their potential energy," Patrizia concluded. "Not from the weak, pole-to-pole repulsion, but from the attractive force between the luxagens. Through Assunto's rule, having identical spins forces the average distance between the luxagens to be greater, which means a higher potential energy. So we're back at the original conclusion: unpaired luxagens really *should* be spinning in the same direction."

Carla paused and ran through the whole analysis again in her head; there were just enough twists in the argument that she was afraid they might have lost track of one of them and proved the opposite of what they'd thought they'd proved. "That does makes sense," she concluded. "But what does it have to do with the rebounder?"

Patrizia said, "In an optical solid we could use the polarization of the light to create the kind of field where each luxagen's spin affects its energy—splitting the usual energy levels by a very small amount. The tiny jump between those closely spaced levels would be a perfect match for the tiny shift in energy for photons rebounding from an imperfect mirror. I'm sure we could have made that work—but wouldn't it be better to do it in an ordinary solid?"

Carla understood the connection now. "Enough luxagens all spinning in the same direction ought to produce a similar kind of polarized field within an ordinary solid. But we never saw any sign of it in the spectra of the clearstone samples."

Patrizia adjusted her grip on the rope. "The spins *within each valley* ought to be aligned—but once you go any further, the waves overlap far less and the force between the luxagens starts cycling back and forth between attraction and repulsion. So we can't rely on Assunto's rule to produce any kind of long-range order. Beyond a certain point, the directions of the spins will just vary at random—producing fields with random polarizations that largely cancel each other out."

"Right." Carla hesitated. "Which is unfortunate, but what can we actually do about it?"

"Maybe nothing," Patrizia conceded. "But there's one thing we could try. If the geometry, the energy levels and the number of unpaired luxagens are all favorable... I think we could 'imprint' the regularity of an optical solid onto a real solid. The field pattern traveling through the optical solids we've made so far isn't moving all that rapidly. There's no reason we couldn't shoot a real solid through the light field at the same speed; that way it would experience a fixed pattern. If we can expose the material to an ordered, polarized field for long enough, we might be able to achieve a long-range alignment between all the unpaired spins."

Carla was speechless. Patrizia had produced her share of follies—and it was possible that this was one of them—but nobody else on the *Peerless* could have thought up this magnificent, audacious scheme.

"If we can identify a good candidate for imprinting," Patrizia continued, "the hard part will be obtaining flawless crystals. This can only work if the geometry is almost perfect, otherwise the fields from the luxagens in different valleys will slip out of phase. But if we start with small granules, and pick out the ones that look homogeneous—"

"Like Sabino when he measured Nereo's force?" Carla interjected.

"Exactly." Patrizia was growing anxious to hear a verdict. "So you agree that it's worth trying?"

Carla said cautiously, "I can't see anything that rules it out. But we need to look at the whole thing more closely; we need to study the dynamics of these unpaired luxagens in an external field—"

Patrizia gave a triumphant chirp. "When do we start?"

Carla had no more classes to teach for the day, and she doubted she'd be able to concentrate on anything else until it was clear whether or not this offered a real chance to salvage the rebounder. "What's wrong with now?"

A woman called out brusquely from the doorway, "Do you know where Carlo is?" It was his colleague, Amanda.

"Not this instant," Carla replied. "He said he was going to see Silvano this morning, but the meeting's probably over by now."

Amanda said, "You need to find him."

She wasn't being rude, Carla realized. She was distressed.

"What's going on?" Carla asked her gently.

"Some men tried to grab me outside my apartment," Amanda replied. "And now I can't find Macaria or Carlo anywhere."

"What men?"

"There were four of them, all wearing masks. Someone helped me fight them off, then they ran away."

Carla felt her whole body grow tense. "You think this is about the arborine experiments?"

Amanda said, "Yes."

Patrizia turned to Carla. "I heard people talking about that this morning. I thought it was nonsense, I just ignored it."

"What were they saying?"

"That Carlo had created an influence that could force women to give birth." Patrizia's tone was scornful. "All he had to do was point a light at your skin!"

"That's not true," Amanda assured her. She gave a quick account of the actual procedure.

Patrizia looked dazed. "You're saying I could have a child and *go on living?*"

"We've only tested it on arborines," Amanda stressed.

"But once you're sure that it works on people—?"

"It still won't be a simple thing," Amanda replied. "It would require surgery before and after the birth."

"And the number of children?" Patrizia asked her.

Amanda said, "One. Always one at a time."

Carla broke in. "I should go and see Silvano, and try to retrace Carlo's movements from there."

"I'll come with you," Amanda offered.

"What about Macaria?"

"I've already spoken to her co. He's gathered some friends and started his own search."

"I'll come too," Patrizia said. "Until we find Carlo, my hands are your hands."

Carla was moved by this vow of solidarity, but as they headed out into the corridor she realized that it came from something more than friendship. Patrizia was not at all dismayed by what Carlo had done. Once the shock had worn off she had shown every sign of welcoming the news.

There were women who would embrace this bizarre intervention. Carlo was not in danger from some confused rabble who'd taken the rumors Patrizia had heard seriously. He was in danger from every man who'd heard the truth about the technology, and feared that his co would use it to dispense with him entirely.

"Carlo hasn't been here," Silvano insisted, turning to shout a curt reprimand into the children's room. "What's this about?"

Carla let Amanda explain most of it: the arborine experiments, Tosco's reaction, the attempt to abduct her, her two missing colleagues. Silvano took the first revelation with admirable poise, but Carla judged that he was not quite so unfazed as to be hiding prior knowledge of the matter.

Patrizia recounted the rumors she'd heard of a new influence. Silvano seemed paralyzed for a moment, but then he said, "I'm going to call an emergency meeting of the Council. I'll ask both Tosco and Amanda to give evidence, so we get both sides of this." He must have seen the growing distress on Carla's face; he said, "I'm sure we'll find Carlo unharmed, very soon. You should put a report out through the relay. What the Council can do is promulgate statements dismissing the rumors, and warning people against taking any kind of action against the researchers."

"People don't already know that abduction is a crime?" Amanda asked sarcastically.

"A reminder that they're risking six years' imprisonment might focus their attention," Silvano replied. Carla stopped herself before interjecting that that wasn't the sentence Tamara's kidnappers had received. It had been Tamara's choice to show them mercy, not the Council's.

She wasn't satisfied, but she didn't know what more Silvano could do, so she left him and Amanda to organize the meeting and headed with Patrizia for the nearest relay station. Harnessed to the paper tape punch, she composed a report describing what she knew of Carlo's movements and appealing for any witnesses to contact her. The punch only had buttons for two dozen basic symbols, but the pared down vocabulary that imposed helped her to keep the message free of adornments and to resist the urge to add threats and accusations. When she was finished she dialled in her private key and waited for the machine to append an encrypted digest of the text as proof of authorship, then she handed the completed tape to the clerk. Within a couple of bells there'd be copies throughout the mountain.

Patrizia had waited for her in the corridor. "Carlo wouldn't have been on his usual route to work," she said. "And they couldn't have known where he was going."

Carla felt sick. "They must have followed him from my place," she said. Somehow they must have known that he'd be with her that night, rather than in his own apartment. Tosco would have been aware of their living arrangements, in general terms, but it was unlikely that he'd committed their precise schedule of cohabitation to memory. Her neighbors, though, knew exactly when Carlo came and went.

"We should retrace the whole route," Patrizia suggested. "It might give us some ideas."

"All right," Carla agreed numbly.

They moved along the corridors slowly, Patrizia surveying the walls around them as if they might bear some physical trace of the event. Carla stared into the faces of the people they passed, as if her angry scrutiny might provoke a flicker of guilt that would allow her to unravel the whole conspiracy.

If someone had tipped off Tosco, as Carlo had believed, other people might have been aware of the arborine experiments for days. No one could organize three kidnappings overnight. But a lot of people had taken sides over Tamara's abduction, and those who'd sympathized with the kidnappers then would not have forgotten which of their friends had shared their views on the proper limits to a woman's freedom. Word of Carlo's research could have spread quickly through a network of like-minded travelers who already knew they could trust each other, as they formed a plan to nip the abhorrent new technology in the bud.

They had almost reached Carla's apartment when Patrizia said, "What's that?"

Carla followed her gaze. A tiny dark object—a cylinder maybe a scant long and a quarter as wide—had settled on the floor of the corridor.

Patrizia pushed away from the rope and deftly retrieved the thing, returning with a well-aimed rebound. She examined it, frowning, then passed it to Carla.

The cylinder was made of wood. It had a thin hollow core that reached almost its full length, but stopped just short of the far end. Carla had seen something similar before, used as a sheath for a needle.

"They must have injected him with something," she said. She handed the object back to Patrizia.

"Who would have access to a drug like that?" Patrizia asked. "A pharmacist? A doctor? A biologist? Maybe that hunter who helped him catch the arborines?"

Carla said, "Anyone could have stolen it."

"But those supplies would be monitored closely," Patrizia replied. "We could check with all the groups who use that kind of thing."

"Starting with Tosco's?" Carla knew she meant well, but begging people to audit their drug inventories would be pointless. "Whoever it is, they'll be asking him about the tapes," she said. "The recordings of the arborine mating."

"If that's all they want, surely he'll just tell them where they are," Patrizia suggested hopefully. "Why would he be stubborn about it?"

"But that's the problem," Carla said. "If he gives up the tapes too easily, they'll understand that they don't really matter: he can always make another recording. He can always do the whole thing again."

Patrizia said, "So you're afraid they'll realize that, and try to kill off all the arborines?"

"That's one possibility. Or maybe they'd think one step beyond that, and understand that sooner or later someone would volunteer to take the arborines' place."

"So if the tapes don't matter, and the arborines don't matter…?" Patrizia struggled to grasp her point.

"If he doesn't fight for the tapes," Carla said, "they'll understand that the only way to end this is to kill him."

"No, no, no." Patrizia reached over and squeezed her shoulder. "Don't say that! If they're so quick to grasp the futility of destroying the tapes and the animals, they should understand one more thing: even if they did kill Carlo—and Macaria and Amanda—it would only take a year or two for someone else to reinvent all the same techniques. Everyone in the mountain understands what's possible now. That can't be undone."

Carla said, "Maybe. But from what I've read of history, lost causes have cost as many lives as any other kind."

Patrizia had no answer to that. She said, "We should go to the Council chambers. They might not let us into the meeting, but at least we can be the first to hear what they decide."

Carla could hear raised voices coming from the chamber, but the words remained indistinct. Why couldn't Carlo have taken his discovery to the Council, before anyone else had had a chance to find out what he'd done? Whether they'd have shut down his research or allowed it to continue, at least the responsibility would have fallen on them.

The meeting stretched on interminably. After half a bell, Macario arrived to join the vigil.

"Any news?" Carla asked him. She barely knew the man, but it was painful to see his haunted demeanor.

"Not yet," he said. "But if Tosco knows where they are, I'll beat it out of him."

"I don't think he's behind this," Carla said. "However angry he was at being kept in the dark, he still had authority over the project. There was a lot more he could have done, legitimately—"

Macario interrupted her. "He told Carlo to put a stop to this, but Carlo ignored him. What 'authority' is that?"

Carla didn't want to have this argument. "Did you send out a report on Macaria?" she asked.

"Of course. And my friends are heading out to search the farms."

"The farms?"

"Where else can you hide someone?"

That did make sense; cries for help would be heard from any apartment or storeroom, and even the noisiest pump room received too many visits from maintenance workers to make a good jail. Tamara's kidnappers had shown the way—and if they'd also made the choice a bit too obvious, their successors might well have reasoned that the other advantages outweighed that.

Carla thought about joining the search party; it seemed Macario had only left his friends to come chasing after Tosco. But first she needed to hear what the Council decided. If they banned the research that might be enough to mollify the kidnappers—in which case it would probably be safer for Carlo if she just waited for news of the decision to spread.

"I think the meeting's breaking up," Patrizia announced.

Carla said, "Your hearing's better than mine."

The Councilors began emerging from the chamber. She searched for Amanda, but Silvano appeared first.

Carla approached him. "What's happening?" she demanded.

"There's going to be a vote," he said. "To determine whether the experiments can proceed."

"*Going to be?* Why haven't you taken one already?"

"The vote will be for everyone," Silvano explained. "That's what we decided. This wasn't an issue when we were elected to the Council, so we agreed that we have no mandate to set a policy. Two stints from now, every adult will be able to cast a vote on the matter."

"Two stints?" Carla stared at him angrily. "A lot of things weren't *issues* when you were elected; that's never stopped you making decisions about them."

"Carla, this is—"

"And how are people going to vote on this, when they don't even know what it's about?" she protested. "Half of them think Carlo built a magical light player that can make women give birth from afar!"

Silvano said, "There'll be information meetings every day until the vote, with Amanda and Tosco setting out the facts."

"*Tosco?*" Carla was about to object that Tosco had already shown himself to be wildly partisan, but then she understood that there was no point arguing about any of this. The vote would go ahead; nothing she said was going to change that. So let Tosco denounce the project, let people believe any rumors they liked: a plague of fission that spread faster than wheat blight, with every woman giving birth to six arborines. If there had to be a vote, what she needed was a foregone conclusion: a certain loss for Carlo's side, so the kidnappers would have no reason to harm him.

Macario had cornered Tosco and was shouting in his face. Carla looked on as Tosco protested his innocence. "Someone left a note in my office," he said. "I have no idea who it was."

Silvano said, "The Council's authorized a search of the *Peerless*. We've diverted two dozen people from the fire-watch roster to carry it out, but I'll show you and Macario the names and you can ask for replacements if you believe anyone has a conflict of interest."

"All right."

"And you're welcome to accompany them on the search, as an observer," Silvano added.

"Thank you." Carla felt a little less hopeless; the Council hadn't abandoned the abductees entirely.

But the kidnappers would be expecting a search; they'd be prepared to shuffle Carlo and Macaria from one site to another. However large the team that scoured the mountain, they couldn't look everywhere at once. Two dozen searchers were better than nothing, but the real power still lay with the voters.

If she wanted to see Carlo alive again, what she needed most of all was a way to turn everyone on the *Peerless* against him.

40

Tamara waited for Livio outside the meeting hall, watching the other participants drag themselves in. The proceedings weren't due to start for another chime, but the sound of all the voices from within was already deafening.

Livio arrived, his arms and chest still bearing traces of white dust. "I'm sorry I'm late," he said. "There was a job I had to finish."

"You're not late." Tamara pointed to the clock.

"Late enough that we'll be at the back of the audience."

"That might be the safest place," Tamara joked.

They made their way into the crowded hall. There was a schedule based on birth dates for the particular meetings people were supposed to attend, but it was not being enforced, and Tamara had chosen to break the rule on principle. If cos were allowed to hear this news together, why not co-steads?

There were no visible gaps anywhere in the hall, but the back ropes were the least densely packed so they forced their way onto one of them. As they settled into place Tamara felt self-conscious; she didn't mind being squashed by the stranger on her right, but she'd never had Livio's skin pressed against her like this.

With Tamaro, the significance of contact had come and gone. As children it had meant nothing when they touched, a pleasure as innocent as a shared joke, but when they reached fertility it became charged with danger, more thrilling and vertiginous day by day. As the compulsion grew, they started sleeping with the scythe between them, the blade a reminder when they woke in the night of exactly what it would mean to give in. And gradually, each accidental brush of skin on skin lost both its sweetness and its threat. The outcome it foretold remained a certainty, but it became second nature to think of it as indefinitely postponed.

With Livio, she didn't know what to feel. She focused her attention on the man to her right, then tried to spread her indifference to him across her whole body.

Councilor Giusta opened the meeting with an appeal for anyone with information about Carlo or Macaria to come forward and speak with her at the end of the proceedings. Most of the audience listened in polite silence, but Tamara heard some amused exchanges in front of her; she didn't catch every word, but the gist was that the *Peerless* was well rid of the traitors.

Amanda spoke next, describing the experiments that she and her colleagues had performed on a small group of arborines. Though she must have believed that the research was worth pursuing, she eschewed advocacy and confined herself to a dispassionate account of the team's interventions into the animals' reproductive cycle.

To Tamara, the lack of rhetoric only made her words more resonant: "The female we'd named Benigna survived the birth. After minor surgery she became mobile again, and took to feeding her daughter. Her co, who was not present at the birth, showed no interest in the child." *Survived the birth. Feeding her daughter.* They sounded like phrases someone had brought back from a second *Peerless*, returning from its own eons-long journey orthogonal to the first.

Amanda was emphatic in dismissing the rumors that they'd created some kind of transmissible agent. "I expect that some of you here tonight must have volunteered to have influences recorded, or you might know someone who was sick at the time and took part in that project. We do believe that some influences spread as infrared light, passing from skin to skin—and it's true that we were searching for a way to get instructions for biparity into an arborine's body that way. But we never found an influence that was taken up by the arborines—and we certainly never assembled a new one with the aim of affecting people in any way."

Tamara heard skeptical noises from the same group who'd found Giusta's appeal so hilarious. She forced herself not to glare at the idiots; there was nothing to be gained by starting a brawl.

Giusta introduced Tosco as an expert whose perspective would balance

Amanda's partisan account.

"You will all have your personal views on the kind of society that these experiments seem to be offering us," Tosco allowed. "And perhaps some people are attracted to this vision of an end to the famine, with women living through the birth of a child and going on to meet the fate of men. But we need to examine the consequences much more closely.

"In such a world, who would raise the children? *Their mothers?* Nature has never had reason to shape women's temperament to that task. We've all heard moving stories of the tenacity of women caring for the children of solos and runaways: these courageous women raised many of our grandparents, whose own mothers had taken to the *Peerless* alone to escape the brutality of their cos. The excess of women among the first travelers was unprecedented, and we should be proud that we survived the disruption that followed. But we can't build a safe, stable society on a state of perpetual emergency. Enduring a calamity is admirable; creating one by choice would be the height of folly.

"Now, you might have heard rumors that some prospect exists for the same kind of procedure to give rise to complete families, with a male co. As Amanda has already explained, no second births have yet been demonstrated, and no male births at all. But let's suppose for the sake of argument that the research continued and it led to such a result.

"The experiments already tell us what the outcome would be. The male arborines showed no interest whatsoever in the children of their cos whose births were induced by the light players. A society of struggling women would be fragile enough—but mixing in an equal number of men, all robbed of their natural purpose, would be disastrous."

"We're not arborines," Tamara muttered irritably. She turned to Livio. "And if the First Generation had such a rough time, surely that was due to the holin shortage? How can he compare your friends fissioning without warning into four children each with a deliberate choice to create a single child of your own?"

Livio didn't answer, but a woman in front of them hummed at Tamara reprovingly.

Tosco proceeded to raise and dismiss a series of ever wilder possibilities. "Perhaps in the distant future, after generations of research, we could redesign our biology completely so that men and women could come together in the usual way, and the only difference in the outcome would be the woman's survival and perfect control over the number of children. How could anyone object to that? I can't—but I don't believe it's anything more than a fantasy. This work began as an honest search for a means to achieve biparity without the famine, so that women would be spared the difficult price they pay for population control. And that's still a worthy target to aim for: a simple drug that will mimic the reproductive effects of starvation, in our daughters' lifetimes—not the remote prospect of our great-great-grandchildren bending every law of biology to their will."

Giusta invited questions from the audience.

"Even if this method as it stands has flaws," a woman asked, "why is that a reason to abandon further research?"

"It's a distraction," Tosco replied.

"A distraction for whom? From what? Which urgent project is suffering such a lack of biologists that three people continuing this work for a few more years would be a tragedy?"

Tosco said, "It distracts us all. Our whole culture is damaged by false promises like this."

"Our culture is damaged?" His interlocutor buzzed. "By a few experiments on arborines? Can you be more specific?"

"I'm sure everyone accepts that we live in a complex, delicately poised—"

The questioner cut him off. "Are you worried that women will start delaying childbirth?"

"That's one possibility," Tosco agreed. This brought a few angry shouts from the audience until Giusta gestured for silence. "I respect women's autonomy absolutely," Tosco declared. "The timing of childbirth is a personal choice. But that doesn't mean we can ignore the problems that would follow if the average age began to rise. If the children aren't born until their grandfather is dead, their father is left to raise them alone—"

"Not if their mother's alive!" a young man interjected. His friends broke into fits of mirth; apparently the idea remained so surreal to them that they couldn't treat it as anything but a joke.

The next question was directed to Amanda, and again, the questioner was a woman. "Why are you defending the elimination of an entire sex?" she demanded angrily. "Is my co not a person to you? My father? My future son?"

Amanda said, "This work has barely begun. That we haven't had a chance to demonstrate a male birth doesn't mean such a thing is impossible."

"But what need will there be for men? Why would anyone give birth to a son, when he'll consume his share of the entitlement for nothing?"

"That's your way of thinking, not mine," Amanda replied stiffly. "I believe this research should continue until we learn exactly what kinds of reproduction are possible. That's all. I'm not calling for any method—new or old—to be imposed on anyone."

"And you can promise that will never happen, can you?" the woman asked sarcastically. "What if some future Council decides to turn half the farms over to another use? If we all had just one child—one girl—we could halve the size of the crop and still live comfortably."

Amanda was bewildered. "We could spend a whole evening imagining the terrible things a future Council might do," she said. "But do we really have to shy away from identifying our choices, out of fear that someone, someday might abuse that knowledge?"

Giusta took two more questions, but they were both phrased so abusively that she decided to call an end to the meeting. As Tamara and Livio made their way toward the exit, Tamara saw a scuffle break out near the front of the hall. Only a few people were actually grappling with each other, but they were surrounded by two much larger groups exchanging taunts.

"You want to vote for genocide?" a man shouted suddenly, brandishing a knife. A second man beside him seized his wrist and they struggled for a moment, then the knife floated away, out of reach of both of them. Tamara glanced anxiously at Livio; he was trying to move along the rope, but someone ahead of them had stopped to watch the brawling.

"Do you want to go around?" he asked her. Other people had already started leaving the rope, pushing off into the empty space above, apparently in the hope that some combination of the hall's weak gravity and a wall-bounce or two would deliver them neatly to the exit.

"I don't think so," Tamara replied. Most people hadn't practiced these kinds of maneuvers since childhood; she watched as two women collided in mid-air and began screaming abuse at each other. The hall could have done with a dozen more ropes to make the whole volume traversable—but there still would have been a crush at the doorway when the extra routes all converged again.

"They shouldn't have packed the hall like this," Livio complained. "It's a miracle nobody's passed out from hyperthermia."

When they finally reached the exit they found people lingering outside, apparently just for the pleasure of shouting at each other. Further from the hall they were passed by two groups of youths engaged in running skirmishes, pummeling each other as they bounced off the walls of the corridor.

Tamara was shaken, but she tried to keep everything in perspective. Nobody could contemplate an upheaval like this with perfect equanimity; just raising the subject was always going to create some bitter divisions. But only a few people had turned violent. And the last thing she wanted to do was vote down the research for the sake of a quiet life.

"It's a shock to hear it put so starkly," she admitted. Even after days of rumors and third-hand accounts, it had taken Amanda's testimony to make the results real to her. "But no one would be forced to use this method. Who can complain about being offered a new choice?"

"No one," Livio replied. "Until a couple want two different things."

His words gave Tamara pause, but she pressed ahead. "Have you decided how you'll vote?" she asked.

"For the research to continue," he said. "And you?"

"The same." Tamara was relieved that he hadn't been intimidated by the turmoil. "You're not worried that it might cause conflict?"

"Of course it will cause conflict," Livio said. "But if they shut down the research now, that would lead to just as much violence. And all the same experiments would be carried out in the end—in secret, probably less safely. There is no perfect solution to this mess."

This *mess?* Tamara continued along the rope in silence for a while, but she couldn't leave things there.

"What would you say if I wanted to have a child this way?" she asked him.

Livio didn't need to consider his answer—but then, he must have known for days that he'd be facing this question eventually. "I'd say you're entitled to do what you wish with your body."

"So you'd have no problem with it?"

He turned to her. "You're not my property, Tamara. But you're not my flesh either. We made an agreement for our mutual benefit, but if one of us reneges on that agreement, it's void. I'm not going to help you raise a child I played no part in creating—and I'm certainly not going to pass my entitlement on to any such child. What I want is a co-stead who will give me two children of my own. If you can't accept that prospect any more, our obligations to each other are over."

When Tamara arrived in the observatory's office, Ada was looking through a sheaf of papers. "Have you seen these?" she asked, holding up one sheet.

"No." Tamara took it.

"It's just a copy," Ada explained. "But Carla signed a digest of the whole thing—with a statement saying she found it in Carlo's apartment."

Tamara read the first sheet, then asked for the rest. It was an autopsy report on two arborines: a mother and her child, one of the births induced by the light players. The mother's body had been found to contain a second blastula, hidden beneath the skin of her chest—grossly malformed, but apparently still growing at the time she'd been euthanised, five days after the birth. The child, the daughter, had abnormal structures in her brain and her gut, and adhesions throughout her malleable tissues.

"So much for the miracle of light," Ada said glumly.

"Amanda didn't mention any of this." Tamara was confused. "I thought all the arborines were sent back to the forest."

"Three mothers and their children did go back. But apparently Amanda hasn't been telling us about the fourth one."

Tamara re-read the report. "How do we know this isn't a forgery?"

"I was suspicious too," Ada admitted. "But I checked the digest."

Tamara hummed impatiently. "I meant, what if someone planted a forgery in the apartment for Carla to find?"

"You'd think she'd know her own co's writing," Ada reasoned.

"Why? Tamaro never saw any of my work notes."

"And look how that turned out," Ada joked.

"I'm serious!" Tamara protested. "They lived apart most of the time; she might not be the best person to authenticate this."

Ada spread her arms. "Who would you prefer? Amanda claims it's not

Carlo's writing, but if she lied about the fourth arborine—"

"And I suppose Tosco says it looks authentic?"

"Yes. All right, he's obviously biased," Ada conceded. "Still, that's two witnesses against one."

Tamara took the report over to the relay station and began checking the digest herself.

"You don't trust *me*, now?" Ada complained.

"Anyone can hit the wrong button by mistake."

"And I did, twice," Ada retorted. "But you know what that gives you." The odds against an error making a forgery look authentic were astronomical.

The machine shuddered and declared the digest valid.

Tamara said, "They should autopsy the other arborines."

"That sounds good in principle, but who's going to identify them?" Ada replied. "Amanda just has to point out some healthy specimens instead of the real ones—"

"I don't believe this!" Tamara punched the desk. "You know what kind of state Carla must be in! Someone's fooled her, that's all!"

Ada jokingly feigned a flinch away from her. "All right! Stay calm! I never said that was impossible."

Tamara gave up arguing the point. "The only way to sort this out is with new research," she said. "That's more important than ever now."

Ada eyed her warily. Tamara said, "Don't you dare tell me you're changing your vote!"

"I'm not!" Ada assured her. "But let's be honest: it's a lost cause now."

Roberto entered the office, back from his shift, so Tamara dropped the subject. The last time she'd raised the vote in his presence his discomfort had been palpable.

"Anything interesting out there?" she asked him.

Roberto stretched his shoulders wearily. "What do you expect?" he replied. "You only get one Object in a lifetime."

In the observatory Tamara sat harnessed to the bench, dutifully searching the sky for passing rocks, but as the shift wore on it grew harder for her to keep her mind on the star trails in front of her. She was tired of having her future dictated by people and events beyond her control. She needed to take her fate into her own hands.

If she gave up on co-steads—and gave up on children—wouldn't that set her free? It was what she should have done the moment she escaped from Tamaro. If she kept taking holin and nothing went wrong, she might live for another six or seven years. What was there to regret in that? She wasn't afraid to go the way of men when the time came.

But a part of her still balked at the decision. She'd never obsessed about the children she'd had no hope of seeing—never named them, never even pictured them—but when she thought about relinquishing all hope of their existence she felt a kind of hollowness pervading her flesh. It was as if she'd spent her life tacitly aware of them, not as ideas but as a physical presence: two latent bodies nestling under her skin, waiting to be born.

She looked away from the telescope, intending to rest her eyes for a moment, but as she gazed out through the transparent dome she caught sight of something that her narrower search had missed. About a third of the way up from the horizon, there was a visible break in the bright orange streak that usually formed part of a single long star trail. The gap was about half an arc-lapse—half the width of her thumb held out at arm's length. If it was a passing rock it was either phenomenally large or phenomenally close; the saner interpretation was that a small piece of detritus had somehow adhered to the clearstone of the dome itself. But she had barely had a chance to ponder the fastest way to test that possibility when the star trail abruptly became whole again.

Tamara cranked the telescope as quickly as she could to the point where she'd seen the thing, estimating the coordinates from half a dozen surrounding features. There was nothing visible at the original location—and nothing nearby on the azimuthal arc along which any obstruction stuck to the rotating dome would have traveled.

After a frantic sweep she finally found it: a silhouette against the background of stars, absurdly huge under this modest magnification. She ran her fingertips over the dials of the clock, then wrote the time and the coordinates on her forearm. The silhouette was moving rapidly, blacking out each streak of color behind it for no more than four pauses. It was hard to discern its precise shape, as it seemed to be spinning as it moved, complicating its outline.

This was no interloper; any object crossing the sky so rapidly had almost certainly come from the *Peerless* itself. Tamara reached over and pulled a lever to ignite the shielded sunstone lamp that powered the coherent light source. The device was just a test rig that Romolo had loaned the astronomers, to try out on the first of Marzio's new beacons. The tuning mirrors tended to slip out of alignment, and she had to spend a couple of lapses adjusting them until the monitoring screen showed a steady pin-prick of red light. That was from a tiny portion of the beam; the full radiance would have blinded her. She slipped the mirror into place that sent the beam to a second small telescope mounted parallel to the main instrument.

A red spot appeared in the center of the silhouette—bright enough to prove that the thing was small and close, not large and distant. Tamara guessed it was at most a few strides across—a rock that had broken away from the mountain's slope, or something discarded from an airlock.

But that made no sense. The mountain's spin could cast objects away, but they'd always be traveling at right angles to its axis. Anything flung off by centrifugal force would, in short order, end up motionless against the stars, a retreating image fixed on the observatory's horizon. Not only was this thing above the horizon, it was ascending. Another force must have altered its trajectory after it had left the mountain.

It was a person, Tamara realized. Someone must have fallen from one of the fire-watch platforms. They'd tried to use their air jet to get back, but they'd panicked and become disoriented.

She tore off her harness and scrambled for the exit.

Ada was still in the office. Tamara explained the situation, and gave her the times and coordinates she'd need to extrapolate the watcher's trajectory into the future.

"I want you to go up and keep the light source trained on them. I'll follow the beam out."

Ada said, "No one's been reported missing. There's a dead-man alarm on every platform; people don't just disappear into the void."

"What did I see, then?" Tamara demanded. "Explain it to me!"

"I have no idea." Ada's expression changed suddenly. "Unless it was deliberate?"

Tamara understood her meaning: someone on fire watch who'd been advocating too loudly for the wrong kind of vote might have had a surprise visitor. The alarm would present no problem: the watchers themselves disabled it for every change of shift.

"Track the beam for me?" Tamara pleaded.

Ada said, "This is crazy! How are you going to see it?"

"I'll improvise. *Please?*"

Ada gave up arguing. "Be careful," she said.

She headed for the observatory. Tamara headed for the airlock.

Out on the slope, Tamara clambered along the guide rails leading up from the airlock until the dome of the observatory came into view. Even from this distance she could see a faint red glow on one of the clearstone panels: scattered light from the beam. She released the rails, waited a moment to fall safely clear of them, then used the air jet strapped to her body to cancel the sideways velocity she'd acquired on her way out to the airlock. The rails receded into the distance as the rock of the slope swept past beside her.

She fired the jet again, to take her toward the peak. Once she was level with the dome she slowed herself, then she used a quick burst to move straight toward the red glow. She struck the dome squarely on the panel she'd been aiming for and gripped the edge tightly with six hands, then glanced down and saw Ada gawping up at her. Tamara freed one hand to wave at her, then another to help tug an empty cooling bag out of her tool pouch and spread it across the panel. The beam showed up as a dazzling red disk half a dozen scants wide, shimmering through the fabric.

She didn't need to use the jet: she pushed off from the dome, rising slowly into the void, holding the white banner stretched out below her. She ignored the stars, the dome, the mountain, fixing her attention on the way the light was drifting across the cooling bag.

She aimed the nozzle of the jet carefully, then opened it for a fraction of a pause. The red disk jerked wildly toward the edge of the fabric, and for a moment she thought she'd lost it, but when she stretched her left arm out a bit further the light reappeared.

Once it was clear that she wouldn't need another correction immediately, Tamara opened her rear eyes and searched for the fire-watcher's silhouette. She trusted Ada to perform her task flawlessly, but if the watcher hadn't noticed the beam alight on them—or in their state of confusion had failed to grasp its meaning—they might have done the worst thing possible and fired their air jet again, changing their trajectory.

Tentatively, she slid the banner out of the beam, allowing the light to continue unobstructed to its original target. For a long time she could see no sign of it above her, but then she picked out a faint red speck surrounded by blackness. The silhouette had been there all along, but the trails behind it were so dim that she could barely make them out; little wonder she'd missed the gaps in them. She waited as long as she dared, hoping the reassuring message of the beam would get through, then she spread the banner out again to check her own alignment.

Ada's tracking was perfect, and the watcher was proving to be an obliging partner in the rendezvous. There were grimmer reasons than presence of mind why someone lost in the void might stop trying to change course, but Tamara didn't want to dwell on them.

The next correction she made would need just the briefest puff of air; Tamara's fingers almost cramped with anxiety at the thought that she might open the valve too wide or for too long. The disk of light jittered, mapping every fluctuation in the nozzle's tiny thrust, but when it settled it was closer to the center of the banner than ever. She chirped to herself to release the tension, then gazed in sudden wonder at the steady red glow. The navigators who'd brought the *Peerless* onto its orthogonal course had worked the marvel of their age, but none of them could have imagined following a beam like this across the void. She was at least four saunters from the mountain now, but the red disk had barely increased its width and was barely diminished in brightness.

The third correction was no less daunting, but she didn't foul it up. Tamara imagined a daughter beside her, learning this skill from her, sharing her delight in the intangible red guide rope.

She could see the figure above her clearly now, almost certainly a woman, spinning slowly in the starlight. Tamara let the beam fall on the woman's cooling bag, but it elicited no response.

Agonizing over their relative velocity would only waste time; she was sure it would not be injuriously high. She stuffed the empty cooling bag back into her tool pouch to free two more hands, aimed herself straight at the woman, and prepared to grab her.

Their bodies collided with a beautiful dull thwack, and Tamara closed six arms around her in a tight embrace. For a moment she almost let go in shock: the skin pressed against her through the fabric was alarmingly hot. She felt around the woman's back for any trace of air wafting out; there was none. There was no canister attached to the bag, and no air jet either. Quickly, Tamara tugged her spare canister out of its pouch and snapped it onto the inlet. Air flowed through the bag, sending a warm breeze spilling out into the void.

How long could someone survive without cooling? Tamara shuddered, trying to remain hopeful. She tied their cooling bags together, then took a moment to get her bearings. They were spinning now, and they'd lost the beam, but it wouldn't be hard to navigate back to the mountain by sight alone.

She pressed her helmet against the woman's. "You're safe now," she promised her. "Just rest if you like. There's no hurry to wake."

Had the woman used up her air jet's tank, then resorted to the cooling air as a substitute? But then, why was the jet gone entirely? The situation only made sense if there'd been no jet in the first place. The woman had fallen into the void with nothing to help her. She'd improvised with the bag's air canister and managed to cancel out some of her velocity, but when she'd lost consciousness the canister had escaped from her hands.

Tamara put the mystery aside and concentrated on reducing their spin. Once the stars were no longer reeling around her, she took sight of the mountain's peak and fired the jet, starting them on their way home.

Ada met them by the airlock.

"How is she?" she asked Tamara.

"Still not conscious." Tamara began untying the safety rope that had bound them together. "Any reports yet? Of people gone missing?"

"No." Ada bent down and helped remove the woman's helmet. "I think I know her," she declared in surprise.

"Would she have been on fire watch?"

Ada said, "I doubt it."

The woman began to stir. Her eyes were still closed, but she started flailing her arms weakly.

Tamara was overjoyed. "Are you all right?" she asked. "Do you remember what happened? Where did you fall from?"

The woman didn't answer.

Ada said, "We should contact her co. We should contact Macario."

41

Carla looked up at the starlit mountain stretched out above the fire-watch platform. The ladder she'd just descended and the platform's bulky support ropes converged in the distance into a single slender wisp. From this vantage, an alert watcher could hardly miss a flash of orthogonal matter against the rock's muted tones, and even a lamp carried out onto the slopes would be sure to catch the eye. But any fine detail in this sweeping panorama that brought no light of its own to the scene would probably be lost in the gloom. A small team working by starlight might well come and go unnoticed, right under the gaze of the most vigilant observer.

Tamara nudged her and handed her the spyglass, then showed her where to look. Carla swept her magnified gaze back and forth several times before finally seeing it: a tent—or hammock—suspended from the rock, a circle of fabric attached at a few points on its rim, sagging down in the middle. On close inspection the camouflage pattern dyed into the fabric looked surprisingly crude—but she'd run the spyglass over the same spot twice without noticing a thing. When she'd first heard Macaria's account of the hideaway it had sounded preposterous, but now she had to admit that the kidnappers had merely been unlucky. If one of their captives hadn't escaped, they might have remained undetected.

She couldn't see any hint of movement in the tent, but if Carlo was under guard he'd be wise to lie meekly still. Macaria had never heard his voice in this airless prison, but when she'd managed to tear open her own confining sack she'd glimpsed another just like it before she'd slipped out past the edge of the tent and fallen into the void.

With impressive—albeit nearly fatal—self-discipline, Macaria hadn't even tried to detach the air tank from her cooling bag until the spin of the *Peerless* had put her out of her captors' line of sight—and if she'd continued in free fall, she would have been too distant to be seen with the naked eye when the mountain came full circle. It was possible that the kidnappers believed she was dead and that her corpse had drifted away undetected. Then again, the mere fact of her escape was sure to have put them on edge.

Carla passed the spyglass to Patrizia and helped her aim it toward the tent, silently thanking Silvano for sending most of the fire watch on a search of the mountain's interior. If Ada and Tamara had had to explain themselves in order to get access to the platform, they might as well have put out a bulletin describing Macaria's rescue and listing all the options for their next move.

Under threat of death, Macaria had told the kidnappers where she'd hidden her copies of the tapes, but she'd had no way of knowing whether Carlo had done the same. Would they have released her in the end, if she hadn't escaped? Perhaps the kidnappers had been waiting for the vote, waiting to get a sense of how much support they had among the travelers, before weighing up their options for that final step. Carla tried to take some comfort from their hesitation. However strong their commitment to their cause, and however fearful they were of being punished, killing another person could not come easily to anyone.

Macaria, Macario and Ada were waiting for them back in the observatory's office, having already made their own reconnaissance trip.

Tamara said, "The six of us are enough. We can do this."

Patrizia glanced at Carla, then protested, "Surely if we take this to the Council, they'll appoint police—"

"Word would get out," Ada said flatly. "We can't risk telling anyone else." They had even kept Amanda in the dark, knowing that their enemies were likely to be watching her closely.

"I counted six attachment points for the tent," Tamara said. "Probably hardstone stakes driven into the rock, but we wouldn't need to pull them out, we could just cut the fabric away around them. Do all six at once, and everything spills. Then if we let ourselves drop alongside the tent, one of us is sure to be able to snatch up Carlo. Macaria thinks the guards will have air jets, but even if they don't there's likely to be only one or two—and I'm prepared to take spares to offer them, if they're needed. So if this all goes smoothly, no one gets hurt and Carlo comes home safely."

Carla tried to analyze the scenario objectively, even as she pictured Carlo free-falling into the void. If the guards were caught by surprise this way, they were unlikely to have a chance to harm him. Outnumbered, but not trapped, their wisest move would be to flee rather than take any kind of stand.

"How do we get so close, undetected?" she asked.

"They can't have lookouts everywhere," Tamara replied. "Starting from here, we go straight out onto the surface, and then we travel as far as we can while sticking to the slope. The guide rails around this airlock won't take us all the way to the tent, so we'll make the last step with air jets. They'll be expecting someone coming the easy way, following the rails from their own nearest airlock; they won't be gazing out at the stars, searching for silhouettes. And if we come in from on high as fast as we can, they won't have much chance to see us and react, whichever way they're looking."

"Coming to a halt against the surface isn't an easy maneuver," Carla pointed out.

"Is there anyone here who *didn't* pass safety training for the fire watch?" Ada inquired.

Nobody owned up to that. It was true that the safety exercises included a soft landing on the spinning slope—using an air jet to hold yourself in place long enough to get a handhold on a guide rail—but avoiding an audible thud against the rock hadn't been part of the assessment criteria.

Carla looked around the room, trying to judge what the response would be if she asked Tamara to heed her wishes and call off the rescue. The kidnappers hadn't harmed Macaria, even after she'd given them the tapes and was of no further use to them. If this raid went badly, anything could happen.

Either choice would be a gamble—and when she'd had no alternative she'd talked herself into believing that the vote alone would make all the difference. But did she want to trust Carlo's life to the skills of her friends and allies, or to some fantasy of generosity-in-victory by the people who'd snatched him in the first place?

"We're going to need to get the timing absolutely right," she said. "If one of us hits the tent too soon, we'll have lost the whole advantage of surprise."

Ada said, "I have an idea about that."

Carla felt the guide rail above her shift slightly as it took her weight. She paused and looked up at the supporting post, daring it to slide right out of the rock and be done with it. Though the safety rope bound her to her five companions, the jolt of her fall might tear out enough adjoining posts to spill them all.

Nothing happened. She glanced down into the stars, mystified that the threat of free fall could disturb her so much more than the condition itself. Having to dangle and swing from the rails wasn't physically arduous, but what was hard to take was the constant feeling that the structures she depended on might give way. Whatever improvements the engineers had made, some of these rails predated the launch itself.

She started moving again. Tamara, ahead of her, was setting the pace and Carla didn't want to slow her. She thought of Carlo, blind in his prison sack, and wondered if he'd recognize the terror of his own sudden fall as a prelude to freedom.

As they advanced, the silhouette of a small dead tree rose up against the orthogonal stars ahead—proof that some things could cling to the rock through any disturbance. A few strides back, Patrizia was advancing briskly, keeping up with Ada, almost mirroring her movements. Carla felt a pang of guilt; why had she allowed her to come along? Whatever loyalty Patrizia felt toward her, and however much respect she had for Carlo's cause, she'd had none of the training and experience of the *Gnat's* crew. If she hadn't been with Carla when Ada came looking for her, there would have been no question of dragging her into this. But it was too late to argue the point and try to send her back.

When Tamara reached the end of the rail, Carla drew her own body to one side to give everyone behind her an unobstructed view of their leader. Tamara waited, looking to the east. She'd chosen the violet end of Sitha's trail—Sitha being one star that all of them could recognize—to mark the direction through the void in which they would be flung.

The bright borderline, where the old star trails ended in a blaze of shifted ultraviolet, marched up from the horizon. Carla saw Sitha rising, but merely sighting it wasn't the cue. The star had to lie at right angles to the zenith—and mercifully, that judgment wasn't hers to make.

Tamara gave the signal, a sweep of her lower right hand, and released her hold on the rail.

Carla did the same, and the six of them fell into the void together. She glanced up to see the mountain receding and felt a rush of pure elation: to do this by choice, not by accident, wasn't frightening at all. A few pauses later the rope joining her to Ada went taut as some small failure of synchronization caught up with them, but the jolt was mild.

Tamara was joined to Carla, but a second safety rope linked her directly all the way back to Macario, who'd been traveling at the rear of the group. Now the two of them started gathering up their ends of that longer rope, pulling themselves together. When they'd shortened it to a marked portion of equal length to the other five ropes, they hitched it to their harnesses, fixing the geometry.

Tamara gestured again, and Carla joined the others in firing a brief horizontal burst from her air jet. The loose hexagon spread out into a slowly turning, almost planar figure. At first everyone bounced around a little; the hexagon wasn't perfectly rigid. But as the ropes dissipated the energy of people's wayward motion, the hexagon's stately rotation remained. Carla looked across at Macaria; behind her, the gaudy streaks of the old stars were changing places with the short, crisp trails of their orthogonal counterparts.

Tamara made a few small corrections on her own, to align the hexagon's plane against the mountain. It was not like flying the *Gnat* or the *Mite*, but with care she could act as their pilot. So long as they were turning, centrifugal force and the rope's deadening effect on any small departures would keep them in an orderly configuration.

The next stage was better handled cooperatively: on Tamara's cue, they began firing their jets in unison toward Sitha, parallel bursts aimed at killing their velocity away from the *Peerless*. With one hand on the jet strapped to her chest and another on the second unit on her back, Carla could keep targeting the star even as the sky wheeled around and sent

Sitha into her rear gaze.

Tamara halted the maneuver; they were approaching the mountain now. Carla glanced up but forced herself not to search for their destination. Tamara had chosen her own landmarks and made her own calculations. Ada had checked everything twice. The only thing to do now was to trust the navigators.

The slope grew closer with alarming speed. They were returning more rapidly than they'd been tossed aside, and the rocks themselves were now swinging around to meet them. Tamara made a series of corrections, tipping their trajectory to the south to take them past the territory they'd been unable to cross by rail. Carla's body tensed at the threatened collision, and this new fear was far harder to dismiss: to fall into the void could be harmless, but there was no recovering from being dashed against the side of a mountain.

Finally, Tamara gestured for them to brake. Carla fired her jet toward the second target star, a nameless dazzle of violet on the borderline. The task kept her eyes away from the rocks, and when she finally stole a glance upward the jagged terrain had assumed an almost leisurely pace. She could see the tent easily now: the camouflage had lost its power for her. The slope around it was deserted. If there were lookouts they were all inside, peering out across the mountainside, expecting any intruders to come straight from the airlock.

Tamara had them shut off their jets. When the hiss from the nozzle fell silent, for a moment Carla felt as if she were suspended above the rock, but she knew that was impossible. A pause later she could see that they were still approaching, very slowly, not quite on target. Ada and Tamara took turns making adjustments, taking pains to keep the hexagon as level as they could. Carla stared up at the approaching ceiling, a few dozen strides away at most, then looked down just in time to catch Tamara's last cue.

In almost perfect synchrony, the six of them unhitched their connecting safety ropes, took the hook-ends of their grappling ropes in one hand, then pointed their jets away from the rock and opened the valves wide to drive them home.

Carla hit the edge of the tent with her free upper hand stretched out above her, faster than she'd meant to, but close to the attachment point she'd aimed for. The jet was easily supporting her centrifugal weight, but it was threatening to send her skidding sideways. She reached up and thrust the hook into the fabric of the tent; the material was thickly woven, but the hardstone barb parted it easily and the supporting loop slipped in.

She shut off her jet, leaving her dangling by the grappling rope. She glanced around quickly: everyone was unharmed, in place, more or less at the same stage she was. Patrizia was fine. *And Carlo was in here, almost free now.* They just had to act quickly before the guards knew what had hit them.

Carla pulled the knife from her tool belt and plunged it in beside the attachment stake; she felt the tip go right through to the rock. She tried to extend the cut by lateral force alone—to slice around the stake's retaining head in a neat circle—but she didn't get far before the fabric resisted the blade. She pulled the knife out and thrust again, making a second cut, trying not to panic at the delay. How much could the guards hear, in airlessness? Rock was a good conductor of sound, but the fabric would carry it much less efficiently.

She made a third cut, a fourth. Together, these arcs still only did half the job. She joined two of them with yet another thrust, then did the same to the opposite pair. Two almost-half-circles enclosed the stake. At the edge of her attention she saw another corner of the tent already falling. If the guards had been oblivious until now, that advantage had just disappeared. Carla stabbed at her unfinished cut, joined the two large arcs on one side, aimed again. But before she could strike, the remnant of fabric tore under the strain and she fell with her corner away from the rock.

It was a short drop; the tent itself was still attached at four points. She looked up, hoping to see inside, but all she could glimpse was some exposed rock: the prison's ceiling, glowing softly with red moss-light.

She lurched down again, as Tamara's corner broke loose on her right. Two large air tanks came sliding down the fabric, almost striking her as they tumbled into the void, but she still couldn't see anyone. She began hoisting herself up the grappling rope, hoping for a better view, but then the tent separated from the mountain completely.

Carla pulled herself over the edge, then unhooked the grappling rope and advanced by grabbing folds of the tent's rough fabric. She saw a guard fleeing, silhouetted against the stars—a man, by the size of him, his air jet carrying him away across the slope. *So where was Carlo?* Had he fallen from the other side? She could see a host of small objects floating around her, but the center of the tent was too dark to show anything, still shaded from starlight by the mountain above. She crawled into the blackness.

Carla found the sack by touch alone. It had been secured to the tent with cords. She felt gently for the shape of Carlo's body within; he started, but then became still. She pressed her helmet against the top of the sack. "It's me," she said. "You're safe." She heard a faint, unintelligible reply, then realized that her helmet was touching, not its double, but an unprotected skull. Inside the sack, Carlo was naked.

That was their response to Macaria's escape: they'd stripped their remaining prisoner of any capacity to survive in the void. They must have set up an improvised cooling system to keep him alive, spraying the sack with air—those tanks that had fallen past her. But now he had nothing.

"It's all right," she said. "It's all right." She unstrapped the air jet tank from her chest and cut a long, vertical slit down the center of her cooling bag. Then she put a hand on Carlo's shoulder, waited until she was sure he would remain still, and slid the knife a short way into the sack. She slipped her hand in beside the blade—so that if he moved, his skin would meet her fingers before it could make contact with the knife—then she made an incision to match her own.

She put away the knife and reached in to lay a palm against his chest; his skin was warm, but he was not in danger yet. He took her hand and squeezed it for a moment, then released it. Carla put one arm around the sack, holding him against her as she cut away the cords threaded through the material of the tent. Then she bound him to her, aligning the air vents as well as she could.

The darkness had lifted; they'd fallen far enough for the stars to show around the mountain. Carla saw Tamara and Patrizia approaching, dragging themselves awkwardly over the limp fabric.

Tamara bumped helmets with Carla. "How is he?"

"No cooling bag, but we're sharing. There was only one guard?"

"Yes."

"So which way do we go back?"

Tamara looked down at Carlo; the setup wasn't ideal for a long trip. "We'll try the closest airlock first. I'll send in an advance party to be sure it's clear."

The others joined them, and they linked up with safety ropes again—clustering together tightly instead of rebuilding the hexagon. As Tamara maneuvered them back toward the mountain, Carla watched the tent falling away, shrinking to a small dark speck.

At the airlock, Ada and Patrizia went through first. Carla stood on the entrance platform, Carlo's body pressed against her. He had barely moved since they'd been joined, and she could feel the heat growing in his flesh. She wondered how many supporters the kidnappers' faction could summon at short notice. She and her friends might yet find themselves outnumbered.

Patrizia emerged and swept her hands toward the ladder, like a host inviting guests into her home.

When the airlock was repressurized, Carla removed the cords she'd tied around the sack and eased Carlo down onto the floor. He lay still. She knelt, intending to cut him free completely, but then he shifted suddenly inside the sack and began working his way out through the slit.

When he'd thrown the sack aside, Carla took him in her arms and rested her head on his shoulder. She realized she was still wearing her helmet.

"Are you all right?" she asked.

"Absolutely." He helped her remove the helmet.

"We should let the others through," she said.

"There are more of you?" He could see Ada standing guard at the doorway, but he must not have realized the full size of the raiding party.

By the time everyone was back inside the *Peerless*, Carlo was moving normally, talking and joking with them, eager to be brought up to date.

"They never got Amanda," Carla explained. "And the Council's ordered a vote; in four days' time, everyone will have a say on what happens with your research."

As Carlo digested that news, Tamara added, "There's not much chance of approval, though, after everyone saw your autopsy notes on the fourth arborine."

"My what? What are you talking about?"

"You didn't autopsy one of the arborines who gave birth? Carla found the report in your apartment."

"No." He turned to Carla, confused, but before he could speak Tamara chirped with delight.

"I knew they were forged!" she said. "I knew it!"

"We have to get the news out," Patrizia urged Carla. "That's going to change everything!"

"No one's going to believe a retraction now," Ada predicted gloomily. "They'll just think it's a strategy to sway the vote."

Carla couldn't meet anyone's gaze. "I forged the autopsy notes," she said. "I just wanted the kidnappers…" She trailed off. Everyone here had risked their lives for the cause she'd tried to destroy. She couldn't start offering them excuses.

It was Tamara who broke the silence. "People will understand why," she said. "Write up something short and we can send it out right now. Your co is finally safe, now you can speak the truth. That's not a strategy, it's just being honest."

Carla looked to Carlo. "It's a good idea," he said. "Let people know what happened." If he was angry with her, he was hiding it.

As the group made their way down the corridor, Carla composed the message in her head. Some passersby recognized Carlo and Macaria and greeted them warmly. Others hurried past, casting looks of disdain.

At the relay station, Carla sat at the paper tape punch. As she began hammering the buttons, Patrizia said, "There's a bulletin here, it just came in a chime ago."

"You haven't heard yet?" The clerk was surprised. "Not good news."

Patrizia read the copy on the wall in silence, then moved aside to let the others see it. Carla couldn't concentrate on her own task any more.

"What is it?" she demanded.

Patrizia didn't answer, but now Macaria had read it too. "The forest," she said, dazed. "We've lost the forest."

"What do you mean, lost it?"

"Someone set it alight. From the sound of this, they must have used sunstone. By the time the fire crews arrived there was nothing they could do. They've closed off all the entrances and left it to burn itself out."

42

When Carlo insisted on seeing for himself exactly what had become of the forest, Tamara joined Ada, Patrizia and Carla to escort him down the axis. Macaria had reached the point where she couldn't face any more bad news. She thanked Tamara and headed home with her co.

As the group entered the central corridor, Tamara could already smell the traces of smoke wafting up through the mountain. She'd seen her father burning off blight often enough to be impressed by the ability of plants to limit the spread of fire: in wheat, at least, there was a skin covering most of the stalk that could be shed if it caught alight. But nothing living was invulnerable, not even the mightiest tree. In the presence of a high enough density of flames, the heat carried through the air alone would be enough to render any kind of organic matter unstable.

By the time they reached the second level above the forest, the smoke was thick enough to scatter the moss-light into a disorienting red haze. Tamara struggled to see a dozen strides ahead; they might as well have sent out invitations for an ambush. The heat was becoming palpable, and Carlo had barely had time to recover from his last bout of hyperthermia. When he started faltering, losing his grip on the guide rope, Carla finally managed to dissuade him from continuing.

"If we're already struggling at this distance," she said, "imagine what it was like inside the chamber. The arborines will be dead. There's nothing we can do about that."

Tamara had reached the same conclusion long ago, but she'd been trying not to think about the consequences. Who would vote for the research to continue now? With reports of disfigured arborines still preying on their minds—notwithstanding Carla's belated retraction—and no prospect of further animal tests to settle the matter, who could endorse such a project?

Carla's apartment wasn't far. Tamara suggested that the two of them rest there, and when she volunteered to stand guard Patrizia and Ada offered to join her.

They turned and headed back up the axis, smoke clinging to their skin. The blight infesting the arborines had been burned away before it could spread. Tamara knew the scent of eradication.

"We can't just accept this!" Patrizia declared angrily. "We need to hit them as hard as they hit us!"

Tamara gestured with a hand to her tympanum. Carla and Carlo were asleep in the next room.

"What happened to the Council appointing police?" Ada replied caustically. "You want to burn a few farms now? Or just kidnap a few people at random?"

Patrizia scowled. "Of course not. But we have to show them what happens when they try to win a vote by force. We have to find a way to hurt them."

"Wars of retribution were hard enough on the ancestors," Ada said. "And we have none of the resilience of a planetary culture. If people start repaying every act of violence in kind, we'll all be dead within a year."

Tamara didn't doubt that. The prospect of her father's mentality triumphing yet again enraged her—but she hadn't quite lost her mind. The *Peerless* could not survive any escalating conflict. The Council would find someone to punish for the kidnappings and the fires, eventually, and she would have to be satisfied with that.

Patrizia swung back and forth on her rope, agitated, unable to let the matter drop. "No violence," she said finally. "But we can still hurt them. We still have the one thing they fear the most."

"That's a bit too cryptic for me," Ada admitted.

Tamara understood. "We still have the tapes," she said. "We could still do one more experiment, before the vote comes in and the Council bans the research."

Ada said, "You mean scale things down, from arborines to voles?"

"No, *scale things up*," Patrizia corrected her. "We need a woman to give birth, before the vote. To prove that it works, to prove that it's safe. To show the whole mountain that it really is possible."

That silenced Ada. It silenced all three of them. Tamara stared at the walls, marveling at the strange disjuncture between the joy she felt at the prospect of the kidnappers and arsonists hearing the first rumors of such a thing, and the visceral sense of panic that gripped her at the thought of what it would take for those rumors to be real.

Patrizia said, "I'll do it, if I have to."

"You're too young," Tamara said flatly.

"What—do you think I'm not fertile yet?"

"I mean you're too young to take the risk."

"Someone has to be the first," Patrizia replied. "There aren't going to be any more arborine tests. Someone has to take the risk of finding out if it's safe for women."

Ada said, "If anyone does this, it would have to be a solo. Nobody's co could come to terms with this in a day: you can't just tell a man he has to give up any chance to be a father in the usual way—no warning, no discussion. No one could accept it, and it wouldn't be fair to demand it of them."

Tamara concurred. "This would be hard enough for anyone, but to get a couple to agree on it before the vote would be impossible."

Patrizia shot her an odd glance, something more than resentment at having the law laid down this way.

Tamara said, "I'd do it myself, but I don't have an entitlement. I can't bring a child into the world if I can't feed her."

Patrizia hesitated, then cast aside her reticence. "There's nothing in the separation agreement for your children?" she asked.

"That's right," Tamara replied. "My co's children will inherit the full entitlement."

"What if I signed over a twelfth of mine?" Patrizia offered.

Tamara held a hand up. "You can't starve your descendants, that's not fair—"

"I wouldn't be starving anyone," Patrizia insisted. "If this method works, the population will fall. No one can afford to sign over fractional entitlements for third and fourth children anymore—which is sad, but there's a brutal logic to it. Doing the same thing for *a woman's sole child* is completely different."

Ada said, "She's right. I'll offer you a twelfth as well. And I'll take this to as many other women as we need—if it's really what you want."

Tamara forced herself to stay calm. No one here was trying to trap her; they were just taking her at her word. If she said no, that would be the end of it.

What did she want? She wanted to defeat the fanatics who'd tried to impose their will throughout the mountain by force. She wanted to be free of all the men who believed that her flesh was their property, to protect and control and finally *to harvest*, as they saw fit.

But she did want a child, on her own terms.

She could leave it to someone else to go first, to test Carlo's method, to see if it was safe. But what would happen if every solo, widow and runaway to whom they put this proposition took the same view? The vote was in four days. If everyone balked at the prospect, everyone would lose the chance.

Tamara said, "Do you think Carlo's up to this?"

"Not remotely," Ada replied. "Nor Macaria. It wouldn't be fair to ask them, and frankly I wouldn't let either of them do surgery on any living creature for the next three stints."

"Which leaves Amanda. I've never even spoken to her." Tamara buzzed softly. Was she really going to invite a stranger to cut her open and shine the light from mating arborines into her body?

"I met her," Patrizia said. "On the day of the kidnappings."

"Then you'd better make the introductions," Tamara suggested. "I probably wouldn't get past her bodyguards myself."

In the back room of her apartment, away from the bodyguards, Amanda listened politely to Tamara's plan. But then she started raising objections.

"We know what these signals do to an arborine," she said. "We don't know what they'll do to a female of another species."

"But how else will you ever find out?" Tamara protested.

"Perhaps we won't need to," Amanda replied. "If these tapes had been recorded from a woman, not an arborine—"

"Do you think we'll find a volunteer for *that* in the next four days?" Tamara couldn't imagine trying to sell the proposition to anyone.

"No."

"After which time, the Council will tally the votes and make it illegal for you to do anything of the kind."

"Perhaps," Amanda conceded.

"You don't seem very worried." Tamara was confused; this was the woman she'd heard making a powerful case for the research to continue.

"We should always try to gather as much information as we can," Amanda said. "But if the vote goes against the use of this method, it won't be the end of fertility research."

"Will it be the end of *survivable childbirth*?" Tamara pressed her.

Amanda thought for a while. "For this generation, probably."

Tamara was beginning to understand her position: she wasn't actually in favor of Carlo's method—but she was still prepared to discuss it with scrupulous honesty.

"So if I do this, what exactly are the risks?" Tamara asked her.

"'Exactly'? You want me to put limits on it?" Amanda spread her arms. "I have no idea how to do that."

"I could die, or I could be injured," Tamara said. "The child could die, or be grossly malformed."

"Yes. All those things are possible."

"I could give birth to a kind of hybrid? Half person, half arborine?"

Amanda hesitated. "I can't rule that out absolutely, but if we're right about the nature of these signals that wouldn't be possible. We don't believe they encode traits from either parent; what we saw with the arborines themselves gave us some evidence against that idea. What these signals seem to be are generic instructions to the flesh to start organizing in a certain manner—with the details already intrinsic to the body itself."

"So the real question," Tamara realized, "is whether or not we use the same signals for that purpose as these cousins of ours?"

Amanda said, "Yes."

"It's less like telling my flesh: do this, and this, and *this*, in every last detail… and more like simply saying: do what you already know how to do, to form a child?"

Amanda widened her eyes in assent.

Tamara said, "It's like a language used by two groups of people, who've lived apart for a while. Maybe they've started using two different words for the same thing, maybe not."

"That's the theory, more or less," Amanda agreed.

"And if you tell my flesh, in the arborine language, to form a child—and the word my flesh would use is different, so it can't understand what your tapes have said—is there really any reason to think it will respond by mutilating my body and creating a damaged child?"

"I can't give you a precise account of how that would happen," Amanda conceded. "But I can't give you a precise account of what this thing we describe metaphorically as a 'language' really is, and how it works."

Tamara recalled Carlo's accident with his hand; things had certainly gone badly wrong there. But as Carla had explained it, that had involved detailed instructions: an endless recitation of precise commands from the tape, not so much misunderstood as mistimed.

"You've been honest with me about the dangers," Tamara said. "I'm grateful for that. But I still want to do this."

Amanda wasn't happy. "I don't know what people's reaction will be. It could make the situation worse."

"Do you want our lives to be controlled by these thugs?" Tamara asked her. "Whoever sets something on fire has the last word?"

"No," Amanda replied softly. "I don't want that."

Tamara hadn't realized how frightened she was. But if they let themselves be cowed, nothing would ever change.

"How soon could you get the machinery together?" Tamara had heard that Carlo's whole workshop had been hastily disassembled.

Amanda pondered the logistics. If her answer was *five or six days*, Tamara thought, who could challenge her on that?

"Within a bell or two," Amanda replied. "But you need to be clear: even if this works perfectly, your recovery could take a couple of days."

Tamara waited in Amanda's apartment as the drugs and equipment they'd need were fetched from different hiding places. Like Macaria, Carlo had eventually told his captors where to find his three copies of the arborine tapes, but Amanda was confident that her own remained secure.

Patrizia kept Tamara company, then after a few chimes Ada joined them. "I have the twelve signatures," she said.

"So I have no excuses left," Tamara replied, trying to make it sound like a joke.

Ada squeezed her shoulder. "Every other woman in history went into this expecting death. If you break that connection, you'll be the hero of all time."

"You sound jealous," Tamara teased her. "Are you sure you don't want to swap?"

"No—the fair thing would be to concede command of the *Gnat* to me, retrospectively," Ada decided. "I always deserved that job. For this one, there's no competition."

Tamara buzzed softly, but it was hard to keep up the façade. *Every other woman went into childbirth expecting death.* That was true, but she felt no comfort from it. She couldn't even summon up the image of a prospective co-stead, to lull her body into believing that she was facing a more ordinary fate. Once she might have surrendered all her fears in Tamaro's embrace—and she had no doubt that her certain annihilation would have felt far less terrifying than this.

She peeked into the front room. It was filling up with strange clockwork and brightly colored vials: the light players and the stupefying drugs.

Amanda arrived with a sack; inside was a wooden box containing the tapes.

"Are you sure no one saw you?" Tamara asked her. Amanda didn't reply; it was an impossible promise to make. If she'd been spotted with the tapes there was a chance of a mob turning up outside the door, eager to burn everything within.

"I'll have to make some holes in the bed for the connections to the light players," Amanda explained.

"All right."

"I'll need to measure some features on your body first."

Amanda stretched a tape measure over Tamara's skin, and marked three locations on her lower back with dye. These were the places the tubes would be inserted.

"You don't have to do this," she said gently. She must have felt Tamara beginning to shake.

"I do, though," Tamara replied. What was there to fear? The drugs would spare her from most of the pain. She could have died on the farm, she could have died on the *Gnat*. And if she brought back this prize—or nudged it within reach of every woman on the *Peerless* before it slipped away into the void—it would be worth infinitely more than the Object.

Amanda began drilling a slanted hole in the calmstone slab of the bed. Tamara dragged herself into the front room so she wouldn't have to watch.

Amando had been standing guard since Tamara had arrived. He nodded to her in greeting.

"What do you think of all this?" she asked him, emboldened by her fear beyond the usual bounds of decorum. "Do you think we're going to wipe men out of existence?"

"No."

"You're not afraid for your grandson?"

Amando gestured toward his co. "We have our own plans," he said. "I don't know what my children will choose, when it's their time. But I'm not afraid of letting them make that decision."

"And what if a dozen generations from now, everyone's decided to do what I'm doing?"

Amando contemplated the scenario. "There'll still be children being born, and people caring for them. If they aren't doing that as well as any man, it will never reach the point you suggest—where it's universal. If they want to call themselves women, let them call themselves women. But who knows? Maybe it's not men who will have vanished from the world: maybe the people who care for children will always be known as men."

Tamara gazed back at him, amused and a little giddy at the thought. "So here's to the extinction of women," she said. "Those irritating creatures who do nothing but complain—and never, ever help with the children."

Amanda called from the bedroom. "Tamara? We're ready for you."

43

Tamara was woken by the pain. It began as a state of raw panic, a sense of damage so urgent that it preceded any notion of the shape of her flesh, but as it dragged her into consciousness it resolved into a distressing tightness in her abdomen, as if some giant clawed creature had seized her body and tried to pinch it in two.

Tried, and perhaps succeeded.

She opened her eyes. Ada clung to a rope beside the bed.

"How long have I been sleeping?" Tamara asked her.

"About a day. How are you feeling?"

"Not great." She tried to read Ada's face. "What happened?"

"You have a daughter, and she's fine," Ada assured her. "Do you want me to bring her to you?"

"No!" Tamara felt a dutiful sense of relief at the outcome, as if she'd just heard that some stranger had survived a brush with death—but the prospect of actually seeing the thing that had torn itself out of her was horrifying. "Not yet," she added, afraid that Ada could read her mind. "I'm still too weak."

She looked down at her body. She'd gone into the procedure limbless, and right now she couldn't imagine ever having the energy to remedy that. Her torso, tapering bizarrely into a kind of wedge, was crisscrossed with stitches that began in the middle of her chest.

"Are you hungry?" Ada asked. "Amanda said you should eat as much as possible."

Tamara was ravenous. "I have no hands," she said.

"I can help you." Ada fetched a loaf from a cupboard by the bed.

Swallowing was painful, but Tamara persisted. When she'd finished the loaf she felt her gut convulsing and the stitches tightening, but she forced herself to keep the food down.

"Is there any news I've missed?" she asked.

"I don't think your daughter's had much competition," Ada replied.

"Do people know? It's not a secret any more?"

"No, it's not a secret," Ada said dryly.

Tamara felt a sudden pang of fear. "And what? Are we under siege?"

"There's a crowd outside the apartment, constantly," Ada said. "Bringing gifts for the child and wishing you well."

Tamara couldn't tell if she was being sarcastic. "Are you serious?"

"Absolutely," Ada replied. "No Councilors yet, but that can only be a matter of time."

Tamara started shivering. She should have been happy, but all she felt was pain and confusion.

Ada said, "You're going to be fine."

Tamara slept. When she opened her eyes she checked the bedside clock: three bells had passed.

Patrizia had taken Ada's place. "Are you hungry?" she asked. Before Tamara could reply, Patrizia was holding out a loaf.

Tamara was starving, but this wasn't right. "I already ate, not long ago."

"The rules have changed," Patrizia said. "There is no famine for you—least of all now."

"No?" For all the sense it made, Tamara still balked at the idea of abandoning a lifetime's habits. "And there I was thinking I could keep all that mass off."

Patrizia moved the loaf toward her mouth; Tamara said, "No, let me..." She closed her eyes and pictured two arms stretching out from her shoulders, but nothing happened.

Meekly, she let Patrizia feed her. She'd lost a lot of flesh, she couldn't expect to be perfectly healthy. *But what if this persisted?*

"Do you want to see the child now?"

Tamara thought about it. The idea no longer repelled her, but she wouldn't even be able to hold her daughter. "I don't know."

"Did you choose a name for her?"

"Not yet."

"What about Yalda?" Patrizia suggested.

Tamara buzzed, against her will; it made her stitches hurt. "Are you a glutton for riots?" No one since the launch had been presumptuous enough to use Yalda's name for a child of their own. Appropriating it for this cause would be the greatest provocation they could have offered, short of the act itself.

"Maybe you need to see her first," Patrizia decided. Before Tamara could reply she slipped through the curtains, out into the front room.

Tamara's wound began to ache with a kind of anticipatory dread, as if the wayward flesh that had done her so much harm might tear her skin wide open again on its return. *She wasn't whole, she wasn't strong, she wasn't ready.*

Patrizia pushed the curtains aside with her head: one hand held the rope, the other the child. "It was hard to get her away from the others," she complained. "You might be fighting off rivals for a while."

Tamara stared at the infant. Her daughter stared back, mildly interested, unafraid.

"She doesn't look much like an arborine," Patrizia observed.

Tamara said, "You can't have everything."

Patrizia approached. She placed the child on Tamara's chest but stayed close, prepared to grab her if she slipped off. The child put one hand on Tamara's shoulder and poked at her face with the other.

Barely thinking, Tamara extruded two arms. The child appeared startled by the feat, though it was something she must have managed herself not long before. She buzzed and wrapped an arm around Tamara's.

"What do you think?" Patrizia pressed her.

"Erminia," Tamara decided.

"After your mother?" Patrizia thought it over, then offered her approval. "Why not? This might be the last time anyone can do that without causing confusion."

"They always told me I was borrowing my mother's flesh," Tamara said. She curled a finger around Erminia's wrist. "She's beautiful." What she felt was the ordinary tenderness she would have felt for any child, no more and no less. Could she learn to protect her as zealously as any father would—while letting Erminia's flesh be Erminia's, not an heirloom held in trust?

"I hope you're not thinking of keeping her," Patrizia said. "The aunties and uncles out there will riot."

"I think I need to sleep again."

Erminia had discovered Tamara's stitches and was trying to unpick them; Patrizia reached over and gently pulled her away.

"Will she be safe?" Tamara asked anxiously. Erminia clung to her chest, blithely spitting half-chewed food onto her shoulder.

"How could anyone answer that?" Amanda replied bluntly. "Maybe all your well-wishers are faking their allegiance. Or maybe just a few of them are. But no one's forcing you to go anywhere; you can stay here with your daughter as long as you wish. I'll swap apartments with you, if you like."

Patrizia said, "If you go out, there'll be people you trust on every side of you. But if you prefer, we could have witnesses come in one at a time to see the baby, so they can tell their friends. Whatever happens, there'll still be doubters and believers on voting day."

"I don't want to be a prisoner here," Tamara said. She looked around the room at all her friends, at the cluster of bodyguards by the door. Erminia might be in danger for her entire life, but the greatest protection would come when she ceased to be unique, then ceased to be unusual. If she had to be treated as a kind of political mascot first—in order for there to be any prospect of such change—it was too late to plot any other course.

She turned to Amanda. "Thank you for your offer, and for all your hospitality. But I think it's time I went home."

Amando and Macario left the apartment first, to ask the people outside to give them some space. Tamara heard excited chatter as the implications spread through the crowd. After a while Amando returned. "We can't clear the whole route in advance," he said. "But this looks like a reasonable start."

All the men made their way out into the corridor, followed by the four women who'd been with Tamara on the raiding party. Clutching her daughter, Tamara approached the doorway, then dragged herself through. Peering past her protectors, she could see the corridor lined with people far into the distance, until its curvature curtailed the view.

Someone nearby spotted Erminia. "That's the child," the woman told her friend quietly. Tamara met her gaze; the woman tipped her head slightly, a greeting that made no demands.

Ada touched Tamara's elbow. "You take the central guide rope; I'll go in front of you, Carla behind, with Patrizia and Macaria on the side ropes."

"All right."

The five women took their places, then Addo and Pio, Amando and Macario completed the ranks. Tamara wondered how long she'd need to travel this way. A couple more days? A couple more years?

The group began dragging themselves down the corridor. Tamara cradled Erminia in her upper right arm, using the other three to keep herself steady and secure on the rope. The child did not seem alarmed by all these strangers; she stared at Tamara and pulled faces at random, pausing only if they elicited mimicry or a buzz of mirth from their target.

With her face bent toward her daughter, Tamara could watch the bystanders ahead with her rear gaze. She'd been afraid that even the most benign of them might try to get too close, eager to interact with Erminia, risking a dangerous crush. But everyone kept a respectful distance, watching intently as mother and daughter approached, speaking quietly among themselves.

There were a few men in the crowd, but if they'd come with ill feelings they were hiding them well: most of their faces lit up at the sight of the child. Apart from the sheer density of people, Tamara didn't sense any danger at all; anyone lunging at her from within this mass of support-ers was likely to be grabbed long before they encountered her official bodyguards. It was strange and daunting to be part of such a spectacle, but she was not afraid.

As the group approached the first turn, Tamara spotted Erminio and Tamaro. She let her gaze slide over them, as if she hadn't recognized them. They were stony-faced, but she could imagine their rage. She concentrated on her daughter and did her best to betray no emotion at all: no gloating over this victory, no fear of retribution. Their lives and hers were disentangled now, surely. Let them follow their rules with anyone who wished to share them, and she'd follow her own.

"Word will spread fast," Patrizia said excitedly. "By tomorrow, there won't be a woman on the *Peerless* who thinks this is too dangerous to pursue."

"Perhaps."

"We should have brought some food, though," Patrizia lamented. "We should have let people see you eating your fill. That would be an image for every woman to take with her on voting day—with every hunger pang reminding her of how she could be rid of the famine."

Tamara said, "Now you're starting to scare me."

They might win the vote, she thought. It was not beyond hope now. But if they did, what would that mean? For everyone who took this first tentative sign of the method's safety as glorious news, there'd be others who'd remain bitterly opposed to it. For every Amando who'd happily classify her as an honorary man, there'd be a Tosco denouncing her as unfit to raise a child as she ushered in the extinction of his sex.

There was no prospect of victory, just a truce enforced by the balance of numbers. Whatever the vote delivered, true freedom still lay generations away.

44

Carlo woke hungry, but he kept the food cupboard locked. He left the apartment as quickly as he could, knowing that if he lingered he'd be tempted to break his routine.

He reached the entrance to the observatory a few chimes early, but Carla was already waiting for him.

"I thought you'd be out there doing final checks," he said.

Carla was amused. "If anything fails after all the tests we've done, it will be too late to fix it now. Today, all I did was wind the springs and set the launch time."

She sounded calmer than he was, and he was doing her no favors by being anxious on her behalf. He widened his eyes and offered her his hand. "Shall we go through, then?"

The weightless observatory platform was crisscrossed with guide ropes for the occasion, but so far only Patrizia and her daughter were present. Carlo greeted them as they approached.

"The big day at last!" he enthused.

"I woke up three bells ago," Leonia replied proudly.

"She did indeed," Patrizia lamented.

"I had trouble sleeping too," Carlo said. "It's not every day you see a new kind of rocket."

Onesto, the archivist, was next to arrive. He'd been following Carla and Patrizia around the mountain ever since they'd started work on the project, taking notes at every step.

"The official witness to history is here," Carlo teased him. "Come to record the moment for future generations."

Onesto said, "In that role, I'm entirely redundant. I'm sure everyone here will pass on the story themselves."

"But you'll do a more professional job," Carlo granted.

"Perhaps," Onesto replied. "I only wish I'd started shadowing the inventors sooner. I was in on some of their early conversations by chance, but I missed the most important ones."

"We've told you as much as we remember!" Carla declared.

"Exactly," Onesto agreed sadly. "Edited and censored and tidied up. I don't blame you, but that's what memory does."

"Does it really matter?" Patrizia wondered. "The techniques that work will be repeated, the results we proved will be taught and retaught. Does anyone need to know how much we blundered about, getting there?"

Onesto said, "Imagine the time, a dozen generations from now, when wave mechanics powers every machine and everyone takes it for granted. Do you really want them thinking that it fell from the sky, fully formed, when the truth is that they owe their good fortune to the most powerful engine of change in history: people arguing about science."

Assunto and Romolo arrived—Carla's ex-boss and ex-student—followed by Tamara and Erminia, then Ada with her co and her daughter Amelia. As Carla reminisced with Ada, Romolo chatted excitedly with Carlo about his last trip to the Object. He seemed to bear no resentment at all toward the colleagues who'd rendered his work there peripheral.

"Soon we'll be testing the luxagen field theory to one part in a gross-to-the-fourth!" Romolo marveled.

"That's impressive." Carlo made a mental note to ask Carla if this really was true, or was just enthusiastic hyperbole.

Half a chime before the moment itself, the twelve Councilors filed in, ending all the small talk. Councilor Massimo made a speech, congratulating Carla and Patrizia for their persistence but hedging his bets in case something went wrong.

When Massimo was done, Leonia took it upon herself to start counting down to the launch. Soon everyone was joining in. Carlo spotted Carla and dragged himself toward her.

"Where is this 'rebounder' thing again?" he joked.

She pointed out of the dome at the cubical device, a stride or so wide, resting against a platform at the top of a short post.

"And you expect us to believe that *that* is going to accelerate forever?"

"Until it overheats," Carla replied. "With luck, it could keep going for half a year."

"Three!" Leonia screamed, eager to be heard over everyone accompanying her. "Two! One!"

Carlo saw blue-white light spilling from the chassis, bright but not remotely as intense as the exhaust from any sunstone engine. A little fuel was being burned in there, but it was not being used for propulsion. The light it emitted was priming Carla's strange device, a crystal whose energy levels had been finely split by its own orderly, polarized light field. For all that Carlo had had the principles explained to him, for all the workshop tests he'd witnessed, if he was honest, a part of him still refused to believe that a lamp in a box could have the power of flight.

But the brashly named *Eternal Flame* did ascend, sliding up along the platform that restrained it against the faint push of centrifugal force, crossing the edge and breaking away painfully slowly. Its exhaust was a coherent beam of ultraviolet light, so there was nothing to be seen with the naked eye but the spillage from its lamp. Carlo was torn between an ecstatic sense of triumph and pride, and unworthy thoughts of just how easily a small concealed air tank could have produced the same results.

When the rocket finally rose above the top of the dome, people began cheering. It seemed to take less than half as much time to double its height. Leonia started nagging Tamara to let her view it through the telescope—and by the time she succeeded that was no longer absurd: Carlo could barely see it with his unaided eyes. When he took his turn at the telescope, Tamara slipped a UV-fluorescing filter into the optics—and the base of the receding rocket was transformed into a dazzling circle. If the beam hadn't been aimed to one side of the dome, it would have been blinding.

Councilor Prospero gave the second speech, reminding everyone that he'd always been opposed to bringing orthogonal matter into the *Peerless*, and welcoming this encouraging sign that such a dangerous strategy would soon be proved unnecessary. Carlo thought of Silvano; he owed his friend a visit. Now that he'd been voted out of high office he was sure to make much better company.

Patrizia handed out food, but tactfully steered away from Carlo. He'd grown used to seeing her beside Carla: one post-maternal, the other fasting, and the difference in their size no longer looked strange to him. But the sight of so many women eating in public was hard to ignore. When he woke in the night with hunger pangs he could remind himself of the burden he was sharing with his co—but to be reminded that the burden itself was redundant was harder to take.

By evening the celebrations were growing muted. One by one, the guests congratulated the experimenters and departed. Leonia sat harnessed at the telescope, tirelessly checking and re-checking the rocket's progress.

Carla approached him. "I'm leaving now," she said. "Can we go together?"

"Of course." Carlo bade farewell to the others, tickling Leonia until she moved aside and let him take a last peek at the *Eternal Flame*.

In the corridor, Carla was pensive.

"How long do you think it will take to scale up now?" he asked her. "To engine size?"

"A dozen years at least," she said. "Maybe twice that."

She'd hinted at a similarly daunting time scale before, but Carlo wasn't convinced. "You've spent too long begging for resources, it's made you pessimistic. Now that you're the Council's favorite, all of that's going to change."

Carla buzzed. "The Council can be as magnanimous as they like, but we're talking about enough spin-polarized clearstone to cover the base of the mountain. We don't even have that much ordinary clearstone, of any kind. We're going to need to find ways to manufacture it."

"I know. But once you get started," Carlo predicted, "you'll find new ideas, new short-cuts, new improvements. Isn't that how it always goes?"

"I hope so," she said. "Maybe Leonia will see the engines completed. Her generation, if things go well."

They'd reached Carlo's apartment.

"Will you invite me in?" she asked him.

He was afraid now. "Why would I do that?"

Carla put a hand on his shoulder. "I've had everything I wanted from life. I've completed everything I hoped to complete. Our children should be born now, before you're much older. Don't you want to see our grandchildren?"

Carlo felt himself shivering. "I don't care about that. I don't want to lose you."

"And I don't want to go the way of men," she said. "It almost happened to me once, out at the Object. That's not the end I want."

"It won't seem as bad if you've seen your own daughter," Carlo promised. "That's what makes it easier for men. You should talk to Patrizia! She'll tell you!"

Carla was unswayed. "You know I made up my mind a long time ago."

"Change it," he pleaded. When he'd joined her in the famine he'd told himself it would help undermine her resolve: by letting her eat a little more, she'd be one step closer to Patrizia—and clear-headed enough to be envious that her own concentration was still not quite as good.

"I can't," Carla said. "It's not in me. Ever since I was a child this is what I've imagined."

"Because you never knew you'd have a choice!" Carlo shuddered and added angrily, "What did I fight for, if it wasn't that choice?"

Carla squeezed his shoulder. "And now I'm making it. You didn't waste your time. Maybe our daughter will choose differently."

She pushed open the door and dragged herself into the apartment. Carlo clung to the rope in the corridor, wondering what she'd do if he simply fled. He did not believe she'd stop taking holin; she'd keep trying to persuade him, without bludgeoning him with a threat like that. But if he kept refusing her—stint after stint, year after year—she'd find a co-stead easily enough.

Ever since I was a child this is what I've imagined. Those words were just as true for him. And when he set aside the part of himself that understood how much more was possible, all he wanted to do was give in to that ache and fulfill that glorious longing.

Carla appeared in the doorway.

"Come to bed," she said. "We should sleep on this. We can lie together and see what the morning brings."

APPENDIX 1:
UNITS AND MEASUREMENTS

Distance			In strides
1 scant			1/144
1 span	=	12 scants	1/12
1 stride	=	12 spans	1
1 stretch	=	12 strides	12
1 saunter	=	12 stretches	144
1 stroll	=	12 saunters	1,728
1 slog	=	12 strolls	20,736
1 separation	=	12 slogs	248,832
1 severance	=	12 separations	2,985,984

Home world's equator = 7.42 severances   22,156,000

Home world's orbital radius = 16,323 severances

48,740,217,000

Time			In pauses
1 flicker			1/12
1 pause	=	12 flickers	1
1 lapse	=	12 pauses	12
1 chime	=	12 lapses	144
1 bell	=	12 chimes	1,728
1 day	=	12 bells	20,736
1 stint	=	12 days	248,832

Peerless's rotational period = 6.8 lapses   82

			In years
1 year	=	43.1 stints	1
1 generation	=	12 years	12
1 era	=	12 generations	144
1 age	=	12 eras	1,728
1 epoch	=	12 ages	20,736
1 eon	=	12 epochs	248,832

Angles

			In revolutions
1 arc-flicker			1/248,832
1 arc-pause	=	12 arc-flickers	1/20,736
1 arc-lapse	=	12 arc-pauses	1/1,728
1 arc-chime	=	12 arc-lapses	1/144
1 arc-bell	=	12 arc-chimes	1/12
1 revolution	=	12 arc-bells	1

Mass

			In hefts
1 scrag			1/144
1 scrood	=	12 scrags	1/12
1 heft	=	12 scroods	1
1 haul	=	12 hefts	12
1 burden	=	12 hauls	144

Prefixes for multiples

ampio-	=	12^3	=	1,728
lauto-	=	12^6	=	2,985,984
vasto-	=	12^9	=	5,159,780,352
generoso-	=	12^{12}	=	8,916,100,448,256
gravido-	=	12^{15}	=	15,407,021,574,586,368

Prefixes for fractions

scarso-	=	$1/12^3$	=	1/1,728
piccolo-	=	$1/12^6$	=	1/2,985,984
piccino-	=	$1/12^9$	=	1/5,159,780,352
minuto-	=	$1/12^{12}$	=	1/8,916,100,448,256
minuscolo-	=	$1/12^{15}$	=	1/15,407,021,574,586,368

APPENDIX 2: LIGHT AND COLORS

The names of colors are translated so that the progression from "red" to "violet" implies shorter wavelengths. In the *Orthogonal* universe this progression is accompanied by a decrease in the light's frequency in time. In our own universe the opposite holds: shorter wavelengths correspond to higher frequencies.

Color	IR Limit	Red	Green	Blue	Violet	UV limit
Wavelength, λ						
(piccolo-scants)	∞	494	391	327	289	231
Spatial frequency, κ						
(gross cycles						
per scant)	0	42	53	63	72	90
Time frequency, ν						
(generoso-cycles						
per pause)	49	43	39	34	29	0
Period, τ						
(minuscolo-pauses)	36	40	44	50	59	∞
Velocity, v						
(severances						
per pause)	0	41	57	78	104	∞
(dimensionless)	0	0.53	0.73	1.0	1.33	∞

The smallest possible wavelength of light, λ_{min}, is about 231 piccolo-scants; this is for light with an infinite velocity, at the "ultraviolet limit". The highest possible time frequency of light, v_{max}, is about 49 generoso-cycles per pause; this is for stationary light, at the "infrared limit".

APPENDIX 3:
VECTOR MULTIPLICATION
AND DIVISION

The travelers on the *Peerless* have developed a way of multiplying and dividing four-dimensional vectors, turning these vectors into a fully fledged number system like the more familiar real and complex numbers. In our own culture, this system is known as the quaternions; it was discovered by William Hamilton in 1843. Just as the real numbers form a one-dimensional line and the complex numbers form a two-dimensional plane, the quaternions form a four-dimensional space, making them the ideal number system for four-dimensional geometry. In our universe the distinction between time and space prevents us making full use of the quaternions, but in the *Orthogonal* universe the geometry of four-space and the arithmetic of the quaternions fit together seamlessly.

In the version used on the *Peerless*, the principal directions in the four dimensions are called East, North, Up and Future, with opposites West, South, Down and Past. The Future direction takes the role of the number one: multiplying or dividing any vector by Future leaves the original vector unchanged. Squaring any of the other three principal directions—East, North and Up—always gives Past, or minus one, so this number system contains three independent square roots of minus one, compared to the single square root of minus one, i, in the complex numbers. (Of course squaring the opposite directions—West, South and Down—also gives Past, just as in the complex numbers squaring $-i$ also gives minus one, but these aren't counted as independent square roots.)

Multiplication in this system is non-commutative: $a \times b$ generally isn't the same as $b \times a$.

Vector multiplication table

×	East	North	Up	Future
East	Past	Up	South	East
North	Down	Past	East	North
Up	North	West	Past	Up
Future	East	North	Up	Future

Vector division table

÷	East	North	Up	Future
East	Future	Down	North	East
North	Up	Future	West	North
Up	South	East	Future	Up
Future	West	South	Down	Future

Every non-zero vector v has a unique reciprocal or inverse, written v^{-1}, which is the vector for which:

$$v \times v^{-1} = v^{-1} \times v = \text{Future}$$

For example, East^{-1} = West, North^{-1} = South, Up^{-1} = Down and Future^{-1} = Future. In the first three cases the inverse of the vector is its opposite, but that's not true in general.

When we divide vectors, $w \div v$ is just multiplication (on the right side) by v^{-1}:

$$w \div v = w \times v^{-1}$$

Because multiplication is non-commutative, we need to be careful with the order of vectors when we take inverses or perform division. Taking the inverse of two or more vectors multiplied together entails *reversing their order*:

$$(v \times w)^{-1} = w^{-1} \times v^{-1}$$

This reversal is necessary to ensure that the original vectors come together in the right sequence to give a final result of Future:

$$(v \times w) \times (w^{-1} \times v^{-1}) = v \times \text{Future} \times v^{-1} = \text{Future}$$
$$(w^{-1} \times v^{-1}) \times (v \times w) = w^{-1} \times \text{Future} \times w = \text{Future}$$

Similarly, when we divide by a product of vectors we need to reverse their order:

$$
\begin{aligned}
u \div (v \times w) \quad &= \quad u \times (v \times w)^{-1} \\
&= \quad u \times w^{-1} \times v^{-1} \\
&= \quad (u \div w) \div v
\end{aligned}
$$

Although the tables only give the results for multiplying and dividing the four principal directions, the same operations can be applied to any vectors at all (with the exception that you can't divide by the zero vector). A completely general vector can be formed by adding together various multiples of the principal directions:

$$v = a \text{ East} + b \text{ North} + c \text{ Up} + d \text{ Future}$$

Here a, b, c and d are real numbers, and they can be positive, negative or zero. Let's define another vector, w, using four other real numbers, A, B, C and D:

$$w = A \text{ East} + B \text{ North} + C \text{ Up} + D \text{ Future}$$

We can multiply v and w together by following the ordinary rules of algebra, taking care with the order in which we write the products of vectors:

$$
\begin{aligned}
v \times w = \quad & (a \text{ East} + b \text{ North} + c \text{ Up} + d \text{ Future}) \\
\times \quad & (A \text{ East} + B \text{ North} + C \text{ Up} + D \text{ Future}) \\
= \quad & a\, A \text{ East} \times \text{East} + a\, B \text{ East} \times \text{North} \\
+ \quad & a\, C \text{ East} \times \text{Up} + a\, D \text{ East} \times \text{Future} \\
+ \quad & b\, A \text{ North} \times \text{East} + b\, B \text{ North} \times \text{North}
\end{aligned}
$$

+	b C North × Up + b D North × Future
+	c A Up × East + c B Up × North
+	c C Up × Up + c D Up × Future
+	d A Future × East + d B Future × North
+	d C Future × Up + d D Future × Future
=	(a D + b C − c B + d A) East
+	(−a C + b D + c A + d B) North
+	(a B − b A + c D + d C) Up
+	(−a A − b B − c C + d D) Future

The length of a vector can be found from the four-dimensional version of Pythagoras's Theorem. We write the length of the vector v as $|v|$, and it is related to the size of its components in each direction by:

$$|v|^2 = a^2 + b^2 + c^2 + d^2$$

When two vectors are multiplied together, the length of the resulting vector is just the product of the lengths of the original vectors:

$$|v \times w| = |v||w|$$

Given a vector v it's often useful to talk about its *conjugate*, which we write as v^* and define as the vector whose components in the three space directions are the opposite of those of v, while its component in the time direction is exactly the same as that of v:

$$v^* = -a \text{ East} - b \text{ North} - c \text{ Up} + d \text{ Future}$$

Multiplying a vector by its own conjugate gives a very simple result:

$$
\begin{aligned}
v \times v^* \quad &= \quad (a^2 + b^2 + c^2 + d^2) \text{ Future} \\
&= \quad |v|^2 \text{ Future}
\end{aligned}
$$

Since the direction Future acts like the number one in this system, if v has a length of one its conjugate v^* will also be its inverse, v^{-1}. If the length of v is not one, we can still find its inverse from its conjugate by dividing by the square of its length:

$$v^{-1} \ = \ v^* \ \div \ |v|^2$$

Because of this close relationship between the *conjugate* of a vector and its *inverse*, it's not hard to see that if we take the conjugate of a product of vectors we need to reverse their order, just as we do with the inverse:

$$(v \ \times \ w)^* \ = \ w^* \ \times \ v^*$$

The Future component of the product of one vector with the conjugate of another, $v \times w^*$, carries some useful geometric information about the two vectors:

$$\text{Future component of } v \times w^* = a\,A + b\,B + c\,C + d\,D$$
$$= \ |v||w| \ (\text{cosine of angle between } v \text{ and } w)$$

The quantity on the right hand side of the first equation, where we multiply the four components (a, b, c, d) of v and (A, B, C, D) of w and add up the results, is known as the *dot product* of the two vectors. As the second equation shows, it depends only on their lengths and the angle between them.

Any rotation of four-dimensional space can be achieved by fixing two vectors whose length is one, say g and h, and then multiplying on the left with g and dividing on the right with h. So the vector v is rotated by:

$$v \ \to \ g \ \times \ v \ \div \ h$$

For example, a rotation that swaps North and South and also Future and Past, while leaving all directions orthogonal to these unchanged, can be achieved by setting $g = $ South and $h = $ North.

How can we be sure that this operation really is a rotation? For a start, it's easy to see that the length of v is unchanged, since $|g|=|h|=|h^{-1}|=1$ and:

$$|g \ \times \ v \ \div \ h| \ = \ |g||v||h^{-1}| \ = \ |v|$$

We can also look at what happens to the angle between two vectors when we perform the same operation on both of them, by looking at the effect on $v \times w^*$:

$$
\begin{array}{rcl}
v & \rightarrow & g \times v \div h \\
w & \rightarrow & g \times w \div h \\
v \times w^* & \rightarrow & (g \times v \div h) \times (g \times w \div h)^* \\
& = & g \times v \times h^{-1} \times (g \times w \times h^{-1})^* \\
& = & g \times v \times h^{-1} \times h \times w^* \times g^{-1} \\
& = & g \times (v \times w^*) \div g
\end{array}
$$

The Future component of $v \times w^*$ is left unchanged by this operation, since $g \times \text{Future} \div g = \text{Future}$. And since the Future component of $v \times w^*$ determines the angle between v and w—along with their lengths, which we know are unchanged—that angle is also unchanged.

All rotations that involve only the three dimensions of space can be achieved by restricting the original formula to the case where $h = g$:

$$ v \rightarrow g \times v \div g $$

For example, rotating everything by half a turn in the horizontal (North-East) plane can be achieved by setting $g = \text{Up}$.

Two other particular kinds of rotation occur when we set $h = \text{Future}$, which amounts to simply multiplying on the left by g:

$$ v \rightarrow g \times v $$

and when we set $g = \text{Future}$, which amounts to simply dividing on the right by h:

$$ v \rightarrow v \div h $$

Both these operations will always rotate in two orthogonal planes simultaneously, and by exactly the same angle in both. For example, multiplying on the left by East will rotate by a quarter-turn in both the Future-East plane *and* the North-Up plane.

Consider a rotation specified by g and h that transforms vectors according to the usual formula:

$$v \rightarrow g \times v \div h$$

There are two other kinds of geometrical objects that can be described by quaternions, but which are *not* vectors because they obey different transformation laws when the same rotation takes place:

$$l \rightarrow g \times l$$
$$r \rightarrow h \times r$$

These curious objects are known as "spinors": l is a "left-handed spinor" and r is a "right-handed spinor". In our own universe the mathematics of spinors isn't quite as simple as it is in the universe of *Orthogonal*, but it's very similar, and in both universes spinors play a crucial role in describing the way certain fundamental particles behave when they're rotated.

AFTERWORD

By the early years of the twentieth century, physicists had identified a variety of deeply puzzling phenomena—some naturally occurring, some the product of laboratory experiments—that could not be explained by the classical laws of mechanics, thermodynamics and electromagnetism. The spectrum of radiation emitted by an incandescently hot object made no sense: it should have contained an almost equal amount of energy at every possible frequency, but instead it tapered off rapidly as the frequency increased, a disparity known as the "ultraviolet catastrophe". And while atoms had been shown to be composed of charged particles, both positive and negative, nobody could explain how they could be stable, or why the spectrum of hydrogen consisted of a set of sharply defined frequencies that followed a simple mathematical rule.

In the *Orthogonal* universe, because there is an upper limit on the frequency of light there is no ultraviolet catastrophe, and the spectrum predicted by classical physics is only slightly different from the true, quantum-mechanical version. And while the puzzle of the stability of charged matter remains, there is no direct equivalent to the hydrogen atom to serve as an elementary test bed for a new theory. What's more, the simple electronics that lay behind many physics experiments during the birth of quantum theory in our universe is not available in the *Orthogonal* universe: the very nature of electromagnetism makes the generation of any appreciable, sustained electrostatic force on anything but a microscopic scale almost impossible.

Carla's tarnished mirrors do have their closest match in one seminal experiment from the early days of quantum theory: the photoelectric effect. This phenomenon brought Nobel prizes in the 1920s to Albert Einstein for his theoretical work and Robert Millikan for his painstaking experiments—though Millikan appears to have been trying to *refute* the theory! The photoelectric effect refers to the release of electrons from a metal surface in a vacuum when the surface is struck by light of various frequencies; the electrons can be collected and their rate of ejection from the surface measured as a current flowing along a wire. The abrupt cessation of this photoelectric current when the frequency of the light striking the metal falls below a critical value supported the idea that light could only be absorbed and emitted in discrete amounts whose energy was proportional to the light's frequency. Since it required a certain amount of energy to tear each electron away from the metal surface, unless each individual quantum of light, or photon, carried that minimum energy the light could not produce a current.

The *Orthogonal* version works somewhat differently: rather than absorbing light to gain energy, the surface is stimulated by the incoming light to radiate light itself, which is accompanied by the production of conventional energy. Also, more than one quantum of light is needed to bridge the energy gap between bound and free luxagens, since a smaller gap would make the material unstable.

With no electronics at her disposal, Carla can only observe the tarnishing itself, along with the scattering of light by the luxagens released into the vacuum. The unexpected way in which free luxagens interact with light echoes another landmark experiment in our universe, in which the X-rays scattered by free electrons in graphite were found by Arthur Compton to betray distinctively particle-like behavior.

Despite all the difficulties they face, the scientists of the *Orthogonal* universe do have one advantage: the mathematics of quantum mechanical spin fits into a beautiful geometrical framework that they would have had good reason to explore, long before the discovery of quantum mechanics itself. In their universe, four-dimensional vectors are naturally identified with the number system that we call quaternions (see Appendix 3 for more details). Remarkably, quaternions can also be used to describe entities known to us as spinors, which correspond to particles such as electrons in our universe, or luxagens in the novel. Having a ready-made mathematical system that can encompass both vectors and spinors offers a powerful short-cut to insights that took many years to achieve in our own history of quantum mechanics. For this insight I'm indebted to John Baez, who explained to me how spinors can be viewed as quaternions.

Although the word "magnetism" appears nowhere in the novel, most readers will recognize Patrizia's ideas about aligning the spins of luxagens in a solid as something closely analogous to the creation of a permanent magnet. Just as an electrostatic force that pulls in one direction over macroscopic distances is impossible in the *Orthogonal* universe, the same is true of magnetism, so there is no long historical tradition of familiarity with this phenomenon. But amazingly enough, the quantum subtleties that Patrizia discovers to be dictating the alignment of spins are even *more* crucial to the existence of permanent magnets in our own universe than in hers! Under our rules, the magnetic force between spinning electrons encourages them to adopt opposite spins and cancel each other's magnetic fields, and it's only the quantum effect that we call the "exchange interaction"—which relies on the way different combinations of spin affect the average distance between electrons, and hence the average electrostatic repulsion between them—that allows a substance like iron to hold a powerful magnetic field.

The "optical solids" described in the novel might sound reminiscent of the "optical lattices" that are used by real-world researchers to trap and study atoms at extremely low temperatures—but in fact these are very different systems. In the *Orthogonal* universe, the hills and valleys of light's electric field can be made to move slowly enough that charged particles can be trapped in the valleys and carried along with the light. A combination of three light beams can sculpt this "energy landscape" so that the valleys confine the trapped particles in all three dimensions.

In our own universe this is impossible: charged particles could never keep up with a traveling light wave, and in a standing wave—where the intensity of the light forms a fixed pattern in space—the electric field is still oscillating in *time*, with each valley becoming a hill, and vice versa, hundreds of trillions of times per second. But while an optical lattice can't trap charged particles in its ever-changing electric field, it can nonetheless exert subtler kinds of forces. These forces relate to the intensity of the light rather than the direction of the electric field, so they retain a consistent direction over time and can be used to confine electrically neutral atoms.

Supplementary material for this novel can be found at **www.gregegan.net**.